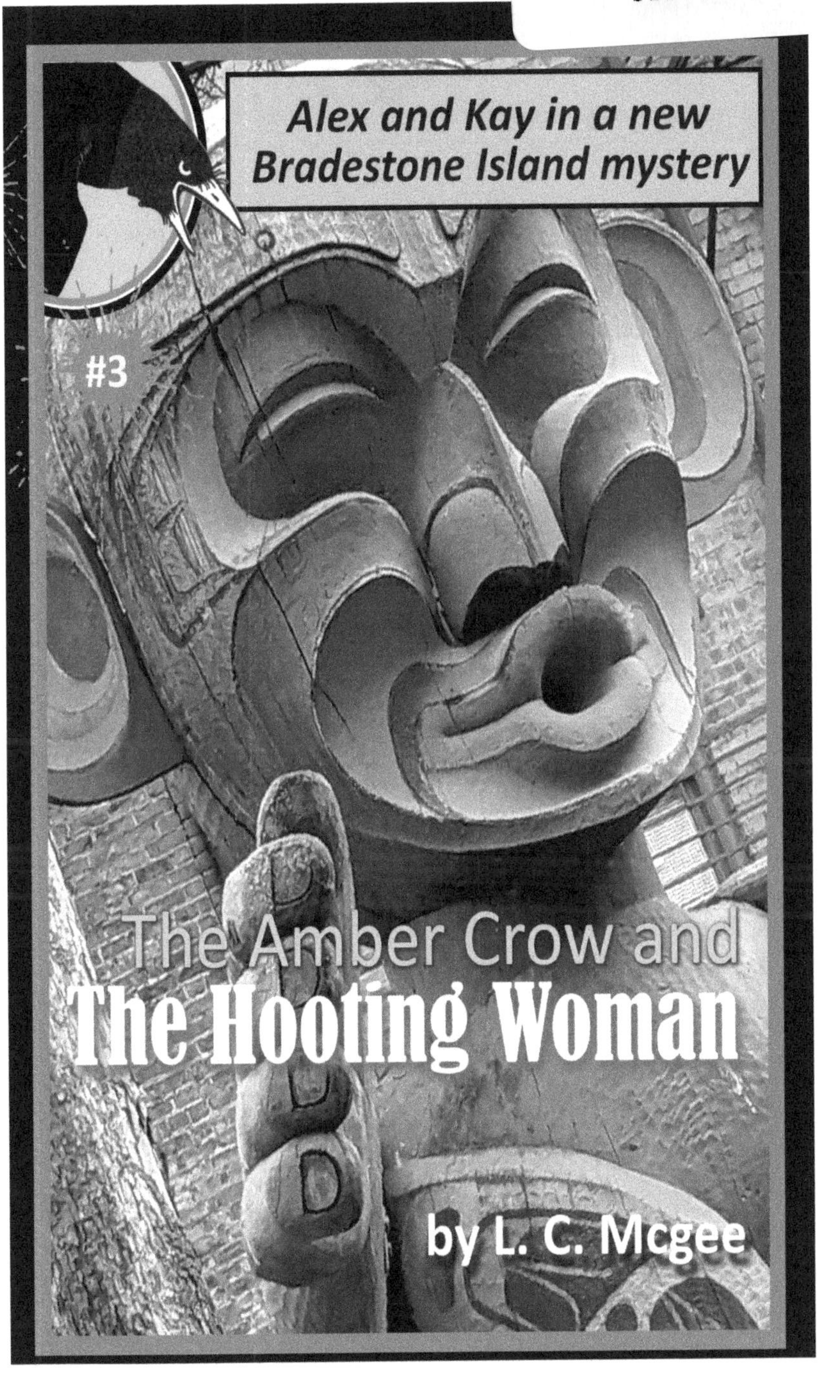
Alex and Kay in a new
Bradestone Island mystery
#3
The Amber Crow and
The Hooting Woman
by L. C. Mcgee

This book is a work of fiction. Names, characters, places, and incidents either are products of the author's imagination or are used ficitiously. Any resemblance to actual events or locales or persons, living or dead, is entirely coincidental.

Copyright © 2025 by L. C. Mcgee

ISBN 978-0-9981564-4-6 (paperback)
ISBN 978-0-9981564-3-9(hardcover)
ISBN 978-0-9981564-5-3 (ebook)

Our crow is adapted from an illustration by Boris Artzybasheff, Crow & Canary. Published by E.P. Dutton, NY, 1922 (Verotchka's Tales) [Public domain], via Wikimedia Commons.

Cover photo by Charles Thompson

Seattle, Washington

www.TwoNewfs.org

Woo, woo, come taste my Witches Brew
Made of eyes of cats, blood of bats
and croaky toads I slew

Hallowe'en invitation, circa 1943, by Leola L. Angelo

Also by L. C. Mcgee

The Amber Crow

The Amber Crow and the Black Mariah

New Halem Tales: 13 Stories by 5 Northwest Authors

CHAPTER 1

Phone Call

Sun glittering off their green and blue head-feathers, two mallards cut vee-shaped wakes across Millers Pond. Loudly quacking, they paddled toward the cattail-lined shore.

Willie loved this kind of morning. The ducks. Crows cawing far away, a chattering kingfisher plunging like a rock into the mirror-like water; then emerging, beak empty and chattering north. The fisher knew there were better pickings in Scoon Bay.

Familiar cawing sounds came closer, bringing fond memories of his first corvid friend, Zondi. An injured raven he raised and trained many years ago. To Willie, an entourage of crows was a familiar visit. They flew erratically, led by Edgar, a half crow, half raven; Zondi's amazing offspring.

Edgar circled gracefully, then glided to a two-point landing on the cabin porch. His Amber and white wings flashed as he tucked them into his amber body. Then he puffed his chest out. Three raucous caws announced his arrival.

None of Edgar's family spoke with his nasal Raven tone, nor had they picked up his remarkable pattern of color. Most sported a mirror-like sheen of black. A few had white and amber feathers evenly dispersed among their wings. They carried his genetic traits, but Edgar's exact amber-combo had skipped them.

Edar glanced at Willie, then strutted into the cabin. What? Not waiting for his usual treats? That saucy gad-about was up to something.

"Mornin' to you too, Edgar. Okay, what's on that peabrain of yourn?" The crow flew and landed on Willie's workbench.

Pausing among the shavings, he stared with a basilisk's eye.

"Oh, oh, I know that look. What's a buggin' you?"

Edgar swaggered to the large pigeon-hole divider on the back of the bench. The unit held some of Willie's finest carvings. With claws clutching the first tier and wings flapping, Edgar jumped to the second tier. Pecking, he worried at a carved wooden clam. Quickly, it dislodged and fell among the wood shavings on the bench. Edgar, with an occasional glance at Willie, pushed the shell toward a partially carved mask. He stared at Willie, then pecked the clam again and jumped on the mask. He cocked his head and cawed three times.

Willie's eyebrows shot up. That mask was his newest project. A half-finished face of Tsonoqua, the legendary hooting woman of the Northwest. The amber crow stuck to his perch and randomly pecked at the large curling lips, hooked nose, and deep-set eyes. It was puzzling. Why had Edgar positioned his intricately carved cockle-shell next to it? A chill crept along Willie's shoulders. Gently, he pushed Edgar aside and looked at the carving. He knew.

* * *

Willie picked up the mask, he usually started a project because of an inspiration. Either something like a rattle that intrigued him or an interesting behest from a potential buyer. Why he'd chosen this particular subject, he couldn't say. But he felt compelled; driven to carve and complete the mask. Its legend didn't draw it to him either. The woman, it could also be a man, snatched an onerous or wandering child, carried the hapless victim to the Tsonoqua long-house, then roasted and ate them; perhaps accompanied by a fish sauce or a condiment of clam and pickled kelp.

It was last week when Willie selected the block of cedarwood. Why this creature? Already there were some ancient and current representations of the cannibalistic monster. Most were individual pieces, created by skilled native artists and non-native artisans. Willie found a few of the interpretations amazing and beautiful.

He grimaced; the spirits had to be speaking to him; but why? Edgar took a last peck at the mask. Then, in a flurry of amber feathers, flew out the door and headed for the woods.

Willie's teeth gritted as he scratched behind his ear. *It's a warning Edgar's tell'n me sumpin and it ain't good.*

Still bothered, he put the mask back on the bench and went outside. Demanding caws greeted him; after all, it was morning treat-time. Shrugging, he thought about the omen later. A three-pipe problem, as Kay would say.

Sparring and raucous, the crows bounce-landed on the patch of grass in front of the cabin. Then, calming down, they waited respectfully while Willie took bread from his coat pocket.

He tossed torn pieces to the mob; Edgar returned with his mate. They landed in front of the clan and crammed as much as they could in their beaks.

"Don't be so consarn hogalish, Edgar. Taught you better table manners than that." Then Willie chuckled. Edgar, bounty in beak; tore off again for the firs. His sleek mate followed.

Still considering Edgar's portent, he threw the remaining bread to the rest of the family. Squawking and flapping, they jostled each other. Those who'd beaked the most took off; the rest dive-bombed in hot pursuit. Willie knew the crow tribe enjoyed the show as much as he did.

Bunch of God-damned clowns, he thought. Every year the thieves assaulted his fig and cherry trees and his grapes. But so did the raccoons and rats. He admired all of them. After all, the creatures possessed their first rights. He was the interloper. They put up with him and his labors. And they took little. He had his vegetable garden and the town market.

Puzzled, but saving serious thoughts till later, he sat down on the porch step, lit his pipe, and reflected upon the beginnings of a fine day.

His friends, Kay and Alex Beahzhi, lived two houses to the north, on one of the high banks of Bradestone Island. They'd bought the old Petoskey farm and were turning it into a mighty fine B&B. Fortunately, Kay loved Edgar as much as he did. At her suggestion, Alex nailed an apple-box nest under their porch eave. Here Edgar would take his-self, depositin' small crab and clam shells, and most of his other treasures.

Puffing away, Willie's thoughts turned to the other times Edgar had warned of dark events. There was the time Edgar saved Kay and Alex's lives by immolating a killer... he tsked... unfortunately, his cabin burned down, too. Nother time, Willie and Edgar saved Alex and his best buddy Role from death by drownin' in the old Packard. Willie shook his head.

Damn, thinking of Role, where was that wonder'n 'dopted son of his anyway? Role ceased writin' and callin' about nine months ago. Even Kay and Alex had heard nary a word. Willie puffed on his pipe. Could be that his nemesis did Dr. Roland Shakleford in the treacherous Mr. Hugo?

But nope. Willie took another draw. Role was alive and excavat'n that dig in Mauritania. He felt it in his bones. But worryingly, just last week, the consarn T.V. rattled on about things gettin' tense over there.

Willie smiled. Ole Role was a sharpie though; he'd figure best when to get the hell out of Dodge. But he'd have to give up all his searchin' for that Juba II's library. Most likely a good thing if'n he did. Yes sir, his searchin' for it last year got him into a passel of trouble.

Dagnabbit was that his phone ringing? Who the hell would call now, interruptin' his morning musings? His feet drug as he entered the cabin and neared the phone. Robo-calls were fast becoming a nuisance. The ancient black candlestick kept up its annoying ring.

No hotshots were gonna convince him to drop the landline, no-siree. The old phone worked without a hitch. That's what Thommy Jay at the antique shop assured him. His first phone was burnt to a crisp in the cabin fire. Willie shook his head. It had eighty years plus on it, and only went out when the lines were down.

The ringing persisted. Better answer the damn thing, he thought.

"Hi there!" Willie shouted; briefly deafening the person on the other end.

"You don't have to yell. I'm not deaf yet. You're comin' in loud and clear. I'm sure you woke up the entire town of New Halem!"

"Oh, 'pologize Cousin Mary," he said sheepishly. "You a-callin' from Oregon?"

"Well, I'm not on a raft, stranded in the middle of the Pacific. If that's what you're asking."

"Ah yeah," he said, then smiled as he considered the pleasant possibility. "How's your health?"

"Why thank you, Willie, it's never been better. And by the decibel count, your health sounds top-notch, too."

Willie lowered his voice. "Sorry, sometimes this damned connection goes on the fritz."

"Hmph, why don't you sell that ancient contraption and join the 21st century? And stop smoking that pipe. It'll shorten your life." Her voice rose, "and it stinks to boot."

"You can't smell it way down thar."

A long silence followed on the other end. "Willie, you know I can… and I can also see you hiding it behind your back… right now."

"You're aspookin' me, Mary." Cursing under his breath, Willie swiftly placed his pipe on a metal tray. Cousin Mary had the sight. Not only was she a shaman but descended from a long line of revered native seers. No way could you fool that woman.

"That's why I called." There was a long silence.

"What, seeing things again? I guess Hallowe'en is next month, heh, heh."

"Don't even try to be funny. There's a… can't quite put my finger on it yet, but I will, eventually."

"What in tarnation are you a-goin' on about?"

"Soon, you're going to need my help, and in spades."

"Are you comin' for a game of poker?" he asked, muffling a chuckle.

"Everything's a big hah, hah to you," Mary said, then sucked in her breath. "But… in another sense I am. There's been a warning in the cards. You need to invite me to Madrona. And the invitation must be handwritten. I'll stay in town, of course… otherwise things, er, might not play out the way they should."

"Oh, good lordy, what things?" Willie grumbled.

"Well, you've got a right to be concerned. There are indications of potent forces and something menacing converging on Bradestone Island. I've consulted the cards nine times, and they still fall the same way, dammit."

"Er… ah, there ain't gonna be no dead people, are they?"

"No, not that I can see… yet. But I get a whiff of spirit interruptions and in transit too. I don't think it happens on the island, though," there was another pause, "unless things seriously get out of hand. You've seen me always doing my best, but the techy fiddling-fingers of fate can muck up the best-laid plans."

"Yeah, true. Most times you, ah… do a pretty good job."

"Thanks for that enthusiastic vote of confidence. However, remember, I must be invited with a handwritten note from you, and soon. Don't forget or put it off, like you usually do. This can't wait. As the cards say, events are now in motion." There was a click of finality on the line.

With a shaky hand, Willie replaced the receiver and looked out the porch door. The sunny day had fled, with threatening clouds boiling in from the southwest. A look of anger came over Willie's face. "What things?" He growled aloud.

CHAPTER 2

The Magpie

Every tribe had at least one, sometimes several. Rumors, manipulation, and people's misery were their raison d'être. And the Magpie wasn't alone in prying, spying, and collecting.

But, in disguising his techniques, the Magpie was the most skillful. He simulated stupidity and perfected a variant persona of the village idiot. Of course, there was always an avid listener. Someone eager to lend a malicious word or perceive something useful in the Magpie's information.

Occasionally, his insinuations, manipulations, and disclosures caused irreversible harm. Shrewdly, he held back the main bits when he unearthed a special gold nugget. After all, the person who wanted more information could offer a little something.

At communal gatherings, the Magpie's mere presence would stir up turmoil and unease among tribal members. Misery and evil followed him and occasionally infected neighboring tribes. He reveled in schadenfreude. He was not liked, but he was listened to.

Singling me out at the Public Market had been his undoing. It was strange. I'd recently met him at one of our tribal gatherings. He knew I always saw through his game of manipulations. As he sidled up, he whispered the necessary tribal greetings, then continued with an exchange of pleasantries. He spoke as if his reputation for conniving never existed.

However, when the Magpie wasn't able to bridle his innate nature, he asked questions. "How was I? What had I been doing all these years?"

I mentioned I was moving, and permanently, but had to take care of a few things. I said I'd followed a different path, shedding the material life. He listened to the string of platitudes I generated for his benefit. More sniffing around, then he brought up the crux of his interest.

Had I really lost everything in the conflagration? He gasped with shock at my description of the devastating fire. "That was terrible, terrible," he said. "Naturally, I'd heard about it," he smiled obliquely, "glad there was no lasting damage to you; so very sorry, I was away." Then he launched into related questions about the intervening years. He'd heard I'd become very well-off. But I carefully avoided mentioning anything of significance that he could use later.

"Yes," he said with upturned puppy eyes. "I won't utter a word about seeing you but remember, I'm going back to the Gulf of Alaska." He shrugged, then smirked and apologized. "A word or two might slip out. After all, I'm much older now and enjoy the drink. Maybe if there was a reminder, a token; to be discreet. You know, the chiefs and elders expect me to entertain them with anecdotes and accounts of my travels. And they will ask me about where you are now and what she's doing." He placed a finger to his lips. "But I won't let my tongue slip. Your reputation and generosity have always preceded you." He smiled and gazed vacantly over the fish and vegetable stalls of the Public Market. "Wasn't it amazing? The spirits must have destined us to cross paths in Seattle, of all places."

He continued to natter on about people we had known. He easily slid into asking specifics about what happened after the fire. Then he proceeded with the recent tittle-tattle. "Wasn't the tragic death of our esteemed chief so unexpected and odd?"

He shuffled, hands in pockets. Remember, a small "reminder of the true events" would help him… recall things correctly. It wouldn't be difficult; a slight rephrasing of events here, an enhanced suggestion there. Things could become confused. Cluttered tribal memories of the past massaged. "Few people ever recall exactly. We're all getting old. And it was so very long ago."

He smiled, then continued. "Over the years, I've taken it upon myself to recall things with slight differences. It's kinder for all of us. Didn't you have a daughter, or was it a son?" He spread his hands and looked bewildered, as if he were only a hapless instrument of malicious spirits.

He shook a finger. "I always recall fondly those who gave me the occasional remittance, and they, in too, recover well from false ideas and terrible rumors, which, if I had not intervened, could otherwise generate harmful and difficult situations... even dangerous ones."

***

That's when I decided and graciously invited him to meet me at my motel room.

"Yes," he replied eagerly. "I know the place where you're staying. It's on that dock near the end of the train tracks. And there's a neon sign that winks like the eyes of an alluring woman. It's not that far from Ivar's, is it?" He rubbed his hands vigorously. "I'll be there at 11:30. There are many things I haven't shared yet." He leaned forward, the smell of whiskey pervasive.

"Recently I worked at the Bureau of Indian Affairs." He put a finger alongside his nose. "There have been meager breakthroughs in negotiations with the non-natives, the usual pandering, but I have some inside information, some good, some bad." There was a leering pause. "Maybe we can use it to our advantage?" I nodded.

That evening, I had tasks to do. A pebble placed in the far exit door with an oily smear on one CCTV camera. My room itself was favorable, near the end of the dock. I got a few stones from the breakwater. The Magpie was skinny and slight; hadn't gained the weight and girth that so many men do over the years. His perennial pea-jacket was perfect, deep pockets.

Because it was Saturday night, many motel guests were prowling the waterfront. They mingled with the crowds, sussing out souvenir places, giving coinage to buskers. Countless tourists visited the Ye Olde Curiosity Shop or dawdled in the bars and eateries further down the street.

Too, a waterfront carnival was well underway. Along with the loud music and hubbub, it was all coming together. No one would give a second glance at two inebriated guests: one short man leaning heavily on a woman's shoulder.

***

The exit door opened quietly. The scent of the sea and tar was strong. There was only one awkward moment. A sailor leaning on the opposite dock-railing took a swig from his paper-wrapped bottle and raised it in salute. "To romance," he slurred, paused, wiped his lips, and blearily gazed as we wobbled past. Then he spat, turned, and walked away. Glancing back, I watched as he sidled into the shadows of the motel and sat on the pavement, his back against the building. He, too, wishing not to be noticed.

We staggered to the far end of the pier. It was in darkness. Several lights were out, a boathook had been useful earlier. Here, there was no railing, only a foot-high border of a creosoted log.

I peered casually around. We stumbled closer. A sudden nudge and he neatly disappeared over the low barrier. The splash, when it came, was barely audible. No flailing, no crying out. The herbs in his drink were quite strong.

Beneath me, a black shadow slipped below the oily waters. Several bubbles burst at the surface, the only sign of passing. I grinned, delighted. The Magpie's chattering and insinuating threats were silenced, forever...or were they? I still had to be careful.

CHAPTER 3

Aunt Maureen

In the first bay window, the one closest to the kitchen, Alex and Kay were having their morning cups of coffee. Alex starred ahead, cup in hand and bleary-eyed; unconcerned at the capricious breezes ruffling Scoon Bay below. Kay fussed loudly and leaned forward in her wing-backed chair. She waved an open letter, as if it were a flag of surrender.

"She will be here the day after tomorrow. Thankfully, she's staying at the Madrona Inn," Kay sputtered. "That's only two days from today the girls arrive on the ferry. We're going to be very busy."

"Let me see," Alex mumbled and reached a hand forward, then sleepily, with the other hand-combed his unruly hair.

Kay snorted. "Here, read it aloud. Hopefully, it'll light a burner under your butt. Oh murder, I'm determined not to panic."

"That's a wise decision," Alex replied slowly, and focused on the delicate script.

Dear Kay,

Thank you for your last letter. I did not want to make contact again until I took care of several problems that were bothering me. I am now in a better frame of mind… and health. I will call, to give you my new number, and we can arrange a meeting. When I first visited Bradestone years ago, it was quite rural. I am sure things have changed since then.

Alex paused. "That must have been way before our time." He cocked an eye. "Did she say anything about this in her last letter?"

"No. But I'm sure she'll tell us later. But I do wonder what brought her here in the past. Anyway, read on Macduff."

During my illness, a dear friend took pictures of everything I thought you might be interested in. All my household objects and the furniture I mentioned. I also directed him to include my imported India rugs, linens, and other things. Those I brought back from my travels in China, Russia, and Europe. My friend put the pictures on something he calls a thumb- drive. Sounds painful to me. He says you can download them on your computer. Everyone seems to have one or two of these machines nowadays. Sad to say, I cannot become enthusiastic about them. I find cars and planes an annoyance too, but necessary. I do not claim to be a Luddite, as I always come to things when I need them. And if certain popular objects become imperative in my life, I will haplessly follow the lemmings to the sea.

I understand you have not opened your B&B yet. I therefore, as I said earlier, booked rooms at the Madrona Inn. I understand it was formerly called Madrona Cottages. Soon, I surmise, they will find themselves in rivalry with your establishment.

Am looking forward to meeting you and your family. I arrive on the 5th of September.

> *Best Wishes,*
> *Maureen Roberts D'Moresby*

Alex grinned. "The Madrona Inn? Hah, not much competition. That's the flea-bitten hostelry where Thommy Jay's guests stayed last year. They said the main building was so vermin-infested that at night they could hear the rugs running up and down the hall."

"I remember, but I'm sure it's not that way now. Ujima's cousin stayed there for two weeks last spring. She said the new owners have completely cleaned it up."

"Hah! If it was only cosmetic, people will come to our B&B in hordes."

"Size-wise we can't accommodate hordes, but our rooms are clean. And, thanks to Aunt Maureen's largesse, will be individually decorated. But, with the view of Scoon Bay, Heron's Hook, and walks on the beach, there won't be any shortage of guests," Kay paused, "I would've asked Aunt Maureen to stay here, but with the girls doing their research, and not everything here being finished..."

"I'm sure she'll understand. But she'll miss our included continental breakfasts." Alex smacked his lips.

"Oh, walking garbage can, I don't know why I caved on that amenity. Oh, I do too. Your feet are always first under the table." She smiled devilishly. "And therefore, I've volunteered you as head cook." She closed her eyes. "All I have to do is make reservations, schmooze with the guests and smile indulgently. Oh, and pat their egos when problems arise."

"Better you than me, Madam. And we shall see about assigned tasks. My duty roster is not yet completed."

"Oh lordy, you and your duty rosters. Those lists drove me and the kids almost over the edge." She laughed. "You know they saluted you behind your back and sometimes I snapped one off myself."

Alex closed his eyes, his face a look of tolerance. "There's nothing like a little army discipline to keep everyone in shape and on task. We made actual progress. And could not we be where we are now if..."

"Spare me your lock-step pontifications." She paused. "Though you're right, it worked perfectly. But now, my dear Major Hoople, a lengthy list of accomplishments would not be beneficial to either you or me."

Alex felt duly chastised. "I know, I'm probably getting over excited about everything."

Kay took back the letter. "I'm very excited, too," she paused, "but I'm curious. What were Maureen's serious health problems?"

"Not to worry. I'm sure we will hear all about them; and in magnificent detail."

Alex pointed at the island paper, the Spindrift. "To shift to other news, did you see where a guy from the east coast has rented the old art studio in Madrona, the one owned by Wick's friend, remember him?"

"How could I forget the unfortunate Mr. Grey."

"Yep, I agree. Being murdered is unfortunate. Anyway, after he left his entire estate to Wick, it's amazing; even though the lawyers took their massive chomps out of things, he made out like a bandito."

"Uh, I'd say that's a bit of hyperbole there; the Spindrift has perfected the art of exaggeration. Does the paper say anything about who's the renter and what's happening to the studio?"

"A new fellow, by the interesting name of Mr. Jinx Buckwass, is putting in a bookstore."

"A bookstore! The poor innocent. He is 'jinxed' and living in the last century or suffering a major brain burp. With e-books, the closing of newspapers, magazines, and the availability of most everything in print on Amazon or the internet; he must have the patron saint of books in his hip pocket."

Alex's look became distant. "I believe that would be Saint Jon." He'd launched into his professorial mode. "My Catholic grandfather said his real name was Joao Duarte Cidade. He led a very fascinating life. Started as a shepherd and…"

Kay rolled her eyes. "I said it as a joke. It seems there's a sainted somebody for everything, even used toothbrushes. Sorry to rouse the pedant in you, not to mention your encyclopedic memory. Oh crap, speaking of memory, you must pick up the girls; they dock in less than an hour!"

"I only remembered the saint's name because my grandpa enjoyed assaulting our ears with historical accounts at a tender age."

"You're assaulting my ears." Kay said in exasperation.

"Let me finish. The stories were always about daring young men who took off to tussle with the world."

"That figures. Daring women always get short shrift."

"Hey, take a deep breath. Anyway, it fascinated my brother and I." Again, a faraway look came over Alex's face. "Role became an archaeologist because of the fantastic stories his uncle told him."

Kay grimaced and pointed at the clock. "The girls, remember? Tales come later."

CHAPTER 4

Ghosts

Leaving West Seattle's Colman Dock, the ferry cut smoothly across Puget Sound. The nameplate, Rhododendron, paid homage to one of the first ferries of the last century. Dead ahead lay Bradestone Island.

On the forward railing, above the car deck, two young ladies, Teri Roberts, and Brooke Hamlin, stood side by side. The late September sun was brilliant and hot on their backs.

Below, at the bow of the ship, gulls wheeled and screeched as a small man cast bread onto the water from the car deck. Brooke picked up her ever-present Leica, steadied herself, and snapped several quick shots. Her stance helped dampen the ship's engine vibrations. Puget Sound, or as Teri liked to call it, South Salish Sea, was calm and as flat as the proverbial duck pond, sans ducks.

Teri was ecstatic. She loved the welcoming signs of home; the constant throbbing engines as the ferry surged ahead, her hair blowing wildly about, and the smell of clean salt air.

She was looking forward to Christmas. Their traditional Solstice celebration is with her mom, Kay, and her mom's fiancé, Alex. Teri smiled. Not to mention Alex's recently discovered son, Wick. There also would be Byron, her brother, with his crazy college stories.

Wick's face flashed before her again. Man, must she let him intrude on her thoughts? Luckily, with her classes and busy study schedule, she'd kept images of him and the eerie events that had happened last summer at a manageable distance. At night, though, dreams were not so charitable. Stop worrying; she said to herself, firmly closed her eyes, and breathed deeply. This new venture was very thrilling.

Kay had e-mailed her the night before. She described the remodeling of the old Petoskey farm. Her mom said they were close to their spring goal next year, with Teri and Brooke's room completed. Alex just finished the trim yesterday. Wow, there'd be a lot of changes.

"Brooke, when we get in, Mom and Alex will want to show us everything they have done to the old place. But I said we'd have lunch first. You're probably as starved as I am. After lunch and our grand tour, I'll drive you to Madrona. It's a dinky town, but there are lots of fun places."

Brooke brushed a strand of black hair from her forehead and checked the camera that hung around her neck. "It's been so busy this week, with planning, packing, and checking what to take, I haven't had a moment to ask about your family," she smiled, "I know more about your crazy brother, Byron, than anyone else."

Teri nodded. "Oh yeah, my brother's unrelenting e-mails and texts."

With her slow, serene smile, Brooke silently agreed, then glanced at her sports watch. "If the ferry is on time, it'll be about 40 minutes before we dock. Why don't you catch me up on some of the Roberts family skeletons? I'd like to know something scandalous about each one. Don't want to be totally out of the picture when I meet them."

Teri laughed. "Brooke, I don't know what scandals I've mentioned and which ones I haven't. I was madly packing, too." She rested her elbows on the railing and cupped her chin in thought. "Well, here goes, and shout 'whoa' if you've heard it before. You've already met my virtual brother, Byron, so we won't go there. And I've told you a lot about my mom, Kay."

Brooke fussed with her ponytail. "I think I'm very interested in your mom's fiancé. His pictures look pretty hunky."

"Humph, I guess Alex is, if you're into older guys."

Brooke shrugged. "For starters, you can tell me how he got that broken nose. He looks like a Mafioso wannabe."

"Easy, a bar fight, but I want you to meet Alex first and check him out on your own. My take is he's nice, considerate, and loves mom. And he's super, because he treats Byron and me like we were his own kids." She noticed a question forming on Brooke's lips. "Well, he is older and has a son named Wick. He came on the scene only two years ago."

Brooke raised her eyebrows.

"Oh, no, no, I'll shut up," Teri said. "Wick and Byron can tell you all about that episode. It's complicated, and Wick is so shy about certain events, and I don't want to mess things up."

"Phooey."

"Well… I can tell you that when Alex was younger, he traveled all over the world. I don't think I mentioned he was often with his buddy, Dr. Roland Shackleford."

"Wow, a doctor?"

"Roland wasn't a doctor then. And most of their wild times happened when they were much younger. It was mainly archaeological work. Roland got his degree later. He's the same age as Alex. But they were working in separate areas," she hesitated, "I think Alex was getting credits towards his Masters in Astronomy." Teri grinned. "Anyway, they were both 'shovel bums' in the summer and showed up where they could earn money for digging and also got to go to places just for the heck of it."

"Where did they meet?" Brooke asked, focusing her camera. The island's dock was approaching.

Teri pointed. "That's Vashon. We'll stop, unload some cars, pick up a few walk-ons, and then go on to Bradestone."

"Anyway, they met when Roland was attending an intra-college consortium about archaeological techniques. Alex is interested in almost everything and he was there, too. Roland convinced Alex to work on sites scheduled by one of his friend's Anthro professors. Digs are always looking for useful bodies and they could earn college credit, make a little money, and eat free, too." Teri's look became distant, "But at other times, some of their side-work became shady." she added in a lower voice. "The pay was better, but it wasn't kosher."

"Oh, now, that is interesting."

"Umm, it sure is. Alex likes to embellish stories, and it's cool if you can finesse him into talking. But he and Roland become tight-lipped about certain subjects, though." She shaded her eyes. "Luckily, I'm a good eavesdropper. I think someone stumbled onto some stolen artifacts and forced them to deal with it"

"That does sound intriguing. Where's this professor working now?"

"Roland is in Morocco working for a private university in Rabat. Mom says that with his background and skills, he's super qualified."

"Outstanding. But in Morocco? Isn't that place dangerous?"

"Now, that is interesting; earlier a prestigious European archaeological group hired him to assist at a site they discovered in the desert, near Mauritania. Dr. Roland, besides having great credentials, is a pretty valuable man, speaks beaucoup languages, even different dialects of Arabic, and has lots of connections in his field. Alex says he easily makes friends and develops great relationships with people on his dig."

"Cool. How did you find out about this Moroccan adventure?"

Teri stood back from the railing, rubbed her hands together, and tapped her nose. "I'm good with this. And big-nose Byron is too. It's all supposed to be very hush-hush," Teri frowned, "but the two men were in serious trouble last year. Almost got killed because of what happened."

Brooke shook her head. "Golly, this sounds like it could be a TV adventure series. Did Byron say what they were doing?"

"There was some brouhaha about an artifact Roland found. The good doctor oversaw a survey near the dig and stumbled on some 'mysterious find' outside the dig area. Byron's words."

"Where was this?"

"Byron said the excavation is in a location that's part of ancient Mauritania. They don't advertise where. Looters, and as we know, some museums and private collectors, have their antennas out for any unusual finds and related artifacts." Brooke nodded in agreement. "I also know that Dr. Roland hopes to find Juba II and his wife Selene's traveling library with notes from their expeditions. Mom and Alex think it's a 'pie in the sky' search."

"That's pretty wild, though. I ran across some fascinating references to Selene and Juba II in Professor Wilson's class. I'd sure like to meet this Doctor Roland and talk to him about it."

"You might. He hinted he might be back on Bradestone next year." She smiled with pride. "I actually worked for him last summer, editing his notes and organizing them. Man, he is exacting. Almost drove me bananas. But I learned a lot in the trenches; you know, about proper procedures and correct field documentation, notes, etc. etc."

"Gee, were you on a dig with him? Maybe he needs a photographer?" She excitedly patted her camera bag.

"Oh, no, not a dig; we were here on Bradestone. Kay and Alex stumbled onto some mummified remains on the farm they purchased. Even the police got involved," she shook her head, "Gad; I'll let Byron tell you that story, too. There's even an old car we found. No doubt they'll take us for a ride in it."

"Now I'm full of questions. But back to Doctor Roland. Underneath, is he just one of those stuffy academics like Professor Wilson?"

Teri pushed away from the railing and laughed. "Far from it. He's well over six feet tall, brawny, broad-shouldered, and one tough character. Alex is like him, only shorter, and you're never aware of Alex's toughness, not until the chips are down. Roland simply doesn't wait."

"Alright, too fantastic, an action man in the instant evaluation department. I like that. Okay, I'll wait until I talk to Byron. It'll be a cool way to break the ice with him."

Teri laughed. "Oh, I don't think there will be any problems there."

* * *

As the ferry pulled away from Vashon, Brooke finished snapping pictures and turned toward Teri. "So… back to Alex; you said he'll meet us at the dock?"

"Oh, he'll be there alright." Teri frowned. "You know Brooke, seriously, at first, I thought it was weird when my mom and Alex bought that wreck of a farmhouse. They pooled their money to buy it. Alex wanted to open the house as a B&B. But, from the beginning, Mom said 'no way.' Of course, I thought it would be a gas, but Mom was adamant: 'no time and no way.' She's into pottery, pine-needle basketry, and teaching yoga at the Burn community center. Everything Mom does takes careful planning. I'm still surprised she changed her mind. Alex must have been very persuasive. Anyway, it's going to be challenging." She shook her head in disbelief and gazed into the distance. "They actually will be owners of a B&B."

"In your pics, Alex looks too young to be retired. What's his story?"

"Alex said he always planned to make a one hundred and eighty from a career in math and astronomy. I guess banging around on digs with Roland made him antsy. And then he met Mom. That was after Alex's brother died, and since Alex was his only living relative, he inherited a fortune and retired right now."

"That's cool. Nothing like a legacy, but how did Alex and your mom get together?"

"At Tesla College, she was taking his Astronomy 101class."

"Moon and stars, how romantic. I hope something like that happens to me someday."

"Well, as my nerdy brother says: 'They leaped into non-contractual conjugal life with all four feet and no brains.'"

Brooke laughed and shrugged. "Marriage isn't the be-all and end-all of life."

"Wow, I never took you for an existentialist," Teri mused, then turned and smiled at Brooke. That was odd. A puzzling look had crept over her friend's face.

Teri shrugged, pulled against the railing, and sucked the salty air through her teeth. "There's Bradestone Island. Isn't it beautiful? We'll be docking in five minutes!" She glanced at Brooke and pointed to the landing. "Look at the line of vehicles waiting to get on, always a big crunch. It's even worse at the beginning of spring. The tourists spend the weekend and then make an early start for Seattle. And in the summer, it just gets crazier, especially when school gets out."

Brooke raised her camera and started taking shots.

Teri admired Brooke's shiny black ponytail as it busily swished back and forth. She knew she was as excited about the working fall and spring quarter as she was. Weird, though, Brooke had lowered her camera. Her puzzled look had returned, and she was gripping the railing with white-knuckled tenacity.

Teri laughed. "I hope you're feeling alright. Thommy Jay said he gets seasick just walking onto the dock." Teri looked closer. "Gosh, you don't look so good. What's up?"

Instead of answering, Brooke stared straight ahead and vaguely mumbled, "Who is Thommy Jay?"

"He's one of Mom and Alex's best friends. He sells antiques

on the island, a hilarious man. Flamboyant to the nth degree; I bet you'll like him," Teri paused, "Hey, you are looking paler than usual."

Brooke closed her eyes and smiled thinly. It annoyed her when someone remarked on her sallow complexion. But now she inexplicably felt panicky and fingered her camera.

"I, I'm sorry Teri, I…I just feel weird." She uttered a short laugh, "I'm not seasick, but I have goosebumps." She shrugged. "I'm apprehensive about… about something and I don't know what nor why."

Teri studied Brooke's rigid profile and then turned away to look at the rapidly approaching island.

"Hope you're not worrying about our study projects. They will be a piece of cake. Your dad helped us a lot. He showed real savvy when he cut through all that red tape. Now we can work on our separate master's programs and have a great time doing it." She nervously looked at Brooke. "Gosh, I can't wait to show you all the cool places on the island. You'll love the old farmhouse; plenty of beautiful scenery, too. Hey, it just dawned on me; you'll be the first guest at their B&B."

Brooke offered a wan smile. "Yeah, I'm keyed up about our projects. You're right, my dad is a great guy. Being the Dean of Brighten-Bush with all of his connections doesn't hurt either." She paused and turned to stare at the tree-lined shore. "No, it's not our research work. It's… it's something else. I can't shake this feeling." Her camera swung around her neck as she rubbed her arms. "I have these thoughts of déjà vu." She gestured helplessly. "And we both know I've never been here before. Isn't this weird?"

Teri stared at Brooke. Very little bothered Brooke. The first time she'd met her new friend, she found her a strong and determined female. And her attitude of 'damn the torpedoes, full speed ahead' was also Teri's motto. Teri shook her head and giggled. "It's not déjà vu all over again, is it?"

Brooke grimaced. "Teri, sometimes I've had these feelings, but never, never this strong."

Both jumped as the ferry horn gave three ear-shattering blasts. A flashy speedboat, with two waving young men, cut across the ferry's bow. Brooke whipped up her Leica.

"Oh murder, that looks like my crazy brother, Byron, and my

stepbrother, Wick." Cupping her hands around her mouth, Teri leaned over the railing and shouted. "You idiots! You're gonna get pulled over by the Coast Guard!" Then she promptly negated her warning by jumping up and down and waving.

Brooke took a deep breath. The show-offs made her smile, but when she stopped taking pictures, she started getting goosebumps again. Whispering hoarsely, she lowered her camera. "It's worse than before Teri, it's a feeling of... of fear and dread. And it's horrible."

Teri turned and snatched her friend's free hand. Tears were running softly down Brooke's face, and she looked at Teri with pleading eyes. "I'm totally creeped out and I don't know why."

CHAPTER 5

The Lone Traveler

On the car deck, below the girls, Jinx Buckwass quickly wrapped his half-eaten sandwich and stuffed it into his shoulder pack.

The announcement for foot passengers to embark had jolted Jinx out of his reverie. He chided himself. Going over the past had not been fruitful. Then, shouldering his backpack, he strode confidently to the stairs.

Standing in queues and crowds at the ferry terminal had stressed him out. But now, with the boat approaching the island, the scent of seaweed, the cry of gulls and the occasional glimpse of green forest was calming. He was content. Though alone, it was reassuring to see Bradstone again.

Jinx turned as the two children pointed and tee-heed. He scowled; they ran. It was always annoying. People react to his gaunt features and pallor. Some stared rudely, even making asides he could hear. He knew his hawk-like nose was his best feature, but really, why should he even care? That was their problem. After all, he told those who asked. He was recovering from a lengthy illness and regaining strength daily.

'Forget the negatives', he murmured, 'be in the moment.' He pinched his wrist and patted his breast pocket. There was a comforting crinkle of paper. I have much to look forward to. The documents are safe. If all went well, I could take possession of the building tomorrow. Sniggering, he knew exactly where it was located and what it looked like. Originally, it had been one of the tumble-down structures on Madrona's main street. But he cajoled himself, the recent remodel was ingenious. It kept the old town features with the wooden outside, and the inside was completely modern. He rubbed his hands together. He thought many things would have changed for the better, maybe even forgotten, since the last time he was here.

Two months ago, the realtor, Rose Bracken, promptly sent him the exterior and interior shots. The insides were perfection. Plenty of space for bookshelves. And the two large bay windows cried for the displays of large publishing companies; they were a great hook to catch the passerby.

New arrivals, best sellers, free refreshments — it all would bring them in. Slowly at first, it would attract people. After all, it was a small populace and also, he gloated, the vote of the people barred from the island, large box stores, and related commercial chains. The argument was that tourists and visitors and homeowners came for the charm and the pace. Serious bargain shoppers could deal with the commercial madhouses on the mainland. Ach yes, he didn't agree completely, but for him it was perfect.

Now, with corporate competition reigned in, he could leisurely familiarize himself with the natives, their preferences, and interests.

Bradestone was the perfect base for his retirement, with profits at his pace. There was the innovation of e-books, ah, another lucrative opportunity. One could never make enough money.

Standing in the passenger line, Jinx's thoughts turned to the name of his business. Book-Wise Wisdoms. It was a catchy spin on his last name, Buckwass. It even kept the glottal stop, which he used loudly, either for respect or intimidation. He relished what his surname stood for. It represented his unique tribal heritage, honoring his ancestors and the ghosts of the past. All his life, he'd been a busy fellow and done his best. Now, no looking back, only forward. He felt his motivations now would be entirely different.

Three deafening horn blasts jumbled his thoughts. Yelling and shouting boomed from the upward deck. Several people, including himself, rushed to a nearby window. What was the fracas all about? Hah, he pointed, there it was. A speedboat had cut between the ferry and the dock. Very dangerous. Typical rural teens, showing off; they had big smiles and were waving to someone above. Then they shot past. The roar of their outboard diminished by three more horn blasts.

Brilliant. Now there was an idea. He would include a teen's gaming section and a young reader's nook in the store. Weren't zombies, vampires, werewolves, and other ghoulish attractions for the current fads? Too, there was fantasy, adventures with wizards and dragons, along with the lucrative genre of science fiction. With special sections decorated just for the youthful readers, he could cater to them all. The interior of the building was certainly large enough. And could easily accommodate any walled-off sections.

He adjusted his shoulder bag, then exited with the walk-ons. He'd be in the chips if he handled everything smoothly. Then he smiled. Well, he always wound up in the chips. After all, wealth was his predilection, his destiny.

CHAPTER 6

Chauffeured

"Not good," Teri said aloud. "I don't see anyone waiting for us." She plopped her backpack on the sidewalk with a thud. Brooke carefully shrugged hers off.

"The boys should have been here 20 minutes ago. Isn't that just like them, messing about in boats?" Teri said.

Brooke was amused. "When I was a kid, I loved Wind in the Willows. Wait…coming over the hill is that…would that be them?"

Teri waved and jumped up and down. "It is it's the old Packard. I heard they'd repainted it. Look at those colors, they're totally different ."

"It's beautiful. I've seen nothing like it. All that shiny chrome. It looks like a Rolls Royce," Brooke said, laughing.

The horn mooed three times. "It's just Dad!" Teri shouted as Alex did a U-turn and pulled up to the curb. "The guys must be still showing off."

"The car's beautiful," Brooke whispered. "I love the cocoa-colored fenders and the latte body paint. Awesome."

"And they've used orange body-striping too, way cool," Teri said, then pointed at the passenger's door. "Wowsers! That's an advert."

Magnetically attached, the poster read:

The Burn Town Puppet Troupe Proudly presents:
"Monsters of the North Woods"
October 1st through October 29th

at the Burn Town Community Center

Tickets are available at Rose's Real Estate, Gilmore's' Hardware and the library.

Prepare to be Haunted and Horrified

Youngsters are welcome. Adults too… if they dare!

Hands to face, Brooke laughed, "It's wonderful; everything on this island seems odd and out of the past."

Alex got out, then stepped down from the running board, walked to their side of the car. He expertly doffed his chauffeur's cap and bowed low.

"Ladies. I assume that you're the first guests to grace the Inn of the Amber Crow." He straightened solemnly and saluted. "Might I store your luggage?"

"Dad, where did you get that wild outfit?" Teri exclaimed, then ran and hugged him. "I've missed you all and I've got zillions of questions to ask."

He grinned, holding her at arm's length. "We've missed you too. You know, young lady, there is called the internet; there is the phone, and now there is Skype." He rolled his eyes. "This is the computer age we're rapidly jetting into." He admonished. "And we're only an hour away by ferry."

Teri hugged him harder. "I know, I know, I've been so busy this quarter. It's no excuse."

He tousled her hair. "No, it isn't … now, who is this lovely young lady, patiently waiting to be introduced?"

Teri took Brooke by the arm. "This is Brooke Hamlin, my best friend, and a photography wizard. Mom must have told you. Brooke is also working on her master's."

"Mr. Beahzhi, it's so nice to meet you. Believe me, I wasn't prepared for all this. I've got to take some shots of you and that cool car. The light's just right," she said, and busily adjusted the camera slung around her neck. "What's the story behind this behemoth?"

Alex wrinkled his brow and carefully replaced his cap.

"Ah, er, Dad and I will tell you all about it later," Teri said and nodded at the plastic sign. "I see Wick is thrilling and chilling his public. How is the new play?"

"I've watched some of it, but major details are hush, hush. Byron and Wick want it to be a big surprise. Naturally, Byron is handling the promo end of things. This placard is just one of your brother's creations."

Teri smiled. "Of course it is. I noticed his inimitable touch. Byron also sent me some of his ideas on brochures for the inn." She shrugged and looked sheepish. "Again, I have had no time to respond."

Alex nodded. "His mockups are pretty...well, creative. But, not to worry, we've got time to sort through the choices, and you can help." He pointed at the car. "Byron is renting the Packard out for weddings and such. He or Wick usually drives. But I'm at the helm only for very special occasions," he grinned, "like this one. Local businesses are eager to advertise with these magnetic signs." Alex shook his head. "Of course, not only do they buy Byron's sign; they have to rent the door space too. Your enterprising brother has even gone so far as to get a business license."

"He's such a capitalist," Teri exclaimed.

"Wick suggested they use this car next year for official transport from the ferry to the inn. Whatever the guys do is fine with me. They went through a lot of trouble with this heap." He smoothed the front of his uniform. "Even spent mucho dinero on my outfit, but enough schmoozing, let's get your gear in the trunk. I'm starving and Kay's got a special lunch going."

Alex arranged their backpacks in the small trunk space and closed the lid. "How do you like this luggage carrier?" He asked and pulled an attached rack down, then pushed it back up and tightened the chromed side-knobs. "These are used for enormous trunks. And we can stack light luggage on top too."

"Mr. Beahzhi, it's beautiful. I can see our reflections on every surface."

"Yep, spit and polish, just like the Army. And please call me Alex," he said, then paused. "Brooke, take a gander at this." He eagerly moved to the front of the car. "This is a new stone guard; it protects the radiator. Pretty sharp, eh? The boys installed it last week."

Brooke gasped. "I wondered what it was. It seems woven out of silver." She cocked an eye. "Gosh, the grille looks fantastic framed by those enormous headlights. Um, go ahead, stand in front. This will make a great shot." Alex tilted his hat, put a booted foot on the bumper, and casually leaned forward, right arm on knee. "How's this?" he asked and puffed out his chest.

"Looks good, but …did Byron and Wick do all the work on this car?" Brooke asked as she rearranged Alex and moved Teri into the picture. "That's perfect. Hold it, guys." After several shots, she gave the okay sign.

"No," Alex answered. "They had plenty of help; got hooked up with a great guy on the Island by the name of Bobo Bentley. He maintains all the old cars here. It's his passion. With this baby, he did the transmission, clutch, and engine restoration. And for free. He says these ancient cars are mobile works of art."

"Enough, I'm beyond hungry," Teri said. "Let's roll."

While the girls settled in the back, Brooke couldn't stop marveling at the interior. "The passenger seat, that folds under the dash… it's amazing. So compact, you hardly notice it. Makes everything cozy and easy to move around back here."

"Yep, that's why this model is called an 'Opera Coupe'. Ladies wouldn't crush their fancy dresses when they got in," Alex said, then thought to himself, the damned seat also saved my life.

"Cool, there's even a cigarette lighter with an ashtray on the armrest by my elbow."

"Yep, all the latest conveniences of the early 1930s. And look at this one." Alex pulled a chrome cylinder from the dash; a thin but retractable electric cord attached to it. The end lit with a red-orange glow.

"It's another lighter!" Brooke exclaimed.

"Right. At your service, Ma'am. It turns on automatically when you pull. It's for the passengers up front. Too, if the armrest lighter didn't work, you could use this one. It stretches to the back." He guided the lighter as it rewound back into the dash.

"Home, James," Teri said, closed her eyes and flicked her hand. They all laughed.

Already familiar with the car's interior quirks, Teri sat back and grinned. She watched as Brooke lowered and raised the silk window shade next to her seat. "Privacy plus," Teri remarked, and pointed out interesting features on the dash as Alex smoothly double-clutched. He used what he called the 'grandma gear' to drive up the steep hill.

"Now isn't this the cat's pajamas?" Teri said with a laugh and wiggled back in the seat. She watched Brooke pick up two pillows and inspect them.

"Hey, Dad, who made these cool crocheted cushions?"

"Your Mom. She said they brightened up the interior. She even suggested we install cut-glass rose vases. They attach to the door jambs. She saw them in a car magazine on classics. But I kiboshed that, too fussy."

"It's such a quiet ride," Brooke exclaimed, then noticed what appeared to be a small, hunchbacked man. He was adjusting his shoulder pack as he determinedly walked up the sidewalk. "Teri, isn't that the man from the ferry, the one we saw feeding the seagulls?"

"Yes. Must have been a walk-on." She tapped Alex's shoulder. "Dad let's pull over and give him a lift. It's a big hike to Madrona from here. Strange, he doesn't have a ride."

The man looked surprised as the large car rolled to a stop. Alex reached across and rolled down the passenger window.

"Hi stranger; if you're heading toward Madrona, we can drop you off somewhere."

The man had lively sparkling eyes, separated by a long-twisted nose. "Oh. Bless you," he said with a grateful smile, removed his hat, and wiped his brow. His dark blue suit was neat and clean, but miserable on a warm day. "I am going to Madrona, and it is hot. Especially with this shoulder pack."

He leaped easily onto the running board and looked in the open window. "Er, oh. There appears to be no passenger seat," he said and smiled at the girls. "I'll hold on here."

"A moment, sir." Alex pulled the jump seat out from beneath the dash and, with a flourish, flipped up the attached backrest. "Now you see it, and at other times you don't."

"This is marvelous," the man said with glee. "It's like magic. What a clever vehicle." He took off his shoulder pack, opened the door, and slid onto the seat. "Kind sir, my name is J. P. Buckwass. The J. stands for Jinx." He shook Alex's hand, then turned toward the girls. "And who are the lovely ladies in the backseat?"

"I'm Alex's adopted daughter," Teri said. She extended her hand.

"And this is my friend, Brooke." Teri sat back. "We're graduate students and we'll be working on our separate master's projects on the island."

"That's fascinating. I'm interested in everything that goes on here. I used to live on Bradestone. Of course, many years ago. It's a beautiful place and I'm delighted to return." He winked.

"Most people don't know that in ancient times, Bradestone was a busy trading locale. Indigenous peoples sailed and traveled all the way from Lower California and down from Alaska. Inland natives came here too, from way east of the mountains." He looked bemused. "It was once regarded as a sacred trading place. Of course, that was long, long ago, before the scourge of the white man."

Eagerly, Teri leaned forward. "Mr. Buckwass, if you have any information about Bradestone's pre-history, I'd like to interview you. That's actually part of my project. My field is Anthropology."

"Well, my dear lady, I would be honored. I'm part Haida myself. But remember, not everything I know or have heard can be officially documented."

This puzzled Brooke. "But Mr. Buckwass, how do you know things that happened so long ago, like in the past? I mean, before there were any, er… written records. You're not that old."

"Ach, thank you, my dear, kind of you to notice. So, when I was young, not like today's generations, I always paid attention to my elders." He smiled. "I've traveled a lot and visited most of this world. And wherever I find myself, I take great care to listen and learn from the knowledge of others." He sighed. "My journeys have been long and satisfying. But now, alas, I am retiring from my work." He smiled. "Don't look so saddened, beautiful ladies. It's not a death sentence. And now I have a gift to lift your spirits." With a sudden snap of fingers, a crepe-paper flower bouquet appeared in his left fist.

Hands flew up in surprise. "You're a magician!" Brooke exclaimed and took the proffered posy. "Why, they even have a floral scent. They're lovely."

He shook his head. "Thank you, but I'm not a magician. Not in the slightest. It's only a hobby of mine. I'm actually a toymaker." He smiled slyly and carefully removed a tissue-wrapped object from his inner pocket. It appeared to be swaddled in hair. "This is for you," he said and handed it to Teri.

"Why it's a doll's head," Teri exclaimed and carefully removed the paper. "It's… so, so realistic. Look, Brooke, even the eyes move." She paused, enchanted. "These are what you make, or made? They're exquisite."

He smiled deprecatingly. "No again. I would like to think

I possess such artistic abilities, but the dolls were only a part of my toy business. As you can see, the head is porcelain, and they're fired and painted by a brilliant artist. I met her years ago, while on my travels in Italy."

Brooke looked carefully at the doll's face and felt inexplicably dizzy; a faint headache threatened. It's too hot, she thought, and with all this stimulus, she massaged her left brow and slowly handed the bouquet back.

"No, no. Keep the flowers and the doll's head too; they are gifts from me." He smiled. "Soon I'll be opening a bookshop here. I insist you visit me and bring your friends."

Alex slowed. "Mr. Buckwass, where do you want to be let off?"

Jinx looked around. "Already here? Main Street is fine. I appreciate the lift. By the way, is there somewhere I can reach you, fine people? I want to thank you appropriately."

Alex down shifted, applied the brakes, and smiled at the man. "There is. It's called the Inn of the Amber Crow. It's a new B&B; everyone in town knows where it is. My fiancé and I are opening it officially next spring."

"Ach, something more to look forward to; how delightful." He opened the passenger door and grabbed his backpack.

The girls thanked Mr. Buckwass profusely. Then all in one motion, he nimbly jumped from the running board, spun around with a bow, and doffed an imaginary hat. "I thank you. It was a most pleasant journey. Amber Crow, you say? What an interesting name, how…"

Alex closed his eyes and shook his head. "It's a long story but ask anyone in town. Not the tourists, of course, but most any of the locals you encounter will spin you quite the tale," he rolled his eyes, "with plenty of embellishments." Alex nodded. "Well, a good day to you, sir. Our lunch is waiting and we're off in a cloud of buffalo chips." With a puzzled smile, Jinx shut the door. Then Alex yahoo'd loudly and engaged the clutch.

"Is your dad always this, er… enthusiastic?" Brooke whispered as she dabbed her brow with a hanky.

Teri, with a know-it-all expression, closed her eyes. "When one is burdened with parents, bordering on senility, you must indulge them. It's kinder for everyone. Home, James." she shouted again.

Fading laughter drifted on the fall breeze as Mr. Buckwass watched the massive car take a left turn at the only traffic light in Madrona.

* * *

Jinx found a park bench, removed his backpack, and wiped his forehead with a handkerchief. Why had he worn a suit? He was miserable. The day was only getting hotter. Was it to impress? To show off wealth? He sneered. He still defaulted toward the white man's successful, business-man image.

He rubbed more sweat from his brow. At least the big-leaf maple above provided some shade, and the dappled gold leaves were his favorite color.

Jinx took off the warm jacket and placed it beside him then, reached into his pack and retrieved the half-eaten sandwich.

Munching, he looked at his watch. Ach, four hours before his appointment with Rose, the realtor. He put his sandwich down. He wasn't starving.

A gurgling noise came from the branches above. Jinx looked up. It sounded like a raven, but there wasn't one. He scanned the foliage meticulously. From behind a clump of maple leaves, a bird moved side wise. Carefully, it edged along the branch, then peered down at him. It was a large crow, an Amber Crow! Unusual. Ach, of course, most likely the one that Mr. Beahzhi had used for the name of the inn. Brilliant.

"Here," Jinx called and shook his sandwich. "You family of beggars are always hungry." The crow, motionless, watched Jinx intently; then moved further along the branch.

"Not interested? Well, here." Jinx threw the sandwich on the ground. The crow gurgled; the sound was deep, questioning. With suspicion and stealth, the bird quietly inched forward. Eventually, it stopped above him.

"Oh, a picky one, are we? Well, there… that's better." He ground the rest of the sandwich into the grass at his feet. "More to the liking of you and your gang of thieves."

Edgar became silent, a frozen statue of a crow.

The bird's stillness unsettled Jinx. In a singsong tone, he raised his voice; it was mocking and shrill. "You don't like me, I don't like you, get yourself lost, or I'll hit you…" Jinx reached down and picked a large stone, "with a rock!"

Edgar squawked loudly and took off toward the old Packard. Amber wings flashed as he raised a continuous alarm call. If he could, he would have said, "Here...here, here, make me cheer."

"Oh, shit!" Jinx jumped up, yelled in anger, and hurled the rock. A well-aimed splat hit his head. Furiously, he wiped at the sticky mess. Jinx clutched his hanky, eyes darting about desperately. A dry clump of grass, yes, yes, dry grass, that would do it. Jinx reached down, grabbed a clump, then stopped. Increasing in volume came the raucous cawing of many crows. Hiding under the trees wouldn't help him. Grabbing his coat, he ran.

CHAPTER 7

Arrival

Kay arose from her yoga mat. In the last year, even on misty mornings, the veranda's top deck was her favorite place. After stepping through her bedroom's French doors, she would move into her asanas. The aroma of fir trees, and the mirroring flashes of Scoon Bay, surround her with pure beauty.

Finished with her meditation, she rested her elbows on the railing. A lone heron sailed lazily over the water. The large bird vented a horrendous squawk. It resounded over the narrow bay below. Kay shivered, imagining a pterodactyl in flight. The blue-gray bird glided to the opposite beach on Heron's Hook, landed gracefully in the shallows and stood like a soldier. A fish breakfast was on its menu.

Kay's stomach grumbled. She glanced into the bedroom. Alex sprawled naked on the top quilt, snoring softly into his pillow. Typical up-and-at-em type of guy, she thought. And it was his turn to fix breakfast. He promised an herbed scramble, accompanied by jam-filled brioches. He bought twelve yesterday. "I put plenty in the pantry for us and those two ravenous girls," he'd said. Kay licked her lips. She savored the thoughts; the breads would go with Caffè Umbria, and naturally brewed in their French press, a fancy gift from their neighbor, Toady.

It would be breakfast for two. The girls had bowed out last night. Teri had convinced Brooke that she and Alex were tired.

"The old folks are, you know... wasted, all that excitement and yakking until 2:00 a.m." Teri grinned as she and Brooke stood at the foot of the stairs. Besides, there's a great buffet breakfast in town. The food was plentiful and spectacular. Afterwards, we can explore the island."

"We heard that!" Alex shouted from upstairs.

Kay chuckled. A youth, only a brief sleep, then the ability to tear off with excitement and boundless energy. Teri is pretty wise, though; it certainly allowed Alex and Kay to catch their collective breaths… and plan for Aunt Maureen's arrival.

Kay liked Brooke and could see why Teri and she had become close friends. Both girls were really thoughtful. They made quite a delightful duo.

She sighed; it was going to be a beautiful day and with no serious to-dos. Shading her eyes, she watched as the sun topped the trees on Heron's Hook. A breeze arose and as the sunlight touched the water, dazzling shards of light bounced off its surface. She inhaled deeply, then let her breath out slowly. Ah, this was communing with nature.

A soft crunching sound came from the gravel drive below. "Now who could that be?" Kay grumbled and peered over the railing.

Cinch's taxi eased on up the road, made a U-turn, then pulled to the front steps of the veranda. Slowly, a markedly tall woman crouched as she backed carefully out of the cab door. Reaching into a capacious handbag, she paid the driver, then seemed frozen as she stared at the vista of the bay and the hook.

The cab moved quietly down the drive. Cinch waved, but the woman did not wave back.

Must be over six feet, Kay thought, and she stood as tall and rigid as this morning's heron. After the motor sounds of the taxi faded to the main road, there was complete silence.

The woman's enormous head swiveled slowly from left to right. A puff of salt-scented breeze ruffled Kay's auburn hair, but the woman's disarray of thick, long black tresses did not move. She seemed transfixed, lost in the bay's beauty and the forested ridge opposite. The sun became warmer.

What, who? Oh Lordy, it had to be Aunt Maureen! A day early and nothing was ready. Kay waved. "Hey, up here." She shouted. What should she call the woman? "Er… Aunt Maureen. It's me, Kay. We'll be down in a few minutes to let you in."

The gigantic woman turned slowly. She looked up. Large, staring eyes glistened. And her face… oh my, those oddly shaped red lips made her look sad. Kay's hands went to her cheeks. Was the woman crying… or was she ill?

"It's me." Kay yelled and jumped once more, then turned and rushed pell-mell into the bedroom; her thoughts were chaotic. Why the early arrival? How come she acts so peculiarly? And what happened to her face?

"Alex, wake up!" Kay shouted, while peeling off her yoga togs and frantically sorting through her dresser drawers. "Aunt Maureen just showed up!" All benefits of Kay's meditative composure had flown.

"What? Huh, what's going on?" Alex, eyes squinting, sat up. He ran hands through his messy hair.

"It's Aunt Maureen. And someone has to let her in," Kay hissed, clutching her bra.

"Uh… no sweat. I'll do it," Alex answered vaguely. He staggered, reached for his pants, and began stumbling into them.

"Wow, are you going commando?" Kay blurted out.

Alex looked down. "I… uh … thought you were in a hurry. Look, I'll put my shirt on and be down in a tic… oh Mama Mia," he groaned and rubbed his face. "I've just remembered breakfast. Got to get breakfast started." He jabbed an arm in a sleeve, made for the door, then stopped. "Oh, well… it's no big thing," he said with a yawn and zipped up his fly.

"You said it, I didn't," Kay snorted.

"Huh? What? Hey, thanks a lot, real funny," Alex drawled as he groped for his sandals in the hall.

Downstairs, he finally finished buttoning his shirt and grabbed a quick gulp of cold coffee. Lipstick! The girl must have left it on the living room side table. Cup still in hand, he straightened his posture and swung wide the front door. Man, Kay was supposed to do the greeting and schmoozing. He wiped his bleary eyes with the back of his free hand and pasted a dutiful grin on his face.

"Greetings Mrs. D'Moresby. Kay will be down…" He hesitated, eyes wide. Not a person in sight. "Huh?" Nothing like talking to thin air, very thin air.

Blinking, and wishing he had a real hot cup of coffee, he looked up and down the gravel drive. Oh, there she was, standing at the trailhead to the beach. The sun was clearing the last tall trees. It cast the woman's shadow across the driveway. My god she's tall and built like a brick, hmmm. No dainty auntie coming to tea, was she? He thought.

Alex yelled and waved. "Hello, hello." He placed the empty cold cup on the railing, walked across the porch, then down the steps. The old girl's probably hard of hearing, he mumbled to himself.

"Hello," he said louder and held out his hand. "My name is Alex Beahzhi. I'm…"

Turning slowly, a drowsy but grave face studied him. "Please, don't shout. I have excellent hearing. And I know who you are. You're Kay's paramour." Her voice was nasal, deep, and firm.

Alex gulped, looked up, and stepped back. Egad, he was roughly six foot three, but she was taller. An odd chill crept along his shoulders, but he managed a solicitous Squire of the Inn voice. "How do you do? I hope your trip was pleasant. Did you come by plane?" She said nothing.

"Um, shortly we'll serve breakfast on this side of the veranda, near the kitchen. Er, do you take tea or coffee, sugar, cream?"

She waved a hand and smiled suddenly, lips curling back in a red tulip-like shape. "I drink coffee, black, and I'm starving," she paused. "I couldn't touch any of that abominable ferry food." Her voice boomed.

She studied him carefully, then engulfed his hand as if it were a child's. "A person eating that nauseating version of white man's food invites days of intestinal disaster… if not death." She threw back her head and roared. Her laugh, long and throaty, reverberated in a hooting sound across the bay. The hackles on Alex's neck stood up. She dropped his crushed hand and slowly moved towards the steps.

"Our friend, Thommy Jay, would agree with you wholeheartedly," Alex said to her back as he massaged his hand, then darted to open the screen door. Stooping, she entered. My God, he thought, before whatever happened to her face, she had been beautiful.

"Scoon Bay is every bit as lovely as Kay described. It reminds me of my younger days. Our tribe was on the Alaskan coast. The place is riddled with odd inlets and bays… but it's wilder and completely isolated and quiet." Her voice was resonant, but wistful.

Kay flew into the living room and held out her arms. If she

was shocked at her aunt's appearance, she didn't show surprise and awkwardly hugged the gigantic woman.

"Aunt Maureen, it's so wonderful to meet you in person." The woman did not return the embrace but looked wearily straight ahead, her eyes half-open. "You must be exhausted from the long trip. Alex and I will bring breakfast out on the side veranda. You just rest. There are comfy chairs and a large lounger to stretch out on. Do you like coffee with your breakfast, or tea maybe?" She knew she was babbling. The woman turned her head slowly and looked down at Kay.

"I told Alex I'd have coffee, but don't fuss, my dear. I'll drink whatever you have at hand." She continued with a long sigh. "It's extremely kind of you to receive me so soon and unannounced. As I wrote, I'm staying at the Madrona Inn. They have a large storage unit for my extra luggage, and the rooms are neat and quiet. I didn't wish to intrude. I know you're not finished with your B&B remodeling."

Aunt Maureen's gaze drifted around the large living room. She closed her eyes. "Ah yes, this house has a fascinating history." There was a long pause. "Spirits of place, speak to me," she said; then appeared to concentrate deeply. Alex and Kay stared at each other. Maureen's eyes popped open. "The ones here are apparently at peace…aligned with their past, and interestingly, your presence." She chuckled deeply. "Of course, there are always unsettled afreets lurking somewhere. You never know what activates the nasty things, nor what they're up to. And usually, not until it's too late."

Alex wiggled his eyebrows at Kay. She took hold of Aunt Maureen's hand. "Thank you for the heads up. We'll certainly be careful but having contented spirits around is a lovely thing to know." She winked at Alex. "Show Aunt Maureen to the breakfast table on the porch. Umm, also lower the bamboo shades. We want it to be airy, but comfortable."

Alex nodded. "Aunt Maureen, if you follow me, there's a shorter way through the hall. I'll settle you in. Breakfast will be out in a tic." *I hope she doesn't flatten the chair;* he thought uncharitably and showed her through. The newly painted furniture was old and the wicker tired.

She sat down, leaned back, and with a contorted grin on her face. She stretched and slowly winked at Alex. "Well, it hasn't collapsed, has it?" Alex blushed. My God, can she read minds too?

Aunt Maureen nodded as if she did. "By the way, I saw lemon, pineapple mint and feverfew. They're in the flower beds, by the stairs. Could you bring a bouquet for the table? The combination of aromas calms nerves." Alex bowed. "At your service." Walking swiftly along the veranda, he turned with a smile, waved nonchalantly; then almost plummeted down the porch steps.

CHAPTER 8

Breakfast Bombshell

Mushrooms, onions and garlic sauteing in butter and olive oil scented the kitchen. Alex gently stirred in the curried eggs and mayonnaise concoction. Towards the finish, he tossed in parmesan cheese, minced oregano and chive. Sniffing with approval, he portioned the large scramble onto three heated plates; sprinkled them with fresh chopped sorrel and closed his eyes. "Ah heaven," he muttered to Kay.

"Give the larger portion to Maureen," Kay said and bumped him with her hip. She placed the carafe of coffee, warmed milk, napkins, utensils, and other items on a separate tray.

Alex shook his head and grabbed the catsup. "The food will certainly be up to snuff, but the view at the table might be a bit off-putting. To quote one of my Army buddies: 'Odd's bodkins, that face has seen at least twenty-five miles of terrible road'."

Kay snorted, then growled. "You're not exactly the Apollo of perfection. A broken nose, hair that looks like someone took an eggbeater to it, and I'm sure you won't forget, a super exaggerated slue-footed limp; not to mention your rather interesting taste in clothes… or lack thereof."

"Hey, thanks a lot, mate. My foot problem is because of that so-called footbridge accident."

"What? Surely that was two years ago."

He sniffed loudly. "The doc told me to favor it. Anyway, she also has a faint cachet of copper metal that drifts about her."

"You're impossible. A preteen's mentality personified. Should I remind you that the smell of sweaty pits and well-worn socks can be challenging, too?"

Alex closed his eyes. "Not possible. I surround myself with the allure of wood, fern, blackberries, and notes of rum…very masculine. The ladies can't resist."

"You wish; after garlic-pasta, fish-wrestling and throwing chicken and horse manure throughout the garden? Dear, even when you divest yourself of clothes and spend a serious hour in the shower, you still have the faint aura of 'Eau-du-barn'." She paused and batted her eyes, "And what, may I ask, is this wood fern scent that turns the ladies' heads?"

He put his fingers to his lips. "That's a state secret, my ever lovely. Harrumph, isn't this tray ready to take out?"

"Yes, excellent diversion. I'll follow with this basket of breakfast pastries; wouldn't want any mysterious disappearances in transit. And don't forget, I have a proprietary interest in those cheese Danishes."

"What? You don't trust your man in transit?"

"That's just the problem, Alex, I do." She paused with a grimace.

"But mainly, I trust you to say and do the right things this morning."

Putting a benevolent smile on his face, he approached the breakfast table and placed the pastry tray on the sideboard. "It's a terrific view of the hook and bay this morning," Alex said. He paused and cocked his head. "It appears our lucky neighbor, Toady, is heading out in his sailboat. Pardon me Aunt Maureen, but I feel the urge." Alex stepped to the railing, cupping his mouth, "Ahoy there, mate!" he shouted.

With an echoing 'Hail me hearty' Toady yelled back, waved, then blasted the ear-piercing boat horn.

Maureen broke into hooting laughter. "Men will always be boys," she shouted, then regarded Alex with sleepy eyes. "I gather you'd rather be out sailing?"

Alex spread his hands. "True, true, I must admit, and I apologize. Sounds carry here."

She slowly shook out her napkin. "Where I grew up, near the Skeena River, the surf was extremely loud. But when the many voices of the sea calmed, human sounds carried for miles."

After the coffee was poured, pastries eaten, and sides of salsa and various jams depleted, Aunt Maureen pushed back from the table, put down her fork and sighed. "Everything was delicious, sumptuous even. I didn't know fresh side-pork was still available."

Kate nodded. "I'm glad you like it, and it keeps well in the warming oven. Our butcher in Madrona wanted us to try it. We're fans now and are going to feature it on the Inn's breakfast menu."

Maureen patted her lips with her napkin. "It is certainly better than bacon."

"He's going to provide all our meat requests," Alex said with a nod.

"It's small-town businesses that cater the best," Maureen said, then paused for a length of time, her eyes half-closed, lips parted. "I really don't know where to start. But I feel it is important that I explain my rather… ah, disturbing facial appearance. I know it bothers some people."

Alex glanced at Kay, who smiled and put down her Danish. "Aunt Maureen, that's unnecessary. We presumed it was an accident."

Maureen focused on her plate; her voice was deeply nasal. "It was more than that. I was caught in a house fire…unfortunately, one that I started; I was in a rage." She looked at their startled glances, then sighed. "My only excuse is that I hadn't been married long and was very young. And horrible circumstances confronted me. There were things I was vaguely aware of but stupidly ignored. What I did was foolish, but even when a child, I suffered from these inexplicable rages. When I go into them, I never know what I'm doing. And now that I'm older, they're more frequent and can come on at the most unexpected times."

Alex shrugged. "Occasionally, we all fly off the handle, over disturbing things… er, how do you cope with them? Our demons, as they say?" He looked sideways at Kay.

Maureen reached into the breast area of her loose and voluminous dress and withdrew a green-glass vial. It hung from a leather lace around her neck. "This contains my medicine for such emergencies. An antidote, if you will. It's most useful when a spell is coming on."

Kay slowly dabbed her napkin at her lips. "Do you have any warning signs when these… er, spells might occur?"

"My physician, a very revered shaman of our tribe, ferreted out the subtle things that can bring on my moods. He's helped me realize key triggers that I frequently curb most attacks."

"Um, how does one administer your medication?" Alex asked.

"One or two teaspoons, usually stirred into a cup of temperate water works the best. I have a large amount already prepared and stored in the refrigerator at my apartment. But she fingered her vial. I use this as an emergency first dose." However, if things become worse, I carry a small flask of three doses in my purse." She dug around until a triangular-shaped, pearly-green bottle appeared in her hand.

"Several swallows of this, and in about ten minutes, I'm completely able to," she eyed Alex, "I believe the correct Army term is stand-down," she said, then leaned back and hooted with laughter.

Kay smiled and pointed. "Well, that is a good idea, and certainly convenient." Alex nodded with an uneasy chuckle.

"Yes, it is. But I also want you to know, when I come out of the state, I've forgotten the incident and, frequently, whatever triggered it."

Alex inhaled deeply. "Thank you for telling us." He looked at Kay. "We have several friends who have sudden attacks of vertigo. They don't know what triggers those either. The spells can come slowly or fast. And they carry a drug; I believe it's called Meclizine. I think it's mainly used for air or seasickness."

"Yes, I'm aware of that medicine. But my condition is quite different." Maureen fastened her gaze to a remote point behind them. "I also felt it was necessary for you both to be aware of my gap that happens after the event."

"If you notice me going into a, shall we say, situation. I usually find this flask on time. It has a delicious taste. I merely hold it to my lips and swallow." She leaned forward. "Our shaman says my condition is very similar to grand-mal, but these spells, are not only harmful to me but others as well."

She reached over and patted Kay's arm. "My dear, I didn't wish to alarm you, but you both should know this odd condition your aunt suffers from."

The remains of breakfast had gone quite cold.

CHAPTER 9

Brooke's Journal Entry #1

Today I downloaded my first pictures of the island. *Beautiful locations with many well-kept farms separated by old split-cedar fences and rolling pastures. There are horses, meadows with munching cows, and lovely stands of old trees. The insanity of covering each inch of the earth with houses, then paving everything hasn't reached here…yet. Driftwood-covered beaches are everywhere and so much wildlife that I'm constantly shooting away… with my camera, of course.*

Madrona is the quintessential calendar picture of a 1950s old town with wooden and newer buildings. There's even a 1920s general store called a Mercantile down one of the back roads; and Teri says, "You have seen nothing yet until you've seen Burn." It has some late 19th-century buildings. They rebuilt the town after a devastating fire. So, I'll be able to put some cool historical shots in my college folio.

Burn has a terrible history though. A conflagration burned Asian farmers out. Some cruel, land-grabbing white settlers started it. Prejudice and misery are everywhere in our history. It's there, even now. No matter how many times people try to white-wash it out.

On the lighter side, Teri's a trooper. She's taken me to special places that I would never find on my own. Tomorrow we're back-packing on Heron's Hook. It has exceptional stretches of old forests and trails. And it's directly across Scoon Bay. Right now, I'm looking out the window and can see the Hook from my bed. When we go over there, we'll be able to see this old farmhouse. It's the opposite. I'll get some excellent shots.

Teri's family is planning to open their B&B by next spring. Teri's mom is letting us sleep in two of the second-floor finished guest rooms.

Love the new French Doors. The rooms aren't pretentious, just right and all different. The ones on the top floor and facing Scoon Bay are my favorites.

The family voted on naming this farmhouse 'The Inn of the Amber Crow'. It's an illustrious name because Kay gives treats to a saucy crow named Edgar. He flies up, from time to time, into an apple box nailed near the top of the veranda. It's below our rooms and we can all feed him snacks. He has amber feathers and a real snarky attitude. When his girlfriend, and sometimes the entire bird family, shows up, it gets extremely noisy.

This remarkable crow lives with a local man, Willie Cloudmaker. He's another person I haven't met yet. And he sounds like an interesting fellow. Teri says he's an excellent woodworker and carves all kinds of Pacific Northwest artwork, like rattles, masks and has even made bentwood boxes.

He's part Tlingit and has an extended family, with relatives in Oregon, the San Juan Islands, Canada, and Alaska. Evidently, Mr. Cloudmaker is a great friend to most of the people here. He lives near a marshy pond, with a stream that feeds into the south end of Scoon Bay. When Teri goes to interview him, I'll go too. It's part of her research proposal for her social ethnography professor. Hope Mr. Cloudmaker likes to have his pictures taken.

Friday, Teri and I will take the dune buggy to the trailhead of heron's hook. The locals call the hook a hogback because of its shape. And it looks like one. I've already skimmed the shoreline with my binocs.

Also, I just walked out on the top deck of the veranda, set up my tripod, and shot away. Then every night I sort through the pics. It takes about an hour to plow through and select the best.

The inn itself is fascinating and has loads of charm. Teri says Alex and Kay started converting it over two years ago. They've kept the character of the old farmhouse; and even if it's not finished, it's a great place to stay. We added new bedrooms, several with bathrooms en suite. The furniture is pretty scant, but Teri's mom has a good friend, Thommy Jay. He's an antique dealer, and he will help her decorate. Teri also said her mom, Kay, will inherit a lot of old furniture from her Aunt Maureen, who is downsizing.

Surprise, surprise, Kay's aunt showed up. It was at breakfast time, this morning, and she wasn't expected till later this week. Odd, I guess she's decided to stay at a motel in Madrona. Teri and I missed meeting her as we were having our own delicious breakfast at Myrtles in Madrona. Then we took off to see the island. We didn't get back till dinner time, which is about in a half hour.

Okay, I should stop stalling and talk about the weird feelings I've been having. Remember, Dad tried to discourage me from coming here. He said I'd be bored and because the island is closer to the ocean; it was cold, foggy, and rainy most of the time. And he said I wouldn't have the convenience of the city.

Too, he emphasized the lack of my friends. He knows I'm with my best friend Teri. If he could think of anything unappealing, he brought it up. He knows I'm not clueless, and it was so obvious he was trying to keep me away. And this place is none of those things. He doesn't seem to get that I'm not frivolous. And even the short time I've been here I like the rural life. In fact, with Teri's enthusiasm, showing me everything, and with her quirky family, it isn't boring at all.

Her stepdad, Alex, is a hunk and always says things like, "Now if this were the Army, we would…" he's so funny. And if Wick or Byron hear him behind his back, they'll make a serious face and salute him. It's hard to keep from laughing. Teri's mom, Kay, and Alex aren't married, but that's all good, real romantic.

And there are handsome and interesting guys here. Teri's brother for one and his friend, Wick Wilding. Mr. Wilding owns and is in charge of the boathouse community center in Burn. Naturally, that's where the Burn Puppet Theater is located. Teri told me he is Alex's son. Must be from a former marriage. Seems awfully young to own a Boathouse. Anyway, Teri's brother Byron is exceptional and funny, but he seems very intense, more about him later.

I'm still avoiding what's bothering me. Well, it's this strange feeling, like I've been here before. It scares me a lot and makes me sad at the same time. I get good vibes and bad vibes depending on where I am. Things seem vaguely familiar and pleasant and then, suddenly; I sense something foreboding and feel lost. It's like having a horrible dream in the middle of the day! Sometimes I'll tear up for no reason at all. It's crazy, like I'm somebody else and not me, at the same time.

I know I'm not insane or even near it. I'm an easy-going, normal person. But, whatever is happening, I'll have to face it head-on. Our family has had many crises and gotten through them, like Mom's dying and then that financial mess at college. Wish Mom were here; she always knew what to do. But I feel there is a connection here to all my fears. And I'm determined to find out what it is!

Anyway, Teri's a rock. So supportive, says she'll help me find what's causing these odd feelings, and she doesn't think I'm losing it either. She says there's a logical reason for anything that happens, whether good or bad. And we aren't always aware of subtle things that trigger our emotions. She helped me through the breakup with Todd. I thought I would die, but I didn't. Maybe, subconsciously, I'm still freaking out about that.

Anyway, on the ride to the inn, we gave a man named Jinx a lift to Madrona. I usually hold any judgment back till I get to know a person, but right off, I didn't like him.

Oh, man. I hear the guys running downstairs and my computer says it's time for dinner. What will it be? Kay and Alex are experimenting with different menus and use us as guinea pigs. Since they're both superb cooks, the food is fantastic. 'Oink, oink', as Byron would say… he's so cute. Bye for now.

CHAPTER 10

New Business

Mr. Jinx Buckwass rubbed his hands together and generated one of his lopsided smiles. Unfortunately, to Rose, it only made him look more sinister. He rarely spoke and when he did, it was in a high voice and his head bobbed. Rose felt uncomfortable standing next to him. The large room had a dank odor.

"Yes, Ms. Bracken, this will do nicely. But I will need a few area rugs and the custom-made bookshelves I mentioned earlier. By the way, the photos you sent me were excellent."

Rose tottered slightly on her heels. "There's a skilled carpenter and a marvelous interior decorator that live on the island. I'll write their names and contact sites on the back of my card before you leave." She moved toward the rear door. "Would you like to see the backyard? It hasn't been looked after in years. I also have the name of a very good lawn guy and gardener. He…"

Mr. Buckwass turned and smiled. "Dear lady, I'm sure you do. I, myself, will tend to any minor problems, but much later. Right now, I must find a place to store my things. The movers come next week," he said. "Do you know if that storage facility I spotted near the dock has any spaces available?" His head waggled even more. "I've been so incredibly busy; I haven't had time to enquire."

"Don't worry; I'll be glad to set up a storage unit for you. I think there are several large ones empty and—"

"I imagine I'll need about 50 to 60 square feet." He interrupted, then pursed his lips. "Probably two will do if the larger ones have already been taken."

"I'll find out for you." Earlier, she noticed when he addressed her, he never looked into her eyes. He concentrated solely on her mouth; it was strange. Maybe he never listened to her either.

"Miss Bracken, you've been so helpful. Let's get back to your office. It's chilly here. Don't want to come down with ague, now do we?"

What on earth did he mean? It sounded like an argument. "No, we absolutely don't. I've got the …"

"Of course, you're very efficient. I noticed those things." He rubbed his thin fingers together. "After the pertinent documents are signed," he hesitated, "the deposit and the first and last month's rent will be in cash. I insist."

"Don't be concerned. That's the usual protocol; my accountant tends to the contracts, and she handles everything through the bank."

"Nice, tidy, and efficient. That's what I like about you. And thank you for honoring my insistence on no inspection and related fees."

"Well, the State…"

He waved and wobbled. "Just another minor problem. By the by, is there a decent seafood restaurant near here? I'm fond of cockles and clams…oysters work in a pinch too." His grin now struck Rose as cadaverous. "Brunch today will be my treat." He paused and ran a finger along his forehead. "I also plan to take two lovely ladies to lunch next week. I think you know them, Miss Teri Roberts, and her friend Brooke Hamlin?"

"Oh, how kind of you. I'm sure they will enjoy that. I haven't met Brook yet. But thank you so much for my invitation. Unfortunately, I have another appointment this afternoon and it too involves a luncheon with clients," she made a show of looking at her watch. "However, Madrona has a pleasant seafood restaurant on the next street over. It's called Myrtles, simple dining, but lovingly prepared and very fresh."

"I'm sure," he said in a faint whisper, "but never mind. Another time perhaps?"

"Er, that would be nice," Rose said and concentrated on opening the front door. She stamped into the sunshine. Mr. Buckwass tugged on a lanyard around his neck and put on his large pair of sunglasses.

"Carry these always. I have a terrible allergy to sunlight. My doctor says that I must always protect my eyes and my skin. I could get cataracts, and I burn so easily."

That would explain his extreme pallor, Rose thought and rummaged through her purse. "I have a similar problem," Rose said with a guilty chuckle, then made a "tsk, tsk" noise, "oh prunes, I've left my sunglasses back at the office."

"Ach, madam, allow me." A pair of expensive sunglasses, including their case, miraculously appeared in his hand.

"My stars! How did you do that?"

He grinned and bowed. "Parlor magic, it's one of my hobbies. But these are a gift from me."

"Oh, I couldn't."

"I always carry an extra pair. I insist."

"Why thank you. I'm amazed they fit perfectly." She shook her head, "and such a lovely case too."

"I think appropriate fashion is important for all sexes."

She smiled. "It's surprising that we still have to wear them so late in the year. Usually, the month of October isn't this cloudless and warm." She turned toward him. "I don't know if you're aware of this, but the Northwest has set record highs through these last five months, and now October has started very warm and dry."

He made a dramatic gesture toward the sky. "Global warming it's here, and Mother Nature is on the move. Recently, I was in France and Italy. Ach, my oh, my. Europe and its environs are having major floods, landslides, and then severe droughts. Our climate is reaching a serious point for all the creatures on this planet." His head wobbled. "We seem to be a species that continually fouls its own nest. I tell you, Miss Bracken, a major change is coming. And when it reaches full steam, it won't be good for anything or anyone. Ach, I'm getting carried away."

Rose strode toward her car. "Many of my friends would agree with you. Thommy Jay says that when it stomps on our tails, it'll all be too late. Maybe we'll go the way of the dinosaurs," she mumbled as she searched her purse for keys.

There was a quick, wriggly movement in the vacant grassy lot across the street. Mr. Buckwass gaped. His eyes became wider. "Wah… what is that?"

Roses squinted; her distance glasses were somewhere in her purse. "Why … I'm not sure. But I bet they're finally going to mow that tall grass. It's a fire hazard." she tsked. "One tossed cigarette and whoosh, the whole thing will go up. I called the owners the other day. I said that..."

Mr. Buckwass shushed with his hands and strained to stand on his toes. "No, no... I think it's something else."

Rose chuckled as she fumbled her regular glasses up under the new sunglasses. "You're right. It looks like someone has put up a scarecrow. It's a witch. Look at the face. Hate to run into her on a stormy night," Rose said with a chuckle, then shook her head. "Tsk, tsk, our kids are up to more shenanigans." She brought out her jangle of keys. "Hallowe'en is about three weeks away and some youngsters can't wait to stir up the islanders. Why I was talking to Cal Smith just the other day about the dry grass on that lot, and..."

The creature appeared to grow outstretched arms. It lurched towards them.

"No, no." Mr. Buckwass shrunk back, hands shaking as he pointed. "It's the witch and she's alive!"

Rose cupped her hands around her mouth and shouted loudly. "Hey over there! Woo, woo, very, very scary, but watch out for the little ones, they might not think it's so funny."

The monster froze, turned cumbersomely, then reeled into a stand of trees and disappeared.

"Corn and confusion. I wonder how they did that?" Rose smiled and turned towards Mr. Buckwass. His face was ashen.

"My God, it's her!" he exclaimed and gave Rose a terrified look. "She's here for revenge."

Flummoxed, Rose stared at Mr. Buckwass, then back at the vacant lot. He must be nuttier than the proverbial fruit cake, she thought. It was one of those rare times when Rose was at a loss for words.

CHAPTER 11

Unit 13

With a self-satisfied smile, Mildred Osprey unlocked the door to storage unit 13. She'd saved this one for today. Who did the new tenant think she was, royalty? Pah!

D'Moresby; just another Indian who thought she was better than everyone else. Probably a pagan too.

Mildred sniffed. As the new owner of the Madrona Inn and a Christian, she had every right to be here. She flicked on the light switch. The dim bulb cast mysterious shadows. Only 25-watt industrial bulbs were allowed. After all, electricity was expensive. And besides, the basement walls had small, slotted windows at the top. They provided sufficient light during the daytime. It would be suspicious if anyone came down at night.

Her trusty penlight threw a narrow beam. She smelled something. The odor was peculiar. Mothballs, but there was something else, the odor of dust and decay.

Quietly and methodically, she removed lids from various containers. Contents scrutinized; she replaced the inspected boxes in their original order.

The one labeled Xmas ornaments felt light and rattled. Carefully removing the lid, she found a torn cardboard sleeve of shiny metal strands. Ah yes, rain. Mildred lightly fingered the tinsel. There were lumps beneath the yellowing tissue. She sniffed. There were only a few small ornaments. She paused, then huffed. Below, and covered in more tissue, were five obscene celluloid dolls, almost naked; with cheap, glittery top hats.

The innocents clutched black canes and wore scanty bits of

feathers. Wide-eyed, they stared back at Mildred. She diverted her attention from their pink nudity, and the spots of feather and glitter. The Devil's work, but she couldn't help studying the carefully wrapped dolls. She recalled that her louche great-grandfather had won something like this at the Multnomah County Fair. He insisted they hung on their Christmas tree every year. Right, they were called Kewpies, disgusting little things. She closed the box hastily.

Hmm, that stack of luggage should contain something of interest. She ran her rubber-gloved hands over the tops and sides. Fancy brass locks adorned the three fine leather cases. Fortunately, the locks easily clicked open. Drat, no flimsy garments or racy peignoir sets, utterly useless; no tittle-tattle here. Mildred shook her head. The woman spends her money foolishly.

Her eager eyes darted to a shiny black cabinet against the back wall. Asian, of course, no doubt Chinese, and made of cheap lacquered wood. Something on the front glinted. She'd save that till the end.

A moth-eaten footstool rested under the tall cabinet. Next to it was a child's oaken rocking chair; and there, a wicker baby-buggy. Why did this strange and ugly person have such ridiculous things?

Mildred shrugged. It made sense, though. Last week, when the woman registered at the desk, she had difficulty talking. And was bored as if she would fall asleep right there. She kept pointing at her letter of confirmation, tapping on the line that stipulated she would rent the apartment for six months. Mildred snorted; did the foolish women think I couldn't read?

Then there was the cough, and a licorice odor. Combined with nasal honking, it was disgusting. Mildred kept her distance. Most likely, the woman had one of those foreign viruses.

She shook her head as she continued to reflect. Also, there was a green tinge to her skin, and the red lipstick was thick and garish. The D'Moresby woman had no sense of simple makeup or dress. Mildred pursed her lips. For all she knew, she could be a dope fiend. It wouldn't be unheard of. She'd seen those types before. Either way, she was obviously unhealthy.

Mildred wondered if she could tolerate the women's presence for a month, let alone six. After all, she kept an up-scale and discrete hotel. The derelicts of life could go elsewhere. She had to consider the other guests and her reputation. She shrugged, but money was money. D'Moresby hadn't been sticky with the dollar, and it would be helpful during the slow time of year.

Mildred carefully lifted the lid of a heavy box. She inspected the contents, only a cracked glass lamp with a metal base, and carelessly wrapped it as well. She regarded the hideous dragonflies, ungodly insects. But then she smiled. They looked appropriately squashed. Carefully, she lifted the shade. Beneath rested a stereoscope and beside it, wrapped with rubber bands, World War One pictures. There were views of the Eiffel Tower and the Arc de Triomphe. "Insipid Frenchie taste," she mumbled. Toady and Thommy Jay, the community fairies, would be thrilled to their toes.

She put everything back. It was a peculiar collection of things, junk for normal people. She backed up, almost toppling a box. Carefully, she admonished herself. Though many of her hotel guests were out for the day, one might unexpectedly return. But she had a perfect reason for being here. Yes, setting traps for RATS, if they ever even dared to enter her establishment.

Now the special black cabinet. Pulling out the tatty footstool beneath, she plumped down. Her fingers traced the inlaid polished stones on the double doors. Humph, Chinese fishing from peculiar boats, and coiling dragons. It looked like and was… another work of the Devil. She crossed herself and pulled on the pear-shaped brass handles. A strong smell of licorice cough drops assailed her nostrils.

Carefully, she probed inside the opening, but the dim-lit bulb made it difficult to see. She again flashed on her penlight. The upper shelf held a long, narrow wooden box. Oddly, someone had haphazardly stuffed old linens on the lower shelves.

She withdrew the box. It was heavy and surprisingly elegant. She shook it gently, the paper rustled, her eyes became slits. "Ah, letters," she said aloud. Finally, she would find something incriminating, something nasty.

With elation, she lifted the lid. Curses! It was some odd-shaped object, wrapped in heavy black velvet; ugh, the smell of mothballs mixed with licorice was strong, almost nauseating.

She unfolded the cloth carefully. It had to go back, just so. Obviously, it was something precious. She held her breath in delight.

Her mind went blank. What was she seeing? A child's clenched fist? Without thinking, Mildred unwrapped the rest. It couldn't be. Attached to the fist was a torn arm, spattered with dried blood.

Mildred hurled the box. Her screams echoed through the basement, then she collapsed in a dead faint.

CHAPTER 12

A Rat

Sergeant Isaac Reynolds shrugged and spread his gloved hands. Arms crossed; Police Sheriff Ujima Washington waited for an answer. He swallowed twice. "The poor woman said she heard rats." He gestured towards an open bag of traps next to unit 13's door. The scent of peanut butter wafted from the action levers.

A corner of Ujima's mouth curled. "I think the only rat here was Mildred Osprey. She's a born snoop and whiner." Ujima toed a piece of debris. "Look at this mess. Ever since she bought this place, she's been prying into her guest's lockers. I've had complaints. Renters find things, either disturbed or missing. She's a definite pain in the rectal area."

Isaac turned to hide his grin.

"Okay Sergeant. Fill me in on the entire story. Would I be too hopeful of imagining an avenging rat attacked her?"

"No such luck," Isaac murmured as he looked at his notes. "A hotel guest, Mr. Arthur Ross, found her. Mrs. Osprey told him she was setting a trap under that cabinet back there, but there's no evidence of that effort." He pulled his nose. "She also said she accidentally bumped into the cabinet, which caused the doors to fly open. I know; I know...anyway, the box fell out. Its contents spilled to the floor. In shock, she flung the 'evidence of murder and mayhem' toward that wall and passed out."

Ujima chuckled and walked over to the 'mayhem' evidence. With gloved hands. She picked up a cloth of black velvet and three pieces of broken arm.

"Humph, I can see this could be quite a surprise." She fitted the sections together and studied the arm closely. "It seems to be ceramic, maybe bisque or porcelain? But it looks real, and it's old. This brown paint; resembles spots of dried blood." Ujima sighed. "We'll have to get it analyzed. Could be some weird stage prop, or someone's disgusting joke. We'll have to interview the owner. Either way, it's damn peculiar."

"How about Thommy Jay?"

"What about Mr. Jay?"

"He has a collection of puppets and dolls in the display case at the back of Toady's shop. He seems to know everything about them. When made, where, and their rarity."

Ujima pursed her lips. "Ah, into dolls, are we?"

Isaac blushed. "Only the grown-up ones! I was in the shop last week. Miss Rose Bracken has her mother's old collection. She wants to sell. Some are called Terry Lee dolls. Man, Mr. Jay went into detailed explanations about them, and then told us, I mean Rose, all about his antique collection in the shop. Some are really old. There was a fantastic Russian doll with actual fur hats and capes. Some of them are rare and worth plenty."

"How did Mr. Jay acquire such a collection?"

Isaac shrugged. "He said, besides Roses', many of them come from residents at Shady Meadows. He sells the dolls on commission. Also, he handles other things they wish to unload."

Ujima smiled. "Before we send this off, consult Mr. Jay. Find out anything you can about … this." She bagged the arm's remnants. "How is Rose these days? Are you and she still an item?"

Isaac stood straighter. "Yes, we are. We're seeing each other and haven't come to blows. We complement one another and she's a smart woman, knows her real estate business inside and out."

"Yes, she is clever. And since the scandal at the other agency, she's the only act in town. You've got a neat lady there. Rose may seem ditzy, but when she's in a tight situation, she's a woman of action."

Isaac laughed. "You mean when she tangled with that rich dame and her Mercedes?"

"Yes, that, and when you two cornered our dear, insane Edith."

"Yep, it's been pretty exciting." Isaac grinned. "Rose is a rock and funny too; though I just wish she wouldn't shop at Sabras all the time. It's expensive."

"True, not cheap, but do I hear a little censorship there?"

"No, no, not that. It's because Sabra always uses Rose for testing a new line in shoes…and other things. Rose falls for it every time. Sabra gets super complimentary and there goes Rose's budget."

"Are you Rose's taste, ethics and monetary manager?"

"Rose has a closet full…she's the Imelda Marcos of Bradestone," he exclaimed.

"So now you're appraising her closet contents. Umm, what else Sergeant Reynolds?"

"Well, you know what she's like; she enjoys showing all the things she has."

Ujima feigned a scandalized look. "So that's how it is."

Isaac's face became purple. "No, no. I didn't mean that!"

Ujima laughed heartily. "But seriously, Sabra creates smart designer looks. However, she also has a practical line of clothing." She paused and winked, "with fashion Sabra makes beautiful wedding dresses… and has, for most of the ladies on the island."

Isaac looked stricken. "Er, er yeah, yeah. She has lots of pretty dresses. Rose always asks me to tag along, says she prefers having a man's opinion." He was perspiring profusely.

Ujima cocked an eye. "The island grapevine has it you bought her a ravishing gold lame dress. Then you two set off for a romantic date at the Seattle opera house."

"Oh yeah, that was a really special evening. We went to see The Tales of Hoffman. Toady said I'd have to rent a tux for opening night and Rose said she had nothing fancy to wear, so she took me to Sabras. Sabra pulled something off the sale rack. I thought it looked great and mentioned I would spring for it since the opera was sorta my idea. Sabra heard me, made a crocodile smile, and says she knows just the thing. From nowhere, this bolt of gold material appears, and whoosh up goes the price tag."

Ujima patted his arm. "Admirable, Sergeant. Rose showed me photos of that night. You both were stunning."

"Ha, I think I was stunned. We followed with dinner at the College Club."

"Sargent, it was a lovely thing to do. Few men find the right way to a woman's heart."

Isaac said nothing but ran a shaky hand over his face.

"Now, back to business. I want you to interview Mrs. Osprey. Wait till she has regained her senses. And don't forget she's a sharp old bird… yes, pun intended. I want to know why she specifically picked this storage unit. And if there are any other private units that she felt she had to protect from rodents. And look for evidence of droppings or other ratty actions. Then find out the name of whoever rents this space. I'll conduct the interview." Ujima cocked her head. "I'm curious to know what this cabinet stores," she scanned the area, "and if anyone has disturbed the contents of these other containers."

"Will do. A few looky-loos came by after the uproar and complained to me about things being gone through." Isaac shrugged. "But what could I do?"

"Basics. Get their names and talk to them. If they have evidence of tampering, or if caught in the act, it would be an invasion of privacy. All complaints should be registered. If there are enough of them, the island rumor-mill will kick in and that's not the publicity one would want. After this incident, if grievances continue, we will apply pressure. I want her to face some sort of accountability."

"Aye, aye. Anything else, Sheriff?"

"Isaac," she said and gestured with the bag of arm parts. "This is grotesquely realistic. Where did it come from? Is it some peculiar stage prop? And why was it wrapped in this carved box and black velvet, and why in this chest?" She frowned. "I've a hunch this is symbolic of something… and I don't care for the variety of conclusions I'm coming to."

CHAPTER 13

Interview

Ujima smiled, shifted her briefcase to her left hand, and stepped forward. "My Name is Sheriff Washington, welcome to Bradestone. I'm very pleased to meet Kay's Aunt Maureen." Ujima looked up. Six foot four, easy, she guessed. No response. "She told me you were coming to visit." The woman stared vacantly. "When did you arrive?"

Maureen yawned. "I flew in last Tuesday on a friend of a friend's plane from Canada. It was called a Gooney Bird. The weather was roughing up a bit. Quite bumpy. But what an appropriate name for the plane." Her laugh was a hooting bray.

"I'm sorry. It's usually a pleasant journey. I'm wondering, what did you do after you landed?"

"I was so shaken and tired. I spent the day here and then met Kay and Alex for breakfast the next morning. I arrived a bit earlier than they expected, but everything has turned out pleasantly." Her large mascara outlined eyes slowly took in her surroundings. "Won't you come through and take a seat on the couch? At present, it is the better piece of my furniture." She slowly looked around the room. "The movers should be here with the rest. I think, by the middle of next week."

The couch was large and comfortable. "Thank you," Ujima muttered as she removed a pad and pencil from her case. Aunt Maureen settled into a straight-backed parson's chair and faced her.

"Oh, I am forgetting myself. Would you care for a cup of tea and a biscuit? I entertained very little in my other home."

"No, thank you. I had a late lunch. But don't let me stop you."

She shook her enormous head. "I am aware of why you're here and am glad you came. It's always nice to meet the local constabulary. It puts one at ease." Maureen leaned forward to take Ujima's hand. She squeezed firmly. It was an awkward moment, her grip long and forceful. Ujima let go. It was like being caught between two chunks of ice. How could one person embody so many unfortunate traits? Probably teased all her life, and there was that odd smell, feint but persistent.

"So, you've heard about what happened in your storage unit?"

"Oh yes. I first noticed the commotion from my room and came out on the landing. The man next door to my apartment told me there was a Sherriff's car out front and an emergency vehicle. They took Mrs. Osprey away. I hoped everything would be satisfactory, but then I became amused. The fellow was so excited he couldn't stop jumping and chattering about it."

"Yes, it was a curious incident. Have you been down there since you put your things in storage?"

"No, but I'm surprised there is a rodent problem. Everything is so clean."

"I was surprised too. Mrs. Osprey said she was setting out rat traps. Evidently, she stumbled, had an unfortunate experience, and lost consciousness. Oh, don't worry. The incident was minor. She will recover. But I am curious. Have you noticed anything like droppings or things being chewed on? You know, rats. If they make their minds up, they can get in just about anywhere."

Maureen's voice was sonorous. "I have seen no vermin. Mrs. Osprey runs an exceptionally clean inn. She was probably taking preventative measures." There was a long pause. "My neighbor said Mrs. Osprey became dizzy and fainted. What was the cause?"

Ujima lifted her leather briefcase onto her lap. "Mrs. Osprey said she stumbled against a large oriental cabinet."

"Oh yes. The one at the back of my unit."

"She also said something fell out that shocked her."

"Indeed. That's the cabinet I wish to give to Kay. There's nothing in it but hand-embroidered linens, cloths, pillowcases, antimacassars, and serviettes. Most of the lacework is beautiful and fits the period of her inn…so you see, there couldn't be anything startling in there." Maureen leaned in with a confidential air. "You know I'm giving everything of mine to Kay. She can use those things. I don't have any need for them anymore."

Ujima stopped opening her briefcase. "That's interesting, and why is that?"

"I mostly grew up mostly in my native winter village, in the wilds of Alaska. Our summer village bordered on an inlet on the coast. All you needed to survive was your clan, the woods, the sea, the animals, and the ever-changing beauty of nature. My family, my people, we were thrilled." She sighed; her eyes unfocused. "My father was a white man, a Norseman, a lovely and kind person, but he'd been brought up, as they say, 'to toe the line' when it came to Scandinavian ways. He rebelled and at fifteen, left to roam the world."

"Hmm, quite the adventuresome sort."

"Oh yes. In his wanderings, he found our village and my mother. He married into our clan, her life. Then they had children. Because he came from a wealthy white family, and was worldly, our father entertained us with his stories of glitter and gaiety." She gave a hooting laugh. "Are there any peoples, who can live without the baubles and enticements of a wondrous world? I don't think so. Who can resist those temptations?"

Ujima leaned back on the couch. "I beg to differ. There are people who can. For instance, certain tribes in South America are trying to keep their cultures from being trampled under the guise of progress. There are people in Africa too. But it is like fighting a steam roller. Missionaries soften them up, then come the entrepreneurs, followed by money grabbing conglomerates, then the state moves in to finish them." Ujima grimaced. "It's strange…oh, I apologize. I was getting on my soapbox. Unfortunately, I do from time to time."

Maureen answered slowly. "No, I understand completely, but the civilization steamroller, as you put it, is colorful, exciting, seductive, but sadly, ultimately destructive. Not everyone's aware that these temptations come with bitter consequences and sacrifice. People in society are expected to conform, and they shun or ridicule anything different or individual, branding it as useless. Subtlety is stamped out." Maureen looked down at the floor. "I've been there… I've seen it happen."

Thinking of humanity's worse phantoms, Ujima shivered.

"This is odd. We've wandered a long way from my interview."

Maureen's face became enigmatic. "I seem to have that influence on, er, certain individuals."

Ujima shook her head and looked at her notes. "I'm curious. Are you really giving everything away?"

"I won't need… those things," Maureen said, and clapped her hands on her knees. "As people say, I'm returning to my roots, to my village, to my real life. I know things have changed, but I have friends. And they're still living there. Together we will ease our journeys… into the rest of our days."

Ujima looked dubious. "Hmm, good luck. Something like that is difficult. And there's the proverbial saying: you can't go home again?"

Maureen hooted; her lips formed a perfect tulip shape. "Ah, Thomas Wolfe." She shook her massive head. "But the ancient philosopher Heraclitus is also credited with that thought. And I'm sure many of our ancestors were before him. They felt the same way." She nodded with closed eyes. "But you see, really, I can go back. I mean, I have no illusions, no expectations."

Ujima smiled wryly. "I wish you the best of luck. But now I have a mystery to clear up." Ujima pulled a carved wooden box out of her briefcase and placed it on the coffee table.

"Where did that come from?"

"Mrs. Osprey said this fell out of your Chinoiserie cabinet. You don't recognize this item?"

"No, I don't." She appeared puzzled. "Let me see that. I wonder where the linens are?" Carefully she removed the lid, then slowly unwound the black velvet.

"What? Where did this come from?" Maureen's puzzled expression quickly turned to outrage. She stood up. "That's… it's, it's…what a horrible thing to do," she said in almost a whisper. Then quickly re-wrapped the arm in the velvet cloth. Shaking, she handed the boxed arm back to Ujima, then stood up. Large tears fell from her eyes.

"My medicine, my medicine. I must take my medicine." Nervously, she tore a vial from her blouse, popped it open, and gulped the green liquid; then limbs loose, she swayed backward, groaned, and crumpled into her chair.

Ujima moved swiftly, her body braced to help. But the flimsy-looking chair held. She lowered her arms as the sound of deep snoring filled the room. Mixed feelings of surprise and consternation changed to annoyance.

The interview was obviously over.

CHAPTER 14

Legend

Kay buttoned the top of her sweater and wound her scarf tighter. Today, the walk to Willie Cloudmaker's cabin was windy and cool. Fall was definitely in the air. The aroma of maple leaves crunching underfoot, quacking ducks in the pond, and the ratcheting call of a kingfisher cheered her.

Ah, there was Willie's Eden. Amazingly, the leaning, moss-covered woodshed was the lone survivor of the terrible fire two years ago. The new house itself nestled near the tall firs. Kay smiled. The cabin was a fugitive beckoning from a fairy tale of long ago. White smoke curled lazily from the river-stone chimney. A scarecrow, sporting a jaunty hat, stood in the vegetable garden; its raggedy arms moved slowly in the breeze.

Kay knocked on the partially opened door and entered the cabin. The aroma of cedar shavings and freshly baked bread greeted her.

Willie thrust a warm mug into her hand. "Saw ya day-dreamin' out there. It's a bit nippy. Got a fire going. Sit thee down." He motioned with his cup toward a well-worn club chair. "Raspberry leaf tea plucked em from the canes, outback. 'Twas mighty hot this summer and fall too, but still a decent berry crop." He took a deep draught. "Yep, tastes mighty fine, don't need no honey."

The tea was indeed wonderful. It relaxed Kay's thoughts, and the taste of ripe raspberries refreshed her.

Willie pulled out the stool from under his workbench and sat. "Morning's cool now but wait till noon. It'll hot up again." He took a moment to study Kay, scratched his head, then turned to his bench. From under a white cloth, he removed a swatch of long black hair. "Workin' on a new mask." With intense concentration, tongue between teeth, he attached the swatch carefully to a carved face. "Like it?"

"How can I tell, covered by all that hair? What is it?"

Mask in hand and elbows on knees, he leaned forward. "Ya know tis interestin'. For some dang reason, old Tsonoqua's been in my dreams these past few weeks."

"Tsonoqua?"

Willie chuckled. "An ancient legend of the Northwest Coast, mostly, and way north, too. Anyway, thought why not give it a shot? Today's folks call it the Hooting Woman. Here, take a gander."

Kay brushed the coarse hair from falling over the mask's face. Then, holding the mask at arm's length, she inhaled sharply. With a long hook nose and massive hirsute brows, the dark, eyeless orbs of the Tsonoqua stared menacingly back.

Willie chuckled. "Not just another pretty face, eh? The story's scary 'nough too; keeps young' uns from wanderin' off. Ya know. Ifin' your work'n, or berry pickin', or clammin'. Can't keep an eye on em all the time."

"Willie, this is…is formidable, especially these empty sockets and lurid red mouth. Ah… I see. These curled lips must intensify the wearer's hooting sounds?" Kay hastily handed it back.

"Yep, if you hear a hoot'n and a toot'n, you'd better make tracks for safety. The old girl is hungry. She's look'n for wander'n young'uns, so she can pick her teeth with their bones afterward." He chuckled. "Edgar hates the damn thing. But I got to carve it."

Kay shivered. "It's very good and the long black hair…it seems almost human!"

"Sure enough 'tis. Sent from my cousin Mary in Oregon. Her friend runs a hair cuttin' place in New Halem, called the Chop Shop. Gal's a wizard barber. Saves hair I need for rattles and some of t'other masks that I've sold. She handles the cuttin's careful like and gives them to Cousin Mary. Mary mails the pieces she thinks I can use." He cupped his chin and studied the back of the mask. "Course there's a male Tsonoqua too. Don't hear much about him. Tales say he's shifty, even changes shape. And don't eat any food he offers either. It'll make you into a sorta ghost, and then he's got controls on you."

"Willie, what a fantastic legend. Even with your stove's comfy heat, I've got the shivers." She paused. "It's odd, vaguely reminds of something I've seen before." She shook her head. "Nope, can't recall it."

Willie nodded, but he hadn't heard. "Yep, there's a lot of spirit power here...not all bad; she sometimes brings money, many wonderful gifts; occasionally, good luck too."

Kay attempted a smile. "I know. This reminds me of our Bigfoot and Yeti legends and, of course, witches. Hah, even Medusa and the Gorgons."

"Maybe." He tapped his head. "But all those monsters could be sumpin' in our memes. These buggers ain't very likable and ancient memories don't let us forget their, um... essence of harm. Sorta like Irish leprechauns on steroids. We're only a couple hundred years from those tales, and people still spot em."

He tapped the mask. "Wouldn't surprise me none if'n right now they're sneakin' around somewhere out on the peninsula or skulk'n in the woods on Vancouver Island...or further...yup, right on to Alaska and all. Might be in plain sight, damn sly at hidin' a foolin' the eyes... stories say, anyway."

"Here! Let me show ya." Willie quickly covered his face, then hunkered down and lurched from his chair. Arms flapping, he crept and leaped across the cabin floor. "Hu, Hu", utterances came from the Tsonoqua's mask. Oddly, the sounds became magnified, then reverberated in the small cabin.

Claustrophobia and light-headedness enveloped Kay. She covered her ears. "Stop! Stop that, Willie. I don't like it."

Swiftly, he removed the mask and placed it on his workbench. "Heh, heh, guess I got carried away. These masks'll do it. Noticed it when I wore an old carving of the ghost spirit. My uncle made it way back. They've a power 'n a life of their own... 'pologize, sorta got taken back with those damn memes. Echoes from the past, I figure."

Kay smiled tentatively. "Maybe your past, not my ye old Anglo-Saxon past."

Willie laughed, then topped off her tea and cocked an eye. "Don't shortchange the boogie man, golems, ogres, flying besoms and the like."

Kay nodded. "And bumps in the night, and those things we choose to ignore. They come to us in a movement, maybe out of the corner of our eye. And sometimes, when I'm walking at night, a slow and eerie feeling tingles up my back. I'm sure something's watching me… or horrors, standing behind me. One's hair fairly rises." Kay laughed nervously. "Wow, here come those creepies. I'm psyching myself out."

Willie apologized and walked over to his kitchen table. Poured more tea, then handed Kay a slice of warm bread slathered in butter. She thanked him and took a sip, then a bite. "Willie, this bread's delicious. You'll have to bake this for our inn."

"Don't come cheap," he said with a grin.

Kay dabbed her lips with a paper napkin. "If you're sharing, the recipe will do." She winked. "I was wondering about those memes. Aren't you thinking in the general terms of Richard Dawkins, the English scientist?"

"Yes ma'am, you got that right."

"So, it's the senses we inherited from our ancestors? They protect us. Like you said, ancient memes, and they're maybe in our genes. Hey, that rhymes." She paused and gestured with her cup. "I think, these times, we have more and more things distracting us from being conscious of our natural world."

"Yu'r darn tootin'. Survivin' skills have gotten weak, and most are gone. Tis a danger."

Kay nodded. "It's likely because of personal avoidance and cultural censoring. But regardless, whether it's mental or physical. Something uncanny is released with that mask on." She paused and smiled. "But I think it's perfect, and terrifically spooky for Hallowe'en. Oh, and I'd like another slice of that fantastic bread."

Willie gave her another piece, then regarded her with a gimlet eye. "It gets a tad weirder. Wick's afinishin' a Hallowe'en puppet play at the boathouse. And it's 'bout monsters of the northwest."

"Yes, I've seen part of it. And if I know Wick. There's a Tsonoqua stomping around somewhere in it."

"Yup, one scene's got the Hootin' Woman." Willie became excited. "'Twas Thursday, last weeknight, we were a jawin' with friends at Rainy Days Tavern.

Outa thin air, Wick says: "Willie, do you know anything about the Northwest Tsonoqua legend or The Hooting Woman?"

Almost fell off my stool. "I said mebbe, cautiously ya ken,

cuz I got a peculiar icy feeling, right in my gut."

Then Wick shoots me a magnificent smile and says: "Fine, Toady said you would. And if you don't have any objections, I'd like to use your expertise on that part of my script. You'll get credit, on the program, as Bradestone's genuine native advisor, for the play."

"Don't figure why, but out pops, 'sure thing'; we shook on it." Willie took a large gulp of tea. "Guess I want Wick to get really close to interpretin' the old legend in 'bout the right way. Ya ken, outa respect for our ancient peoples and their folktales."

Kay nodded. "I think that's wonderful. We need elders like you who are sharp and remember the old stories. It keeps us newbies on track."

"But." Willie said sharply and shook his finger. "Ever since, things have been a happen'n…things that can't be splained." He spread his hands. "It's as if I loosened some sorta spirit and it's a startin' to meddle. Edgar's awarnin' me too." He paused. "And it's nay a good thing. Cousin Mary told me 'sumpin was up. I just don't like it, not one bit... and I'm worried…that, that bad things are gonna happen."

CHAPTER 15

Gorgon

In the smooth waters of Scoon Bay, the current tugged gently. Easing the oars, Alex shifted his weight. In the stern, neatly coiled ropes of a crab trap pushed into the soles of his bare feet. It was another beautiful October day as the sun's rays rose over the forested ridge of Heron's Hook.

"Goddamn, what a tippy tub," Alex mumbled, as he moved cautiously and peered over the side of the small dinghy. Gently, he pulled the crab pot to the surface. He smiled at his catch. He was pushing it. Crab season was over, but if he didn't get caught, there would be plenty for dinner tonight. The innocent crabs were voraciously working on chopped fish parts. Ah, their last meal before their succulent contribution to Crab Vermouth. He could already smell the aroma of Kay's remarkable sauce of wine, butter, and herbs.

Licking salty lips in anticipation, he looped the pot line over a starboard cleat near the transom, rearranged several cushions to accommodate his long frame, then stretched back. Head nestled in his cupped hands; his eyes closed.

Man, he was tired. Should've had that third cup of coffee. And the sun felt good. Taking a deep breath, his thoughts drifted into sleepy reflections on the curious warmth of the October day and his more curious morning workout.

He was running down the path from the farmhouse to the beach, past Willie's cabin and onto the trailhead of Heron's Hook. The jog path was long, but misty and invigorating. The cool, pleasant damp made the forest wonderfully silent. He padded down the first of the fir-needle covered trails that crisscrossed the long hook. It was heaven, the clean aroma of fir, moss, and fern; all mixed with other mysterious scents drifted across the forest trail.

Alex glanced up. He'd sensed a sudden movement on the path ahead. A large brown shape swiftly flashed across the trail ahead of him and into the underbrush. A deer? Often, they swam over in the shallow channel that flowed between Bradestone Island and the Olympic Peninsula. He chuckled; thinking of the island farmers who complained about deer ravaging their apple crops.

Cal Smith, the editor of the Spindrift, the island paper, had laughed too. "The farmers get tetchy if one apple disappears down the throat of Bambi. And their wives get upset if their prize roses are nibbled on. Sure, there are a few deer here. But I noticed that come hunting season, some, not to be named, islanders put tasty venison on their tables. Also, several guys make a tidy profit on sales to the mainlanders."

Cal droned on. "There are chefs who covet the wild meat for their fancy restaurants." He snorted. "These days it's considered a delicacy, like elk. So, restaurants and patrons buy exotica. Of course, menu prices ratchet up accordingly." He shook his shaggy head. "But you gotta have a chef with the know-how and a flair for fixing it. Why I remember, the medallions of an elk dish I had in Sedona. Couldn't get enough. And man, there was that venison roast with Jaeger sauce in Mainz, Germany." He grinned. "Few cooks can prepare wild game properly. And I wager less in Seattle. Too, they gotta know the best beer or wine that goes with the meat."

Alex nestled back further into the boat cushions and smiled. He recalled that he, Kay, and Sabra had eaten an excellent wild boar meal in Olde Burien on the mainland. Thommy Jay agreed. The restaurant, the 909, was one of the best places to eat near Seattle. It was close too, just a few miles from the Coleman dock.

A cacophony of crows interrupted Alex's daydreams. Opening one eye, he counted six sleek black flyers in the sky. The seventh, covered in a distinctive pattern of amber feathers, was the leader of the raucous pack. Hah, Edgar and his motley clan; no doubt heading towards Willie Cloudmaker's cabin at the end of the bay. They were excited about something, probably Willie's fig trees. They bore late this year, and thieves delighted in plundering the sweet fruit; or it could be Willie's late-season grapes that were on the menu. Alex chuckled; Willie didn't mind. "After all, Edgar and his tribe have to eat too," he'd say with a wink.

Edgar was Willie's special friend, an unusual, amber-feathered crow. Two years ago, he'd rescued the bird from two hungry foxes, and nourished it to adulthood. Now Edgar had found a mate. Alex grinned; Willie predicted that 'come next spring' a noisy family would be born at the top of the giant Douglas Fir near his cabin. Kay named Edgar's present flying family the magnificent seven, or when they were up to no good, a murder of crows. Although, the actual number in the murder depended on the person who did the counting.

The family seemed exceptionally riled this morning. Alex scanned the sky for the usual culprit, an eagle. A crow's ever-present enemy. Nary a one in sight, he thought, then chuckled; too much time spent with his Tlingit neighbor Willie Cloudmaker. He was picking up the old-timer's lingo.

The clan's cawing intensified, and the crows changed direction. They swooped towards the sandy beach at the base of the hook. Clearly agitated, they dipped, circled, and squawked at something in the woods. Abruptly and eerily, they became silent; circled once more and then soared high. Calling one another, they resumed their scattered progress towards Willie's cabin.

Odd... an unsettling feeling teased at the nape of Alex's neck. Feeling uncomfortable, he sat up. Slightly, he shifted his weight. The tipsy boat rocked.

Shading his eyes, he scanned the far shore. What? A shape moved out of the brush and onto the beach. He blinked to focus. A bear reared up and stared. Alex started. It was probably the brown bear, rather than a deer, he'd seen on his morning run.

He recalled one of Cal's news articles several years ago. A bear swam from the peninsula and emerged on the beach near the coastal town of Des Moines. They captured and released the hapless animal somewhere into the wilds of the Cascades.

Alex blinked. Uh-oh, the creature looked quite un-bear-like. It was tall, thin-shaped, with long hairy arms moving in slow motion. Was it beckoning him? He squinted. Whew, what looked like scraggly black snakes tumbled and coiled from the creature's head. The mouth was large and looked covered in blood. Cripes! Was this thing a Sasquatch or, what some of his friends at the local bar would insist, a Bigfoot?

A spine-chilling hooting echoed over the bay. Gad, the facial skin of the thing, had a greenish cast. He had to get a closer look. Some idiot was clearly having fun. Who was it?

Forgetting the drag of the crab pot, he scrambled to place the oars on the tholepins. The boat rocked, then slewed. With a yelp, Alex pitched headlong into Scoon Bay. Spitting salt water and treading noisily, he cursed Toady's old dinghy. Emblazoned in white on the stern, the boat mocked him. Fanny-Dunker II.

Angrily, he swam to the damn thing before it drifted out of reach. Kicking, he latched onto the stern. Then, carefully balancing, he eased his weight into the skittery craft. The water, usually chilly, was surprisingly warm. Probably because of the scorching days of the lingering summer. Sitting up and grabbing the thwarts, he vigorously shook the water out of his hair, then spotted the creature's back, rapidly blending into the trees.

Well, whatever it was, there had to be footprints. He pulled in his crab pot and quickly, but cautiously, rowed toward the sandy beach of the hook.

CHAPTER 16

Becalmed

Alex shucked his squishy shoes. Then, dripping tee and running shorts hit the porch. Shivering, he walked into the kitchen and massaged his muscular arms. "Did you get…get… my robe?" he said through chattering teeth.

"Oh yes, master, but use the beach towel first." Kay threw it at him. "Tsk, tsk, you're getting salt water all over our new kitchen tiles."

She broke into a laugh. "I watched you through the binocs. That was a marvelous cartwheel over the side. Trying out for the Cirque-du-Soleil, are we?"

"Argh, wench. Dangerous to joke with a wet rooster. Give me my bathrobe and look lively about it."

Kay frowned and handed him the robe. "Yes, master. But no life preserver. That's not standard navy, or army procedure," she chided and shoved a hot cup of tea into his hands.

Alex growled, drank the steaming cup, asked for another, then wrapped himself in the heavy terry and sat down. "Ah, the ever-sympathetic lass. I merely wanted to get a closer look at something on the opposite shore and craps, lost my balance." He raised a skeptical eye. "Hey, I didn't hear any complaints about the crabs for dinner tonight."

Kay turned to prepare lunch. "No, you did not. They're plump and beautiful. I put them in the shade. What were you looking at, a stranded mermaid?"

"I wish. That would have been fantasque." Alex rose out of his chair, arms waving above him. "But it was a beast, a bête noire, gigantesque!" He snarled loudly and, arms extended, lurched forward. His robe flew open.

"Yipe," Kay giggled. "Monsieur, did he speak French and carry such an enormous weapon?"

A lustful grin spread over Alex's face. "He did not … but I can't help it. You know I always rise to the…er occasion and you look fetching in that frilly apron."

Kay quickly removed the garment. "We'd better calm the beast right now, or lunch will not get done." She looked at her watch. "The girls won't be back for over an hour," she stepped forward, smiling. "Oh delicious, you smell like the sea."

***

Alex punched his pillows into shape and rose on his elbow. Taking a tress of Kay's auburn hair, he slowly wound it around his finger.

Kay looked up. "What is it?"

"I'm feeling a little rueful about the other morning." He sighed. "I want to apologize for being flippant about your aunt Maureen." He shrugged… "but you know me. Sometimes I like making light of things." Kay nodded as he continued. "At one time, your auntie was a handsome woman, before the accident, I mean. You can tell if you really study her face."

Kay nestled up to Alex. "I love being mother confessor," she sighed, "but I thought so too. Whoever botched the surgery was a novice. It must be hell to live with. Something like that, you would never get used to."

She rubbed her forehead. "You can see lines where the surgery was done, mainly around her eyes and lips." Kay rearranged her coverlet. "I'm sure she's had plenty of negative comments behind her back. You can't totally inure yourself to something like that. Every time you need to use a mirror, it's there."

Alex pushed more pillows behind his back and sat up. "Man, also her description of her medical condition…it blew me away."

"Me too; I can't imagine living alone and having one of those spells. It would totally freak me out."

"I'm glad she told us everything, though." Alex ran his fingers through Kay's hair. "I know she'll want us to tell the girls. They need to understand what to do if something happens. It's a major safety factor. Forewarned is forearmed."

"I agree." Kay plumped her pillows and sat up. "When you were over at Wick's barn in Burn, Aunt Maureen gave me two cups of her green medicine to store in the fridge. That makes me feel better if something untoward happens. Oh, and she brought over pics of the furniture and other items. I pointed out only a few things. But Maureen insisted we should take it all; use what we can and decide later about the other pieces. Oh, there's so much stuff!"

Alex stroked his chin. "No problem. We can store the excess in the basement."

"I thought so too. And I'm going to ask Thom if he wouldn't mind handling the rest, on consignment, at the shop. Maureen said that most is in excellent condition and would be easy to sell."

Alex shook his head. "I never know who's in charge of that shop. Sometimes it's Toady and then it's Thom."

Kay laughed. "I think each has their own half-interest, so they toss the running back and forth like a relay stick. It's pretty convenient when one takes a trip or, as in Toady's case, starts a new venture like the Bloated Toad."

Alex rolled his eyes. "What a crazy name for a restaurant. But, getting back to antiques and old stuff, aren't they passé? Today's young people couldn't be less interested. They like fresh, simple, and clean. Dust-catchers are definitely out the door."

"My, what a sweeping statement," Kay said with a grin. Alex groaned. "Anyway, like any fad, these things go in cycles. And I wouldn't say all young people, but most."

She threw off her coverlet. "I'm going to leave it up to Thom. He can determine what looks good and where." She shrugged. "I want things to be attractive but useful, not just sitting about. And Thom has that uncanny ability to pick just the right thing and the right spot."

"He's got the knack alright," Alex said and sat bolt upright. "Hey, isn't it great having the girls here? Really peps things up." He swung himself out of bed. "Time to hit the shower. Want to join me?"

"As long as it's only a shower. Teri is giving Brooke a tour of the island and they'll be back soon. Not to mention," she rolled her eyes, "starved! I told them we'd have lunch around two thirty."

"Come on then, let's have a quick douche."

Kay giggled. "No frolicking now, let's get serious. I have to put the brioches in the oven, and you have to do the scramble."

Alex grabbed Kay and wiggled his eyebrows. "Baby, I can scramble, and in double time, even in close quarters."

CHAPTER 17

Haunted House

"Stop!" Brooke shouted. Teri slammed on the brakes.

They'd been traveling country lanes; switching back and forth; encountering remote beaches, farms, inland stands of trees, then back to roads log-strewn sands. When Teri took sharp corners and tromped on the accelerator, they laughed and screamed. Visions of reports, projects, and picky professors were fast blown away. The ever-shifting scent of woodland, salt air, and freedom was exhilarating.

As they sped along another paved secondary road in the open dune buggy, Teri's thoughts sobered. Byron would have her guts for garters at the risks she took. But she argued with herself. The boys drove the souped-up Squash-Bug the same way, their sobriquet for the yellow monster.

"What is it?" Teri looked sideways at Brooke. The camera hung loosely around her neck. She had ceased taking shots and was staring intently behind them. "That Y junction in the road, back there. See it."

Checking the rearview mirror, Teri spotted a weathered sign pointing to Dark Hollow. She remembered hearing about the abandoned ranch and its intriguing name. But like many of the island's mysterious places, she'd put it off. Another thing to explore later.

"What, did you see a deer?"

Brooke's features were pinched. "No. It's a house I glimpsed. It's on the smaller road." She shook her head and looked helplessly at Teri. "Can you believe it? I suddenly got that weird feeling, you know, like on the Ferry."

Oh lordy, Teri thought, here we go. "I didn't see any house and besides, we have to get back in time for lunch." She frowned. "The boys gave us a rather limited window. And if we want to borrow the Squash-Bug again, we…"

"You're right, but lunch is around two. I'd like to look at that house; maybe even take a few shots?"

"Sure," Teri said, shrugged, then quickly backed onto the verge. She spun the dune buggy around and stopped.

Brooke eyed Teri. "Remember, in Dr. Taylor's psyche class?"

"Yes?"

"He felt that if you face things head-on, whatever hold they have usually goes away," she whispered.

"Thank you, Doctor Freud, or is it Doctor Fraud?" Teri said with a wink and smiled.

"Look Teri, you know I'm worried about these…these feelings. Maybe my subconscious somehow associates this island with an unpleasant experience or dream. I think if I deal with whatever's giving me fits, I'll feel loads better, okay?"

Teri paused. "Okay, I'm in for it." She engaged the clutch.

Brooke's laugh was shaky, but she sat up straight and raised her camera. "Oh, wise one, just indulge me. We can analyze any psychobabble later… over lunch, maybe?"

Teri turned onto the narrow gravel road. A huge willow came into view, then came a broken cedar fence. Hidden behind the ancient tree was the collapsing porch of a Victorian mansion. Weathered and worn, the house nestled in the grassy hillside. One roof had a turret. It reminded Teri of a witch's hat. Patches of shingles had blown away and sections of plank siding were missing. "Turn of the 19th century, but the bones are good." Teri liked that, saying it sounded all-knowing and sophisticated. She switched off the engine.

"Without a doubt, a carpenter's masterpiece at one time," Brooke said. "Too bad it's been let go."

The dirt road up to the house was unused for years. Hip-high brown grass covered the road, then grew over it to join a once-hayed hillside.

"We'll take a quick look, then head back," Teri said and glanced at Brooke. Her friend hadn't moved. She sat transfixed, staring at the house. "Brooke, if you would rather just take a couple of shots, we can take off now."

"No… I want to get some interior pictures." With Leica in hand, she jumped gracefully out of the 'bug' and turned to Teri. "It's interesting, this place. I have to see it." She struck out. Leading up to the house was an animal trail. Wading through the sea of dried grass, Teri quickly followed.

Parts of the porch had fallen through. There was a sweeping view of the land across the road. Some were being farmed, but on the side, near the house, everything had reverted to the wild. Old-willows, and tall Rowans, still bearing dried berry clusters, grew along the ditch below. Red-wing blackbirds mewed to one another as they flitted through the brown cattails.

"There, over there," Brooke pointed. "It used to be a swamp. It stretched to that plowed land. But why? Why am I so sure? We both know I've never been to Bradestone in my life."

Teri folded her arms. "You must have… probably when you were very young. Your family most likely visited a friend or a relative nearby. Ask your dad, he'd know." Teri grinned. "No mystery. You're recalling things from your past, that's all."

"Maybe, but look, I've got goosebumps and that bizarre feeling, again."

"You may have had an awful experience. You can call or email your dad tonight; he'll straighten things out." Teri glanced at her watch. "We'd better go."

"You're probably right, that's it." Brooke shot some pictures, then took a deep breath. "But I want to go inside."

Teri rolled her eyes and pushed through the broken door to a hall. She hesitated. It ponged badly. "Yeah, I want to see it, too. But, with that smell, we'll have to make it short."

The interior was a wreck. Broken furniture and rotten mattresses were in the main rooms, empty beer cans and bottles tossed into corners. Almost everywhere, holes in the plaster walls punched through to the lath. Huge graffiti murals covered a few. The once elegant fireplace smelled like a urinal.

Teri folded her arms and grunted with approval. "There's quite a good tag artist on this island."

Brooke nodded, then covering her nose, headed for the trashed kitchen. The appliances were long gone. Broken plaster and smashed glass crunched underfoot.

"Whew," Teri exclaimed. "It reeks and, worse, looks dangerous."

"Yes," Brooke replied vaguely. She didn't seem to hear Teri and hesitated at an open doorway. A rickety stairwell led down to the basement.

Teri froze. "We're not going down there. It's ready to collapse!"

"I'll go," Brooke replied in a monotone. "The railing looks solid." She pulled on it. "It's safe. I'll stay close to the wall." She tested the first step and gingerly moved down.

"You're not going alone," Teri muttered through clenched teeth. She waited until Brooke was off the step at the bottom.

"Watch your footing, and keep both hands on the railing," Brooke whispered back as she cautiously moved into the large room. Another overpowering odor assailed their nostrils; something earthy and rank.

"Was this trip really necessary?" Teri asked flippantly, hands-on-hips.

"It has to be here." There were tears in Brooke's eyes.

Teri glanced around the cavernous room. Scattered across the floor were toys and broken parts of a tricycle. Yellow light filtered through shattered grimy windows. They barely illuminated the ruinous mess.

Brooke moved into what appeared to be a hall. Small rooms branched off the sides. Teri thought of prison cells in a horror film.

Brooke's voice became muffled as she turned around a corner. "It's here. It has to be here."

Teri spread her hands in frustration. "What? What, Brooke? What are you talking about?" There was no reply.

Teri tiptoed carefully to where she had last heard Brooke's voice. Empty boxes and packing material were prolific.

"The rooms here must have been mainly used for storage. Strange, some putz hasn't burned the place down," she said sarcastically. A huge, but empty coal bin loomed ahead of her. The basement was larger than it first appeared. She stopped to listen, nothing. Teri shouted: "Brooke, Brooke, where are you?"

There was no reply, only a faint scrabbling noise, like rats. Great, now we're in a real horror film, Teri thought and headed toward the sound. The way was better lit. She grimaced thinly, then gulped. At the far end, beneath what had been a small three-paned window, was the remains of a once upright piano.

"Just gets better." Were Teri's thoughts as shreds of cobwebs brushed her face. Arms swiping from side to side, she steadily followed the sounds of quiet weeping.

Turning a corner, Teri entered a small bedroom. She blinked to adjust her eyes. Near an open closet, there was a small floorboard. Brooke sat, smiling and rocking. She clutched something to her chest.

"She's still here. Matilda is still here." Tearfully, she held up a small body. "They hurt her. So, I hid her." Cobwebs and dirt clung to the tiny, tattered white shoes of an armless, nearly headless doll.

CHAPTER 18

Brunch and Bivalves

Teri opened the invitation. "Oh bother, remember Mr. Buckwass? He's invited us to lunch this afternoon."

"After yesterday, I don't feel like doing anything," Brooke groaned.

"Look, we've talked over all possibilities from down to up. Your dad will give us answers when he gets your message. Besides, even if we're psyched from yesterday, the change will do us good. When we gave Mr. Buckwass that lift, he sounded knowledgeable, especially about the island's prehistory. Brooke, he's a really valuable source for our projects. Come on, don't look like that."

***

They glanced into the café window. Jinx Buckwass was at a corner table. He stood up as they entered the café, flourished his napkin, and bowed low. "Jinx Buckwass at your service my dear ladies," he cocked an eye, "won't you two lovelies join me at my table?" Oh, merde! Teri thought. Ham on the rocks with socks. As they sat down, Brooke nodded with a thin smile. She felt the same way Teri did.

In a conspiratorial manner, Jinx leaned forward. "What's the problem with this restaurant? No flowers at the table to give ambiance and stimulate digestion? What do you ladies think?"

"But there is feverfew, and roses by the register. They're from the garden out front." Teri looked around the room. "I know Myrtle is trying to upgrade things." She lowered her voice. "Mom said this place used to be a real greasy spoon."

"Flowers at the table would be nice, though," Brooke said. "But I don't mind. The dining room is clean and just as inviting without them."

Jinx thrust his chin forward. "I, for one, feel that fresh flowers lend a more romantic aura to dining, so…." His left hand moved into his jacket. "Voila, instant ambiance." He flourished a bouquet.

"Gosh, they're red roses and in a crystal vase, too," Brooke exclaimed. "These are real. How did you do that without spilling the water?"

Jinx shook his head as he placed the flowers on the table. "That's my secret. But I enjoy surprising people. It gives me great pleasure. My mother told me since I was three, I was into playing pranks. That's how I got the name Jinx." He grinned. "I would hide things or create funny situations by teasing, or making things appear, then disappear. It drove my parents wild." He chuckled. "And they were forever trying to amend some indiscretion I had a hand in."

Teri laughed. "My brother Byron is always up to something, too. It keeps the family's adrenalin flowing."

Jinx nodded. "For me, tricks are the sustenance of life; many people lack a sense of humor. But that's their problem. I will never reform; and become more adult, as people say I should."

Feeling more relaxed, Brooke chimed in. "A philosopher, I don't remember who, once said, 'If you take life too seriously, life will start taking you seriously and then you're in deep trouble'. That's why…"

"Thank you for answering my invitation to brunch," Jinx interrupted. "I promised you a treat after the lift in that amazing cool car. Isn't 'cool' the appropriate new-age adjective nowadays?"

Teri said that some linguists felt it originated with black entertainers in the 1930s jazz era. But ignoring her, Jinx gabbled on.

"So, Teri, your dad and mum were too busy to come?" He shook his finger. "They're forgiven for now, but not next time." He smiled. "I've asked our chef to prepare something just for us. They're cockles, prepared in wine and garlic. It is a delicious dish that I first tasted in Italy. Notice the menu offers cheesy-garlic bread with seafood selections. But I want us to enjoy the cockles, unsullied. No bread or anything else for me."

"Cockles?" Brooke looked surprised. "I didn't know they were edible."

"Oh, yes." He licked his lips. "They're one of the tastiest creatures from the sea. You must try them." He smirked. "Brought a basketful to the chef; I gathered them this morning."

Brooke shook her head. "That's so kind, but I have to eat lightly. After yesterday, my tummy is off." She made a slight moue at Teri, then peered at the menu.

"Sorry, I'll pass too, Mr. Buckwass. I've got my eyes on the razor clams. They're frozen, but they're delicious and hard to get. Byron says the new chef, Myrtle hired, cooks them just right. The clams come out tender, not chewy. Evidently, she breads them in a special seasoned flour, dips each one into a whipped egg, then sautés them quickly in butter. Yummy."

Brooke nodded. "Mr. Buckwass, Teri, and I appreciate the trouble you've gone to, and we'll enjoy the cockles another time."

"Well, I am disappointed," he said and flapped his napkin. Then he smiled slyly. "But not to worry, you can taste a portion of mine, and you'll find out how delicious they are."

"Of course," they chorused together, paused, looked at each other, then laughed.

"Ah, that's settled then," he said with a self-satisfied grin. "I guarantee you won't regret it. Here comes the server. We can place our orders. Brooke, have you decided?"

"Yes, I've determined to eat lightly. Buttered toast and herbal tea with honey, and I think the fresh papaya would be good too; it aids in digestion."

Teri stared at her. "Getting a case of the punies, are we?"

"Yes," she hissed, quietly. "It started when I came in."

"I'll have tea too," Teri announced firmly, "with lemon. And I'm sticking with the razor clams."

Jinx sniffed, and the cry of a seagull interrupted. "Pardon me, ladies. My phone." He frowned. "I must take this call. Excuse me." After he left. They could hear his quiet murmuring coming from the hall to the restrooms.

Teri teasingly poked Brooke. "You're not pregnant, are you?"

Brooke winked. "Not that I know of, but I understand there's always a remote possibility of virgin births."

Teri laughed, then Brooke became serious.

"I thought I was really handling this weird Matilda thing. As you said, it must have a logical explanation. But until I hear from Dad, I know I'll be upset and nervy."

Teri nodded sympathetically, then noticed a busboy carrying a large pitcher of water, staring at them. He seemed at a loss for words. "This is water for your table."

"Oh. I thought it was for us," Teri shot back, straight-faced. The boy's complexion turned pink. "Ice or no ice?" he said through tight lips.

Teri pointed at Brooke. "Ice for her. She thinks she's having a hot flash and might be pregnant." The boy's face turned beet red. Quickly he filled the glasses and stumbled a retreat.

The girls were giggling hysterically as Jinx returned to the table. He regarded them with a twisted smile. "I see you're enjoying yourselves. I'm glad. And I apologize for the cell phone disruption. Rose, my realtor, informed me that my plans to do a bit of building remodel on Main Street have gone through."

Teri poked Brooke and blotted her eyes with her napkin. "We were sharing a silly joke about girl problems." Brooke responded with a giggle. "And I know Rose Bracken; she's a good friend of my mom's and Alex. They bought their old farmhouse from her. Which building in Madrona are you talking about?"

"A Wick Wilding will be my landlord. You're probably familiar with the site. The previous owner had some sort of studio in there. It's a surprisingly roomy building, spotless and up to date."

Teri looked serious. "Uh-huh, that was Martin Gray's old studio. He willed it to Wick. It was not under the best of circumstances."

"Ah. I see you know Mr. Wilding. I want to learn all the scuttlebutt about what's happened on the island since I left many years ago." He squirmed in his seat. "I'm very satisfied with this property agreement and plan to open a bookstore. Of course, the books won't be the only draw. I also will have a gift section featuring some of the European art that I've collected during my travels. I have both old and contemporary pieces. Also, I'm going to include antiques and current works of Pacific Northwest artists." He seemed to grow taller. "I have many important pieces in my collection. And through my contacts, I'll be able to acquire more objects from around the world. You would be amazed at what I've stumbled upon in my travels and what comes up for sale."

"Not really," Teri said and took a casual sip of water. "Brooke and I have part-time jobs at the campus museum. It's funny what people bring in to have evaluated or try to sell. Sometimes we find out the items were stolen from private collections," she turned and laughed at Brooke, "and some had even been stolen from the museum."

Brooke chimed in, "there were even masks smuggled in from Canada. And a few were so expertly faked that our museum gurus, who should have known better, only found out later after they'd documented and catalogued them as the real thing."

Jinx looked extremely uncomfortable. "That can happen to anyone. I've been taken in too, but I usually get to the truth, and then I get even."

"I hope you'll include some porcelain pieces," Brooke interrupted to defray the tension. "You know, like the one you gave Teri in the car."

Jinx smiled. "Ah yes, the doll's head from Madame Roma Ragatzi's studios. She's an excellent China decorator. I'll include those... a few, anyway." His eyes widened. "Incidentally, you can have them made to order. If you have a friend, parent, or child and a suitable picture of them, Madame Ragatzi can create a remarkable copy, an avatar if you will. In our long association over the years, I've never had a disappointed client. Oh, and I have hand puppets too, along with string marionettes, many from Rumania. I'm sure your young friend, Wick, and his company will be very interested... if not envious."

Their chef appeared with a large tray. Beside her, the busboy set a voluminous pot of tea down. He left quickly.

"Your luncheon orders are ready," she announced and carefully distributed their dishes around the table. "Does anyone need cream or sugar?" They shook their heads in unison. "Anything else I should bring?" When there were no answers, she smartly whipped the tray under her arm. "If you find that, you need something. Jim, your table boy, will alert me. Enjoy!" She said, a little too loudly, and left for the kitchen.

Brooke raised her eyebrows. "Did she say stable-boy?" The girls broke into giggles again, Jinx smiled indulgently.

"The razor clams are delicious. Would you like to taste one,

Mr. Buckwass?"

"No, but thank you," he said and poured tea into the girls' cups. "But here, try one of my cockles." He placed one each on Teri's, then Brooke's plate.

Brooke sipped her tea tentatively. "It's minted. It should work wonders." She took another sip. "Yes, why I think I'm feeling better already. But I'll save my cockle for later, thank you."

"Don't wait too long, ladies. They're best hot. And if I have my way, you'll become devotees, if not captives of cockle-clam-cuisine," he muttered into his tea with a giggle.

"Excuse me, sir," the chef returned, wiping her hands on her apron. "An odd thing just happened. Someone stole into our new kitchen and took the rest of your cockles… right out of the chill pantry."

"What?!" Jinx snarled and shot up. The tea slopped as he bumped the table askew. "You don't have any security in your kitchen?"

"Mr. Buckwass, I assure you, nothing like this has ever happened before. The kitchen boy, Mel, was peeling tonight's potatoes and noticed a forager out back, by the garbage cans. I tell my helpers not to shoo any people away." She shrugged. "Many times, we leave food items out, just for the needy. Well, the next thing Mel noticed was this person. He thinks it was a woman, carrying the sack of cockles over her shoulder and hurrying out the door. Mel was so surprised. He thought he was seeing things, but when he went to check the bottom shelf, your bag was gone!"

Jinx trembled. "I'll call the health department. I'll see that you're shut down. Reinstatement can take months." He glowered at her. "They'll take you apart. If you think I care about altruistic twaddle and social consciousness, you're very much mistaken. Those marginal peoples bring nothing but disease, dirt, and criminal activities with them."

Teri and Brooke looked askance at each other and pushed their chairs back.

Mel darted in from the kitchen, eyes wide. He'd been listening. "It was an old woman, looked like a witch. She even cackled as she disappeared down the alley. I think she's one of those monsters that Cal Smith has been warning everyone about in the Spindrift."

A few startled diners stopped eating.

Jinx's height appeared to increase miraculously. His black eyes glittered ominously. It was as if he were unfolding. "A woman!" He gritted his teeth. "I know of an evil woman that would do that. But she's dead, dead, long dead... and was as mad as a hatter... and vindictive, always trying to harm me and my... family." His voice became lower, his eyes stared into a distant past. "Anything I did for that woman was not good enough, or too good. She ultimately destroyed everything." He was repeatedly stabbing the tablecloth with his fork, punctuating each word.

He whined. "She can't be here now. The thief must be a member of her tribe, but how? No one knows where I am."

Teri and Brooke watched, wide-eyed. The chef stood more erect. Her face red, fists clenched.

"Mr. Buckwass, it is not the end of the world. We on this island help anyone that needs help, shelter, or whatever, to survive. I was just surprised at the thief's audacity of entering the kitchen. It's posted strictly off-limits, obviously for health reasons." She took a breath. "My son Jimmy and I will go out at low tide tomorrow morning and collect cockles. They will be fresh and I'll gladly..."

"NO!" He thundered. "Those were special. Only I know where and how they must be collected." Waving his fork in the air, he commanded, "Go!" as he sat down. A glaze came over his eyes. He wiped his napkin back and forth across his mouth. He stopped, took a deep breath, then white-faced automatically began straightening the table. "I don't know what came over me." He appeared to diminish in size, grinning sheepishly at Teri and winking at Brooke.

"I've never been this upset. I deeply apologize." He shook his head. "It's the tension I've been under lately. I've mixed feelings about returning to Bradestone and settling here. Also, I've been worried about the shipment of my delicate collections and their safe arrival at my storage units." He paused. "Other odd things are happening, too. Recently, a close partner of mine has gone missing. He was scheduled to be here... at least two weeks before me."

He wrung his hands. "My friend never showed up on Bradestone, and I thank the Gods the Seattle police are now looking for him." He became silent. Pleadingly, he looked at Teri and Brooke, his face a mixture of apprehension and helplessness.

"I hope you ladies will excuse my uncalled for and wretched behavior."

Brooke and Teri thanked him for the lunch. Then said they were sorry about the theft, understood why he was upset and as politely as they could, excused themselves.

CHAPTER 19

Homework

"Teri, we're having such a good time, we'll talk about that creepy house later." Brooke adjusted her sunglasses. "Let's just chill out." They were relaxing outside their bedrooms. The veranda's view, Adirondacks and rail enclosed roof-top, had not been resisted.

"Not a bad idea," Teri said, hands behind her head, and nestling back into her chair. She glanced sideways at Brooke. "I could live here, permanently. It's a perfect place to get your head on straight." She paused. "But I'm having a slight problem with my master's program." She chuckled. "You know, Dr. Corey is a so-so advisor. His guidance suggestions date from the Pleistocene."

Brooke looked at Teri. "I don't think Dr. Corey is that bad. Besides, the undergrads think he's cool." She held up five fingers. "One: they applaud his sudden lecture asides on love, two: on sex… naturally, three: his radical views on the ingenuity and the importance of Neanderthals. Four: of course, his weird politics, and Five: his weekly lamentations on the state of the world's civilizations."

Teri laughed. "That's right; you took his Psych 305 course as an elective."

Brooke nodded. "I did. And now he's asked me to become a T.A. I think I'll do it. The class pumped up my morale. An older and experienced nurse was also taking the course, and we both wound up with A-pluses, and on all our papers."

"I remember you mentioning that. The real plus is as a T.A.

you'll learn a lot more, but the obvious negative is the pay is nil."

Brooke grimaced. "I can't imagine anyone in it for the money, and I'll be busier than last quarter, but what's this about your problem?"

Teri rolled her eyes. "What I'm moaning about is finding a cool way to ease into my interviews with the islanders. Dr. Corey looked over my proposed questionnaire and said Bradestone was a good place to start. And this spring, no problem with people signing the waiver slips, but my inquiries are like pulling teeth."

"Really? Most islanders seem to me to be very open. And a few have fascinating stories to tell, so I wind up spending a lot of time schmoozing." She paused. "Of course, that makes my photo sessions longer, but easier. Almost everyone likes their pictures taken." Brooke paused. "Teri, if I pick up on any info you can use, I'll let you know… but I'm wondering, could it be the order in which you ask your questions? And I don't mean to sound critical, but also maybe the way you're asking them?"

"Oh probably, I can get a bit gung-ho, as Alex would say, and I have to admit I have a hidden agenda."

"Oh, what's that?"

"I'm more excited about finding information on the ancient sites of native settlements." She grimaced. "As you know, few people can remember what happened last week, let alone fifty or more years ago. Some ramble, others make up stories, and some embellish. It's only human nature." Teri shrugged. "Hah, the difficulty of separating the 'wheat from the chaff,' that Dr. Corey goes on and on about."

"Well, let's see if we can tweak your approach. Like, tell your interviewees you are conducting the first in-depth study of the island…which you are also let them know their contributions will be acknowledged in your research. Then slip in questions on local lore. Hey, I'm sure you'll trigger things they aren't even aware of." Brooke became excited.

"Too, you could ask them if they have old photo albums, diaries, or whatever. They always like to drag out pictures they've taken, and it can get kinda boring." She looked thoughtful for a while. "Remember when your mom and dad talked about Shady Meadows? Well, I asked at the desk for the go-ahead and took some great shots there. Lots of retired people. They could also be another source for you."

"Hmm, I like that, a captive audience. Remember what Mr. Buckwass said?"

"Really Terry, I'd just like to forget him."

"Well, he seemed to know a lot about the pre-history of this island, and he is a First Nations person. Too, what he said seemed to back up Dr. Corey's idea that Bradestone was part of extensive trading routes. You know, linking Asia, Polynesia and the Aleutian Islands, including inland native tribes, and even as far down as lower California. And he said, clear to Tierra del Fuego."

"Ugh, you can talk to that man. What a creep. After the restaurant fiasco, I want nothing to do with him."

"Yeah, he was pretty rude. But remember, in the car, to me, it sounded like he knows more about the ancient history of the island than I've found in any of my preliminary interviews."

Brooke reached down into her bag and pulled out a small recording device. "Remember the fun we had with this in the dorm? Well, now I take it on my photo interviews and ask the people if they don't mind. It's amazing. When I hit playback, I clue in on important things that I missed when taking notes."

"Hey Brooke, that's a great idea. When we're in Madrona, tomorrow I'll pick one up. And your suggestion to use current history remembrances first will ease my way of asking about the more distant past. But I still think I'll begin with Mr. Buckwass." She giggled. "He likes to appear as a know it all, so it's as good a place to start as any."

"Better you than me," Brooke said. "And remember earlier, when the island's primary librarian, Solange, let us review the existing materials on Bradestone? There were only shipping documents and a few micro-fiche files of old diaries. Your inquiries may be tough now, but any pre-history monographs you write, even if the evidence is fragmentary, will provide important documentation, before it's lost, forever."

Teri made an exasperated sound. "Oh, I know my research is valuable. But I'd rather be locating ancient sites. If what Mr. Buckwass says is true. This island must be peppered with them." Teri looked discouraged. "But right now, there's little evidence of anything. In this wet climate, wood and woven objects are lost when they rot or get buried in mud."

Teri sighed, but her mood quickly changed to excitement. "Brooke, I don't think I've mentioned this before, but there are some curious shell middens I discovered two years ago. I also found blue trade beads in Edgar's nest. I know he likes things that sparkle. And if I find further evidence of native occupation, Dr. Corey says he might," Teri made air quotes, "Persuade the powers that be, to float a grant and set up excavation sites for next spring quarter. Man, I'd be the first there, muck-stick at the ready." She grimaced. "But I'm determined to ask Mr. Buckwass. I feel he knows a lot about Bradestone." Teri made a horrible face, raised her hands like claws, and lowered her voice. "Even where the skeletons are buried."

Brooke looked troubled. "You may joke, but unfortunately, I agree, he's probably an excellent source. Even in my art-photography interviews, I occasionally have to grit my teeth and ask a creepy person some questions. Good luck."

CHAPTER 20

Ah, Tabloids

Cal Smith, the editor of the Spindrift, pushed his office chair back and stood. His bear-like size always impressed Rose. He leaned forward and shook her hand.

"Hey, Ms. Bracken. I got your message; glad you had time to come in." Grinning broadly, Cal gestured at the pile on his desk. "Got a lot of reports and mail to catch up on, and wouldn't you know, my computer is having fits." With a thud, he flopped back into the chair and scratched his tangle of red hair. "Please sit down… so, so what's this all about?"

Rose had seen Cal several times in Madrona. For a big guy, he moved amazingly fast. Frequently, he was on a story or the scent of one. Rose admired his muscular tattooed forearms and rugged looks. No wedding ring, that was interesting. She cleared her throat. "I'm not criticizing the police, but they're busy with misdemeanors and local concerns. I read the Spindrift all the time, so I know I'm not totally off the map."

"Er, what exactly do you mean, Ms. Bracken?" She was still standing and appeared to be furiously collecting her thoughts.

"Oh, oh… please, call me Rose." She teetered for a moment. "Remember, this is confidential, and I want to know if I'm being silly, or if there are, as you've written, strange happenings on this island." She paused and peered cautiously around his office.

Cal rubbed his jaw. Does she think someone's listening? "Um Ms. Bracken, ah… Rose. If you want to see Carly, my secretary, she's on her lunch break."

Rose looked at him blankly. He wanted to snap his fingers.

"Uh... can you be more specific? Is this about the mayor's cabinet member selections, recent alien sightings, or the island's organic movement, or what? My articles have covered all..."

"Well, yes, it is about that... I think the second one." Rose yanked the strap on her shoulder purse. "I'm not sure where to start...it seems foolish now." She looked at him with reservations. "I'm not making this up to get attention. And I certainly don't want my name in the paper on this, no way."

Rose seemed scatty, but Cal knew she was a competent realtor with an excellent reputation. He recalled her role in breaking up the corrupt dealings of the other land agency. At present, she was the only act in town. No doubt, much sharper than she seemed. Cal smiled, confidentially, opened his large hands and shrugged.

"I always advise people to relax, take time, put their thoughts together." He pointed again. "Pull up that chair, rest your feet. Then start slowly... at the beginning, when you're ready." She appeared to have balance problems. Possibly those extremely high heels he'd noticed when she walked through the door.

Rose smiled and sat down. She liked Cal Smith better and better. "Well, okay. It was Monday, two weeks ago. I was showing a rental to a client and in the vacant lot, across the street... I think it was two kids, I mean. Anyway, a huge scarecrow-like creature stood. And when I shouted at it, the thing made threatening gestures and started lumbering around." Rose rolled her eyes. "I know Hallowe'en is at the end of this month. So, I wasn't surprised. But what surprised me was the reaction of my client. He almost went to pieces, telling me it was 'her' and she'd come to kill him or some such nonsense."

"Well Rose, some people get hysterical over the slightest thing. Er, did it approach you?"

Rose waved her hand back and forth. "No, no, it just disappeared."

Cal looked at the ceiling and made a helpless gesture with his hands.

She took a deep breath. "Wait, there's more. I know it has to be some sort of prank. But, last week, I was showing the old Anderson farm to a prospective buyer. You know, it's 24 acres of prime farmland near Clovis Passage." She smiled. "It has a terrific 180-degree view."

Cal nodded. He really didn't know but gaped encouragingly.

"The clients were dressed as if they were going to a cocktail party. Can you imagine, out there?" She grimaced, "And, they were over an hour later, to begin with."

"And did something… happen?"

"Yes, yes, it did. After they'd left. I was locking up. As you're well aware, this time of year it's getting darker and darker." She leaned forward, an amazed look on her face. "You won't believe it. They came in a huge limousine, and…"

Cal stared at her. For a newspaper editor, cum-reporter, he was unusually patient.

"Excuse me, Miss Bracken… where is this going?"

"Well, after they'd left, there it was, moving across the lower field. I suspect it came from a shed. At first, I thought it was a cow. Of course, I put on my glasses to see better. Then I thought the man had returned." She shook her head. "Even now it gives me the willies."

Cal's newsy nose perked up as he unburied a lined notepad. "What man?"

"The husband, naturally."

"Oh, of course," he paused, pen in hand, "but had he?" Cal shook his head. Even he was confused.

"No, silly me, it wasn't him. Not even a cow. It was another person. Much larger and wearing some outlandish, and I might add, very tacky fur coat. But the face when it turned toward me… oh, I can't forget that! Dark green hollows for eyes, bright red lips, and the hair, her hair was a mess. She saw me and naturally tried to hide her face."

"She, her? I thought you said it was a man."

"Yes, that was the first thing that came to mind. It walked like a man. Sort of erratic. Of course, I became frightened and immediately ran back to the house, locked the door, and called the police." Her look again was far away. "Sergeant Isaac Reynolds answered the phone and came at once. He scouted the area. You know he's quite the detective, actually found peculiar footprints by that shed."

"I've had several interactions with Sergeant Reynolds. The officer is a definite asset to Chief Washington's department."

Rose nodded. "Oh yes, the Sergeant is that…" She leaned back. "But I must say he can be bull-headed. At first, he insisted I saw a deer; and it was probably standing, nibbling leaves." Rose blushed, then picked a pen off Cal's desk and tapped her other hand with it. "I don't always wear my glasses. They're so... so uncomfortable. I've tried contacts, but oh my, I've dry-eye syndrome. They are terrible the contacts I mean," she paused and frowned, "Cal, there aren't any nuts that have escaped from a loony-bin and running around the island... are there? If the public is not alerted, things could get dangerous."

Cal busied himself with his pen. "Rose, it's not P.C. to refer to mental institutions as loony-bins, and you meant someone suffering from a psychiatric disorder?"

"Whatever. Political correctness can be silly and in the long run, don't you think it's colorless and non-specific?"

"Well, that's the point, isn't it? Not to offend. Using tact has the added advantage of forcing one to be clearer in meaning and definition."

"Humph... I suppose so. I'll have to think about that one."

Cal cleared his throat. "What interests me is your reference to this creature as a she and not a he. What makes you so certain?"

"One thing, the hair was long and looked greasy, another you couldn't mistake the lips, bright red and very pouty...really an overuse of lipstick there: not to mention the excessive eye shadow. Of course, it was at a distance, and I was hurrying to get inside the house. But when the thing started across the pasture, it moved like a man."

Cal chuckled. "Sounds like another teenager running around and having fun. My suspicions are, as you've said, Hallowe'en's coming up shortly and some people love cosplay. I think that's what all these sightings are about." Cal grinned, "but oddball, weird, and alien sells papers."

Rose made a face. "I suppose so, but I think it's damn peculiar. Way out there in the woods. Going around scaring and even threatening people, it's ridiculous. I was out there all alone."

"Did he or she threaten you?"

"Well, no, but the thing's attitude was certainly threatening."

"I see." Cal frowned and slowly fingered his tablet. "You've been confidential with me and now I'd like what I'm about to say, to go no further than this office."

Rose's ears eagerly perked up. "Oh, you can count on me. I

won't breathe a word." she said and crossed her fingers behind her shoulder bag.

Cal smiled reassuringly, lowered his eyelids and reflected. Um, here I go. It's island rumor time. The news wasn't slow, not with all the recent bizarre happenings on the island, but this might get the ink flowing even better.

"I've had…er, many irregular calls coming in the last couple of weeks. Oh, there's the usual hoopla. UFO sightings, alien kidnappings; but at least seven of them fall into a different category." He tapped the pad. "They're claims about seeing Bigfoot, Sasquatch, even a Yeti; very similar to the thing you saw." Cal shrugged. "Some sightings come from fairly trustworthy individuals. And when they go into details, I've noticed major commonalities. A. It's very tall, B. has huge black or dark-green shaded eyes, C. long scraggly black to yellowish hair and D. every one of them mentions the open and very red lips."

"Oh yes, one can't forget the lips, garish color, poor shade."

Cal grimaced. "And one other curious thing." He glanced at another pad on his desk. "Four sightings mention a basket. A woven basket, attached to the person's back. Yes, whatever it was, that's what they saw. And it was when the creature was running away."

"You mean like a backpack?"

"Yes. They described it in detail."

Rose shivered. "That's sooo eerie."

Cal stroked his chin, hiding his smile. "It is truly odd. But if you, or anyone else you know, sees or hears of something similar, I would appreciate your calling immediately. And if I'm not here, you can give Carly all the details." He rifled through his papers, then handed her a sheaf of notes and colorful sketches.

"Could any of this fit what you saw?"

"A Yeti? That's quite impossible. On the boob-tube, they're white." Rose pointed at another paper. "Bigfoot, why they look like huge gorillas. And these, these creepy aliens have gigantic slant eyes. No, no one could mistake those for what I saw. This monster was entirely different."

"Ms. Bracken, if I can be candid, most of this is B.S. But keep your ears to the ground. Something's going on and whatever it is, it's great for newspaper sales."

Rose stood in indignation. "B.S.?" She thrust the pictures

back. "Well, what I saw was ghastly and real… not one of these hokey things." She stuck out her chin, then reached across to shake Cal's hand. "Certainly, I'll ask my clients if they saw anything when they left… I'll start there. And I will keep my eyes open. I'm not the only person seeing peculiar characters." She shouldered her purse. "And it wasn't a cow or deer nibbling in the woods." She insisted sternly. "But thank you for listening." In a flash, Rose saw Sgt. Reynolds. Tall, neatly dressed, always in command. A man of action, not a doubting desk jockey. Oh, she admonished herself, that wasn't fair to Cal.

As she walked down the stairs to the street, her thoughts turned again to Isaac. Hmph, he too had been dismissive. Damn him, damn all men who judged women out of hand. She sighed. Of course, Sergeant Isaac Reynolds was far from perfect. What man could be? She walked toward her office; thank heavens it had turned out to be a very warm day for October. Her smile was as radiant as the sun. Isaac looked extremely dashing in his crisp uniform.

CHAPTER 21

Refuge

The soft ticking of the wall and table clocks accented the still-ness of the antique shop. An ancient grandfather bonged the hour deeply. Other than that, the atmosphere was peaceful.

At the last solemn stroke, the silence was torn by a shriek; "Ole!" Thommy Jay yelled, jumped up from his desk, clapped his hands and flung himself into serious flamenco moves down the aisle. At last! The business belonged to him. "Mon! Mon!", he shouted. He'd bought Toady's half. Toad Hall was his. The deal closed officially at that hour.

Thom clapped his hands. The re-opening of Toady's restaurant, The Bloated Toad, could now be the young man's focus. Toady had already said goodbye to the Gym and his tennis-pro activities. The Restaurant's name was Toady's idea. It played on his epithet and, too; the eatery bordered a large lake-like pond. Croaking bullfrogs were everywhere. Thom stomped out his feelings; I wish him the very best. The fire, last year, had been devastating.

After he'd danced and clapped his version of palms up and down every aisle, he would have jumped on la tabla, if he had one. Ah, memories of that cantina near Barcelona. Those were the days.

Winded, Thom leaned gratefully against the frame of the first bay window and gazed out at the dismal weather.

Oh prunes, it appeared to be the start of the perennial October rains. Humph! Yesterday, it had been brilliant sunshine.

Ah, yesterday. He vividly remembered Toady asking him if

he could handle the tourist trade on his own. Thom snorted. "Do you really think I'm that feeble? My God, I've subbed for you many a time."

He then cast a withering stare at Toady. "For your information, next week, I must be back in West Seattle. Possibly, you may recall, my house is closing. And, unless I find someone with experience to run the shop; well, I'll close. Yes, everything; and that week." He glared at Toady. "Unless you know someone?" Toady shook his head and gloated. "Hah, not my worry. Do what you must do. I have enough to handle with my restaurant." He'd answered with a sniff of indifference, then swaggered away.

Bitch, Thom thought. He'd known for weeks that I'd be moving. Probably jealous of my new and, not to mention, sumptuous residence on the island.

Since his house was sold in West Seattle, Thom was frustrated. Downsizing wasn't as smooth as his compadres built it up to be. Every packing detail demanded his personal attention. Nobody realized that each one of his irreplaceable acquisitions was… special and held its own unique story. He wiped a mental tear from the corner of his eye.

Immediately, with a burst of laughter, Thom quickly shed his peevish mood. He recalled that last week, the two dears, Toady and Rain, were all a-flutter when they'd left for the mainland.

Toady's madcap plan was to visit organic food outlets, including wholesale and retail on the mainland. The dear wanted only "top-notch comestibles" for his restaurant. With Rain's advice, he'd already scheduled provisions from the island's organic farms. However, backup was essential when shortages or unavailabilities occurred.

Then a roadblock happened.

Rain insisted on going too. Mercy, Rain was hell-bent on sussing out small farms in Puyallup, Snoqualmie, and Mount Vernon. His logic was typical of Rain. "I've already formed an organic cooperative with Bradestone Island's small farms. I must go with you. Really Toady, I will be a benefit. I know some wholesalers and where the best is located!" Rain had said, voice raised. Thom smiled. The poor boy was so cute, blushing and fuming.

Thom tsked to himself. But Rain's nit-picky thoroughness would take more hours than Toady could imagine. The distances, negotiating deals; why the time involved would easily eat up a week, maybe more. Toady sensed that. Oh, oh, Rain set his jaw. Toady's eyes flashed. It was a major impasse. Thom sighed. He just had to intervene.

"No!" Thom bellowed. "Remember, sillies, when you pack, don't forget your special soaps, shampoos, toothbrushes and deodorant." He pursed his lips. "Nobody likes potential customers that may be odiferous and lordy, look like rough trade." They all stared at each other. The first to laugh was Rain, then all hilarity broke out. Tensions were defused. They left together the next day.

* * *

Thom's reflections were wrenched back to the drizzly afternoon. Dogs were barking furiously, followed by shouts from boys running down the street. "Oh mercy, not tourists, certainly the ferry hasn't arrived yet!" He groaned aloud.

In a flurry of movement to his right, the shop door burst open. Thom stumbled back from the window. A woman, moving surprisingly fast for her size, slammed the door behind her; the shop bell flew off the wall.

"Those dreadful children with their dogs," Maureen choked out. Short of breath, she turned her huge, dark eyes on Thom. "Mr. Jay, I hope you don't mind. I'm seeking refuge." She smiled sardonically. "Those boys are devils. Their mothers should have pinched their heads off the moment they were born." Thommy Jay moved quickly and replaced the Open sign with Closed. He locked the door.

Crossing his arms, he studied the rowdies. Laughing, they pushed and shoved each other in the doorway. Then, flashing rude gestures, they shouted "Queery, queers!"

Thom turned to the large woman and smiled. "I wouldn't suggest the permanent pinching method. I'd opt for neutering. It's more effective and saves the planet from further environmental deprivation."

From somewhere, a large handkerchief appeared as Maureen's head fell back, and with a roar of laughter, she blotted her eyes. "It started a block away; they materialized out of nowhere and assembled like black beetles. They're poison personified."

Thom puffed out his chest. Lips in a snarl, he whipped his cellphone to his ear. The boys stuck out their tongues, then ran off, yelling and shoving each other.

Thom glanced at the woman. She appeared to have a crazed smile on her face. My God, those lips! Someone ought to tell her that the shade of red was simply not her color.

He pointed at the window. "I know those boys. They enjoy stirring up trouble. But their parents are very supportive. I'll ring them now. The little shits will be surprised…er pardon my German." He winked. "And, if I'm not mistaken, they're skipping school…"

He buzzed one of the mothers. Then gleefully nodded in agreement as to the consequences offered by the raised voice. He turned to the rankled woman; his best-beatific-beam pasted on his face.

My God, she looked over seven feet tall. An unkind thought lurched across his mind: an escapee from Dr. Frankenstein's laboratory?

"Please, have a seat, my dear, and I'll brew some tea. Those brats can rile the most congenial of persons."

She plunked herself down on the Louis XIV chaise near the window. Thom held his breath. Ah, it hadn't collapsed. The poor woman was flustered. She kept dabbing her eyes. The boys really had been beasts.

Certainly, she was different, a recognizable outcast, like him. Society always taunted the unusual, either in action or appearance. What was the maxim? The nail that sticks out gets hammered down.

"I'll fetch a tray. There's nothing that a little tea and sympathy won't cure." Hurrying to the back room, he set the kettle to boil. His anger surprised him as he dialed the rest of the parents.

Ten minutes later, cobbled together on a bamboo tray, came cookies, a few day-old scones, and little jars of various jams. In the middle of the circling goodies was an ancient Chinese tea set. Thom shouted: "Ta, da." On the piecrust table between them, he artfully arranged it all, just-so. The woman was sound asleep.

Nudging her gently, she slowly nodded awake. Then, with a sweeping gesture that encompassed the entire shop, Thom said: "Welcome to 'Toad Hall'. Moi's newest business venture. I bought it this week."

"Oh, thank you," she replied in a deep, hollow voice. "I have had nothing since breakfast." Thom sat down next to her, handed out lace napkins, and said, "Tuck in. I'll play mother. Sugar, cream, lemon?" He was a devoted anglophile.

The delicious aroma of Russian Caravans, a smoky flavored tea, wafted over the table. "Mr. Jay, this beautiful establishment is yours?" she asked through a mouthful of crumbling scones.

Thom's corduroy jacket puffed, this time with pride. "Yes, I purchased it from a dear friend, Mr. Raymond Toda...who, by the way, prefers everyone to call him Toady."

Thom rolled his eyes and poured more tea. Toady would curse him. He was using one of his recently gained treasures. But, oh well, if you had special things, they were to be used. Not "always saved for good," as his grandmother would have admonished. After all, it was a fact, good sometimes never came.

"Instead of Mr. Jay," he beamed, "please call me Thom. I'm temporarily a shop wrangler until I find someone with a few brains to run this place."

"Isn't Mr. Toda, er, Toady available to help you?"

"My good friend and his partner Rain are disporting themselves on the mainland." He took a leisurely sip of tea and studied her over the rim of his cup. Of course! This was Kay's infamous aunt from the East Coast.

She laughed, in a low hooting sound. "Mr. Jay... Thom, as you wish. I see you've discerned that I'm Kay's aunt, Maureen. The one bearing gifts for my niece, who, as far as I know, is my only relative." She studied him. "I understand you're one of her best friends," she said as she selected a lemon cookie.

"I refreshed those, along with the scones, in the microwave and one hopes they're edible."

"It all tastes excellent," she said as crumbs cascaded down her large bosom. "You're rescuing a starving woman. I'm very grateful."

In that instant, Thom knew he liked her. She must've suffered some terrible accident when young and had no intention of hiding herself away from others.

"When we're finished, I'll show you around the store. You may find something that calls to you, or you can't possibly live without."

Maureen looked up. "Thom, that's very kind, but I have everything I could ever need," she paused and cocked her head. "However, there is something. Maybe the island rumor mill hasn't reached you yet, but I'm moving from back east and intend to settle on the Alaskan coast, to spend the last of my days. I already have the basics to survive there. I'm sure you've heard that I've left all my worldly goods to Kay."

Thom maintained his ramrod posture. "But my dear, you aren't…"

"Let me finish, please. The place I'm returning to has everything. It is a simpler way of life. I'll be living with nature, as my ancestors did." She paused. "I thought, when Kay finishes sorting through everything for her B and B, maybe you could help with the remainders. I assume you take things on consignment. It would be easier for Kay to eliminate the rest of the bits and pieces here on the island."

"I'd love to. Kay and I actually discussed this several days ago. Fortunately, I have contacts in Seattle; they would be quite interested."

"Thank you, Thom." She selected another scone.

He grinned. "My pleasure. And when we top off our tea, I'll give you the Grande tour of my new shop."

"Actually, I am finished and would be delighted. However, I have to take care of a few things at the bank, so it will have to be brief." With care, she folded her lace napkin on the table, then delicately placed an untouched scone in a capacious pocket.

Moving down the aisles, Thom selected paths that Maureen could easily negotiate. "I must show you Toady and Moi's most recent acquisitions," he said and looked back with a smirk. "It's a set of exquisite dolls. We spotted them in the Antique Emporium in Seattle. They aren't old. I know, as I'm a professional collector; however, many are unique." He moved a three-paneled Chinese screen aside and bowed in a sweeping flourish.

He clapped his hands. "I visualize them tête-à-tête at a long, tres elegant tea table. The little dears sharing cocoa and goodies. That Meissen set there, to the left. It's extremely rare and…" He faltered. Maureen had become rigid, a horrific look on her face. Thom trembled.

The howl came first, then burst into a bellowing roar. Maureen slammed into the table. Her arms flailing, dolls and China flew in all directions.

Screaming, Thom jumped up and down. Shaken with shock, he fumbled out his cell phone and speed-dialed 911.

CHAPTER 22

The Session

"You look really serious," Alex said. He took her hand and led her to the living room chair. "How's Maureen doing?"

Kay shrugged as she sat down. "The doctor says her vital signs are good, and she is resting. However, he's concerned about drug interactions after I informed him that Thom gave her a dose of the herbal medication she carries. But what could he do? She was on the floor, thrashing around. Thom was only following what she motioned for him to do."

"How did he know about the stuff?"

"Evidently, she yanked the vial free and had enough presence of mind to gesture to him." Kay shook her head. "Thom was so upset when the medics arrived, he simply forgot to mention he'd administered the drug. They were the ones that gave her a mild sedative before taking her to the clinic so they could treat her lacerations and the damage to her hands."

"Whew, that must have been trying for him, not to mention Maureen. What's the prognoses from here on out?"

Kay massaged her forehead. "Tentative, of course. It seems there is no care directive, or instructions or health provider noted anywhere. The clinic and Ujima's office are sorting through the mess. I know they're attempting to contact her tribal shaman. And that is tenuous at best. But the doctor said he'd keep us in the picture, maybe later today, with an update. The nurse said that regardless, call her at 9:15 tomorrow. But for now, Maureen is stabilized. And the Doc doesn't want any extra stress to put upon her. However, he's hoping that maybe she'll be able to talk tomorrow."

Alec sat down. "So, no visitors and we wait for a call, possibly later today." He paused. "What is Ujima's take on things?"

"She said she'll discuss things with us after she has more information from Thom." Kay inhaled deeply. "But that's not the only problem we're facing."

"What!"

"Umm, Willie's Cousin Mary called me this morning. I filled her in on yesterday's fiasco; And she's coming over to do some sort of session at 2:00, this afternoon. It sounds like Willie's coming too."

"That's insane. We've got enough on your plate. I would cancel … what if we have to go to the clinic this afternoon?"

"I know. But she said it was extremely urgent. Things were happening faster than she thought, and she might shed more light on Aunt Maureen, and her problems in the bargain."

"Shish, what things?"

"I don't really know, but it's better than just sitting here twiddling our thumbs." She patted Alex on his knee. "Come on, let's get some tea ready."

"Okay. But right now, I'm heading for my best brandy." He arched his brows. "Do you wish to share?"

Kay looked surprised. "Do you have to ask?"

* * *

Kay turned the ring in her hand as she sat at the kitchen table.

"What is this? A seance?" Alex snorted as he came into the room.

"No." Cousin Mary said. "I intend to use Maureen's ring to get a better sense of her being. A session with her past, if you will."

"Wared yah find that?" Willie said, a surprised look on his face.

Kay passed the ring back to Mary. "Aunt Maureen wanted me to have it. It was hers; handed down through only the women in her family. It's carved ivory, and that's gold inlay."

"Ah. It is lovely. But cousin Mary, how can you, er use it?" Alex asked and scooted closer to the table.

The ring seemed to glow as Mary turned it in her hand. "I

only have to hold it, like so." Everyone was quiet. "And thank you, Alex, for moving the wing chair in here. I feel more at ease in the kitchen."

Willie nodded. "Yep, tis the heart of a place."

"I must, of course, relax, lean back, probably will go to sleep. Maybe mumble something. But I need a respectful silence," Mary said, and slowly closed her eyes.

"Yep. I've seen her do this afore. Real spooky. Snores; usually after discovering what's thar, and..."

Mary arched her left eye. "Willie. I said I needed silence."

CHAPTER 23

Rescue

Somewhere, years ago, in the much-contested Alaskan panhandle.

A wave of saltwater flushed through the woven-reed basket of oysters. Maureen carefully wedged it between the barnacle covered rocks.

She smiled at their size. A few more and there would be plenty for dinner. Shaking her head, she recalled the ancient taboo against eating and gathering shellfish. "Eating them was only for poor people, and warriors would lose their strength." Thanks to the Gods, a Norwegian wanderer had set the elders straight. Truth be told, there were those that always ate them, anyway. The oysters were delicious.

She waded out further. The soft sand and incoming tide tugged at her feet. Carefully, she avoided the protrusions of sharp rocks. Uncle David had drilled holes in the sides of her old shoes. They protected her feet, and the water ran out quickly. Maureen waded deeper into the inlet.

Noisy seagulls wheeled and dipped over her head. They seemed unusually interested in the next division between the cliffs to her left. The oft-disputed coast of this northern part of Canada was rugged. But Maureen found, in this area, she could move easily from one craggy inlet to another.

Mother nature had connected some of the small inlets with stretches of rounded stone, log-covered sand, or both. Some coves were very short, but each nurtured the bounty of life.

Moist salty air blew in on a gusty breeze. Maureen inhaled

deeply. Mustn't dawdle, she admonished herself, or Lucy would paddle her butt. Although Maureen towered at 6 feet 4 inches, her cousin, Lucy, came in at 5 feet, but she was a feisty, bossy woman; and wouldn't put up with any drifting and dreaming, even if it was a glorious summer day.

She spied on two more shelled beauties knocked off the oyster bed and reached down into the clearer water. Further out she knew it was deeper, the waves dangerous. They could knock an unwary person off their feet, then drag them down into tangles of seaweed. Already strings of emerald, green clung to the hem of her dress.

What was that? High above the roar of crashing waves, a mewing sound drifted on the wind. Could it be a sea creature in distress? Already the thundering surf was pummeling the mouths of the many inlets. There it was again, fainter, but coming from the other cove. Maureen, sensing urgency, dashed up on the beach, then turned the sandy corner into the next inlet. Shading her eyes, she scanned the top of the dividing grass-covered ridge. Waves lapped at its rocky irregular base.

At first, she didn't see them. Then movement. Stranded on a flat-topped rocky ledge, a girl and boy sat sideways. When the girl stood up, the boy clung to her legs, sobbing and wailing. The girl, older, maintained a stoic stance then, wiping tears, cupped her mouth and shouted for help. But the wind and crashing waves tore the sounds from her lips. It shocked Maureen. How did the children get there? She didn't recall any white families staying near the summer village. Most visited the small cannery to the south, near the landing dock. Her eyes widened.

The wee ones couldn't wade back to the beach. The incoming tide surge would carry them away.

Moving too rapidly, she slipped. The cold water of the inlet covered her. She brushed at the green and brown seaweed as she emerged. It clung tenaciously to her face, shoulders, and long black hair.

Maureen cupped her mouth and shouted in English: "Stay there. Don't move. I'm coming." Both children pointed at her and screamed.

"The Sea Monster, no, no, no, go away, go away!"

Startled, Maureen looked behind her then gasped; it was her; they were pointing at her. The boy stood up. The children clutched each other, wailing uncontrollably.

Maureen shook with rage. She remembered the taunts and jokes that came her way because of her size. "I'm not a sea monster," she yelled. "I've come to rescue you."

She took powerful strides, but the water here was waist-deep, and the chaotic rhythm of the waves kept pushing at her.

"What are your names?" She shouted. "Mine is Maureen." She glanced out to sea. "We have to move quickly."

"Th…Theodore, he's my brother," the girl said through chattering teeth. "I'm Jessie…are you going to eat us?"

Maureen shook her head vigorously as she picked her way up the slippery rock. "I have to get you to the beach before the tide swallows you up. I'll take your brother first." He was the smallest and most fragile. The sister was taller and had a presence. Maureen reached for the shivering child. "Nooo, you're going to eat me," he howled and gripped his sister's leg tighter.

Maureen pointed to the sandy beach, yards away. "Would you rather get warm by that rock wall or drown in this cold water?" She stressed each of her next words: "We have little time."

The girl wiped her eyes, sniffed, then pushed her brother. "Go, we don't have a choice." He fell from the unexpected shove and toppled into Maureen's outstretched arms. They both went under. Maureen could see small fish darting away as she pushed the boy to the surface. "We have to hurry," she spluttered through a mouth of water. "The tide's moving fast." Clutching the shivering and crying boy, she made it to the beach. "Go over to that wall of rock," she commanded sternly, "and take off those wet clothes. The sand is warm there. Push it over and around your body. I've got to get your sister."

Carefully descending the rock, the girl desperately tried to balance as waves surged over her legs. Maureen would have to swim. She hoped the child could, too.

"Cling to the rocks behind you!" She yelled and dove into the water. To her, not that cold. She had grown up fishing and swimming in these inlets. It had made her hardy, and the sea gave her an almost supernatural surge of strength.

With pushing and splashing, they finally drug themselves onto the sandy beach. "Jessie, remove your clothes and join Theodore by that warm rock wall." Maureen shivered; she too had to get warm.

"I've left my oyster basket and carryall in the next inlet over. When I get back, I'll build a fire. But for now, spread your clothes out on those pieces of drift. They'll dry with the sun and the wind."

* * *

Halos of sand fell from the children's bodies as they held up their arms and danced to the warmth of the flames.

Maureen smiled. Being in the sun and building the fire had warmed her, too. "Rub yourselves vigorously, especially your arms and legs. I'm going to get more dry driftwood. There's plenty hung up there in the rocks."

"We're all naked," the boy muttered, studying Maureen's strong and well-muscled brown body.

Maureen turned to face the children. "In an emergency like this, we must get completely warm and dry. Wet clothes would make things worse. As my cousin Lucy says: 'you'll catch your death staying in wet clothes'."

On feeding the dry wood, the fire crackled higher. Maureen set her leather carryall on a convenient log. Carefully, she portioned out dried fish, dried hazelnuts, and dried berries. The children, between sniffing and thanking her, devoured their food.

After eating, and polite murmurs of approval, Jessie thrust her fingers into the sand and assumed an air of authority. "Theodore, Maureen is right. We are in what father calls a 'dangerous situation'. In order to survive, we must use all our 'wiles and cunning', and sometimes we have to do things we don't like." Jessie smiled lovingly at Theodore, who continued to eat. Then Jessie looked solemnly at Maureen for approval.

Maureen smiled at the wise reproof, nodded, and busied herself sorting through the bottom of her oyster basket. A few small ones, roasted in the coals of the fire, would be nourishing. "Speaking of your father, where are your parents?"

The girl shook her head and pointed to the sun. "They're very late. They told us they would return before noon." She looked down. "I know they didn't want us to climb rocks, but we were worried and thought we could spot them from up there," she pointed, "on that grassy top. But we couldn't see them anywhere." She sniffed. "Then the tide was coming in and cut us off from the beach. The only safe place was on that ledge."

"Why didn't you go back up to the grassy top? It's safer there."

"I know," she said and wiped her eyes, "but Theodore had skinned his knees. He was tired and so was I. We had had no breakfast."

Maureen frowned to herself. Where were the parents? It was far after the middle of the day.

* * *

Willie and Kay looked at each other. "Hasn't your cousin Mary been in that session a little longish? I'm getting anxious," Kay said.

Alex came back into the room and put a bottle of brandy and four tulip shaped glasses on the kitchen table. He looked at his watch. "Yeah, it's been about an hour."

"She's comin' round now,' Willie said and placed a reassuring hand on Kay's arm. "Seen her do this afore."

Mary rubbed her eyes and glanced around the table. Her gaze was vacant.

Willie chuckled. "Welcome to the present, Cousin Mary. Meet any ghosts out thar?"

"Oh, hah, hah. You and your ever-making jokes," she muttered. "But now, there's so much more. It was the beginning of things." Mary looked puzzled. "But how did she change into... and what?" Mary paused for a long time. "Well, I'll have to find out more later. But the picture of Maureen's past was informative."

Mary shook her head, glanced at her observers, and chortled. "You look like a trio of startled chickens." Then her eyelids fluttered, and her voice softened. "Don't be troubled about the way I do things. It's all part of the game." She stretched and yawned deeply. "But now I need sleep. Deep, deep sleep. "Her mumblings became softer. Her head fell back to rest in the chair's wing.

Hearing her snoring softly, and seeing a slight smile on her lips, Kay fetched a blanket from the window seat and gently tucked it around Mary's tiny frame

CHAPTER 24

Brooke's Journal Entry #2

I've been unbelievably busy *getting my portfolios in shape. This last week, everything went totally ballistic.*

It started with Kay's Aunt Maureen. The poor woman freaked out in Thommy Jay's antique shop. And in a rant, she broke a lot of valuable things. I guess there's no way to predict what triggers her spells. It's odd, most of the time she appears very lethargic.

Kind Mr. Jay isn't pressing charges. Chief Ujima Washington is another terrific person and head of the small police department, here. The medics called and treated her. Kay was able to visit Aunt Maureen a day later. Then Alex and Kay took her back to her apartment and stayed with her through the evening until she fell asleep.

When Kay's aunt first came to the island, Kay and Alex clued us in on what to do if she goes into a "mood-change". I guess she can have blackouts afterward and not remember anything. There's a vial of medicine around her neck and Kay now keeps several bottles of the correct dosages in the refrigerator. I guess there weren't any warning signs, or maybe Aunt Maureen and Mr. Jay couldn't get to the medicine in time. So, the island rumor mill is running fast and mean. Sadly, most people don't like her and think she's lost it. It's because they haven't got to know her. The few times Teri and I were with her, she was gracious, interested in our projects, and kind. And a rare thing, she listens to what you're saying.

Speaking of other eccentric people, Mr. Jynx Buckwass takes the prize. I get the weirdest feeling when I'm around him. He took me and Teri to lunch the other day, and it was a disaster. Very weird, worse than the Mad Hatter's tea party. He kept trying to make us eat cockles he'd gathered, especially at the beach that morning. Ugh. I like seafood, but the way he kept pushing made me feel… suspicious. I wasn't feeling well, anyway.

Then, talk about a person getting angry. He shouted, putting people down, and just being very nasty. It was all because some hungry, poor person made off with his stupid bag of cockles. They took them from the restaurant cooler. We left as soon as we could. It was embarrassing.

Then a weirder thing happened to Rose Bracken last week. After she had shown Mr. Buckwass his rental property, they'd stepped outside, and he became not angry, but all hysterical when he saw some kids in a field. Rose said they were larking about in a Hallowe'en costume. Mr. Buckwass got bug-eyed and yelled something silly, like: "She's come to get me!" I think he's mental.

Of course, I can't be too superior. An awful thing happened to me too. Teri and I were exploring an abandoned house. Weirdly, I felt drawn by the place and its setting. All I intended to do was take pictures. But what creeped me out was a battered doll in the basement. The odd thing is, I knew right where it was! I nearly lost it in front of Teri. I was very frightened by the experience. She has been wonderful, though, helping me see reason and calming me. Now it all seems like a vague nightmare. But the doll is real. We cleaned it, and now it's in my bedroom.

Teri didn't want to be in the ruined house at all. But she followed me in. I even knew the doll's name, Matilda! Teri and I think I must have visited that horrible house at one time. It's a creepy place, but I'm going to ask Dad. Unfortunately, he's at an important conference in Spokane this week. I'll have to call him again next week when he gets back. My petite hysteria can wait.

There's more strange news. There seems to be a monster, vampire, whatever, lurking on the island and it sometimes stalks people. Woo, woo, very scary. Most sightings are during the day and at dusk. It's kind of spooky with Hallowe'en looming in two weeks. But I think it's humorous, in a way, if it doesn't scare small kids. I bet I know who's behind it.

Rose said that Mr. Calhoun Smith, the editor, and publisher of the island paper (who really promotes UFO mania), thinks the sightings are pranksters, gearing up for the 31st. With an eye for profit, Cal Smith embellishes the accounts and puts sensational headlines on the front page.

Naturally, rumors are everywhere, and the paper circulation is off the map. I think the most believable account is when Rose saw whatever it was on a real-estate deal in the hills. But then, Alex saw it too, when he was out crabbing. Chief Washington claims it's a lot of nonsense and said soberly, "It better not get out of hand, or they will have to deal with me. And I'm the actual monster around here."

Willie Cloudmaker, the island's local guru, told Alex he thinks something psycho-serious is up, like the visitation of a Tsonoqua spirit. Yes, Tsonoqua. It's an indigenous legendary creature who steals and eats kids. Really? Today, that would give any monster serious digestion problems.

My oh my, this island is an exciting place. Peculiar things never stop happening. Here's to Hannibal Lector, munch, crunch, munch.

More later.

CHAPTER 25

Titans

Three days after Mary's consultation, she sat on one of the inn's window seats with a large pillow propped behind her. Comfortable, she gazed at Scoon Bay below. The weather was warm, allowing a heavy mist to creep over Heron's Hook. The sounds became muted, making the morning peaceful.

Kay had suggested that Mary and Maureen meet at the inn. She said it should be a comfortable setting. Willy had also volunteered to help. Mary smiled. She could smell the makings of breakfast drifting into the large front room. Her stomach rumbled. She rubbed her eyes. Forget my stomach. I must organize my thoughts; this first meeting is going to be a major challenge.

What had she learned about Maureen's past? When a young woman she rescued two abandoned children. And now she seemed possessed by a negative force. It compelled her to do... do what exactly, and... why?

Mary knew it was necessary to meet with Maureen as soon as possible. Kay's aunt held the key to the Island's peculiar events and the ominous premonitions that Mary felt. Whatever the problems were, they lay in Maureen's realm.

From what she'd been able to determine, Maureen had some shamanistic capabilities, too. And even if they were from different northwest areas, they should be able to come to some sort of common ground.

Mary nodded to herself; it was perfect having the use of the inn. The two charming young ladies were away on their separate projects. Alex was in Burn helping Wick on the new play and Kay was also in Burn, teaching a yoga class with her new hire.

Willie was in the Inn's enormous kitchen and gleefully taking advantage of the goodies in the pantry. He prepared an egg and bacon sandwich for himself and assembled Mary's favorite breakfast: a pot of boiling, dark chocolate. She liked it spiced with chili, nutmeg and honey, and then a plate of raisin-cinnamon toast, slathered in crunchy peanut-butter at the side.

Willie devoured his own breakfast, then set Mary's on the large kitchen table. "Come and get it," he hollered. Shae didn't wait for a second urging. He winked as she sliced her three pieces of toast, then dunked one into her oversized cup of Mexican hot chocolate.

"Willie, this is heavenly." She grinned back. "Thanks for remembering." Willie bowed, put on his cap, told her he had already finished his breakfast, then politely excused himself.

"Got to mosey into Madrona for some groceries," he said. Wished her a "good chat" and quickly headed for his truck and just as quickly, set off for town.

Mary smiled. Typical Willie, get out of Dodge before the fireworks start.

The morning fog had burned off. A good omen. Scoon Bay was a mirror. Great, now they could have an intimate breakfast on the veranda.

After she brought the plates and napkins, including her breakfast, to the outside table. She sat straight-backed in her wicker chair, emptying her mind. Must become extremely perceptive to any tiny nuances in the conversation, Mary thought. She would do her best.

The gravel drive crunched. Maureen's cab stopped at the foot of the wide stairway leading up to the veranda. Paying Cinch, the cab driver, she laughed at something he said, then turned and waved at Mary. Mary waved back.

As Maureen approached, Mary could feel an aura of dominance and danger. This was not a person to be trifled with.

"Hello Cousin Mary," Maureen called, her voice nasal, as she slowly negotiated the stairs. "I hope dear Kay has set aside some breakfast; I'm starved."

"Hello Maureen. Actually, Willie was our chef. Your breakfast is being kept warm in the oven." Mary got up. "I'll fetch a tray. Please sit in the other chair. Would you like some hot cocoa? It's ready in the kitchen."

"That sounds jolly. I would indeed." She heavily sat down.

Soon, Mary brought out the tray. Maureen, not saying another word, slurped cocoa, while gobbling her quiche, a brioche, and ham. She belched into her napkin. "Pardon me. I was so hungry, and these days have been very stressful. I hope there's more."

"There certainly is. In a bit, I'm going back for seconds, myself. But tell me, if you can't wait," she said and dipped another piece of toast in her cup.

Maureen leaned back and peered at Mary intently. "I can definitely wait. The doctor says it is best for my digestion." A protracted silence ensued. Maureen eyed Mary. "I understand you're a seer and a healer...of the old school... as they say."

"My grandmother and special members of our tribe trained me. I try to help others when I can." Oddly, she felt nervous, like a naïve child. "Things don't always work out cleanly, though. They can become muddled."

Maureen waved her hand. "I'm well aware of the limitations of Shamans and Seers. It comes with the metaphysical territory." She chuckled, "Similar to the amazing discoveries in quantum physics, very mysterious. But that aside, I think you can help me."

"Mary, I'm at a loss. You are, I imagine, and I hope, a dispassionate observer. Thus, you may see a connection, or reasons certain things are happening to me." She took another sip of her coffee. "Where I live, life has been pleasant, and I've been happy. However, since I've come here, evil has approached me. There is an ominous presence, but I can't define it. So, I'm experiencing certain, shall we say, uncontrollable reactions? And they can become dangerous when I become upset... even memory lapses occur."

She fingered the vial of green liquid attached to her necklace. "I'm sure you know I take this medicine when things go awry. It works well. But now I can't always recall things that happened, or what precipitated a bad spell. Here, on this island, it seems to get worse... and more frequent. Our tribal shaman, who made this for me, said that I will heal once I get closer to home."

"And where is your home?"

"It is to the far north, in the Alaskan panhandle. We keep the location secret. I intend to go there after I settle everything with Kay." She paused. "It's a sanctuary, protected by my family and our tribe."

"How long has this sacred place existed?"

"It seems, since forever. Of course, I grew up there and that's where I intend to end my days." Her fist suddenly slammed the table. "But I may never live that long with this wretched thing plaguing me. These malignant forces are driving me to the edge." She fingered the tablecloth, and her voice became low, even menacing. "I've heard of you. The rumors of your powers and helping those who have curses or spells put on them." She looked up with her huge, haunting eyes. "I'm pleading for you to help me. These ominous sensations are worsening. It feel I'm manipulated by something, something beyond my abilities."

Mary paused for a length of time. She must parse the odious waves of deception and menace that emanated from this woman. Though Maureen's core vibes were solid, there was a much stronger overlay of malevolence. She could and would find the source.

"Of course. I'll do everything I can to help," she replied in a level tone and clamped down on her own repellant feelings. "We should start with your past. Most of these troubling memes originate there and we, unfortunately, carry the burden either consciously or unconsciously." Mary had a vague vision of trees. "I don't wish to disturb you further. But was there an occurrence, or possibly traumatic experience you had in your life, one that you've willfully suppressed, denied? I'm seeing an ancient forest and smelling the scent of fir trees."

Maureen dropped her head and nodded. The silence was eerie. Her voice, when it came, was hollow, distant. "Yes. It's rather, rather horrible. It happened a long time ago. I was very young." Maureen's eyes became glazed and unfocused. "I've told no one." She shuddered. "I...I think it's when everything wretched must have begun."

Mary sat back, closed her eyes, and willed her mind to become neutral. A blank screen. As Maureen's voice droned on, Mary's vision became vivid. People, objects, unblurred into a 3-D photograph. Then they move. The first things she saw were tears of desperation.

CHAPTER 26

Transformation

Maureen wept. She could not believe what he had done and what he was doing. It was vile, not real. She had been such a fool. I've got to get away. The forest: yes, she'd run into the forest. It would protect her.

Blindly, Maureen leaped over logs and bracken. She staggered onto an animal trail that snaked into the woods. Wringing her hands, she ran faster. Sobs of loss made her stop. Gasping for breath, she fell to her knees. Head back, she roared. Trees, ground, sky, offered no pity. Rage overwhelmed her. Crows cawing wildly circled above her. Were they following her and leading her to where she could die of the shame and her own stupidity?

Furiously, she wiped her eyes. Anger, anger was better than madness. She grabbed a dead branch, and, gritting her teeth, snarled. She battered the vegetation in her path. Soon she subsided again into sobs and gasps for air. With a spasm of all her muscles, she fell headlong into the ferns by the path.

Hollowed out nothing left. She lay face down, stunned by the attack on her world. The crow's raucous screams faded. Above, the canopy of giant trees sighed. She turned in total pain, but the almond scent of crushed fern and moist earth slowly, gently, calmed her.

Ahead, long gray streamers of beard moss draped the fir branches. A breeze eased over them. Voices murmured and whispered through the moving trees above. It was the wise and reassuring conversations of the ancients who had gone long ago.

Eerily, an owl's voice, asking who? emerged from the whispers. Who? Who? The call was for her. She slowly stood. Pieces of fir needles, soil, and twigs cascaded from her body. She brushed furiously, then like a wet bear, shook off the rest.

Maureen froze. Before her was an ominous human shape. Amid hazelnut branches and huckleberry fir stumps stood a gigantic gray-haired woman. Clumps of snowberries sprouted from her head. With enormous arms outstretched, Tsonoqua beckoned. A tongue moved inside the large O-shaped mouth. The movement transformed into a startled owl. It screeched and swiftly soared over Maureen's head.

In awe, she approached the monster. With each step, the shape became larger, more threatening, and oddly, more beautiful. Clinging ferns waved from her shoulders and the exquisitely hewn outstretched limbs. The right arm, rotted off at the elbow, left a giant hand thrusting palm up from the blackberry bushes at her feet.

Sunlight, filtering through the tall trees, fell on the ancient totem. It brought life to the hooting mouth… the chipped red lips, and the deep-piercing eyes. The visible torso above the brush appeared at least twenty feet high. Terrified, Maureen wanted to turn, run. It was too magnificent, too real.

Fashioned by forgotten peoples of long ago, the ancient ancestral totem beckoned. Compelled, Maureen kneeled before the sacred, carved colossus. She ran her hand over the grooves in the weathered cedar, breathing in the scent of it. The aroma was wonderful, complex. Almond scents of green fern mixed with the earthiness of the forest floor. It was an aroma stirring the deep wildness of human nature.

In a flash of understanding, she knew … it was chilling. The terrifying aspects of human beings would plague the species until the end of their time. Then, another animal would dominate this earth. Would it suffer the miseries of hatred, atrocities, meanness with all the eons of confrontations for greed and survival inherited from an atavistic past?

These feelings overwhelmed her until, behind her, she heard snorting and trampling of the brush. She turned slowly. A great shaggy beast stood erect, monstrous fur-covered shoulders visible.

A giant grizzly, sensitive nose twitching, searched for her

scent. It hadn't seen her yet. Quietly, on all fours, she backed up. Where could she hide? There, there behind the Tsonoqua was what appeared to be a hollow. She crawled into it. She thanked the spirits; the scent of a bear was not here. But it was an animal tunnel, a lynx's pathway, perhaps? Good, she knew how to alarm them.

As she crawled further into the passageway, the berry bushes and bracken became less dense. But a few arched overhead, tunnel-like. Still, on hands and knees, she felt an abrupt change in the dirt. It was on the edge of a wooden floor.

Carefully, she stood. Dappled sunlight illuminated cedar roofing and support beams that were rotting into the soft ground. It had once been a magnificent longhouse. Branches and brambles hid her. But because of her tallness, she could peer over them. Another snort echoed through the woods. The bear turned; light shimmering off its large rear and shoulders as it lumbered away.

Disoriented, she turned to stare at the remains of the immense longhouse. It appeared to go on forever; broken walls and fallen beams receding into the forest. In the distance and tilted at odd angles, were different rotting totem poles. Their weathered faces seemed to stare accusingly. It was strange. The ruins were close to her own tribal village, but no one had ever mentioned them. She walked forward in wonder, then stopped when something soft yielded underfoot.

Looking down, she realized she was standing in the remains of one of the grand house fire-pits. Her foot sensed something buried in dirt and ashes. Scraping away the ancient debris, she found a soft object. It was a leather bag, small and rotten with mold. Out of the deerskin fell six blue trade beads and five drilled cowry shells. It was odd they were shiny, almost new, as if recently placed there. The objects formed a bracelet. Remarkably, the connecting chord still held them together. She clasped the object to her breast. It was a sign, an offering. She immediately knew what she had to do...purify, cleanse.

Later, the villagers found her burned and barely alive, the house, in ashes. The tribe agreed it should be rebuilt to heal the bleak wound in the earth, but the Shaman knew the scars on her body and mind would last the rest of her life.

* * *

Mary sat stunned. The visions she'd witnessed were sacred and, by their implication, more compounded. Future events would be difficult for everyone.

Quietly, Mary studied Maureen's face of misery. The woman stared blindly ahead; eyes blurred with tears. Then slowly, exhausted by the telling of her terrifying experiences, Maureen's head drooped.

Mary pursed her lips. So, more damned difficulties were approaching. And more blasted obstructions to peel back. Mary liked a challenge, but... shaking her head, she gazed at the exhausted woman.

Maureen slumped in her chair, snoring softly. With her mind lost in forgetfulness, she appeared almost beautiful. And totally oblivious to the growing dangers.

CHAPTER 27

A Policeman's lot is...

Ujima put her feet on the desk and stuck the wrong end of the pen in her mouth. "Oh Bletch! When am I going to stop this filthy habit?"

Kay laughed. "When you have someone permanently around, to get on your case, like Role. He was…" Ujima's feet hit the floor, loudly. "I'm sorry, I didn't mean…"

"It's alright Kay. Roland isn't in the running, anyway." She picked up three papers from her desk and carefully straightened them. "There is a certain Gerald Vandermeer I met in Curaçao. Remember my vacation last winter? He seems to be seriously interested."

"I assume that's a letter from him?"

Ujima shook her head. "No, my memo pad. We communicate by e-mail." She made several notations on the top paper, then looked up. "Met him at my dad's liquor store. Gerald is quite the connoisseur. He bought a case of fine vintage wines my dad had shipped from Europe; afterward, he asked me out. And that night we went to an excellent French restaurant." She smiled. "He and the food were quite captivating, and in that order."

"Hmm, Vandermeer, an interesting last name, Dutch?"

"Yes, with a bit of Carib-Indonesian mixed in, a luscious combination. And he speaks German, English, French, and Island Patois well."

Ujima raised her hand. "Before you ask; he works for the TSONEX Corporation. In fact, he owns it."

Kay stared, wide-eyed.

"Yes, that TSONEX--- he can write his own ticket anywhere on this planet. Well, almost anywhere." She raised her eyebrows. "He hit it off with my aunties and dad, too."

"Sounds intriguing, and I'm glad for you. So, Roland is definitely out of the picture?"

"Yes. Yes, he is. The last missive I received from him," she fiddled with the papers, "was… anyway, he's following a lead on that mysterious beloved of his. Now in Cairo, of all places."

"Cairo! I thought she disappeared in a sandstorm in Mauretania."

"She did. But she somehow survived and was taken to a hospital in Cairo."

Kay spread her hands. "For Roland's sake, I hope she's okay. And what about the potentially fabulous discovery of the great Juba II's and Selene's library?" Kay ahemmed. "Which, and I quote, 'will rock the archaeological world to its roots.' Did that pan out?"

Ujima rearranged the papers on her desk. "He said they found something, but as usual, he was very secretive. As you're aware, their encampment is under strong surveillance." She shook her head. "You and Alex have known Roland much longer than I have. But, to me he has the romantic vision of a 16-year-old. He appears happy with the desert, sand, stars, and the continual pursuit of adventure. He'll never change."

"Humph, for all his promises, you've heard from him more than we have. The last communication we had was that he'd made it safely to Morocco. After that, no response. Alex facetiously said that the mysterious Mr. Hugo probably trussed him up for shark bait." She paused. "But since he's alive and breathing, I'll attempt to contact him. I have some, not too difficult, requests in mind."

"Good luck," Ujima said, and grimaced. "I don't know why he felt it necessary to contact me." She arched an eyebrow. "His letter is curious, though. I'll share it with you and maybe you can help. I need a Rosetta stone to interpret the damned thing. He's avoiding any concrete information if it drops into Mr. Hugo's hands. And you can tell, by the clumsy opening and resealing, someone has read it. So, I can see why he's been purposely abstruse." She pushed the flimsy papers toward Kay. "What do you make of it?"

"He'll still be a good friend of yours, I hope," Kay mumbled as she perused the top sheet. The writing was small, almost illegible. And to put it mildly, confusing from the get-go. Funny, Ujima was an ace at resolving cryptic communications. Uhm, Ujima had made excellent notations in the margins. Why did she think I could do any better? This is a puzzling paragraph, looks like code. With her finger on the passage, she leaned forward. Ujima's phone rang.

It was welcome, giving Kay time to scan the rest of the papers. My, there was a helluva a lot more than she wanted to ask. But Ujima was involved. The conversation consisted mainly of head nods and hand gestures. Ujima made a quick entry on her computer and carefully placed her desk phone back in its cradle. With a peculiar look, she glanced at Kay. "Later, later I'll share that letter with you… and with Alex too. He's more familiar with his old buddy's eccentricities."

Kay nodded. "I think we should also pull Teri in on this. As you're aware. Two years ago, Role was her tutor on that dead body she found." She placed the letter back on Ujima's desk. "Now, what's up?"

"I don't know." Ujima, her forearms on her desk, fiddled with her pen and tablet. "I've had beaucoup complaints coming into this office. People say they've seen monsters, bigfoot, aliens, etc. For Pete's sake, Hallowe'en is a few weeks away; but this is the umpteenth time."

"I'm getting to be a very annoying and unpleasant person. Fortunately, Sgt. Reynolds has followed through on the first five sightings, and there's nothing. Everything seems bogus, just hearsay."

"No solid evidence?"

"Oh, he's found footprints. Usually, water-proof boot prints. A very common variety, available and cheap. An islander must have them when we're in the wet. You can buy them at the hardware store, and the Mercantile. Every farmer and her grandmother have a pair… if not two."

"Actually, at the inn, we have six."

Ujima grumbled, "Must be some kook, or a cos-play group who needs attention…" Ujima stopped and looked at the expression on Kay's face.

"What?"

"I guess you'll have to add another sighting. Alex spotted a weird creature when he was crabbing on Wednesday of last week. I think he had an excellent view of the thing."

"You're putting me on."

"I wish I were. Alex is a fairly excellent observer. It was romping on the beach at Heron's Hook. Alex said. It gestured to him. When he went to investigate, he found very large prints that were jumbled in the sand. But Alex felt weirded-out enough to mention it to Willie. Then Willie became serious, said these sightings are ominous and people should stop messing around with something they know nothing about. He told Alex he's very relieved that his cousin Mary is visiting from New Halem, Oregon."

"Really? What's the significance of this Cousin Mary waiting in the wings?"

"She's a relative on his mother's side. You're aware that Willie comes from an extended family. Lots of aunts, uncles, and cousins. Anyway, they're all very close." Kay shrugged. "We know Willie senses things we don't. I guess his cousin does, too. She's some sort of tribal shaman."

"Well, that's jolly. Now we have another woo-woo factor to deal with."

"Well, he told Alex that since she is a seer, she may nip all this brouhaha in the bud, possibly prevent further disruption or even serious trouble."

"He hit the nail on the head there. It's agitating the populace and taking up our valuable time when we have more serious policing to tend to. What else did Willie say?"

"He says it's … a… well… malicious interference, of a Tsonoqua."

"What the hell is a Tsonoqua?"

"It's an evil spirited monster that captures children and eats them."

"Oh, that's not necessarily a bad thing," Ujima said with a laugh. Then her expression changed. "However, to be serious, we have similar legends in the Caribbean. They're useful in stopping young children from talking to strangers. Or going places and doing things they shouldn't. Obviously, these legends are symbolic of the evil nature of humankind, very much like the witch in Hansel and Gretel, you know, or the classic bogey."

"Willie told Alex about the same thing. The Tsonoqua legend is present up and down the Northwest coast. Of course, in other tribal groups, the thing goes by different names."

"Okay, I follow. But how does this Tsonoqua gig, theoretically, affect us?"

"Willie says that no matter what; by monkeying around with this very dangerous meme, it can stir up evil things, yet to come."

"Oh fun. You and Alex don't believe in all this hoopla, do you?"

"Ujima, I feel there's always a smidgen of truth in any legend. Willie didn't say what would happen. But cousin Mary seems to be the genuine article, an actual seer. To me, she's extremely concerned and wary."

"You mentioned you met her. Somehow, I missed her visiting the island. What's she like?"

"Well, enchanting comes to mind. Even politely, out of the blue, she requested a first-time meeting with Aunt Maureen."

Ujima leaned forward, memo-pad in hand. "Ah, continue."

"Anyway, the morning of their first face-to-face meeting, they had breakfast together. They wanted a private meeting the next day, so Willie, Alex and I and the girls made ourselves scarce."

"When did you come back to the inn?"

"When Willie and I finished our to-do lists. Then we met for coffee. We arrived after about two hours. That's the window Mary requested. Interestingly. Maureen wasn't there. She'd taken Cinch's cab back to Madrona."

"What was the upshot?"

"When we came into the living room. Mary was coming out of what I would call a trance. She calls it a session. It's very unusual. But afterward, for me, it was quite an informative experience. Mary said she and Maureen had a wonderful talk, but she revealed little about it. Mary said she was satisfied with what she, er… envisioned, or saw. And the presences she senses here. I believe hippies would call it bad vibes. Evidently, they are close, real and dangerous."

"I believe I heard a plural there." Ujima rolled her eyes. "Oh goody, I can see this rapidly becoming a real Spook Fest. I will have a talk with her." Ujima smiled. "Maybe find out what the spirit world has to say." She gave a short laugh. "Possibly meet a few auras and ghosts from my past. The more the merrier." She paused, then looked at the ceiling and frowned. "You said that the session was informative for you. What did you mean...."

Kay shrugged. "The bomb shell I discovered...is that Brooke's adopted. And her father, or mother, never told her."

"Hmm, nothing we can do there, but that is curious. Let's keep a lid on it for now. What else did our resourceful Kay come away with?"

Kay spread her hands. "Well, I was impressed with Mary's demeanor; she's not at all over the top, and I found her extremely sweet and very intelligent." Kay's eyes arched. "I was the one that suggested they meet at the inn, since Mary requested the initial part be private. I know. But it all went well. The inn proved to be a calm and peaceful setting."

Ujima clapped her hands. "What? No items flung off the walls, no broken bits of crystal ball, nor spewing heads to clean up after?"

"Oh ha, ha. Though, it's weird. I have the feeling we'll be glad to have her in our corner and not on the, er...spooky, wacky side." She regarded Ujima's face with amazement. "I'm just saying."

Their laughter of hilarity was genuine but tempered with an undertone of apprehension.

CHAPTER 28

Brook's Journal Entry #3
Concerns

Kay invited me and Teri to lunch with Aunt Maureen. It was awful. I know the woman's not stupid, but she wouldn't talk, ate nothing and just stared. She made Kay's entire luncheon weird. It didn't seem like one of her spells, however, Teri and I thought it might be a mild one. Her mom excused us early, but before we left, Kay said her aunt just wasn't feeling well after what she'd been through.

Later, I asked Teri if she noticed the weird change. She said of course she did. And then brought me up to speed with a brief history of Aunt Maureen. When she was young, the poor woman got caught in a house fire, had a mental breakdown, and they finally confined her in a rehabilitation institution in Canada.

Maybe she has PTSD after what happened at Thommy Jay's.

Teri thinks that all these events coupled with her disabilities just make things worse. She will most likely have these episodes for the rest of her life.

Gosh, there's been awful news this week. The new restaurant that was being built on the edge of a millpond, north of Madrona, caught fire. The rumor is that Kay's aunt had something to do with it. Evidently, an anonymous phone call said she was around the building at the time of the fire.

Ugh, I know it is unreasonable and irrational, but I don't enjoy being around her. It's unfortunate, but she seems to be vaguer and more ponderous.

Oh, and back to the fire. The local paper, the Spindrift, says that the police think it was arson and there may have been an accelerant used. It started on the outside deck, then destroyed the dining room. Luckily, the kitchen survived.

Mr. Raymond Toda, the owner, named his restaurant, The Bloated Toad. Teri and I think it's hilarious, all his friends call him Toady. He used to be the owner of Toad Hall, an antique store in Madrona.

Byron and Teri know Mr. Toda, and he's a close friend of the family. He sounds resilient. He told them he'll start rebuilding in January.

Getting back to that weird lunch this afternoon, I'm still thinking about it. It was so horrible. Intense waves of dislike toward Aunt Maureen overwhelmed me. It was surprising because the first time we met I liked her. I'm non-judgmental and I know it takes time to really know a person. But she's changed somehow and is completely different. Her eyes are unblinking. She looks right through a person as if they're not there. I just get chills thinking about it.

Maybe I remind Aunt Maureen of someone in her past. Someone she detested. Teri and I agreed she looked at me with pity, and it seemed there were looks of anger and disgust.

She sat to the right of Kay. If I said something, she'd look at Kay and make an unrelated remark. It was really uncomfortable. She ignored Teri and sometimes there were long silences, then when she talked, it was monotone and real slow. You'd think she was stupid, or in a trance. When she laughs, it's honking way and has a nasty edge to it. I'm sure the fire damaged her lungs, and her throat, too. I should feel sorry for her, but I don't and trying to rationalize why I've reacted this way.

At first, I thought she was cool and unique. I hate it. It's like when you have a premonition of something awful about to happen when someone acts so weird.

Everything is confusing. I just don't want to be wherever she is, so Teri and I have spent the day in Burn. There we can explore the town and bounce ideas off each other. After we get back, we'll follow up by summarizing the first phases of our projects. I know we'll have fun. And Aunt Maureen will have left for the Madrona Inn by this evening.

It's amazing. Teri seems unfazed by any of Maureen's strange behavior, and even my weird, ominous feelings. Teri just shrugs and shoots me her familiar lop-sided smile, then says, "Whatever?"

I wish I had her strength and confidence.

CHAPTER 29

Roma Ragazzi

In the remote Italian hilltop town of Fierro, the morning was golden. Roma Ragazzi sat at her palazzo's terrace table, sipping espresso and regarding the tray of letters before her. Still sleepy, she smiled as an impish breeze teased her airy robe, bringing with it the wonderful scent of fresh rain that earlier had graced the fields below. Now fog buried the farms. But Roma knew the mist would burn off by noon and the day would be hot and glorious.

She was famished, and when Sophia brought her mail, she promised her breakfast would be up shortly. Roma sorted through the various envelopes. Then sat back and sighed. With extreme curiosity, she scanned the return address on the large brown envelope.

The postmark was Bradestone Island, U.S.A. It had to be him. Interesting. What did he want now? It was close to two years, and she hadn't heard a word. She smiled. He never texted, used email, faxed, or the phone; always secretive. He told her it made things less complicated.

Tsking and shaking her head, she picked up the table knife and slit open the flap. She examined the three photos that dropped out, then picked up the enclosed letter accompanying them.

Dear Roma, as you know it has been a while. I've been busy tending to loose ends in Canada and I'm now back in the United States. I'm sure this the last order to fill out will surprise you. After retiring soon, I purchased a small villa in Sardinia. It's been a long time since we have seen one another, so let's get together when I'm in Italy. I won't be that far away; we can sync our schedules and meet at that small café. Remember where I first met you? That's if it's still there. So many things have changed.

Fondly, J.B.

What's this? Was Jinx finally tired of the wet and the cold? She thought it would be more in his nature to retire to Alaska. Wasn't that where his village was? She shook her head. He was one of her more wealthy and eccentric clients. She never liked the fact that he would not share how he marketed his dolls. Oh well, she was through asking him questions, and his recompense was beyond excellent.

Really, she owed much to him. She wouldn't have been able to live here, and she wouldn't have met her wonderful Phillip if it weren't for him. Thinking of Phillip, she looked up to the balcony. Bougainvillea tumbled elegantly over the palazzo terrace. The colors dazzled as they moved in the light breeze. Wasn't he awake yet? The doors are shut. She tsked, then eyed the geraniums. She'd have to ask Sophia to water them.

Roma thought of the new girl. Sophia was so conscientious. She'd obviously allowed Phillip to sleep in. Well, he'd be down later, for lunch. After a night out with his amici in the village, he'd be more than hungry and brimming with local gossip. She chuckled and took another sip of expresso. In her long life, she'd determined that most men were worse chatterboxes than women. Her eyes drifted back to the photos and letter. She skimmed to the more important part. She could hear his voice.

As you can see, this is a lovely little girl, and her parents want this to be one of your very special creations. Pay close attention to the clothes and especially the color of her hair. They must be exact.

Odd, didn't she always do that? Over the years, he'd been effusive about her work. She picked up one photo and studied it more carefully. A pretty girl, yes, and a pretty smile; it would be easy to capture her features. And there were several bisque blanks to hand. Hopefully, this was his last order. He must finally complete his collection, and as usual, he required one for himself and one for his client.

Roma's eyes were not as good as they used to be, but her hearing was excellent. Last weekend, Marie, the wife of her son Carlos, brought the grandchildren to visit and play. Carlos routinely comes early so that he and Mama could have a quiet chat time; before the children arrived.

Later in the evening, Maria and Carlos had gotten into the habit of sitting together in the terrace alcove. It was very romantic. They held hands and watched the children. But recently, Marie chided her husband about Roma's new projects.

"Carlos, I think your mother should retire. She's worked so hard. She could continue her museum contracts, restoration, etc. But the larger artworks, only. Your mother should hire one of her abler students to do the finer pieces. There's Eleni. She's sharp and trained very well, and you and I both like her work."

Carlos would nod his head sagely and say, "Marie, please give me a little more time, then I'll talk to mama. She's very sensitive when I bring up anything related to aging, as you know."

Roma pretended to be drowsing in her favorite lounge chair but could hear every word. She smiled. What Marie and Carlos didn't realize was that she was already using Eleni. She looked forward to the astonishment on their faces when she would tell them that Eleni had done all the work in the last two years and a half and Roma had deeded the entire business to Eleni. The girl's eagerness and quality of work would carry on the studio's reputation. This delighted Roma's husband, Phillip, who already planned a trip for them to Brazil. They would visit his family there and then meet all his cousins, too. She sighed. Roma wished she'd decided four years ago. It was long overdue.

* * *

Later, when everyone was gone, she picked up the enclosed check. Her eyebrows rose; three times her usual fee and more. This wasn't a mistake. He wanted this project to be the last work from her studio. She would not let him down.

CHAPTER 30

The Fates at Play

It was her, that treacherous woman. She was alive! Jinx couldn't believe it. Face white with anger, he jabbed at his laptop. Did she have an accomplice? What convoluted mix of forces had brought her madness to Bradestone? He soon found where she was staying. He wrung his hands.

Why, why was she here? Only spiteful spirits could answer that. He must have a session with the shells, they would tell him. It was not a coincidence. He would stay completely out of her sight. Yes, he had his resources; he'd call on them and drive her away. It wouldn't be difficult. She was unstable. He struck when her underlying insanity broke through. Then she would be vulnerable.

That accounted for the strange incidents on the island. And, most likely, the other inexplicable events. She had that innate power. He knew she'd plotted to destroy and disrupt his livelihood several times. He grinned. But he had survived. He had skillfully eluded her traps and spites. His last scheme would be perfect. The record folder he titled the Final Contract, appropriate. He'd underline it double.

He scanned the room. The fates were with him now, and now he understood why he'd felt the aura of a tranquil sea when he entered this new shop.

The old storage units were gone. The replacement bookshelves were almost completed, and the carpets installed. Rose really had been very helpful. She keyed him into finding comfortable and attractive furniture for his reading nooks. And her judgment on the installed lighting was fresh and subtle. The county and city's encumbering inspections were all passed. He nodded. In a week, he would move his merchandise from the storage facilities near town. Ready for business in three weeks. That was his goal.

The porcelains would be as eye-catching as ever. They would shine exquisitely, placed here and there, among the gifts and notions on the shelves. He patted his laptop. The photos and ancillary papers were in his protected computer file. The paper backups were locked and safe in his fireproof file cabinet.

The final number of five was prophetic. Five, five clients to complete his lucky number. But the fifth one, still active, was the most difficult. The other four were strictly doll collectors, easy. The fifth was his swan song. Roma would retire as a millionaire and he would too, but twice over. Even though Roma now worked from Italy, there was surprisingly little difficulty in financial exchanges, and recently, the same with products.

Roma's work was impeccable. The first time he'd met her professionally was in her small studio off the Rue du Sénat in Paris. After viewing the exceptional intricacy of her work, he asked her out to dinner. He pursed his lips. It'd been pricey. She loved good food and expensive wines. But the meal was well worth it. When she saw his plans and what he wanted to accomplish, she'd readily agreed. Roma had two small girls and a boy, and her husband worked in a clockmaker's shop. She was delighted to have a contract that would more than supplement the family's income.

"A good education comes at an exceptionally high price these days. And now my husband and I can send the children to schools we've only dreamed about. Thank you so very much, Monsieur."

It wasn't long after that, because of Jinx's flourishing business, her earnings far surpassed her husband's. When they'd met again, she clasped Jinx's icy hands. "My husband and children are all so happy. We have my sister in Italy. She's always wanted my family to come and live with hers, and now we'll be able to. Also, we'll now be able to visit my husband's family in Brazil," she said excitedly.

When Jinx had seen his Roma's first commission work, they were exceptional. Even when his team couldn't catch all the details in their photos, Roma had the uncanny ability to interpret even the haziest of shots. Clothes, expressions, she could render an almost perfect likeness, even to the shoes, if they wore them.

Jinx snorted. There were a few unsatisfied customers, obviously the type that would complain about anything. But in the end, some of the fussy ones made the purchase they had initially rejected. His company had earned the exclusive reputation of people being 99% satisfied with what they made and their follow-through.

Avatars Angéliques Animes had a five-star reputation. And there were no other competitors vying for his elite clientele, nor able to provide his unique results.

CHAPTER 31

Ghostly Gala

Raymond Toda brooded as he stared at his garden below. Outside, wearing his go-to gardener's leather vest, Rain was weeding, then spreading his winter mulch. The sound of Thom's sports car disrupted Toady's thoughts coming up the driveway. Toady grimaced. He did not need this.

Thom tooted his horn and got out, removed something from the trunk, and strolled over to chat with Rain. The exchange seemed serious. Then, spotting Toady in the window, he waved, and was soon trotting toward the house; carelessly swinging his tattered briefcase.

Not bothering to knock, Thom thrust open the door to make a dramatic entrance. He stopped, sniffed the air. Ah, something unpleasant. Then tottered over to the granite-topped kitchen island. Gently, he placed his tatty briefcase on the stone surface. The island was a divider between the kitchen and Toady's spacious living room.

"Oh, sad and mournful one, I know just the thing to cheer you up."

"What? About forty martinis?" Toady said and grimaced.

"Well, we could start, say with a tray, of drinkies, but only six. Nay, my sad sir, I'm not thinking of your excellent libations, but more in the line of a delightful debauchery, say... a P-A-R-T-Y?"

"Oh sure, that'll be a big help."

"Darling, I'm suggesting a Hallowe'en Party. It's your favorite time of the year. It'll be the bash of Bradestone. Rose, Kay, and

Solange are already excited," he paused, "even stodgy old Alex agreed to my idea."

"A Hallowe'en Party? You are all out of your collective minds. I'm not interested in something so juvenile. And I certainly won't cater it. I'm not in the mood. Maybe next year, hah, or maybe never." He exclaimed, then flung his arms in exasperation.

"Oh, poor, poor boy, a pity party does not become you. After the smoke out at the Bloated Toad and Cal's dramatic write-up, I'd think you would want to prove to the community, and yourself, that even a disaster won't set back Mr. Raymond Toda. Latch on to the Brave Brit Brigade. Are you familiar with the clichés? Chin up, put your shoulder to the wheel, full steam ahead, all colors flying, etc., etc., ad nauseum. Where did your spunky, up-for-anything-side, go?"

Toady's shoulders slumped. "It didn't go anywhere. I'm thinking of all the work everyone did, and then phut! Thank the Gods, everything was insured up the yin-yang." Toady paused, running his fingers through his mop of hair. "Oh. Maybe you're right. Something ridiculous. A lavish bash. It'd squelch the rumors that I've lost my shirt and drifting into bankruptcy." Toady's eyes flashed. "Throw that crap into the ashcan, where it belongs."

"That's it. Hear, hear!" Thom shouted, jumped off his bar stool, and started clapping his hands as he executed perfect pirouettes. While performing his twirling-dance he thought, I should have gone into PR and sales; I would have been bitchin'… and on wheels, too!

Thom stopped, gasped, and steadied himself. "So, hunk, what do you thunk?" He nodded toward the window. "And how will our rabidly weeding rustic feel about a party?"

Toady shrugged. "Rain? He's been moping too; burying himself in his new organic gardening venture." He smiled thin-ly. "Pun intended. Though I think the idea has some merit. He'll be able to shed his long face, and if he doesn't." Toady smiled. "I'll kick him in his beautiful ass."

"That's the spicy Toda Sauce I know; comes out mercilessly, throwing punches and kicking." They both laughed. Thom suddenly grabbed Toady in a hug, pounded him on the back, then held him at arm's length. "OMG, guess what? Oh wow, oh my wondrous mind! I'm having a brilliant epiphany right now. It must have been the spinning!" He suddenly looked demure. "I know, I'm being modest…actually, to a fault. But why not?"

"Why not what?"

"Why not make it a serious costume event? Decorations, entertainment, drinks and pull out all the stops. A Gay Gorgeous, Gala!"

Toady wiggled his eyebrows and snapped his fingers like flamenco castanets. "Thom, that's a fabulous idea. And I've a brain bomb too. We'll start things off with a pumpkin carving contest at the boathouse in Burn. Maybe two pumpkins for an entrant, with 1st, 2nd, and 3rd prizes. Afterwards, we can use them as decorations for the party." Excited, he seized his phone. "I'll call Rain right now. Marrows swamped his hardy farmer mates this year. I'll see if he can pick up fifty assorted pumpkins from Island Farm's Co-op. They can donate them. We'll note it in the announcements. They have a huge pumpkin patch. They'll love us." He hit speed dial.

Thom slouched casually against the bar. "While you're talking to gorgeous, tell him we'll need volunteers for clean-up, and any grunt work, etc. Your carving contest will be fun, but a super involved activity. And what a great intro to the party."

Toady nodded, conveyed the information to Rain, then hung up. "It's a go. And he's going to enlist Alex, Kay, and Rose to be on the contest committee. Of course, we'll have to dig up the goodies. And I think I'll serve a spiked punch." He winked. "Maybe, a lovely libation of Trader Vic's Zombies. Naturally, only for those who wish to ease their cramped hands. Medicinal purposes, obviously." Toady grinned. "Hey Thom… thanks for getting me and Rain out of the boondocks."

"My pleasure." Thom said and flexed his hands. "I'll reserve the carving for the arty types. Of course, I'll be more than happy to supervise." He exaggerated a shiver. "Cold pumpkin pulp will never touch these sensitive hands. Why…why they could become arthritic." Clasping his brow, Thom closed his eyes. "Oh, never again to play Papa Hayden…quelle tragédie."

Toady snorted. "Maestro, you could wear rubber gloves. You are the diva of the kitchen. How can you prepare your famous squash bisque with stringy guts, seeds, and all? It must be hilarious to watch."

"Let's just say… I manage," Thom said stiffly, then tapped his briefcase on the counter. "And to prove to you I'm not avoiding work … I brought you a collection of antique Hallowe'en post-cards. Naturally with assorted artworks; all related to the season. We'll need things inspirational, and in spirit, pun intended, to advertise this fete." With a flourish, he dumped the contents of the case on the counter.

"What! Old movie shots of Frankenstein, the Mummy, whoa, and this sexy, naked Wolfman, sans fur? That's a new one. Remember Thom, this is a family affair… ho, ho, zees peecture of zee Count Dracula? Hmm," he paused, hand to chin. "Why do the words passé and trite, even old-fashioned, come to mind?"

Thom stood still, offended, nose in the air, eyes closed. "You know well that I detest the current indulgence in guts and gore. Those obscenities literally bleed into our favorite autumnal celebrations. Hallowe'en is sacred, a recognition of the harvest season, and feeling the first chill breath of old man winter. Yes, it's a time for ghost stories and lighting fires and pumpkins; a time to scare away demons, real or not. But what happened to the charm, the fun, the elegance… the creativity of yesteryear? Not to mention the spell of mystery. I ask you." He took a deep breath and growled. "Today, it's revolting violence and blood-dripping knives." With a sniff, he pointed at the collection and expertly fanned the holiday cards and posters on the top of the bar.

"Thom, you grew up in different times. There were different mores. Some were old… very old school. But, at the base of our Hallowe'en is the simple fact that many people like to be scared, even terrified. It's become boringly graphic, even tacky. I'll tell Rain we will go for the more traditional approach. And temper the grislier aspects."

"I hope so. It should be fun. And another thing, let's make this a charity raising event. Say, donating to my favorite one; Medicines Sans Frontières."

"You're on. That's a great idea." Toady smiled inwardly. He knew from Thom's presentation that he'd been planning this assault on their misery all along. He shook his head, then scanned the display of materials.

"Actually, I like these Thom. Where did you get them?"

"Oh, here and there; I haunted many a spooky soiree in my lifetime, and in lavish style."

Toady smiled. "I'm sure you did." He raised an eyebrow. "On

the invitations we'll have to specify, full costume a must. It'll be a requirement to get past the doorman."

"Is he cute?"

"The doorman? I think so, but a better word that comes to mind is handsome. It'll have to be Wick, Alex's son."

"Alas, he's straight as an arrow. Why? Ah, I see, we must clear the use of the Burn activity center with him. Crap." Thom looked worried. "I hope it won't interfere with his present puppet play."

"Look, the play is over on the 31st, and our party will be a winner. Wick will garner even more publicity for his center. With this event, advertised as topping the evening off. Trust me."

He turned and sorted the sundry items into groups. "Yeah, okay Thom. Some are really cool." He pointed. "And we can make enlargements of this group for wall-posters."

"I really like this one of Elsa Lanchester, as The Bride of Frankenstein. Her hair style is fantastic. I think I'll go with that costume."

"Well, Thom, it is an electrifying drag."

"Oh, ha, ha."

"Of course, we'll have to check if these are in the public domain. I like them all. They have that certain, early 20th century cachet. Wow, I'd like to go as Boris Karloff's mummy."

Thom nodded. "If you look closer, I think you'll see it's his daddy." Toady rolled his eyes.

Thom became serious. "Yesterday, I ran these by Rose. She suggested we advertise the event through our neighborhood-watch site. I exploded. I told her that would be crass, strictly déclassé, and très unimaginative. Whereas a missive in the mail has a definite personal touch, and they're tactile too." He closed his eyes. "These cards are a work of art. They modulate space. One can place it on a table, mantle or a piano to admire from time to time. And it adds to the anticipation of the coming event." He shrugged. "Of course, when I stressed this with her, it didn't come off well."

"Thom, you are so Victorian, and naturally, in your grandiose ideas, you've forgotten to consider the cost of printing, addressing, stamping, and mailing. I'm sure there'll be easily over two hundred people wanting to come. And in the past, the boathouse had a 200-capacity limit. We'll have to check with

Burn's city manager. Oh, and we'll have to use a hand stamp, as people will wander out and about."

Thom waggled his head and hands. "It's overwhelming. My God, I'm so giddy. I feel I'm Judy Garland planning a play in someone's barn with Mickey Rooney."

"Thom don't go over the top. The whole gig is about giving back to the community and having fun."

"You're right, it just that now there seems so much to do. But anyway… have you noticed any special invitation design? Anything that's popped out at you?"

Hand hovering, Toady pulled a card from Thom's possibility pile. "I like this one. The picture on the front, it's homey, hand-made, and cheery," he paused for a moment as he opened it up, "yet… it's oddly, quite ominous."

"Hah, I know that one. You prefer it because one of your hopping namesakes is clinging to a cattail, and her family is cavorting in the lily pads below."

"Oh, ha, ha, anyway… ahem, I'll read this aloud." Toady lowered his voice to a nasal and raspy sound.

"Woo, woo,
come taste my witch's brew.
Made of eyes of cats,
blood of bats,
and croaky toads I slew."

"Hmm, Auntie Thom actually likes it, and it doesn't scream commercial." Hand to chin, he studied the card. "The orange, craft-paper background, the black owl cutout in the gnarly tree… it is rather haunting."

"I agree. It reminds one of things past."

"And dear, don't forget, I can take anything your little heart desires to my printer friend in Seattle. He gives me quite a deal on things. Even makes excellent blowups, and it doesn't cost me any body parts."

Toady laughed and nudged Thom. "Maybe something else, eh?"

"Could be, he is cute…"

Toady studied the card's verse. "Hmm, the eyes of cats. Maybe stuffed olives, and the blood of bats…hmm, a stiff bran-dy and rum punch with a little unsweetened cranberry juice.

Something akin to that delicious drink you served last year. Wasn't it called Lord Nelson's Blood?"

"Absolutely perfect for Hallowe'en, and it's easy to make. But how do we handle the prissy pusses who wish to bring their own beloved beverages?"

"We can headache that one out with Rose and the others later." He paused. "Say…those slain croaky toads. They could be my frog legs on a stick. They're still in the freezer. At least that wasn't damaged. And I've got tons made up."

"Real frog legs?" Thom squeaked.

"Come on, they're tiny chicken drumettes."

"I hope you'll have a selection of dipping sauces," Thom mumbled as he put on his reading glasses to study the card. "Umm, yes… damn, old boy. I think you picked the right one. You know it is weird… there's something indefinable, almost creepy, about the invitation…and this hand drawn Le Chat Noir, on the back. I love it."

CHAPTER 32

The Haunting of the North Woods

Wick's eyes flashed. "Yes. I'm sure the auditorium will fill. There's an incredible amount of interest in the new play."

Kay was upstairs in Wick's boathouse. Together, they were peering out the office window and watching the chair crew on the spacious floor below.

"I'm not surprised," Kay said. "From the get-go, your puppeteer group has earned very positive press, even on the mainland." As they turned to sit down, she nodded back toward the window. "You certainly have room for it. Of course, I really love the smaller room where I taught yoga."

"As even you found out. The cool thing is most everyone in Burn is supportive of what we do here. And it's not only younger kids, but teens too. And there're even adults working with the volunteers below."

Kay nodded, then looked thoughtful. "Has Toady spoken to you about the Hallowe'en dance that goes before your play?"

"Oh yeah, Toady and Thom came here Tuesday, and we talked it over. Since we finished the day before the dance. We can incorporate their decorations and pumpkins into our theme. Plus, we'll use our last curtain call to give the event an enormous boost. They've even asked me if I'd like to be the doorman."

"Will you?"

"Ha, I'm thinking about it." He smiled wryly. "Since I act with puppets behind the stage, I don't think I'll be embarrassed in front of it."

Kay leaned back in her chair. She couldn't ask for a better adopted son. He was a younger version of Alex, bright and in love with life. "Now, I'm going to pry. And I won't let the proverbial cat out of the bag; but I've got to know roughly what the play is about."

Wick chuckled. "It's okay. Pretty much everyone knows and is yakking about it. It's all good. It piques people's interest and then they want to see the real thing." His voice transformed into an eerie, deep tone. "Prepare your-selves for scary myths and creepy monsters of the ancient Northwest."

"Hmm, I've got chills already. I suppose you start the play with that?"

He grinned. "Yep, it's the opener. The story begins in Russia. The land of ancient folklore and monsters. A gnarly stepfather has cast a brother and sister out of their home. In their flight, they run afoul of the legendary witch, Baba-Yaga. Oh yes! To escape her clutches, they hide in the haunted forest. Then enters Baba Yaga's much nicer sister, Baba-Ghanoush."

"What, she has a sister?"

"You got it. The operator of our Ghanoush puppet is unbelievably funny, so we asked her to take double duty as the storyteller. You know. Cracking jokes, setting expectations, really providing simple transitions between scenes."

Kay giggled. "Seriously, a talking eggplant?"

"Not to laugh. But sort of. She's purplish, plump, and pleasing. You might say she has a very maternal persona. After all, there are kids out there." He cocked an eye. "But her operator's lines are mature enough to make adults laugh. Anyway, because Baba-Yaga is intending to eat the kids and have a nice dinner. Baba-Ghanoush. and her familiar, a white crow, show the kids how to escape."

"Ah, the fun begins! Any clues about what happens next?"

"Yeah, here." He shoved a detailed outline of the play across the desk to her. "Read it. Here, use this note pad. I'm gonna make us coffee while you skim it. Got questions, or suggestions… we can talk."

"Okay, thanks." Kay read carefully, making notations where necessary.

"Ah, coffee, the magic potion." Wick announced placed a tray on his desk and sat down. "Milk sugar?"

"No, just high octane," she said, and frowned.

Wick poured. "Oh, oh, I see you have questions."

She winked. "My, the coffee's good. But umm, what do you do about the young and the restless?"

"Oh, there are two intermissions. And with our troupe encouraging audience participation, we get a feel for the spectators and change things or ad-lib if we have to. It's very organic." He peered over his cup.

"Humm, it still seems quite busy and the troupe having to be extemporaneous isn't that difficult?"

He shook his head. "Oh, no. it's an intense and together group." He paused. "We're ready to roll right now. It's going to be a fun shoo-in for Hallowe'en. And a big hype for the trick-or-treaters."

Kay rolled her eyes. "I pity the parents! But, for me, what I really like is linking the legends and including the ancient paths of humans." She stopped and looked thoughtful. "This seems weird, but this one character here, Tsonoqua, keeps cropping up, and seemingly everywhere. She's causing quite a lot of local hoopla." Kay's smile was indulgent. "I have a feeling you know more about this than Cal at the Spindrift."

Wick gestured helplessly. "Egad, I know. I didn't mean to for it get out of hand."

Kay laughed. "That's your dad's expression, the archaic Egad; but what do you mean, get out of hand?"

"What can I say? Dad's a card. I enjoy riffing on his eccentricities….anyway, back to your question about the Tsonoqua. It was…well, Brian and I." He shrugged. "We thought it would be a good promo move for the play. You know, running around in costumes and shaking our booties."

"Uh, huh? Alex and I wondered about that. It is an excellent idea… to begin with."

"Yeah. At first, it was so cool. Even Willie was for it. But then Cal gave it outrageous press, and the uninformed took it seriously. Then suddenly, there're copycats springing up. That's when it sorta got out of hand. Willie told us to pull back. And he was right. So, we did. Stopped all together. But the sightings continued. It was those crazy imitators. Just guys into cosplay and having fun. We thought, why not, more the merrier, but Willie became extremely upset."

"I know. At first, he seemed intrigued by the Tsonoqua legend. Even made the scariest, life-sized mask. He was dancing with it, and it took on a life of its own. Wow, it was unsettling. Oddly, it got to him too. It was curious. Even Edgar didn't like the mask and pecked at it."

"No kidding? That's a kick. You know, Edgar's in the play."

"Edgar, how?"

"Remember the white familiar?" Kay nodded. "Will Yaga gets ticked off at her sister and turns it amber. We use him as a great kibitzer."

"That is clever. But getting back to the many places of Tsonoqua."

"Yeah," Wick said and took a gulp of his coffee. "Willie mumbled something about repercussions. But I sensed there was more there. When I tried to pin him down on what he meant, he wouldn't say." Wick became anxious. "And, I know of one repercussion, because of all this copy-crap-caper, has caused Ujima to get steamed!"

"Yes, and very much so. Mary and Willie had a conference with Alex and me. Both Maureen and Mary feel some… well, all I can say, that aroused bizarre energies center on Bradestone. Being seers, they're not sure why here, or how, but they're trying to find out."

Wick laughed nervously. "So, the Ghostbuster's league is on the loose…Wow!... Woo-Woo, what you gonna do? Who you gonna call?"

"Um, I really can't say Wick; but it's not funny… to them. They're quite serious. They really believe something ominous is happening. Besides, I don't think you've experienced any of the peculiar things going on; but Alex, Rose, Mr. Buckwass and I have."

Wick took on a toothy, Dracula-like grin. "Vell, I guess it's time to say, may the Varce be Vith us."

"I know it sounds funny." Kay smiled. "And, in a way, it is. But your dad said that in his Army days, ignoring peculiar things, for instance, can have the bad habit of turning around and biting you in the butt. Of course, he used a different term, for butt."

CHAPTER 33

Kidnapped

The Jack-o'-lantern bounced along the top of the fence. Glittering eyes dipped, then peaked through the slats at her. Renée laughed in delight.

The gate latch clicked. A pointy witch's hat emerged. Below the wide brim, a winking bulbous eye peered through a tumble of gray hair. The old woman smiled and held the sparkling-eyed pumpkin near her face. "A present, sweet dearie." The crone cackled. "Just for you. Do you have anything for me?"

* * *

Judy Johnson immersed her hands in the dishpan. The hot water felt good. It was the first really cool morning in October and the chill had seeped into the old house. The ancient heating system groaned, doing its best to keep up, but barely succeeding.

From her kitchen window, between the back porch and the tool shed, she noticed a light frost on the grass. The leaves of the old cherry tree in her backyard were brown and falling. Kay, her new friend, told her the Farmer's Almanac predicted a cold and snowy winter for the Northwest. Judy shivered.

She wore Ted's old blue sweater. Even though the days were still warm, the cool dawn and nights took a little time to adjust to.

Her mind drifted as she slowly scrubbed the breakfast plates. Recently, they moved from California. Compared to Sacramento's sunny climate, it seemed to be always wet and cold on Bradestone Island. Her husband, Ted, grew up in Seattle and said she might have a little trouble adapting, but she wanted the move. His new job, at the Bradestone Clinic, was perfect for him. And when Renée was ready for kindergarten, they'd both agreed Judy would pursue her career as a children's librarian.

She ran more hot water onto the soapy dishes, then placed the rinsed ones to the left in the new wooden dish rack. Already, in the few short weeks, she had picked up several kitchen things at the country mercantile. While shopping, she had met Kay Reynolds and her hunky boyfriend, Alex. She found that they too had used Rose Bracken as their real estate agent, and now we're lovingly restoring an old farmhouse; about four miles down the road. She loved the location. The farm had a breath-taking view of Scoon Bay, Heron's Hook… and beyond that, the misty banks of West Seattle.

Judy was excited and scared at the same time. It was difficult, all the places she had to remember. Where was Hood's Canal? Which body of water was Elliott Bay? and what was the extent of Puget Sound? Some people referred to it as the Salish Sea, a lovely name. Kay had given her a map, and she'd immediately pinned it on the living room wall. She grinned; it was a big help. Ted used it to map out weekend excursions.

It was amazing how athletically fit Ted had become since Renée's birth. He was always buff, but now, she would say, he'd become a hunk. Thinking of hunky men, there was another one called Toady, a friend of Kay and Alex. He was gay, but not like the few she had met; stuck up and rolling their eyes.

Judy laughed aloud at the antics of their land agent, Rose Bracken. She was always flirting with Toady, and he gallantly flirted back. Rose appeared not to have a clue. But Judy bet she did.

Now Toady's partner, Rain, was, as they say, a different ket-tle of fish; very eccentric and a real back-to-nature type of guy. He was the opposite of Toady, silent, sometimes painfully shy, and seemed to be always outdoors. She liked Rain. Everything, in his view, had to be natural and strictly organic. In gardening, he tossed his cloak of shyness aside. He'd even started a move-ment among the islanders; convincing those who had land, and the time, to turn their acreage, front, or backyards, or both, into organic gardens.

"Growing locally organic produce, and establishing an island farmer's market, was the way to go," Rain said. He even taught gardening courses at the newly renovated community center in Burn. Rain also told her he was determined to make Bradestone Island the poster boy of the Pacific Farmland Trust. Judy giggled. He was pushing the use of mulch so heavily that Ted latched whole-heartedly onto the Earth First! Movement. And the next two days he'd mulched all their beds.

She studied the backyard. They shoveled the long-neglected raised garden into shape. Her aching arm muscles attested to that. Ted had planted a variety of winter vegetables, recommended by the organic man, Rain, of course.

Judy took a deep breath. The house may be old, but the island was so beautiful, and she was getting a sense of what island time was all about. It felt safe here, rested, protected…so different from Sacramento. However, she drew the line at leaving her doors unlocked, even though Rose implied real islanders did.

A raucous cawing jarred her reverie. Seven crows swooped into their cherry tree and began raising hell. An amazing, amber-colored individual was fanning his tail feathers and making the most unusual sounds. Judy chuckled. The bird sounded almost like a scolding parent. It wasn't too surprising. Recently, she discovered that the ball of amber feathers was Edgar, the semi-domesticated pet of Willie Cloudmaker.

One had to smile. Willie adamantly insisted that Edgar was not a pet, but an intelligent fellow friend; just a neighbor that lived near his cabin. The crow family's actual abode was on the top of a fir tree on Willie's property. But Willie proudly showed her how the crows liked to fly in and out of a cage that Willie had built when he first found Edgar. Judy shook her head; Edgar even flew to Kay's house to visit and look for treats. He was quite a beggar.

Wiping her hands on a towel, looped through the apron belt, she went to the fridge. The marauders seemed almost in a frenzy, probably begging for bits of stale bread. It was Ted's idea to keep their bread bits fresher in a plastic bag.

"Mommy, can we go out and play? The crows are here." Renée had stumbled into the room. Her shoes were on the wrong feet.

Judy stooped down and helped her correct the difficulty. "Sure, Sweetie but let me get your winter jacket. It's chilly out there. Honey, what toy would you like to play with?"

Renée grinned through her reddish curls. "The crows want

Mr. Giraffe. That's the one I want too. It's pretty." Renée was a precocious child and very certain of everything she needed or wanted. No dithering for her.

They stood in the yard, throwing bread at the crows. Without fear, but still noisy, they glided down to snatch their treats. Some flew away to hide their food in a private cache. Willie said that some crows tackled their stash at a later time, avoiding competition.

True to his sly nature, Edgar crammed the most he could in his beak, strutted up and down, then flew to the birdbath to give them a good dunk. After losing some soggy pieces, he then took off to a secret place. Judy knew he stashed crusts in the garage gutters, while making sure other crows weren't watching.

Soon the band moved on, except for Edgar. He perched on the top branch of the cherry tree and made curious cracking noises. Judy felt a chill. His voice seemed almost human; it was as if he were warning her.

That's silly. She was letting her imagination run away after listening to Willie. However, his tales frequently had a ring of truth to them. But wow, they were very eerie. Judy loved that he would answer her questions, no matter how ignorant, then patiently explain things in his mellow, reassuring voice.

It was special when Renée and even Ted would ask him to tell stories. Usually, he was carving his wonderful Indian pieces. Some were delightful, even magical. They were about the amazing things Edgar would do or how he could communicate with Willie and others. Judy laughed; as if crows could talk; but then again, maybe…

Kay told her that Willie was a wise and kindly old man. And he liked to share things he'd experienced long ago, because he didn't want the histories and legends to die with him.

"Come on, Renée, let's play in the front yard. It's drier, and you left Ms. Squeaky out there last night. Here, put on your yellow raincoat." Renée squirmed into the coat and took her mother's hand. They skipped through the house.

"Oh squeaky, squeaky… sneaky squeaky. She likes to play hide and seeky." They sang together.

Renée ran to the sandbox, threw Mr. Giraffe down, and quickly helped Squeaky build a leaf and stick house.

Judy studied the new fence. Ted had insisted on doing the

job himself, pouring the footings, selecting the lumber and, with her help, spacing the boards. It was a substantial barrier between the sidewalk and their house.

Her gaze went past the fence. Rose had found them in the right house in an attractive neighborhood. Old maple trees and lovely shrubs lined the street. And since it was an older part of Madrona, there weren't many houses, so the lots were larger. Almost all houses were two-stories, and had towering, tulgey rhododendrons looming near them.

This part of island suburbia had seen little change. Only a single streetlight was at the corner. Over the years, the narrow concrete walk had yielded it's even surface to the underground roots of the giant maples; it had become a quaint, bumpy side-walk. Except for the new hydrants, Rose said that the paved street was the only improvement in years.

Judy went to the sandbox, crouched down, and took Renée's hand. "Mommy's going inside for a moment. Mommy is going to finish the dishes and then she'll be right back out to play. Okay?"

Renée looked up. "Mommy, be right back," she stated firmly and giggled when the twig and leaf house collapsed on squeaky.

Judy straightened, startled by the whooshing sound of beat-ing wings behind her. There was Edgar again. He'd flown to the front yard's maple tree and seemed to mumble to himself. Weirdly, he sounded like the soft cry of a child saying, "I don't know, I don't know."

Judy shook her head at the jumble of her curious thoughts and went into the kitchen. Five minutes later, she dried the last dish and placed it in the cupboard.

Ted promised a dishwasher, but later, after his second pay-check. They had to be frugal. Repaying the student loans had been brutal, but grants helped. Even though the starting pay was low, at the small island clinic, his new position elated them. Times were tough, even for doctors with new MDs. Luckily, out of ten applicants, they selected him because of his background. After introductory training courses, he would work with older adults and, with a full-time psychiatrist, that Ted immediately liked.

Golly, Edgar was making a disturbance out front. Nervously, she pulled off her apron, shrugged into her leather jacket, and stepped out the door onto the porch.

The crow was now in the one ancient rowan tree across the street and cawing loudly. Then he flew furiously up the block.

From the top of the porch steps, Judy could see the scolding crow. Below him, a bent old woman, dressed all in black and wearing a hooded cape, walked oddly. On her shoulders was a backpack. It appeared to be a woven basket. Jerkily, the crone scuttled around the corner and out of sight. Judy laughed; in a few weeks, the woman would be a real scare for trick-or-treaters.

"Renée," Judy called, looking around. "You've left squeaky by the gate…. Renée… Renée… Honey?"

Judy froze. Renée wasn't in the sandbox and wasn't hiding in the overgrown lilac at the corner of the chimney. The peculiar chill she felt in the kitchen intensified and made her legs shake.

"Renée! Renée!" She shouted and ran down the steps. Renée couldn't be in the house; the screen door would have screeched. Quickly, Judy checked the side and backyards. There was no sign of her. She ran to the gate. It was slightly ajar. She felt dizzy. Renée could never have reached for the latch.

Scanning up and down the street, Judy cupped her hands and yelled, "Renée, Renée!"

She ran. Glancing in alleyways, front yards. "Renée, Renée honey, where are you?" Nothing, not even a glimpse of her yellow slicker. Then she saw it, Giraffe; the toy was on a pile of leaves. Absurd, Renée hadn't even been playing with Mr. giraffe! Her hands shook. I've got to calm down. But Renée must have dropped it here. Why would she even have it? Judy glanced at a nearby fence and steadied herself. Tears ran down her face as her thoughts spun. Didn't any of the neighbors hear her? They couldn't all be at work.

She quickly picked up Giraffe. and shook her head. I've got to get help. I've got to stop running and shouting. Her grandmother always said, "it doesn't help a damn thing." But she felt so alone, so helpless. Renée would have answered her…then the words seared her brain, if she could! "No, it's pointless to go there." Judy said aloud and ran back to the house.

Hands shaking, she dropped her cellphone twice before punching in 911.

"Hello, hello! This is Judy Johnson on Maple Drive. Renée, my Renée is gone!"

Patiently, the first responder said, "Ma'am, Ma'am, please

calm down. What is your name? And I'll need your complete address. Where are you located?"

Judy shuddered then with an intake of breath, steeled herself, and firmly answered the questions. Toward the end of the call, her voice broke. "I've looked everywhere. I need help, and now. Oh please, I...I...think she's been taken!"

CHAPTER 34

The Search

Ujima braked. Was that a broken pumpkin against the curb? She got out of her black and white to see orange chunks strewn across the sidewalk. Part of a leering grin hid beneath the maple leaves. It was the only unusual thing she'd noticed since commencing the search for Renée.

So far, none of the quickly assembled volunteer searchers had contacted her. Thank the Gods, most had their own cellphones.

From the branch above, a crow squawked. Startled, Ujima crossed her arms and looked up. "Edgar, what are you doing there?" If in answer, he preened his feathers, then shook his body. "You just didn't pop by, did you?" The Amber Crow looked down at her. He was a welcome relief to the beginning of her worrying day.

Abruptly, Edgar flew down to the sidewalk and pecked at the pumpkin pieces. Ujima chuckled. "What are you trying to say, my friendly bird brain?" He regarded Ujima with a basilisk like look, cawed sharply three times, then whooshed over her head and down the street. Interesting, she thought. In Edgar's random scratching and pecking, revealed more of the Jack-o'-lantern. Ujima removed a large plastic bag. She collected most of the pieces. It was peculiar. Hallowe'en was about two weeks away. It may be nothing… yet.

Ujima stared. Entangled in the weedy grass bordering the sidewalk, glinted the stub of a pink candle. Picking it up, she grimaced. It reeked of a powerful and disgusting odor. Was that ether? Quickly, she placed it in the evidence bag. Strangely, she felt unsteady.

Scanning for any more peculiar objects, she felt the uncomfortable sense of being watched. Nonsense. She pinched her eyes, just a momentary spell of vertigo. *I stood too fast;* she chided herself, then placed the bag in her car. But the back of her neck still prickled. She turned around.

A cold gust of wind rushed down the street; it rattled the crossed limbs of the bone-naked maple trees and sent dried leaves cackling along the pavement. Behind, in the shadows of a crooked laurel bush, stood a partially hidden shape.

"Good morning, Sheriff Washington," the woman said, then shrugged. "I'm attempting to return to the Madrona Inn, but I've become turned around." Maureen D'Moresby stepped forward. She wore her backpack and held a netted bag at her side. It was heavy with books.

"I've been to the library. Solange, the librarian, is amazingly helpful. I'm learning more and more about this island and its fascinating history." She held up her book bag as her choking laugh carried on the wind. "I can never have enough books to read. But I must get them in large print, my poor eyesight ..." her voice trailed off.

Ujima looked up and down the street. "Solange is one of the best," she said, then paused. "Where were you in the last hour? Surely not standing there in this chilly wind?"

Wide-eyed, Maureen vigorously shook her head. "Oh no, Solange asked me to assist her in opening the library. I was there too early. And one of the Pages was late. The girl never called in. Solange insisted that the Page, I believe her name is Sandy, is very reliable."

Ujima was curious. Oddly, the woman was a veritable chatterbox this morning. And Ujima had the feeling that she had been standing there for some time.

Maureen nattered on. "Solange said people drop off used magazines and old books all the time. She asked me to sort through them, then place them on the sale table in the foyer. There are many copies of National Geographic, hu, hu, hu," she chortled. "If I had to do that task daily, I'd disappear into the woods, never to be seen again."

"After you left the library and while you were walking, did

you see anyone… or anything unusual?"

"No, nothing out of the ordinary," she drawled, then paused.

Ujima hastily removed her trusty pad and pen. She made a concerted effort not to lick the nib. "Did you notice the type of van or the plate number?"

"No, I'm terrible with makes of vehicles. I remember that the color was…gray, dull gray." She shifted her weight slowly from foot to foot. "Oh…yes, the back of the vehicle and license were covered with fresh mud, thought it was odd, as it hasn't rained this week." She looked uncomfortable. "Why, has something happened?"

Shortly, it'll be all over the island. Ujima thought. "I'm investigating the disappearance of a child. It most likely occurred in the last hour. So, if you've noticed anything…"

Maureen's red lips formed a perfect O. Her enormous eyes stared. "It happened… near here?" She sounded incredulous.

"Well, yes, and I'm just guessing. The girl was playing in her yard and the mother was in the house. The child might have wandered away. She's about five and she couldn't walk too far…"

Maureen dropped her book bag. Her lips again formed a perfect circle. "Oh no," she said in a whisper. "That's not possible, not here." She quickly covered her mouth.

"What's not possible here? What are you saying?"

Tears washed down her eyes, heavy mascara ran in rivulets. She pulled out a large handkerchief and blotted futilely.

"I…I meant to say, this is a safe island, too removed from…"

"What? Too removed from what?"

"The spirits of evil," she moaned. "Of course, I'm not saying they couldn't be here. You have the Bog of the Medusa," she bent over, fumbled for a book, then shook it at Ujima, "don't you?" She gazed accusingly at Ujima, then seemed to freeze.

This woman definitely had problems, but her challenge made Ujima hesitate. Maureen D'Moresby knew something. There is something more hidden there, and I won't give up.

"Could you give me a rough idea of where you were walking? Landmarks, names of streets would help, and…"

Appearing not to have heard, Maureen sobbed quietly. Crap, she's got to be calmed down, or she'll have one of those accursed spells, Ujima thought. Maybe she'll become more coherent if I can engage her; this chilly wind isn't helping. With a flourish,

Ujima put her notepad in her pocket.

"If you don't mind a lift in my patrol car, I'll get you back to the Madrona Inn. But I warn you. It'll take more time, since I'll be searching. But you, you can be a great help, looking for anything that appears out of the ordinary. Immediately call it to my attention. Are you with me?"

Maureen kept dabbing at her eyes but nodded. She placed her books back into her bag, then ponderously moved toward the black and white.

CHAPTER 35

Home Base

As Ujima pulled away from the Madrona Inn, she reflected on the peculiar things Maureen had confusedly mumbled. Were they true?

"Last night, I...I dreamed that a cloaked figure was on a mountain, ominous. A little girl threw a yellow toy, waving its arms and legs...to...to be eaten. An enormous bird flew at the phantom, but it was still there, it... it pointed at me." Shaking, she buried her face in her hands. Tears burst through Maureen's fingers. "The look was terrible." She gulped. "I've seen that...that look before."

On the drive to the Inn, Ujima coaxed Maureen to tell the rest of her dream, but she maintained the silence of a stone. I'll interview her later; about her supposed forewarning, after the poor woman becomes much calmer.

Cruising the area near the Johnson's residence, she again scanned houses, visible yards, and driveways. Occasionally, a door-to-door search volunteer would wave at her, but Maple Drive was empty. Slowly, Ujima again covered the adjoining streets, and listened intently to the occasional conversations over her squawk-box. Sadly, nothing of significance was reported, nor were any of the call-ins informative.

From nowhere, a group of rowdy crows flew over her car, then down seventh toward Elm Street. Renée Johnson couldn't have wandered that far in such a short time. Unless somebody else...she shook the thoughts away. It was too soon to go there.

Because of the mayor and his cohorts on the city council,

her department was again short-handed this year. Budget cuts meant Sergeant Reynolds was in charge of the call center at the station. Thankfully, his focus on tasks-at-hand had dramatically improved since last summer. Sergeant Lavalon, the new hire, screened phone calls and updated an hourly record of vital information. Most services were 911 now, the volunteer fire department included, but hopefully, there would be no need for them…yet.

Carefully, she made a U-turn and guided her cruiser up on the verge. There was no surprise when she saw Alex and Kay's farm truck. As she set her brake, she reflected on how fast Kay and Judy Johnson had become friends. Ujima's smile was grim. Whatever the outcome, Kay would be a considerable comfort.

Ujima picked up her notebook and pencil. She was not an aficionado of recording gadgets. They were great for the 'with-it' crowd, but she preferred the intimate and calming effect of writing things down. Too, it allowed her time to observe body language, organize her thoughts, probe creatively, and make notations discretely.

The garden gate and front door were wide open. Ujima tapped lightly on the screen door. "It's Sherriff Washington," she called down the hall.

"Chief Washington's here," Kay said. "No Judy, stay there. I'll get the door. Just drink that tea Willie brought." Her voice became louder as she appeared in the kitchen doorway. Kay nodded at Ujima, then glanced back over her shoulder. The tea would be drunk.

Opening the screen door, Kay took Ujima's hand. "We've looked everywhere, not a sign," Ujima whispered. "Even had time to check out the playfield at Elm and Sixth."

Kay gave an expectant look. "Nothing useful from the volunteers?"

"Not yet."

"Were you able to reach Ted?"

"No luck, but we know why."

Ujima shrugged. "According to clinic records, he's attending an impromptu two-day workshop. Interestingly, the head honcho didn't bother to tell his secretary after the group moved the location. All she knows is that it's being held somewhere. It might even be on the Bellevue campus."

"But, not to worry, we discovered that bit of info fairly early. Sergeant Reynolds is already checking hotel registrations. And before you ask, the people attending most likely have their cellphones turned off or were told to leave them in their rooms." She shrugged. "For some esoteric reason, the meeting venue is hush-hush. But we will get through to the husband."

As they entered the kitchen, Ujima could detect the aura of grief, the fading aroma of baby talc, and Judy's quiet, disjointed sobbing. Ujima nodded at Willie. He had come with Kay and was talking softly to Judy. Kay pulled out a chair, and Ujima sat down. Willie nodded back, got up and pushed a hot cup of tea in front of her. He winked and whispered, "Gave Judy a special kinda tea, calms nerves. Yours, just plain."

Ujima frowned and whispered back. "Thank you, Dr. Cloudmaker. I hope you know what you're doing." He nodded reassuringly and smiled.

A month ago, Ujima had 'accidentally' met the Johnsons in town. When she could, she maneuvered casual meetings with newbies to the island. She judged it was an efficient way to identify any potential situations and prevent them from becoming major situations.

Ujima took Judy's trembling hand. "This tea is excellent, Mrs. Johnson. Now… I want you to take your time. I know you've talked to the dispatcher, but when you feel like it, tell me again how it happened." She paused and added gently, "Be as thorough as you can. Even the slightest thing might be important." Judy's sobs quieted and her tear-stained face looked up.

Calmly and succinctly, Judy related the events leading up to Renée's disappearance. Only occasionally was it necessary to reach for the tissue box. Ujima noticed Kay didn't hover. She knew from first-hand experience, when faced with an emergency or tragedy, Kay had a no-nonsense attitude. Ujima briefly recalled the well incident. The almost disastrous situation that they had faced in the past. Kay had a cool head. There was a lull as Judy wiped her eyes and sipped her tea.

Ujima reviewed her previous notes. Ted and Judy Johnson had recently settled on Bradestone. He, a recent graduate, with a Ph.D. in psychology and Judy, a first degree in librarianship. They appeared to be devoted parents. Ujima wasn't aware of any friction between the two. But Ted Johnson might be the variable to watch. Rare, but children could quickly become innocent victims of family squabbles.

"Mrs. Johnson, I want you to know a full alert is out. I've notified the people on Vashon and in Seattle. Also, the ferry personnel were alerted. They are very effective in all situations. But I will need a recent and clear photo of Renée. I'll fax her picture to the ferry officials from my car outside." Judy looked up in a panic.

"However," Ujima hastily added, "she should still be on the island. And we're in luck. The next ferry doesn't leave for 45 minutes. That gives us a larger window of time. And, of course, we will search every vehicle thoroughly before boarding."

Judy's lower lip trembled.

"Now, Mrs. Johnson, you said the only person you noticed was an old woman dressed in black." She referred to her notes. "And she was turning left at the corner of Sixth and Maple." Judy nodded vigorously. "Now think. Do you remember anything else? It sometimes helps if you close your eyes and visualize. I know it's painful, but there might be something you've missed."

Judy paused and concentrated. "Yes, yes. There was something else. The woman had what looked like a backpack and a walking stick. She was leaning heavily on it and walked… surprisingly fast." She sniffed. "The only reason I remember was because of Willie Cloudmaker's pet crow." Smiling weakly, she nodded at Willie.

"Edgar was squawking loudly and jumping from tree to tree. He was above the old woman." She looked perplexed. "It seems…. it seems as if he was following her."

Willie nodded. "Edgars got a sixth sense, Ma'am. Many's the time he gave me a warnin', and I've been better for it."

Kay and Ujima exchanged glances. They both knew that in the past, Edgar had been a harbinger of unusual and disastrous events. And in his own peculiar way, extremely helpful.

Ujima put her cup of tea down and stood quickly. "We alerted all the right people, and the search has been ongoing since you called. The description you first provided has been extremely helpful. But I need that photo to post immediately."

Kay stood, too. "Willie and I are staying with Judy. I've canceled the rest of the week's work roster at the inn. Alex, Rain, and Thommy Jay had to go into the hardware store in Madrona this morning. They're picking up last-minute scenery materials for Wick's puppet play. But they were the only ones I've talked to." Kay noticed Ujima's rigid stare. "Don't get ruffled, I have told no one else, and the guys won't either. But they will be on the lookout."

"I wasn't ruffled, as you put it. It most likely is over the island already. I'm just imagining how the volunteer newbies are handling their public enquiries. Some of the old hands know the procedures, but I'm concerned about how little the time we had for briefing the newbies."

Willie glanced over the top of his glasses. "Of course, then thars that fella, Brace…sometimes pulls a stretch at the Spindrift. The sneaky varmit monitors police calls. It'll be over the darn island anyway, even afore the Spindrift's Friday paper."

Judy took a deep breath, then calmly got up and went into the front room. After a few moments, she returned and handed Ujima a large photo of Renée. Judy brushed her eyes. "What will Ted say? I…I shouldn't have let her out of my sight…not for an instant. What will he say?"

Ujima hid her exasperation. "Don't blame yourself, it won't help. These things can happen, even in a crowd."

Kay nodded. "Sixteen years ago, Teri wandered away. It was only for a moment. It happened while I was in Rhodes, trying on a pair of sandals in the shoe department. One minute she was beside me, then the next, gone. Bargain hunters crowded the store. And if it weren't for some observant salespeople, I don't know what I would have done."

"Listen to Kay. These things can happen in an instant and it's no one's fault." Ujima took Judy's hand. "Remember, Mrs. Johnson, use this number and we will keep you informed." She handed her card over, then studied Renée's picture. "This is excellent; I'll fax it right away." She turned to walk down the hall.

Judy swayed a little. "Oh, I'm so tired…exhausted really… I need to lie down." Kay shoved a chair out of her way and quickly put an arm around Judy's shoulder. "Steady, I'll help you to the bedroom."

Willie followed Ujima and whispered, "That thar tea's a brew Mary suggested. Heh, heh, sorta makes a body feel that they're aviewin' everythin' from the ceiling, just seeing things from above, no part of the action. Real calmin'; 'ventually, like watching a slow movie."

"Thanks, Doctor Cloudmaker. That's certainly more information than I needed to know," Ujima growled as she opened the screen door.

Kay appeared behind them. "Judy fell instantly asleep; I tucked her in and she was out." She frowned at Willie. "What did you put in her tea?"

"Trust me, you don't want to know," Ujima said dryly.

Willie looked seriously at Ujima. "What are you gonna do about that thar old lady she saw?"

"I have a person making inquiries at the private home for seniors. Judy said the elderly lady had a limp and a cane, but even she might have seen something."

Willie's lips pressed into a thin line, then he wiped his mouth with the back of his hand. "Maybe more… what else happened?"

Kay shrugged. "Well, Judy said Edgar and his crow cohorts showed up. They all seemed to have a ruckus, particularly near that poor old lady. You've seen crows pester people. No wonder, even having to use a cane, she was trying to hurry along."

"Yep, that figures." Willie said, then paused for a while and pulled at his beard. "Yep, Edgar hates the Tsonoqua. Why, seen him peck at her mask I'm carvin'. Heh, heh, when he thinks I ain't a-lookin'."

Kay's eyes widened. "You don't think that old lady had something to do with Renée's disappearance?"

Willie grimaced and steepled his fingers. "For sure she did; had everythin' to do with it." He sighed, "Yep, yep, sure nuff, 'twas the Hooting Woman."

"What, you're not serious?" Kay exclaimed.

Ujima scowled, then closed her eyes and made a sound of exasperation. With a shake of her head, she acknowledged Willie's remark, waved, then hurried down the porch steps.

CHAPTER 36

Background

At the police station, Kay selected a pencil from Ujima's vast collection. She tapped it aimlessly. Someone abducted Renee; but by whom? When Ujima and Sergeant Reynolds questioned Aunt Maureen, it had not gone well. She had lost complete control. The result was a dust-up between the Sergeant and Aunt Maureen. Fortunately, she was now back at the island clinic and under sedation.

With an annoying squeak, the door opened to her left, and Ujima came into the room. "Sorry I'm late. Had to take care of one of our overnight cell guests. The poor woman is sobering up after some reckless driving." Ujima slipped into her desk chair and glanced at the door. "That hinge needs oiling." She smiled and cocked an eye at Kay. "How's everything going?"

"I was wondering if you have any current information on Aunt Maureen." Kay grimaced. "I heard by the island grapevine, that she didn't take to questioning docilely. Don't worry. I knew it had to be done. This morning, I called the facility… again, and again they said no visitors. How bad are things for her?"

"I, too, checked earlier this morning and her doctor feels she's best sedated until her vital signs return to normal. Thankfully, she's not in critical condition."

"Any hints when Alex and I can see her?"

"Doctor Butler, the same one as last time, said that most likely tomorrow is in the picture. And when you get the okay, I'd like to see her too… I have a few other questions to ask. I know she tolerates me, but with concerned family members present, it would most likely be a much better atmosphere."

"Do you think she did it?"

"Kay, the time… being in the area, her reticence, those things are suggestive, but circumstantial. And, unless she had a helper, I'm uncertain how she would have managed. When we talked in the car yesterday. She was her normal eccentric self. But it was when I drove her back to the inn, she said something odd."

"What? What did she say?"

"She mentioned that from a dream. She knew this was going to happen, but then totally clammed up." Ujima spread her hands. "Until we can get her to talk intelligibly, I can't make any meaningful decisions." Ujima chuckled. "However, I wish Sergeant Reynolds had been a little more, er…gentle. But she is a large woman."

Kay shook her head. "Did he get punched? Rumors say it was quite a tussle."

Ujima pursed her lips, then smiled. "I won't ask about your sources, but when Sergeant Reynolds is in a situation, he can be as agile as an eel. Even though she'd collapsed on the floor, she was kicking out. After handcuffing, he had to sit on her until she became exhausted." Ujima smiled. "He said it was very much like busting a bronco. Then, I remember him mentioning, as a teenager on his uncle's ranch, he handled horses." She raised her hands and chuckled. "I know. In this business, the more variety of experiences you've had, the better."

"So, no one suffered any serious injury?"

"Only a few scrapes and bruises. Thankfully, no bleeding."

Kay slumped in her chair. "I'm glad to hear that. She's suffered a great deal of misery on this island."

"That's a sore fact. I've been following her exploits. This incident is a little better than what happened at Toad Hall, but not by much. It seems she may have lost or forgotten her vial of medicine. It was nowhere on her person."

"That's odd, but she keeps some back in our refrigerator."

Ujima raised her hand. "At my request, Teri already checked. It's not there. And on top of everything, they could not find her prescribed medications, either. We even went through her motel room and the infamous storage unit 13."

"How can it all disappear and come from our house, too?" Kay asked in alarm.

"That's the strange thing. But, with your permission, I'd like to check your windows, doors and locks. Teri mentioned the back door was left unlatched often."

"Of course you can search. But it's true, it sticks. We've been so busy with other things. There're workers going in and out, so we often forget to give it a push." Kay closed her eyes and shook her head. "But why, why would she do it…why kidnap a child?"

"We don't have any answers yet. She was speaking, then muttering in her native tongue. We could make out nothing. Dr. Butler said, besides being incoherent, she doesn't react well to sedation. We contacted her doctor in Canada and she's sending her medications by private plane and should arrive this afternoon."

"I hope they include the green stuff. It helps almost immediately," Kay said, then looked startled. "Private plane? Doesn't that entail a lot of money?"

"Er, yes. You know your aunt is extremely wealthy?"

Kay paused. "Funny, she mentioned nothing, and we never thought about it."

"From the few directives we found in her apartment, she hobnobs with fairly flush associates." Ujima paused. "We also found that she's married. Didn't she tell you that, either?"

"Married?" Kay was shocked. "No, but about her earlier life, Aunt Maureen isn't very forthcoming. We thought she was a widow. I don't know why. She never mentioned it and we never asked. Gosh, married?"

"Oh yes. We've been checking her background. Since she, more or less, arrived out of the blue; and what you told me about her; an unknown relation, bearing gifts; I was concerned that you might become involved in some sort of nefarious scheme. You know I'm a perpetual snoop when it comes to strangers, particularly on my turf." Ujima cocked an eyebrow. "Of course, it's not always strangers. Forewarned is forearmed, I say. A super cliché: but I've found it's worked well for me."

"Okay, I'm floored and listening; what other… marvelous things have you learned?"

"Well, prepare yourself. This is beyond interesting. The man I believe she's still married to is Mr. Jinx Buckwass."

"You mean that little strange man who opened the bookshop on Main Street?"

"The same. And I've had a devil of a time finding out much about him. He seems to be quite a world traveler, and we know he made his living in toy manufacturing. Specifically, exquisite dolls for a very wealthy clientele. And yet, anything else has been hard, if not impossible, to pin down."

"Those weren't the dolls she destroyed on that rampage in Thommy Jay's shop?"

"The very same. Mr. Buckwass inveigled Mr. Jay to sell them with the pitch of celebrating ongoing European artistry. He told Thom they were remainders and needed to get rid of them. They're not cheap, and Mr. Jay earned a tidy commission. He also felt it would help with sagging sales. The desire for antiques is diminishing, especially among the younger set. 'Très hors de mode,' Mr. Jay says."

Kay placed her hands over her ears. "Egad, my mind is whirling. Any other major bombs you want to drop?"

"Um, Maureen has a computer and quite a file system. Sergeant Reynolds is an ace at cracking code and presently working on passwords. We're not there yet, but he assures me it will be soon. I'll let you know what we find. Other than that, there's not much else that I can add."

"Whew, thank the lordy. Well, Sergeant Reynold's may seem a bit distracted, but comes up with sudden and remarkable ways of solving things."

Ujima nodded and folded her hands. "And he's become quite skilled at hacking." She paused and sniffed. "Everything he does is legal, of course."

Kay winked. "Of course, I've never doubted it. I really hesitate to ask, anything else?"

"Well, I've information about a more pleasant nature. Reynolds and Rose are engaged."

"Rose! The stinker. She never told me. I know they've been pretty thick recently, but I did not know."

"He said they intend to announce their engagement in December. Possibly a wedding in spring."

Kay grinned. "Ujima, you are the original nosy parker."

Ujima feigned amazement. "Kay, me? You're aware it's the most important part of my job description."

"Hmm, spring. That's our grand opening of the inn. Oh, all-knowing one, do they intend to stay here or move to the mainland? Alex and I would hate to lose such good friends."

"Reynolds says he's happy here, likes the rural atmosphere; the pace of the island and Rose has her own successful reality business. Besides," Ujima placed a hand over her heart. "He stalwartly claimed he wanted to work and die where his ancestors lived."

"My, a real homeboy. I'm wondering if they'd consider having their wedding at our inn. Everything is new or refurbished and there's plenty of room for the party. And I'm pretty sure Rose will run the gauntlet; she likes things done traditionally."

"I'm not surprised but ask Rose. I got the impression they're having it at her houseboat. A different venue might be something for her to consider. She is planning to remodel the boat. But we know that will be accomplished on island time." She sat back in her chair. "I wouldn't want to be married in an unfinished building site, but one never knows about Rose. Naturally, Sabra is panting to create a wedding dress."

"OMG, and no doubt design shoes to go with it. Poor Rose, she'll totter up the aisle, then topple at the altar. I'll try to convince her to wear comfortable flats." She paused. "Or on second thought… it would be very romantic if she fell into the Sergeant's arms."

"Romantic? Well, good luck. With fashion, she only listens to Sabra. Besides, Reynolds is strong, he can hold her up." Ujima laughed. "Can't you just see that?"

"I can, I can," Kay said and giggled.

"More info. She's asked Toady to give her away. He's a tennis pro, so she might at least make it down the aisle without creating a debacle." Kay and Ujima fell into helpless laughter.

Kay wiped her eyes. "I needed something hilarious at this time, thank you."

There was the cry of a startled seagull. "Just ono memento. I have a message on my phone." Ujima stepped out of the room. Kay resumed distracting herself by tapping the pencil on the desk.

Ujima returned quickly. "That was the clinic. It appears your aunt has recovered sufficiently to talk. Can you come with me? In the company of family, it might be more settling for her."

"I definitely can." Kay paused. "Everything is such a muddle. Until something comes to light, I don't know what's fact or fiction with Aunt Maureen."

"I'm not assuming anything either. There's still a lot of information to uncover; what is in those computer files, for one?"

"You don't think she was actually behind Renée's kidnapping, do you?"

"I'm straddling the fence on this one. There's been no ransom demands, no notes. So far, I would say, the evidence is tentative at best." Ujima looked at her watch. "Can you be ready within the hour? It'll take about 20 minutes. And I'm sure you don't mind traveling a la patrol car." She said with a grin.

Kay pointed to her face. "Just have to touch up the old war paint… and a chauffeur is most welcome."

"Good. Later, I'm going to Normandy Park, on the mainland. The Chief of Police wants to have a 'face to face' on a certain felon; it most likely will take a sizeable chunk out of the afternoon." Ujima looked at her watch again. "I have to catch the 12:00 ferry, so I'll leave you at the clinic. You could call Mr. Cinch's cab or arrange for someone to pick you up. It's one busy day for me."

Kay scratched her ear. "I'm thinking. I have nothing on this afternoon. Why don't I travel with you?" She patted her shoulder bag. "While you're in conference, I have a Louise Penny I can finish," Kay smiled. "And I'll treat you to a late lunch. "

"More like an early dinner," Ujima said, then pointed toward the hall. "Freshen up in the bathroom down the hall. I'm ready to go now." She grabbed her hat.

Kay stood and saluted. "Yes, ma'am! And since today's lunch is on me, let's go to the 909 in Burien. It has excellent service and food. It reminds me of a European bistro, friendly. Luckily, it's only a few miles from the Coleman ferry dock."

Ujima made a thumbs up. "Cool, you're on. Now hustle."

The Seer

"Shh," Teri said, finger to lips, as she stepped from the porch into the kitchen.

"What is it?" Brooke whispered.

"It's Cousin Mary and Mom." Teri chuckled. "Sounds like they've had a little to drink." Brooke heard chatting and laughter coming from the front room. She shut the door behind them gently.

Teri turned to her. "Alex is in Seattle attending his Tesla University's class reunion. Said it was a 'guy's night out'. So, it seems Cousin Mary and Mom had a girl's night in." Brooke stifled a giggle.

"Let's not disturb them. We can go to our rooms via the back stairs, and…"

"Hello girls," Kay's voice carried into the kitchen. "Why don't you join us? There's a bottle of white wine in the fridge. Sancerre, I believe. Cousin Mary and I are drinking brandy. And it is so smooth!" There was the tittering and clicking of glasses.

Teri spotted the bottle on the hall tray. "Eck, there hitting the Decourtet, Dad's favorite brandy."

"I thought they said cognac?"

"It's both, but Decourtet is made in the cognac area of France." Teri paused. "It's just a fancy-shmancy name, and it's a special blend of only grapes. But don't tell any serious wine drinker I said that."

With the bottle of chilled white and glasses in hand, they walked into the room. Fire crackled in the hearth, and the two rosy-cheeked women lifted their snifters in salute.

"Welcome girls, won't you join our petite soiree?" Kay asked with a wink, took another sip. "Et comment était le film?"

"OMG, they're talking in French," Teri hissed and looked at Brooke.

"It was… okay," Teri answered loudly. "And we'll have just a glass of wine, and then it's upstairs for us. Got a few reports to finish on our computers."

Brooke frowned as they pulled up two chairs into a comfy circle. "Teri said it was blah, but I liked the old film. Even though it was in black-and-white, it was still cool."

Cousin Mary nodded. "Rebecca, est un chef-d'œuvre. Et réalisé par Alfred Hitchcock. Un réalisateur sans égal," she paused, "you ladies should read the book, c'est un mystère extraordinaire… and also read, The House on the Strand. It's about using drugs, très moderne, if I recall. But those period books are usually for us older folks, who are long in tooth."

Brooke stared at Teri. "What did Cousin Mary say?"

Teri laughed aloud. "It must be the French cognac, right?" Cousin Mary and Kay grinned.

"Oh bother. Well, here goes. Loosely, Hitchcock is a director without equal and Rebecca is an extraordinary mystery."

"Right on," Cousin Mary said with a smile.

Teri raised her wineglass. "I propose a toast to Monsieur Hitchcock, an excellent director. But we've just seen the movie. So, the book would be boring. We already know who done-it."

Cousin Mary and Kay laughed as they leaned forward. Everyone clicked glasses.

Kay raised her glass. "And I raise a toast to the young and unmindful."

"Thanks, a bundle," Teri replied with a note of cynicism. They clicked glasses again.

"Movie discussion aside, I sense Brooke has something more on her mind." Cousin Mary set her glass down. And with a smile, turned to Brooke. "And how are you doing, my dear?"

"I think she's been here before," Teri burst out, then cocked her head. "Most likely when she was very young." She took a healthy swallow from her glass. "And when she was here, well… it wasn't an enjoyable experience." She shrugged. "It isn't rocket science."

Cousin Mary stared at Brooke. "My dear, I understand. From what Kay said, you wanted to talk to me. Is that what's bothering you?"

Brooke glanced at Teri.

"For heaven's sake, Brooke, drink up and tell her. Willie said Cousin Mary had the er…er gift; and might help. Right, Cousin Mary?"

Mary put her snifter down. "I do… and what it means dears, is at times I see and feel what other people simply don't. Actually, Willie has that capacity too; he doesn't push it though. I use my gift to assist people, if they want it." She wiped her lips with a napkin. "Now Brooke, maybe I can be of some help?"

"Okay, since I came to Bradestone, I've had…unpleasant … feelings, I guess one could call them." She grimaced at Teri, who nodded in agreement.

"And it wasn't the food," Teri guffawed, then looked embarrassed.

Kay rolled her eyes, but Cousin Mary continued. "Brooke, has there been anything, or a person who has triggered these… umm disagreeable feelings?"

Brooke regarded her empty glass and hesitated. "Well…"

Teri spoke out again. "Brooke, remember when we were in that grotty house, you went exactly to the place where the old doll was? That was seriously way out."

"It was strange Cousin Mary. I even remembered the doll's name, Matilda. But also, there is that awful man. Teri doesn't mind the person. She even interviewed him. But he gives me the creeps, and every time I see him, even if he's smiling at me, I feel scared, lost, and alone. And it's getting worse."

Mary leaned forward and took Brooke's hand. "My dear, is this the man called Jinx who owns the new bookstore in Madrona?"

Brooke shivered, then broke into tears. "Yes, yes, I don't know why, but I can't stand him."

Mary looked up, then said softly, "Kay, Teri …would you ladies mind if I talked to Brooke…alone?"

"Not at all. Teri, refill your glass and I'll pour another little snoot- full of your dad's cognac. Oh, that look on your face. Don't worry, there's an unopened bottle in the pantry." She focused on Teri's approving smile. "We'll go up to your room for a real mother-daughter chat, which we haven't been able to have since you got here."

"Mom, you're on," Teri said, and grabbing the bottle of Sancerre, turned to Brooke. "More wine?"

"No, no thanks. I want to have a clear head," Brooke whispered with a smile.

"Ah. More for me," Teri gloated, making Brooke laugh.

Cousin Mary looked into her glass. "Kay, dear, I seem to have hit bottom."

"No problem." Kay poured a splash more. "Brooke, why don't you take my chair? It's more comfortable."

"If you don't mind?"

"Mama Mia, why would I?" Kay waved her snifter around. "I'll be snug in that marvelous chaise Thommy Jay put in your bedroom. It's so Gloria Swanson, Thom would say."

"Gloria who?" Brooke asked.

"Oh, never mind dear. I'll tell you later," Kay said with a wave and stood up.

"Mom, I'll help you on the stairs. Take my arm."

"What, you'll what? Teri… in my day I could drink Alex and his cronies under the table." Kay grabbed the railing and hustled up the stairs… ahead of Teri.

Cousin Mary smiled as she looked at the living room ceiling. "I hear them moving around. Now we can talk, uninterrupted." She swirled her cognac, inhaled, then paused, her voice confidential. "Has this Mr. Buckwass asked you to have a meal with him, or wanted you to share some of his food, say clams, specifically cockles?"

Startled, Brooke sat back. "How did you know that? He invited Teri and I to lunch. Then kept insisting we eat some cockles." Brooke shook her head. "He'd gathered them fresh, that morning."

Cousin Mary put her glass down and peered closely at Brooke. "You and Teri…you didn't share any with him, did you?"

"No, no. We really thought it was weird. Why?"

"Ah, I thought not. But I wanted to make sure," Cousin Mary took a sip. "I'm glad to hear it. Never, and I mean never, eat any food that man offers; particularly cockles."

"Why, why? Is he trying to poison us!?"

"No, no…mmm, well, not exactly," Cousin Mary paused,

to sip her brandy and think. "Kay's right. This is fantastic. But, now to your question. No, not poison. It wouldn't make you ill or kill you, dear. But if you believe in one of our ancient coastal legends, for some it would be far worse."

"What could be worse than death...I mean," Brooke gestured helplessly.

"Complete control of your ability to think forever."

Brooke blanched. "Well, he was very cross when we didn't. Then, because someone snuck into the kitchen and stole his gunnysack of clams, he got furious and created a ridiculous scene. We couldn't wait to get away."

"I'm not surprised. You see, there are certain individuals, and sometimes, groups of persons, who believe that a person of Jinx's shamanistic background can control a person, particularly if one eats the food he insists on."

"That would explain his pushiness, but really Cousin Mary, it couldn't be true. It's ridiculous."

Cousin Mary toed the pattern in the carpet. "There are many, many things we don't know about the mind." She looked up. "Even in today's culture, the power of some individuals influences us. We call it charisma, elan, seduction, magnetism, crowd swayers, whatever. Control goes by many names. In our culture, these concepts are accepted."

"Remember Jonestown, and others. If one runs afoul of a person who has credence or professes belief in this kind of power or has devoted cohorts; at first one will say rubbish, it's impossible. But something in your mind niggles. It says: well, what if? Then you fall into at least the margins of, shall we say... the suggestion of the idea. This then can insidiously make inroads into the logical reasoning one feels they have."

"So, my golden rule is to be wary and alert to various unusual things. Things that have possibilities. One then can proceed in life with examination, curiosity, and a liberal splash of caution. Just the fact that I am now explaining this nebulous idea of control that Mr. Jinx may or may not have incorporated into your thoughts."

Brooke shivered. "Oh, Cousin Mary, you're creeping me out even more."

"It shouldn't. You're a bright young lady and so is Teri. We can expose ourselves to these ideas. But once you take time to observe them and recognize them, this is important. Analyze how they work, not to mention how insidious they can be; you've armed yourself with protection. Awareness of information and the source… about anything is key."

"Hmm, if you put it that way." Brooke sighed. "Then I feel a little better about my autonomy and…"

"Yes, freedom of choice is directly related to what I'm talking about, but on that subject, there is a larger area of pros and cons to explore. So, it's extremely debatable; we'll have to save that discussion for another time."

"That certainly helps me in handling my negative feelings about Mr. Buckwass and Kay's cousin, Mrs. De Moresby. But about these…" Brooke wrung her hands.

"Ominous feelings? The ones you've been experiencing?" Mary completed Brooke's thoughts.

"Yes," Brooke said faintly.

"My Dear, let's examine them. Do you think Teri's ideas might bear any of this?"

"Teri knows a lot about me. And she's been a rock while helping me handle this muddle. And yes. We were on the ferry. That's where I first felt the weirdness begin; then there was that dreadful house."

"Hmm, let's start with that. Teri thinks you've been to Bradestone before, probably when very young. Do you feel that's reasonable?"

"It would seem so. As my first photos of the Island set me off, then that house where I found the doll. I knew right where Matilda was."

"So, it's possible that you were here in the past?"

"It is." Brooke looked at her hands. "But, but my mother and my dad never, ever mentioned it." She paused. "It was strange. Dad actually tried to discourage me from coming here."

"What did he say?"

"That I would be bored. That it was rainy and foggy, and I wouldn't have anything to do…just like I was a clueless teenager. He…now that I think about it, he attempted to keep me from coming here. But I felt he was being gloomy, since I'd be away for such a longer stretch of time."

"Brooke, what if he was afraid? Fearful that you might remember things…unpleasant things."

"You mean he was trying to protect me?"

"Let's parse this together. He didn't want you to come to Bradestone. Something is here he didn't want you to encounter." Mary paused. "The thing I found most interesting is when Teri said you wanted to go into that house, then downstairs. And you went directly to Matilda. You both saw a variety of toys there and all were well used. So, most likely, at one time, you weren't the only child there."

"You mean it might have been a nursery?"

"It seems possible. You both saw tiny beds and things children would play with…for a while." Cousin Mary looked thoughtful. "Have you tried or ever had a memory of someone else? Perhaps another child?"

Elbows on the arms of the chair, Brooke cupped her ears and leaned forward. "I…I've had an odd dream. It frightens me. It's not like a nightmare, but it's scary. There's a girl in a pink dress, and I remember her on a pink tricycle. When my dreams get frightening, she comes to me, talks to me, calms me. I don't understand what is being said, but then I fall into a deep sleep," Brooke brushed her black tresses back and laughed nervously. "It isn't my mother, but someone else. I remember her hair. It's long, soft and blond."

"Brooke, what do you think this dream may mean? You saw the basement of this house. What thoughts do you have?"

There was a long silence. "I couldn't have been visiting friends. The bedrooms were downstairs, with walls made of plywood, and the doors had lever locks on the outside. Teri and I thought it was more like a prison. Some of the tiny outside windows still had bars in them. It felt to us like the rooms, were… were holding pens. It had to be for children, because the large room was a common and strewn with broken pieces of toys." Brooke sniffed. "I remember that even the pink tricycle was there, wheelless, in the corner."

"And your father, he said nothing about this period in your life?"

"No, never. It's as if that time never existed. That's what I told Teri, like that bad dream, it was just like I… I never existed."

"Hmm, did Teri share any other thoughts with you?"

Brooke hesitated. "Well, she found a large white envelope that was crumpled in the corner. It had the delivery address of some sort of adoption agency. Something like Angelic Aviators. We couldn't completely make it out. Teri laughed, then joked that the place was probably for adopted angels, or maybe flying children. It wasn't funny."

"Dear me, but what did you think?"

Brooke became cautious. "That maybe I was adopted. But my parents never told me. I've known other friends that were adopted, and informed the minute they could articulate thoughts and soon knew what adoption meant." Brooke cried softly; her hands shook. "If I was adopted. I know my parents would have told me." She wiped her eyes, "they would have. Why would they keep it secret? Why?"

"Brooke. Say it were true, most adults who adopt feel they should decide when they feel it's the right time to tell the child. Maybe for your parents, the right time never came."

Brooke sobbed. "But they were always honest and…loving, why wouldn't they?"

Mary leaned back in her chair and sighed. "Dear, some people find it difficult. And some think it won't make any difference in the long run. Of course, that's a big mistake. Somehow or other, the children find out."

"What am I to do?"

"My advice is to talk to your father, ask him. It'll be difficult for you both. But there's a reason he was discouraging your coming here."

"I don't think I can. It would ruin our trust in each other, our relationship."

Mary sighed again. "When you confront the truth, it will be a release for you both. You and Teri have given me the impression that your mother was wonderful, and your father is, too. That will never change. And it's obvious they raised you with care and love. As to whatever the outcome, I should think your relationship would become even stronger. Remember, they nurtured you from the get-go. Adopted or not. They raised you, you are their child, and no one else's."

CHAPTER 38

Commodity

Brooke counted to ten. I'm not going to. I have all the reasons to cry…but it won't help, it won't help at all. Her Dad was taking on his office phone.

She pushed back in her chair, as far as she could, and studied her father. It was as if he were far away, and she was watching him through a tunnel. She loved him and loved him dearly, but she felt stomach, nerves, aching. She was floating in a pool of pain. Fear filled her entire being. The pool had no bottom. She forced herself to breathe calmly and gripped the chair arms. Yes, focus on the chair, yes, the reality of her chair. Her fingers ran along the worn needlepoint, the rough side of the seat cushion, and the faded comforting arms. Since she was a child, this was her favorite chair in his campus office. The pattern of leaf colors always recalled Miss Quigley and her second-grade science fieldtrips, to Hiawatha Park, in West Seattle.

Miss Quigley had introduced her students to the names, variety, and beauty of fall leaves. Since that time, Brooke loved science. They labeled and pasted the leaves in their collection books; then at the side, sketched pictures of the trees that shed them. They learned facts about local plants and the growth of giant trees, facts she would never forget.

Brooke sat in her childhood adventure chair. The chair where they considered everyday matters. Her father, Michael Hamlin, Dean of the college, and her mother, Evelyn, delighted in the clothes she picked to wear for school that day. Of course, her mother helped, but with gentle suggestions. They all took time to discuss. What were the things she liked about grade school? Any new friends? Did she like her teachers? Was the cafeteria food good? It took little bits of her daily time, and she valued those moments.

When Brooke became older, they discussed adult matters. Her father respected her input on the new campus science building and wondered how she felt about certain classes. He was always interested in her opinions. Particularly, whether her new teachers were capable, and made the subject interesting.

Before Brooke's mother became ill, she would come in laughing with breakfast on a tray. When settled, the three would discuss Brooke's growing interests in photography. They considered everything important here.

After the "jawing and jokes session," her father's moniker for their morning get-togethers, she left with her friends. Then her dad walked her mother to the campus library, where she was head librarian. There, he waved goodbye and returned to his office.

Today, delighted with her unexpected visit, he quickly finished his phone conversations. He was humming an ABBA tune. And with eyes bright and questioning, leaning forward, hands clasped on his desk. His manner radiated complete parental indulgence and love.

"Oh Brooke, sorry, I had to take those calls. But you caught me at a good time." He glanced around the walls. "Summer quarter is quite slow this year, thank God. As you know, I'm not so harried." He perked up. "But I was delighted to hear about your work on Bradestone. It sounds like you're having a good time. I will admit, though, after your flurries of texting, I became worried when you just shut off. I knew it couldn't be too serious, or you would have phoned."

He grinned sheepishly and tapped the ancient rotary monster on his desk. "I still prefer chatting on this when you call. It's old-fashioned, but I grew up with it," he winked, "One of my secret pleasures."

Brooke squirmed, then nodded and smiled faintly. "I know, Dad. That's why I came in person, it's…"

He interrupted and gestured at the walls. "I'll tell you I'm very excited about your new photos. My, the unusual people you've encountered, not to mention some of their stories; and then there are your photos. They're top-notch. I'm sending," he gestured again at the wall. "These old ratty things off to the storage room and having your pictures enlarged and framed." He shook his head. "You do them with such artistry and skill, not to mention attention to beauty…they inspire me far more than this typical office schlock. You remember my secretary, Mrs. Caulfield? She'll be upset, but it's time I showed everyone what my daughter can do."

Brooke looked at the balled moist handkerchief crushed in her hands. How could she ask him? She loved him so. But love also meant trust, understanding, and awareness of what was important to their lives.

Michael was shocked. "Why Brooke, you have tears in your eyes. Has some young man stolen your heart, or worse, insulted you? Why I'll take care of things…dear heart, why, what's wrong?"

"Dad, you always said to be open and not hide important things. You know, things that matter to both of us. I must tell you…it's like a tear in my heart. Everything I've known and felt was true and real has changed. My world is dissolving around me. It's like I've slipped into another dimension." She gestured helplessly. "You see, I know. I know I am adopted. That I'm not your biological daughter."

Michael's face turned white. He groaned softly and dropped his head into his hands. "It wasn't my fault," he mumbled. "I knew we should have told you, from the beginning. But Evelyn, my lovely Evelyn, felt… she felt we should wait. Wait till you were older and could understand…and then, then she died… that long and terrible death. Afterward, I didn't have the sense or courage; I was lost. There was only you and me, nothing else. That's all that mattered. We were strong together."

Brooke inhaled deeply. "That's when you should have told me, when mom was dying."

"Brooke, there was so much happening, then to add another trauma…" he ran his fingers through his hair, "I was unbelievably busier than ever, and you were creating your own young life, which is as it should be. I thought about telling you but shoved it away. It would have been another major stress. I'm so sorry…sorry I didn't have the courage, the wherewithal." His voice faded. "Excuses, excuses," he said and gestured feebly.

"But you could have even told me after mom died. My friends, who were adopted, knew from square one; some, when they were barely toddlers. It wasn't any dark secret, something to be hidden, avoided. Now I've found out from a stranger, no less. Willie's cousin Mary, she's such a kind person. I do not know how she knew, but she did."

"Willie who? Mary? Who are these people?"

"Oh dad, I told you about Willie Cloudmaker. Well, his Cousin Mary is visiting him. She's from New Halem; it's in Oregon, on the coast."

"She also said Mr. Buckwass knows, too. And he's a person I detest. He makes me ill when I hear his voice or see his face." She dabbed her eyes with the handkerchief.

It was as if Michael hadn't heard her. "Evelyn and I thought it was best. Why should you know? You were our beautiful daughter, our beloved child. We wanted to protect you from a mean and chaotic world. What value would it be knowing about your real parentage?"

"Truth. Then I could answer other's questions truthfully, and it would have saved me from the smugness of a terrible person. My background, or whatever you want to call it, should not have been a secret, something to be avoided. I know you didn't want things to turn out this way. Love is trust, truth, and caring...since you are my... father and I love you; you should have been honest with me as I am with you. Honesty and love are the only really important things we humans can give each other. Love, and helping the ones you love, to find the truth, and...and trust each other." By now, tears were running down her face. She futilely wiped at them.

"Brooke, I've been a fool. I accept my failure in this. Sometimes we think things are for the best and stumble inanely around. Then we wind up saying I'm sorry, when being sorry does not even touch the enormity of the hurt. We hide things out of fear." He swallowed. "I'll somehow right this with you."

He pushed his fingers through his thick gray hair. "How I wish your mother were here. She always could explain things clearly, rationally...set things right in my mind. We knew sometimes we must tell you, but the cue I needed, never came, or I refused to recognize it when it did... and I never thought of anything else, except your mother's dying and our love and strength with each other."

"I know, Dad, but there is never a so-called right time. And I need that time now. I must know everything, every detail. Mary knew, and she carefully led me to conclude the obvious. But some horrible person like Mr. Buckwass knows it too. How is that possible?"

It was as if she had hit him. "Buckwass? Mr. Jinx Buckwass? He must be dead. Everyone said he was dead. I... I'd forgotten him. Blotted that name out, even his existence. Your mother didn't like him and refused to talk to him. But, despite every-thing, he gave us the greatest gift imaginable...you." Michael rocked his head. "I hated that man. A born manipulator, con-man, conniver. Whatever things call him, he was malignant. But he...he came through completely on his end of our bargain... I suppose one could say, with the devil. Evelyn always referred to it as a Mephistophelian pact."

Brooke closed her eyes, head down. "So, I was a bargain? Something to be haggled over?" Her voice trailed off.

"No, no, it wasn't like that at all. Please, let me explain. Your mother and I were on a special college cruise. Our first one through the Mediterranean. There were many couples aboard, like us. Almost all academics and naturally, we got to know one another. So, it wasn't long before intimate friendships formed, and sadly, we found out we were not the only couple that couldn't have children.

Our common interests grew. And we became close to two couples who traveled together and had known each other for a long time. Both pairs adopted through what they vaguely referred to as an 'agency.' When we asked; it turned out not to be an ordinary adoption service.

The couples convinced us to use the... er, service as it was an agency where potential parents saw the child before they adopt-ed. They received a replica, an avatar if you will. The name of the private business was Angelic Avatar Animators, Inc. When we enquired, he sent an elaborate doll. The company said it was a sample and there was no charge for the service."

"A doll?!"

"Yes, the clothes, facial features, hair, and body type were authentic looking. Everything in exquisite detail. The couples had shown us photos of the children they adopted. Two children, the one couple adopted and the other couple only one. The oldest child was six, if I remember correctly. Of course, they were wealthy and able to afford the service. The greatest attraction to them was… no red tape, no going through bureaucratic channels, and the worst part, finding out later of hidden medical conditions."

Michael spread his hands. "So, there was neither endless waiting nor health vetting and it all came with a guarantee. The children would be in the 4th or 5th year of their childhood."

"How horrible! It sounds awful," Brooke said tearfully.

"But darling, we were told their actual parents abandoned or sold the children. Poverty, desperation, whatever the reasons that drove parents to give up their child; we were never to know. However, it wasn't till later, after we committed, that one member of our adoptive circle found out that some children were stolen."

Brooke said, "Oh, how horrible, no, no." Hands to ears, she was shaking her head. Michael's voice became pleading.

"It was also a terrible shock to your mother and I, but what were we to do? We couldn't go to the authorities. As a group, we swore secrecy, and legally, we would be criminals. All potential parents had to sign a very strict and binding contract with Mr. Buckwass. He said he could destroy us if anyone said anything.

Soon, we knew he had this power, as his agency was extensive with many tentacles. His business operated off the radar and was throughout Europe, parts of the East, Australia, and, of course, the Americas." Michael took a shaky breath.

"But… but was I stolen or given up?"

Michael grimaced. "We found out later that you were stolen."

"That's terrible, terrible." Brooke covered her face.

"It is, and I know it. But I could see where, in desperate situations, people may have to sell their children or give them up. They're hoping that they will find better lives, maybe not starve to death… gambling that their children would have more of a chance than they did, something out of their realm, maybe something they couldn't even imagine. Looking back, I know we were desperate too and very naïve, or just stupid."

Brooke gestured helplessly. "I know you're trying to put the best imaginable spin on this. But the children could've been sold into slavery, maybe even sexual exploitation."

"No, never; Mr. Buckwass assured us that would never be. He completely vetted all the backgrounds of his applicants. It was amazing what he knew about Evelyn and me, even back to incidents involving our grandparents. His dossiers were uncannily accurate. He made sure that his 'adopters' were wealthy, or well off, and led exemplary lives. We were in a small group of eight and had become very close."

"His promises, his papers don't guarantee a damn thing. He is an evil man," Brooke said angrily.

Michael made a calming gesture. "I know, I know, but he gave us hope, and we truly believed things would be in the children's best interest."

"But it's a nightmare. Some of those people must have been caring individuals forced to do a terrible thing. Some parents will always wonder, wonder if their child is alive and healthy, or living a wretched existence, or dead…somewhere on this planet."

Michael picked at his desk blotter, then slammed his fist. "The one virtue Buckwass had was integrity."

"Integrity, him? How?" Brooke said scornfully.

"I meant that in the selection and handling of the children and the exhaustive vetting of the potential parents; he made sure that the fit was right, that there would be little if any margin for mistakes."

"You make it sound like a shopping agency. It involves the initial enquiry, accepting the goods and then gaining the product. No consideration at all that the children are human beings; or of their lives and the intricacies of the family's lives connecting them."

"Brooke, fieri non protos," he moaned in a tiny voice.

"I think I remember. What's done is done. And cannot be undone?"

"Cannot be undone," Michael murmured.

"Please know you are the only exquisite thing that ever happened to us." He fiddled with the desk pen. "I suppose you will want to trace your original parents; most adopted children do. But remember, it can be a shock to… to both sides."

He looked down at his clasped hands resting on the desk. "Mr. Buckwass keeps… kept detailed records on everyone. He let us see our folders. He said there were always little things other people wished to keep quiet and not see the light of day. The implication was that if there ever was a leak, he would take care of things, and not nicely."

"At first, he sent us a picture of you. Afterward, when we committed to the adoption, he sent the doll. It is identical in every way, hair color, eyes, skin tone." There were tears in his eyes. "It is you… when you were four."

Brooke rubbed her eyes, her mind spinning with a myriad of thoughts. "Searching for my biological parents is a question Teri and I have already discussed. You already know she's my closest friend."

Brooke sniffed, mouthing her words slowly. "We agreed to do nothing." She looked imploringly at her father. "Teri said asking would benefit from knowing but could also open a can of worms. She took a deep breath. "Besides, you're my real father… and mom was my real mom. Nothing else matters to me."

She paused. There was a long silence. "Where, where is this doll?"

"We gave it to one of Mr. Buckwass's assistants to let you play with, and you lost it. When we picked you up at that house, he called the 'processing center'. No one could find it."

"Where was this center?" Brooke asked dully; but she already knew.

"It was in an old Victorian house on Bradestone; probably torn down years ago." Michael firmly put his pen down, got up, wiped his eyes, then went to Brooke and enfolded her in his arms. "That's why I didn't want you to go there. I, I knew…knew somehow, that it would bring us bad luck." Holding on to her, he rocked back and forth. "If you ever change your mind, Brooke, I will help you find them and… and we'll do it together, as the loving team we are."

CHAPTER 39

The Uninvited Guest

Rose sneezed into her handkerchief. "Damn allergies," she mumbled and waved as Barney's truck pulled away. Her car was in his garage.

"It won't take long; don't worry, call after 1:00 and I'll come pick you up," he said, loudly popping his gum. What a great guy, Rose thought.

Rose turned to look at the house. Easy to sell, late 1980s remodel, new exterior paint. Not bad. She turned and walked up the steps to the front door. What? Somebody forgot to lock the key box. She looked down. Oh, not good. The coco mat was partially sitting in a muddy puddle. Carefully, she skirted the edge and lifted the soggy end. No key there. Odd, the door was ajar.

Jean Benning, the owner, said she had been back to pick up a few items the movers left. Rose tisked, what carelessness. She scanned the gravel drive. The house was close to the main road. Vandals, maybe? She cautiously pushed the door open.

Rose punched the doorbell several times, then called. "Hello, hello, anybody home?" No answer.

Ms. Benning was one of her new listings, lived in Seattle, and sounded extremely panicky. "When can we stage the house for a show? Could it be next week?"

Cripes, Benning, had lived here for over five years. One of those nervous twits. Hadn't she ever heard of island time? And Rose had just received the listing. Rose stepped over the threshold carefully. Her cross to bear, scatter-brained clients!

The hall was dark and empty. She flicked the light switch.

Ha, Ms. Benning said the power was still on. That's why the doorbell rang. At least one plus mark in her corner.

Rose grimaced. It was the first time she had been to this property. The hall carpet was a rather off-putting. Oh lordy, if she recalled the listing correctly; it ran around the corner to the kitchen door. She looked to her left. The bilious color also went up the large stairway. The stairs ended at a gallery-railed landing. Rose closed her eyes. Most likely, the same gaudy thing was lurking up there. The taste of some people! Rose yelped, lurched forward and grabbed the balustrade. Her right stiletto heel had caught on to the rug, giving her a much closer look at the pattern than she would have preferred.

What? Footprints, fading up to the third step! A pair of large running shoes? She reached down and felt the tread. The mud was dry and crumbly, probably left by one mover. But Rose understood they'd been here two weeks ago. Humph, that's the trouble with not having a washable mat inside and outside the front door. She had one with Wipe Your Feet clearly printed on it. It was obvious Ms. Benning hadn't a clue about sensible house care. Hopefully, there was a broom and dustpan in the coat closet. She'd have a look later.

From the basement came a loud clunk. Rose held her breath and listened intently. Ah, only the furnace kicking in. Well, at least the temp was comfortable. Mrs. Benning insisted on the thermostat remaining at 55 degrees. Kept the damp out. Rose agreed. It was an older house and no doubt poorly insulated. Jean Benning just gained another plus mark.

Rose headed down the hall toward the kitchen. She sniffed. What was that off odor? Beginning to unbutton her coat, she hesitated. Oddly, she felt a presence. "Hallo? hallo? It's Rose the realtor," she shouted. No response. Cautiously, she stepped through the kitchen doorway. Taking out a hanky, she sneezed violently. There it was again, even stronger. The smoky smell of burned toast.

Rose's heels clicked smartly. Oh, what lovely travertine tile, another plus for Mrs. Benning. Hanky to nose, she walked over to the large sink. What? Was that toaster thingy at the side? She sneezed again. Someone had burned bread and scraped crumbs into the sink. Recently too. Humph, dirty dishes everywhere. The woman had left a mess.

Annemarie, Rose's house cleaner, would have to be called. That would be a loss of three plus marks, and more. Thankfully, Annemarie was the go-to person when readying a 'problem' house for opening. Wiping her nose, she stepped into the living room.

"Hallo?" Rose yelled again. No reply. She stopped. Was that a rustling sound? Most likely Mice or worse, rats? 'Call Terminator-Ted, the friendly Exterminator!' The local T.V. ad flashed through her mind. Rose smiled; he was a good kid, dependable, honest and quick.

Hanky at the ready. She blew her nose and sniffed gently. Behind the burned- toast smell was a funny odor of staleness. She grimaced; the house had stood empty for almost a month.

A thorough cleaning by Annemarie was definitely in order.

Hmm, after the cleaning and the staging, she would put the house on the market. That new family, moving from Tacoma, wanted a quiet place to raise their two kids. This house would be perfect for them.

Mentally, she wrestled with herself. But there was the remoteness of the house from schools, not to mention rural transportation problems. However, the house was in a lovely setting and surrounded by trees. Of course, the closest town was Burn. Not exactly a teeming metropolis, even so artsy and fun.

Now, the living room has possibilities. The papered inside wall was a forest of bamboo. A little busy, but nice. I think we can work with that. What? An overturned chair beside a dinky side table. Mrs. Benning didn't get the rest of her furniture? Rose glanced at her watch. The woman said she'd arrive at 10:00 to discuss the house. She should have been here 20 minutes ago. It's useless keeping track of plus points, Rose thought. "No doubt, fashionably late. After all, the peons can wait." Her voice of frustration echoed loudly in the empty room.

Then she sneezed violently; something was really getting to her. Ah, there, there's the culprit, an ugly dried arrangement near the small table on the floor. Using her kerchief like a gas-mask she warily approached. The vase had tipped over, and the flowers appeared to be feverfew, lemon mint, and something else, wild oregano? Her eyes watered. Ghastly weeds! But the vase was beautiful, old cut glass. We could use that, if there was a nicer table somewhere.

Sneezing, she quickly exited through the side door. Interestingly, it came out at the base of the stairs. Startled, she looked up. There was that noise again; like something snuffling around. She dialed Ms. Benning's cellphone. It rang continuously; no answer, not even a 'please leave a message' response. With the scratching came feeble whining noises. Odd, sounded like a dog. Quietly, she tiptoed to the front door.

I don't like this. I'm going to call Isaac. Standing in the open door, she speed-dialed Sergeant Reynolds.

"Hi Rose, what's up? Or should I say, darling, what's up?"

"Oh yes do, of course," she tittered, blushed, then her voice became a whisper. "I'm in an empty house. The owner was supposed to be here," she glanced at her watch, "an hour ago. I think someone, or a dog, or both is moving about upstairs. They even left a mess in the kitchen. I've called out and called out, but there's no answer. I tried to contact Ms. Benning, but no answer there either, and I am feeling... well, it's getting really scary. And with all those crazy things happening near town..."

"What's the address?"

"1929 Mill Marsh Road SW."

"Way out there, on that unpaved road, back in the sticks?"

"Yes," she said meekly.

"Where's your car?"

"Barney's garage. He dropped me off. I've had problems with the transmission thingy and..."

"Listen carefully, Rose. I'm on my way. Go outside; find a clump of trees or brush, somewhere you can hide. Maybe there's a carport you can duck behind but watch the road. Anyway, make yourself scarce. I'll be there in roughly, uh, ten minutes. I'm already rolling."

CHAPTER 40

Rescue the Fair Maidens

Disjointed words, loud static, then nothing from Isaac's phone. Rose raised her eyes to the skies. Ah, technology. Another bad reception area. Well, here goes, one more time. She punched the buttons.

"Isaac, are you still there?" She thought she heard a yes. "But Isaac, I'm wearing my designer shoes from Sabras! And it's muddy off the driveway. There's no carport and," she hissed as she peered out the front door, "no convenient clump of anything. Only trees. Have you forgotten? It rained torrents last night."

His voice came through, choppy but intelligible. "Look Rose, er darling, I'll buy you a new pair, maybe four. Just get the hell out of there. Head for the trees. Hide!"

"But…" He'd rung off.

Hah, hide in the trees. She went back into the hall and opened the coat closet. Ah, there was a broom and a pan! But damn and blast, the light bulb was out. Rose shook her head. Ms. Benning had lost so many points, anyway. She stepped into the dark closet and quietly shut the door.

* * *

She could hear stealthy footsteps. Then silence. The closet door flew open. Rose yelling, hurled the dustpan at the intruder. The broom was next. With quick reflexes, Issac deflected the dustpan, grabbed the broom, and gripped it firmly.

"Yeesh! That's the most bloodcurdling Banshee yell I've ever heard!" Isaac growled through gritted teeth.

"What the be-Jesus. It's you. You scared the hell out of me!"

Rose howled in an accusatory tone, then grinned sheepishly.

"I thought I told you to hide outside."

Rose drew to her full height, including her deadly six-inch heels, and stuck out her chin. "You'll notice, my manly man. It's a lot drier in here."

"Well, we've blown any cover we had. If there was someone here, they have either shot through the roof, or lost their hearing and are now rolling outside, clutching their ears."

"Oh, ha, ha," Rose mocked. A loud thunk, then scratching resounded from upstairs. Rose gripped Isaac's arm. "See, they're still here!"

"Okay, okay. But keep the front door open and blow this… if you see anything, and I mean anything." He gave her his police whistle, paused, then started up the stairs. "The black and white, out front, should deter anyone," he mumbled over his shoulder.

Rose placed the whistle's lanyard around her neck, then, leaning against the wall, removed her shoes and stuffed them in her purse. If she had to make tracks, she was now ready, and nylons were cheap.

Sergeant Reynolds crept up the stairs; his gun drawn. Seeing the weapon, Rose's eyes widened. At the top, he froze and listened at the left door. It was the first one on the landing.

It was thrilling. Would he kick it open and charge in, guns blasting, as they did on T.V.?

Isaac seemed to listen for a long time, then leaned forward, his ear closer. He must have heard something, something horrible. Rose shivered and braced herself.

Slowly, slowly Isaac opened the door, then, like a cat, crept out of view. Silence… Rose was all atremble. What's going on? He's taking his sweet time. Humph, I'm going up.

Like a wraith, Sergeant Reynolds materialized at the head of the stairs. He held a finger to his lips and a puppy in his right arm. He shook his head, then cupped his free hand at the side of his mouth.

"Rose," he whispered, "my darling Rose, be silent." He paused. "Call Ujima at the station, tell her to come quickly, no bells, no whistles. Medics too. This is an emergency."

Rose opened her mouth. Isaac glared, slashed an emphatic finger across his throat; his lips formed a silent, "NOW". Rose was thrilled. Isaac was so masterful and in charge, and because of his skills, no one was shot. But what the hell had he meant by no bells, no whistles? She looked at the one in her hand.

Stepping out to the porch, Rose made her call. Ujima shouted, "Roger, got that!" Then a crackle, and the phone went dead. Rose rolled her eyes, always iffy reception in the boonies. "Gahh, gad!" Spasms of shock flew up her legs.

Oh prunes, the doormat was a sponge of water. Teeth clenched, Rose hopped inside, tore her stockings off, and worked her toes into what had now become a wonderful, warm carpet. Movements above made her look up.

Sergeant Reynolds was quietly descending the stairs. In the crook of one arm was a sleepy spaniel puppy. Wearily, it tried to lick Isaac's firm jaw. Tossed over his right shoulder, and supported in the crook of his other arm, he cradled what seemed to be a bundle of laundry. Only from it, two tiny legs and two tiny arms drooped.

Rose knew immediately. She dropped her precious purse and socks; hands flew to her mouth, and Sergeant Reynolds paused. He nodded and whispered: "Yes, yes, it's baby Renée."

CHAPTER 41

Interviews

"Thanks, Seargent Reynolds. You and Rose did a fine job. Renee and her parents were taken to Swedish hospital in Seatle. The baby is none the worse for wear. And whatever drug they gave Renee, and the puppy was wearing off."

"It sounds like her parents are adding the spaniel to their family. As in Shakespeare's play, All's Well That Ends Well. And it seems Kay is preparing your favorite chocolate cake and setting aside Roses's favorite champagne in tribute to you both. And I'm invited too. Wouldn't miss Kay's chocolate German cake for anything. You did a good job."

Isaac blushed. "We really did nothing that anyone else wouldn't do."

"Oh, don't be so modest. We all know you really did it for the cake."

After their laughter subsided, Ujima nodded. "Now please send in those medics. They did the actual work. They look too young to have champagne, but I'm sure they'll gobble some of Kay's cake."

There was more laughing.

* * *

They both were exhausted. One medic slumped in the corner office chair. The other leaned on Ujima's desk. My God, they were very young. Could that boy even shave yet?

She knew they'd completed their rigorous medical training with honors and valued at the clinic. But both looked barely 18. When did she grow so old?

The girl, with the blonde crew cut and nose ring, leaned further forward. "Sorry Sheriff, we're beat. It's been a busy night."

Brad, the one in the chair, shook his long black mane and spoke. "Yeah, one heart attack, then a lost dude with Alzheimer's wandering around, near Shady Meadows." He looked up, ran a tattooed hand through his locks, and looked at his coworker. "Jess, what happened to those dopers in the schoolyard?"

The girl grimaced. "They're starting to detox. And Doc says we got 'em just in time. That gangly kid who was threatening to end it all?" She shook her head. "He was on something really nasty. Doc was having a helluva time trying to find out what it was. Then there was that middle-aged dude, who couldn't pee, actually about to explode? The jerk finally admitted he took a couple of hits of heroin after he cleaned his mom's place. Honestly, Sheriff, drugs are becoming a real hairy problem here."

Ujima nodded. "Thanks, Jess, we're working on it. The Narc squad from Seattle is a big help. But catch me up on the Renée kid. What did you and Brad find out?"

"Well, plenty. "Jess scratched her chin. "The kid and the dog were both on some kind of herbal tranquilizer. The lab guys are trying to analyze it… as we speak." She shook her head. "The exceptional thing is the vital signs of the kid and dog are strong. They're just in another world." She reached into her pocket and pulled out a plastic bag. "This is the vial with the green stuff. The lab has two more. They wanted you to have this one for the evidence room."

Ujima rotated the bag in her hand. "Thanks, this appears all too familiar." She looked up. "So, they're both recovering, and the mother's, okay?"

Jess nodded. "Yep, and her friend Kay Roberts is with her."

"Good news all around. Well, you two are off duty, so go home and get some sleep. That's an order!" Jess grinned at Brad. "We got the same static from the boss. It won't be difficult to comply." They dragged their tired bodies to the office door.

"Oh, one more thing." Ujima held up her finger. "Could you tell Miss Rose Bracken I'd like to see her now? She's the one with the plastic bag labeled SABRAS. Can't miss her."

"Roger, Sheriff," both chorused and exited.

Ujima stretched and yawned as Rose came into the room. "Pardon my rudeness, Rose. It's been quite a 15 plus hours." She swiveled in her chair, switched off the recorder, and placed her notes on the medic's interviews in a manila folder.

Rose waved her hand. "Understand completely. I'm going home right after this and taking a long snooze."

"Did my hostess with the mostest, out front, bring you coffee?"

"She did. Filled my cup twice." Rose looked to make sure she'd closed the door, then whispered. "She's new, isn't she? Er, seems to be, well… a bit robotic?"

Ujima laughed. "Her name is officer Lavalon. I hired her because she's bright and efficient, doesn't bog down when it's the least expected, not like some A.I. devices."

Rose smiled meekly. "Love your coffee. Hope it doesn't interfere with my sleep."

"You'll most likely sleep like a log. You've been through a lot."

"Here," Ujima said, handing Rose her witness statement. "I think it's ready but read it over carefully. Then, if it's accurate, your signature is required on the dotted line."

Rose took the time to peruse the document, signed it, and handed it back to Ujima.

"Thanks again. I would say you have a keen eye for detail. That makes an excellent witness." Ujima glanced at the wall clock. "Could you tell Sergeant Reynolds I'll be ready for him in about 20 minutes? I've more questions and want time to collect my thoughts." She smiled as she opened another folder. "And I'm sure you'll want a few moments to chat with Isaac."

As Rose stood, she twisted her engagement ring. "I can't help it. It's so beautiful," she murmured nervously.

"It is that. When is the grand occasion?"

Rose took a deep breath. "We're going to wait till a week after Kay and Alex have their grand opening of the inn." She arched her eyebrows. "We've pinpointed the date and reserved a wedding suite on Salt Spring Island in the Canadian San Juans. And if the good sergeant can have that week off, we're going to take the ferry to Sidney first. Canada is so dreamy that time of year and…"

Ujima jotted a note on her desk pad. "It is that Rose. And I'm sure I can arrange for Sergeant Reynold's leave. But please make certain he submits his request and the specific dates… yesterday." Rose tittered and Ujima regarded her steadily. "You're aware of how easily he can get sidetracked. I must plan for his absence, and it's not that easy."

Rose nodded. "Not to worry, I'll keep Isaac on his toes. You said you wanted to see him in twenty minutes?"

Ujima waved her hand. "Twenty or thirty, no rush." Rose tottered cautiously toward the door and closed it softly behind her.

It was always her damn shoes. It's a wonder Rose didn't break her neck. Sabra has a lot to answer for, using Rose as a guinea pig. Of course, Rose could say no.

Ujima shook her head, then picked up the memo on her desk. So, the Spaniel sold a month ago, from a Seattle pet shop. Thanks to the chip, the store was located. Not surprising that they paid for the little pup in cash. Of course, the purchaser's address was bogus.

Betty at "Betty's Vet Clinic & Beautification Parlor", had been very helpful. The quickly sent fax showed that the animal was up to date on its shots and in excellent health. Ujima chuckled. Judy Johnson told Kay the kid wouldn't let the wiggle-worm out of her sight.

Ujima frowned. It was looking more likely that Kay's Aunt Maureen kidnapped. Her fingerprints were on the toaster and other items in the kitchen. Then there was that odd bouquet of herbs on the living room rug. Too, her medicine-come-tranquilizer, was in the upstairs bedroom. And then there was her extremely odd behavior.

Most were circumstantial, with the medicine and prints being the exception. Acting strange, however, seemed to be the woman's modus operandi. The result of trauma? Mental illness? How unfortunate for Kay and Alex.

Ujima punched up a file on her computer screen. The woman had not been quite truthful about events in her past and there were huge blanks regarding her movements in Canada and Europe. Some of her claims had been impossible to confirm. But what would be her motive for kidnapping in the first place?

Well, it was for the better. She would be placed under house arrest at Kay's. At least she would take her new medicine on schedule and be among the family. The Johnsons didn't say they would, but pressing charges might be down the road. Anyway, the first thing she looked forward to was getting info back from the Poulsbo forensic team. They were always thorough and professional and had been a tremendous help in past cases.

Was it really mental illness was behind all this? Ujima pondered. It was a world she couldn't even imagine. Kay, however, handled the situation with ease. Eventually, they would have to find the right "home" or placement for Aunt Maureen. In her personal experiences, such behavior only got worse.

Ujima shrugged. Thank God it wasn't her problem. But it came without saying that she would help Kay. Naturally, within the parameters that were professional and legally allowed.

There was a tentative but familiar knock at the door. "Come in, Sergeant Reynolds, and set yourself down."

Isaac gave Rose a quick peck on the cheek, mumbled something to her, then closed the door. Saluting smartly, he sat down, back ramrod straight.

Ujima rolled her eyes in exasperation. "You don't have to be so formal Isaac and yes, I'll arrange for a sub. But I need the dates, post-haste. Sounds like the newlyweds are going to have a cool time in Canada." She winked.

Sergeant Reynolds blushed and nodded. "Thank you, Ma'am. We'll be gone for five days. And when we get back, Toady's wedding present is loaning us his sailboat. He thought we'd like to take her out and tool around during the rest of my leave."

A flash of intense memory crossed Ujima's mind. She opened the folder on her desk. "I would advise you to check all the exterior and interior fittings before you set sail," she said dryly.

"Yes ma'am," Isaac said and, recalled Ujima and Kay's close call. Was it three years ago? "Toady and I will make certain everything's shipshape, and nobody's been fooling around, absolutely nobody. Not to worry."

"Great. Besides granting leave, thank you again for the intelligent and sensitive way you handled yesterday's difficult situation. Renée's mother was ecstatic. Both Renée and the pup well have a clean bill of health, and hopefully, down the line, no psychological repercussions for either of them. I'm writing a commendation to put in your file."

"Thank you, ma'am."

"You're welcome. You know Isaac, you have improved exponentially since first joining the force. Things haven't been easy. Even though we live on a small island, we have the occasional bizarre situation thrown at our feet. If our lives were in a book, we could blame it on the artless writer."

Sergeant Reynolds laughed. He remembered their wild adventures last year. Chuckled again and nodded vigorously. "So true. But Ma'am, I love it here and so does Rose. We don't have the real messy crimes that occur in the big cities, but inevitably the unusual one comes our way. After all, it's the Fates playing games, like this current case."

"Yes, I'm sad to say, in this instance, the evidence points only in one direction. But again, I want you to go over what happened. Visualize you're there now; just let the words come. Start with the call Rose gave you," she paused, "and relax Isaac. Things don't have to be in order. Remember, I'm always interested in anything peculiar, out of the norm… any detail, even if it doesn't seem related to the investigation, you know the drill."

"Curious you should mention that, Sheriff." He nodded at the recorder. "I'd like to show you something. It's odd." Ujima reached over and switched off the machine. "And what would that be?"

"Just a moment." He got up quickly, stepped outside, and returned with a bulging white plastic garbage bag. "After Renée was taken to the clinic, I returned to the house. I didn't go in because the forensic team would have hysterics. There was enough mucking about when we found her, but…"

Ujima twiddled the pencil in hand. "Yes Sergeant, carry on."

"Well, I was searching the outside grounds in ever-increasing circles. Of course, I picked up cigarette butts, the occasional wine or beer bottle; and yes, the items are in individual specimen bags and their location duly noted."

"Excellent, Sergeant, what else?"

He grinned. "You know Edgar and his motley crew?"

"I most certainly do."

"Well, he and his family were having quite a to-do with a pair of gulls. The argument was about fifty feet into a swampy area of grass. I slogged over there to see what the squabble was about and found these."

He carefully placed double sheets of newspaper, overlapping them, on her desk; and emptied the bag.

"Clamshells, sand, and burned wood?" She paused and sniffed, "Ah, thank you Isaac, for this rather, er odiferous gift."

"I thought you would be as curious as I am. And there's more. Whoever dumped them, cooked there. They left a circuitous but definite path trampled through the reeds. And it went towards the house."

"Now, this is interesting. Go back there. Particularly focus on what's left in the remains of the campfire. Then, using that point as your center, make larger and larger circles from there. It'll be slow going. See if you can recruit Alex to help. He catches on quick and likes this sort of thing."

"Yes ma'am, will do."

Leaning forward, she poked at the pile with her pencil. A surprised look came over her face. "You know Isaac, this might cast another slant on our case. I'm sure this wasn't just a cook-out for the wildlife."

CHAPTER 42

October 30th

Alex put a marker in the Wilbur Smith novel and rested it on his lap. He stretched leisurely in his wingback chair and looked out the living room window. A dense evening fog was creeping into Scoon Bay. Tomorrow's forecast predicted clear and dry. Alex grinned; wouldn't a mist create just the perfect, eerie atmosphere for trick-or-treaters?

The evening brought back memories of a Hallowe'en night, years ago. The trick-or treaters were long gone. Grandad told him to bring in the jack-o'-lanterns, and dump them into the pigsty, out back. The pigs were sure happy, but Alex wasn't. When he returned, somebody dowsed the porch lights. Oh, too funny… no doubt, it was his brother Matt, always up to something.

It, too, was a foggy night. And the old streetlight on the corner glowed feebly. It barely illuminated a small circle at the base of the pole. He chuckled. Grandad always said, "The blamed thing was a typical waste of taxpayers' money."

Alex stepped back onto the porch. He'd think of a good one to play on Matt. The crunch of heavy boots on the gravel road below startled him. Someone, late for treats, was coming. Out of the fog, and down near the mailbox, a gigantic figure slowly materialized. Alex gulped and stared. Wow, the person had no head! Instant goosebumps. What a terrific idea for Hallowe'en. Hesitating, Alex waved, then shouted. He hoped his voice didn't shake.

"That's a great costume. Still got some candy left; I'll turn…" The thing didn't acknowledge him, arms slowly swinging, disappeared into the foggy night.

Kay, standing behind Alex's chair, patted his shoulder. Alex jumped; his book flying.

"For Chris-sakes Kay, don't creep up on a fellow like that. I did not know you were there."

"My, my, aren't we jumpy tonight? Expecting something ghostly to materialize from the fog?" She'd rested her arms on the back of his chair and peered out the window with him.

"Er, no."

"I wanted to tell you that Aunt Maureen has settled into the side-porch-room nicely. We gave her a light supper and, with the aid of her green medication, she's fast asleep. I'm glad Ujima felt the ankle bracelet was unnecessary. Maureen's been through too much, as it is. Besides, she hasn't the means to go anywhere."

"When did you last check on her?" Alex asked.

"About a half an hour ago, and she looks so sweet, sleeping. I can't believe…"

"Hmm, if you say so, dear. When do you want me to pull check-in duty?" he asked as he looked up at her.

"In about two hours. She's really out." Kay clapped his shoulders. "I'm surprised you haven't made a duty roster for us."

"That's coming," he replied sotto voce.

"Well, that's certainly a cheery answer. Anyway, I've some interesting things to do that may liven our evening; but for now, I'll be putting clothes away, upstairs. The girls are in the kitchen." She looked at her watch. "Dear, you have thirty more minutes to read before dinner," she said, tapping him on the head, then headed for the stairs.

The aroma of pumpkin pies drifted in from the kitchen. Teri and Brooke had baked them. They had changed their minds and stuck around for the weekend. They volunteered to monitor Aunt Maureen.

Too, they also said they'd be glad to answer the door with treats tomorrow night. And it would be an excellent time to make modifications to their computer files; and they'd welcome any diversions. Kay thought they might have other plans but said nothing.

Alex could hear their excited voices as the ladies came into the living room. Both carried party bowls; one brimming with popcorn, the other with peanuts and chocolate-covered pretzels.

"I don't think we'll get many kids tomorrow night," Teri said and turned to Brooke. "Few dare to come up our road. It's dark and unlit. And if any real cool costumes make it to the door, I'll take pictures with my phone. On previous Hallowe'ens, some tricksters were really into it." She chewed thoughtfully on a pretzel. "One dressed as a walking box of McDonald's French fries. The girl had to peek out from between the yellow-foam potatoes. She had it down pat. The box was the correct shape, bright red, with golden arches; and the cool thing is, she made it herself." Teri took another pretzel.

"That's so outstanding. Wish I'd seen it." Brooke loudly munched on a handful of popcorn. "One time, at our house, we had a group of six. They sang Hallowe'en carols. All of them were in Charlie Brown costumes. They went through several songs and really had beautiful voices." Chewing thoughtfully, Brooke offered her bowl to Teri. "Your mom made some tasty treats."

"I know. I can't keep away from them either." Teri grabbed a handful of peanuts. "Gosh, I hope we leave enough for the kids."

Brooke giggled. "Seriously Teri, why don't we 'scare up' something to wear when we answer the door? If the few trick-or-treaters make the effort, we should, too." She wistfully gazed out the living room window. I bet there'll be amazing costumes at the Hallowe'en party tomorrow night."

Teri stifled a yawn. "It'll be a bore. You know, mostly the Metamucil set, trying to get down and funky while playing oldies."

"I heard that," Alex grumbled from his chair. "And don't keep eating that crap. You'll spoil your dinners."

Teri and Brooke jumped. "Whoa, we didn't see you there. Mom told us you were helping finish the decorations at the community center."

Alex stretched and yawned. "It's all done. Wick, Byron and others actually took time from the puppet play to help. We're finished, a fait accompli. I was only there till this afternoon, helping with the small stuff. It's gonna be great."

"Didn't it interfere with their puppet play? I heard the last show was tonight."

"No," Alex said with a smile. "The guys have been thrilled with it. Said it would be super spooky for the Grand Finale.

And that's a matinee, tomorrow afternoon. It's popular, so they extended it."

"What's so cool about it?" Teri asked eagerly.

"Well, the place looks like the insides of an Adam's Family mansion. There's even a haunted staircase. It is a mechanical alteration of the actual stairway that leads to the landing. The one in front of Wick's office loft."

Teri laughed. "Woo, that is scary. And what exactly is a haunted staircase?"

"Something that goes thumpity-thump in the night." Brooke said in a very low voice.

"Well, actually, yes. It randomly groans and shrieks when you trod on it. And there's an automated Sasquatch underneath. He reaches out his hairy arm out and growls. I rigged the center's sound system and dedicated parts of it to several animated surprises. It's rather cleverly laid out."

Brooke frowned. "Wouldn't that be an annoyance for anyone wanting to use the upstairs office?"

"Yeah Dad; and what's the purpose, anyway?"

"Mainly for fun. Adults have to run the gauntlet if they want to pick up any awards they win during our pre-Hallowe'en party."

"That sounds cool. Awards? They're giving out awards at the Hallowe'en dance?" Teri exclaimed.

"Yeah, and quite a few. The guys came up with a clever costume category, and best impersonations for the actors on stage. You know, a terrific Lip-sync category and one for the most original performance."

Teri looked at Brooke. "Oh, now I want to go. It sounds like fun."

"Count me in," Brooke said, raising her free arm.

"Hmm, remember? You ladies volunteered to answer the door. And Teri particularly wanted to avoid mixing with the Geritol set. And of course, Aunt Maureen is the number one priority."

"It's the Metamucil set, Dad. What's Geritol? Anyway, I might figure out something," she whispered to Brooke.

"Geritol is a sort of health supplement. You can Google it," Brooke said, then paused. "Alex, I was wondering when they installed the stairs, and how do you keep kids from hurting themselves, or keep them off during the plays?"

"Actually, they're the original 1910 stairs. And, during the play, to keep the wild child, or adult from harm, there's a keyed, off-button. Of course, the spooky stuff sometimes breaks down. But hey, that's what mechanical things do."

"When did they change the staircase?" Teri asked. "I really want to try it."

"They originally altered the stairs for the puppet play's debut at the end of September. The guy's enlisted friends who are audio-buffs. They're all from Seattle and brought some knock-your-socks-off electronic stuff. But then they added more tricks for the adults on Hallowe'en night. You know, Byron, he wants Wick to charge a small fee for anyone who wants to try them out."

"Hum, typical Madison-Avenue Byron." Teri remarked with a bored look at Brooke. "It sounds… maybe interesting. But since we're obligated for Hallowe'en night, let's take a tour when it's over. Wick and company will want to show it all off."

An eerie clacking noise echoed around the room. "What the hell is that!" Alex exclaimed and came up out of his chair. They turned in unison. The noise came from the top of the stairs.

Teri pointed and poked Brooke in the ribs. "Well, my, my, it's our resident ghost and… and it's… it's going camping?"

Kay stopped in mid-decent, hand on the railing, and struck a dramatic pose. A wide brimmed straw hat topped her auburn hair. A thick belt cinched a long-sleeved man's white shirt, tucked around her waist.

Her liberally festooned belt had clacking equipment of all kinds; a dented canteen, a sewing kit, a small hammer, scissors, etc. Her voluminous split-skirt flowed below. To complete her ensemble, she brandished a giant umbrella. It had an extremely pointy end.

Alex was gob smacked, then roared with laughter. "What? You've just returned from Roland's dig in Mauretania?"

Kay walked daintily down to the bottom of the stairs and made a pirouette. Her accouterments rattled. Adjusting her jaunty hat with one hand and using her umbrella as a cane with the other, she stubbornly shot her chin forward.

"Actually, if you must know, Role was a big help. Remember that mysterious shipment I wouldn't let you open in September?" Alex nodded, a foolish grin on his face. "It contained not only this ancient topper," she tapped the brim, "but all these necessary tools. It's all for the intrepid archaeologist that I am. How do you like it?"

Alex slapped his brow. "You're going to the party as an archaeologist, like that? If you fall over, it'll take three powerful men to pick you up. I certainly can't," he snorted. "And you sound like a walking garbage can… who in the hell are you supposed to be, some sort of mummy exterminator?"

Teri, laughing, stood back and squinted. "I know exactly who she is."

"Whom, shall I dare ask?" Kay struck another pose with closed eyes. Her voice had taken on plumy, English tones.

Teri laughed so hard she was gasping. "Mrs. Amelia P…P, Peabody Emerson."

"Wow, the eminent Egyptian archaeologist!" Brooke shouted with a gasp.

"Ah, very observant, my dears. And take note. I've just returned from a bat-infested king's chamber inside a pyramid at Sakkara, naturally."

Brooke shook her head, then held her hands to her ears. "Teri's right. You're the spitting image. If I may use such a vulgar term."

"You may."

"I love that canvass-covered canteen on your belt. We have several in the college museum collection," she said and gasped, to wipe tears off from her eyes.

"Indeed, my dear. How very astute of you. Role was exceptionally thorough. I believe he procured most, if not all, of these marvelous accouterments, er… dated circa 1912; in an Arabian souk."

"The man's definitely in the right place," Teri said, still laughing.

"Now, now I'm wondering, who is going to be your faithful, famous, and… and intrepid companion?" Brooke choked out.

Kay, thrusting her umbrella dramatically, pointed at Alex. "There stands one of the foremost Egyptian Archaeologists of all time, Emerson Radcliffe." She leaned back, free hand to chin and assumed a professorial air of concentration.

"A salt and pepper wig, a touch of tan grease paint, and a

stained billowy, white shirt…opened at the neck, of course," she pointed her parasol, "exposing his manly chest. Yes, a fine specimen. I reckon he's about the right height, too."

Teri, shaking her head, closed her eyes. "I can visualize him now. Strutting masterfully and… and saying bloody curses."

"Yes, yes," Brooke interjected. "But they all have to be 19th-century curses."

Alex's eyes bulged. "What? This is insane. Wigs? They're hot and itchy. The hair gets in your mouth, eyes, and everything else." Alex became exasperated. "And cursing? Who might I be so bold to ask, is this… this Emerson Radcliffe? I am going as a zombie pirate!"

"Argh! Quel ennui," Kay grumbled. "It's a simple decision. You'll make a splendid Emerson. My mind is made up."

Brooke hooted and clapped her hands. "Kay, you sound like I imagine Amelia would sound. What a fantastic idea! You guys will take the couple's category tomorrow night. Hands down."

Teri stood soldier stiff and saluted Alex. "Calm yourself, sir. You'll make a perfect Radcliffe. And for your edification, Emerson is and, I may be permitted to quote, 'one of the greatest Egyptologist of the 19th century, or any century'. Oh, and your sobriquet in Egypt is, The Father of Curses."

Brooke laughed. "You must read the first two mysteries in the series. They're by Elizabeth Peters, an actual Egyptologist. I guarantee you'll be blown away."

Eyes batting, Teri chimed in. "The mysteries are super romantic, but serious too, with lots of fun and harrowing things going on. Pip, pip I'd say, quite over the top."

Brooke nodded, then spoke solemnly. "Solange, our resident librarian, says the books are researched, cover authentic historical facts, and reveal past events of the time."

Alex's eyes rolled. "Oh blazes, all I need is lectures from you two." He pulled a desperate look. "I suppose I can't get out of this one. I bet you've already picked out a wig and clothing. Haven't you… er… Mrs. Emerson?"

Kay smiled. "Right my dear Radcliffe. I have indeed. All your fittings are ready and waiting in the bedroom. But I digress. From now on, you must refer to me as Peabody. The name embodies your undying dedication and affection for me."

Teri grinned widely. "Oh, this I've got to see. Look, you guys, go up and change, then come down and model for us. It'll be a trial run. Brooke and I'll finish dinner. And for the next two days, we'll fix dinner, as a bribe. You know, to see the marvelous couple first."

Alex's eyes rolled. He groaned loudly.

"Teri, on Saturday, we'll have to create an authentic Mediterranean menu. My dad and mom loved the foods they had in Iran. So, I'll get my practice arm in gear. It'll be fun." Brooke took on a serious look. "It'll take a little time, though. We have to round up the correct ingredients; Persian prep can be exacting."

"Since you're both doing the cooking, I'll be happy to eat at any time. I'm sure your suggestion includes cleanup as well?" Kay said with an arched eyebrow.

Teri guffawed. "Don't worry, with two famous archaeologists in the house, it'll be top-notch, and exceptional."

Kay shook her umbrella and headed for the stairs. "Now don't forget this is my trusty parasol." She turned and looked at Alex. "You're absolutely right, wigs can be miserable. I know. We can dye your hair black. Up the stairs, Emerson."

Alex's hands shot to his head. "Dye! My god, it'll take time to wash out. I'll be a…a laughingstock." Then he became sober and muttered, "Besides, my chest hairs are turning gray."

"Humph, then we'll dye those, too. Nothing is beyond us, Emerson."

"What! This is an outrage, and, and, unmanly," Alex growled through clenched teeth.

"My word, that's fantastic. Now, get red in the face then snort at me…oh, and yell, 'Bah', or 'Bloody Nonsense'. And any other curse that suits the occasion. It's quite in your manly character." Kay glanced at Teri and Brooke. "Don't we agree, ladies?"

"Yes, oh yes," the girls giggled. "And we know just the right brand of hair color to use."

Alex looked scandalized at the prospect, then his phone rang. "Curse it, er, excuse me, ladies. Ujima, yes? What's up? Huh!" He stared at everyone's questioning faces and shook his phone at them. "I'm taking this in the hall."

Faintly, they could hear him say, "What? Tell me that again." There was silence, followed by a muffled oath. "But that, that's not only improbable but quite impossible. She was fast asleep the last time we checked."

CHAPTER 43

Answers

"Okay. What's going on?" Kay said. They were getting ready for bed. "You were remarkably deft at fielding the girl's questions at dinner. Then you stepped out to get some fresh air? Remember, I know you."

"Uh, let's keep it down," Alex whispered. "Ujima suggested I should tell only you. Somehow, Aunt Maureen has escaped from her bedroom."

"What? The last time we checked, she was fast asleep!"

"Right, but that's not all. Ujima thinks Mary is in on it."

"Fantastic! That's all we need."

"How they did it is beyond me. I didn't hear any vehicles come up the road. Checked for tire tracks on the drive, nada. However, the back window screen is on the ground." He gestured toward the door. "I told the girls we'd take over room duty tonight."

"Clever, but I know they will suspect something's up. You were not silent on the phone."

"I thought it best not to get everyone in an uproar till tomorrow. Anyway, we can tell them at breakfast; hopefully we'll know more by then."

Kay shook her head. "Why am I not surprised? It's been a chaotic and insane month. Especially since Aunt Maureen got here. Okay, so you've checked outside. But how does Ujima know about the great escape?"

"She didn't say. But she's pretty pissed."

"No doubt someone saw them," Kay mumbled. "Cripes, they

must be on foot."

Alex shrugged. "I don't think so. Apparently, they have Mary's truck."

"I'm sure you use the meaning of 'truck' lightly, but you said you heard nothing?"

"No." He rolled his eyes. "And if I were Mary, I would've parked on the road below. They're a sneaky bunch."

"Hmm, any way you look at it, it's double trouble. And on ours and Ujima's watch too. Now the question is, what are the ladies up to?"

"Odd's bodkins. I'll admit I have a respectably sneaky mind, but how should I know?" Alex retorted, then shrugged. "But Ujima did hint she felt that Aunt Maureen was set up."

"I'm not surprised. I never thought Maureen would abduct that child. She had no reason to." Kay became angry. "She's a kind person. Maybe a bit mentally over the edge, but she means well."

"A bit? You're being way generous there." He paused. "It wouldn't surprise me if the ladies are at Willie's. And I'll wager the slippery duo are planning to flush out the real kidnapper or kidnappers." Alex looked puzzled. "You don't seem too excited about this. What gives?"

"Of course, I'm worried about them, but they're over twenty-one. And yes, I'm definitely curious about what their devious minds are planning. Whatever it is, they could get into serious trouble. But what really ticks me off is the idea that Aunt Maureen might have had something to do with the kidnapping."

Alex frowned. "All along, I've had a gut feeling that the whole imbroglio is some sort of frame-up. My enormous nose smells something, and something ain't right. But I'll be damned if I can figure out what... or worse, even know what we can do about it."

Kay shook her head. "Ujima told me she suspects Maureen knows something; like how it happened, and most likely who did it. That's why Ujima confined her here." Kay rolled her eyes. "Ah yes... in our 'familiar home environment', she might loosen up. But dear auntie has not said boo."

"No, silent as the proverbial tomb."

"And unless we have some hard evidence of a person, or persons involved, there's nothing much we can do." Kay thought for a moment. "I'll drop in on Willie. He'll know what's going on. He's been upset about everything since Mary got here."

Alex hesitated. "Uh, well… I'd thought of actually calling Willie. But if they're working on a strategy, they know what they're doing. As you said, they're adults. And if I were planning something, I wouldn't want the added burden of worrying about meddlers and snoops. Ujima and company are on the alert, and prepared… well, those are my thoughts. But do what you think's best." He shrugged, stripped to the buff, and dropped onto the bed.

"Hmm, you have a point. I think I'll lie in the weeds, too… see what's going on." Kay grimaced. "Unfortunately, it's about twenty-four hours away from the Hallowe'en do. And we've got enough worries."

Alex pulled the covers up, and rested, hands behind his head. "Ujima actually wanted to talk to you, but since I answered the call, she felt I could fill you in on…er, the correct information."

"Holding back, are we?" Kay punched her pillow into shape. "Okay shoot, what else did Ujima say?" She threw it at him.

He caught it easily. "Hey, thanks. Well anyway, since the next day is Hallowe'en, Ujima said her department will be mucho busy." He tossed the pillow back at her. "Good catch! So, you and I are to keep our eyes peeled…yeah, peeled eyes sound ghoulishly appropriate; but seriously, if we notice anything odd or peculiar, we are to contact her immediately, if not sooner."

"So, she wants us there as spies. Hah, see anything odd, at a Hallowe'en party?" Kay made a face. "Isn't that some sort of wandering oxymoron?"

"The oxymoron will probably be there too." Alex paused. "Hmm, that's an interesting concept for a Hallowe'en costume. Now, how would one dress as an oxymoron?" He wiggled his brows at Kay. "Yes, keep that thought."

"Well, smarty, you don't know everything. I know Ujima will circulate at the party and Sergeant Reynolds will be in his patrol car and occasionally making sweeps through the parking lot. Our sheriff also deputized two of her dependable bar buddies. They'll be patrolling in unmarked cars on roads around the island."

"A nifty idea. Usually, the major action is in Madrona or Burn. So, the volunteer fire department is on standby." Alex closed his eyes and smiled. "Ergo, most of the island is covered."

"Ha," Kay exclaimed. "Just when everything seems it can't go wrong, good ole Kismet steps in to kick us in the slats."

"Ujima's aware of that." He smiled. "Said she's got her fingers and toes crossed since the 'fit hit the shan'. That's her words." He patted the bed. "Now the Father of Curses wants to take Amelia Peabody in hand."

"Why, Emerson, you're so masterful. How can I resist?"

CHAPTER 44

The Grand Entrance

"You want me to drive, er… Amelia?" Alex asked as Kay opened the passenger door of the Packard.

"Yes Emerson. Most certainly. I think it's imperative you handle the machine. I feel Madame Pompadour will need all the help I can muster." Her utility belt clanked. "I have a sewing kit for him and a filled whiskey flask for me." More clanking as she felt along her belt. "Now that flask, it has to be somewhere. I'm sure I attached it earlier this evening."

Alex laughed and opened the left glove box. A silver flagon flashed in the overhead light. "Ah, are you looking for this, my dear?" Whiskey sloshed in the container. "I hope you intend to share. Spying makes one thirsty."

"What? You're our designated driver. Now, unhand that potable beverage. I always carry it on my belt. As a restorative, of course. We can only surmise what perilous situations we may encounter this evening."

Alex chuckled. "You're right. And I think Thom's Madame whatever costume may be the premier peril of all perils."

The loud laughter ensued as the Packard lurched forward.

"There's Thom," Kay shouted and pointed. "Pull up front. He seems to have difficulty with his costume."

"I think you mean she is having difficulty," Alex replied, wiggling his brows.

"I'll open the door for him/her," Kay said as Alex maneuvered the Packard to the front of the steps.

"My God," Alex exclaimed. "That white wig. It's at least a

mile high and the dress…she looks like a Spanish galleon, with all sails flying. How is she ever going to fit in the back?"

"I'm sure that's exactly what this Opera Coupe was built for," Kay mumbled, then shouted and waved. "Thom, it'll be easier over here… on my side." She jumped out and flipped the passenger seat under the dash.

A wall of perfume engulfed the Packard. Alex plunged his face into his handkerchief. "Gasp, choke, gag… Thom, what is that, er, stunning olfactory scent you've doused yourself with? My nose is running. Egad, I think my eyes are dissolving!" Alex said and cranked down the side window.

With his white-gloved hand on the door, Thom paused. "Really, Emerson, I haven't even entered this perilous machine and you're complaining. It's so plebeian." Plumping his wig, he tsked haughtily. "What other aroma could I possibly surround myself with? Naturalmente, Evening in Paris? It's de rigueur for such a grande gala."

Kay sneezed. "I'm sure you'll cut a large and perfumy swath." She sneezed again. "Are you aware that many people are extremely sensitive to, er… remarkable scents?"

"I know, my dear Amelia. I'm, so not PC; and simply so-so in other ways." He exhaled. "Remember, a girl's gotta do what a girl's gotta do." Thom shrugged and peered down at where the running board should be. "Really, I can't see a damn thing… It's so gauche to wear glasses, and these damn boobs are…"

Kay choked, then collapsed the passenger seat under the dash, and offered a guiding hand. "Here, let me… there's so, so much… er material."

"Bless you, dear Amelia and thank the car gods, for running boards," Thom simpered, then bunched his enormous dress, groaned loudly, and fell into the backseat. His wig bumped overhead and promptly lurched forward. "Accursed thing. It has a life of its own; it acts like a giant worm!"

Kay studied Thom and chuckled. "Possibly, a baby sand-worm, from Dune?" Alex guffawed loudly. "Just being snarky," she said. There was a pause. "Thom, are you sure they wore black-mesh stockings, er, back in the day?"

"My dear Amelia, the French have, and had, everything… back in the day. But oh, my aching arse, they're hot!"

"That's why I've always hated pantyhose," Kay said. "Er,

Thom, could you help bunch your dress so I can get in?" She slammed the car door with emphasis.

Alex cleared his throat. "Thom, who are you supposed to be? Marie Antoinette?"

"My dear and very dashing Emerson, you seem to never, never listen." Thom punched his wig back into shape. "I'm the famous and fabulous Madame du Pompadour. Chief mistress of Mon amour, Louis XV." Thom tsked. "I simply detest Marie. She's so, so capricious."

Alex shook his head, double-clutched, and rumbled down the driveway. "I wonder if someone will come as Madame Defarge. I mean, I'd sure feel bad if you lost your head over tonight's party."

Thom closed his eyes. "Oh, ha,ha, Emerson. Consider the historical, or some would say, hysterical circumstances. After my brave death (cough, cough) from consumption. It was Madame Dubarry and that cheese-cakey Marie who lost their heads over Mon amour...alas, poor Louis."

"Thom, who did your makeup?" Kay asked, trying not to laugh.

"I did Amelia. Once I toured with a theater group." Thom fiddled with his extremely long eyelashes. "Damned sticky things, ouch! They've already stabbed moi in the eyes, twice!" He blinked rapidly. "Ah, that's much better." He hesitated. "Isn't it rather warm in here, or am I having a hot flash?"

"It's all that bedding you're wearing," Alex said and grinned into the rear-view mirror.

"Emerson, you're just jealous," Thom shot back, then popped his enormous fan and whipped it back and forth.

Kay was in awe. "I can't believe it. That creates quite a wind-tunnel effect." Thom nodded demurely and thrashed the fan more about as Kay continued. "You may be right historically, Thom, but hysterically, I know someone is coming as the Red Queen."

Thom, clutching his neck, swallowed loudly, then growled, "If she even comes near me, I'll drop a rabid mouse down her cleavage, the bitch."

"Off with their heads!" they shouted in unison. The threesome broke into uproarious laughter as the Packard rolled to a stop at the boathouse.

A tall, caped vampire stepped out of the doorway, bowed low, and hissed. "Mesdames and Monsieur. Velcome to De Count Dracula's Castle. Vot is the cause of svetch hilarity?"

"I'd know that lisp anywhere," Thom announced as Kay helped him unfold from the backseat. He rearranged his undergarments dramatically. Then, holding onto his wig, straightened up and regarded the vampire with a jaundiced eye. "Aren't your fangs a tad long, my dear?" Thom leaned forward. "My stars, you poor thing. I've never seen such an overbite."

"Yeath, but they're very effectith," Wick shot back with slurping sounds, then drew himself up to look at Thom critically. "Madame, hath the leaning Tower of Pitha fallen on your tete?"

Thom readjusted his magnificent bosom. "Such an insulting question. Really dear, you wouldn't know a Belle if she walked up to you and stepped on your toes. Go play with your puppets."

Vampire Wick clutched his chest. "Maadaam! Like a vooden shtake you shtabbed me to the hearth."

Alex snorted. "Count, before you curl up your toes and turn to dust, I'm going to park the Packard there." He pointed. "In the reserved spot near the door. Don't want any dents or heavy breathers peeling the paint… plus, the ticket-taker can monitor it. By the way, who is the ticket taker?"

"Me, sir!" Rain shouted and jumped onto the path. He was clad as the Green Man.

Thom sniffed and whipped out an oversized lorgnette from between his bosoms. "Oh, my word, it's that hunky gardener, umm… what deliciously tight leotards."

Rain blushed, then replied, in his fractured Scot's accent, "Ha, me lassie, you not be awearin' your usual specs. Couldn't that be a wee bit dangerous this evening?"

Thom thrust Rain aside, hiked his skirts and sailed regally toward the entry. Then he stopped and turned and looked haughtily at Rain. "Dahhhling… dangerous is my middle name!"

* * *

Alex took Kay by the arm as he returned from parking the car. "Wow," he cupped his ear. "It sounds like Thom's entrance not only stunned me but the cheering crowd too. Come on Peabody, let's not dally. Why, the Bloody Gods in Hell, they're playing our song."

"Emerson, tut, tut, your language. It would make a statue blush. And don't you remember? You detest dancing."

"Curse it, Amelia. Along with the waltz, the jitterbug is my thing."

"This isn't a jitterbug, Emerson… it's a polka."

Alex shrugged. "Whatever." He grabbed her waist and jumped into the fray.

* * *

The emcee, dressed as a frog, sported a candy-striped waistcoat and maroon tie. Clasping the microphone in one flipper, he waved with the other. "Thanks to our Daphne and Chloe duet, and their lovely tune, 'Makin' Whoopee', from the romantic movie Sleepless in Seattle." The applause died down.

"And now, our last lip-sync entertainment, for this part of the evening: Madame de Pompadour and her very special interpretation of Johnny Mercer's hit, along with the Pied Pipers; the 1945 classic, 'Personality'. Let's give the Madame a big hand."

Thom minced up the steps to the stage, coquettishly turned to the mic, mimed a welcoming embrace, then threw a kiss to the audience. He paused, fan to chin. The raucous noise faded. Smiling, he batted his outrageous eyelashes. Then, with eyes closed, made three exaggerated hefts to his bosoms. The crowd went wild.

Tsk-tsking and pretending to be scandalized, he tested the mic with kissing sounds and tapped it gently with his fan. There were a few titters, then quiet.

"Dahlings," Thom drawled. "Most of you sweeties out there asked me if I was the beautiful, but extremely slutty, Madame du Barry. Au contraire, mes amis. I'm the sharp-witted and lovely Madame de Pompadour." Thom plumped his wig, then dropped the lorgnettes into his ample cleavage.

Frogee, the emcee, gaped. The audience yelled and stomped.

"Now Dahlings … my, what an enthusiastic crowd we have tonight. Don't forget dears, Dolly Parton has nothing on me." There was more yelling and whistling. Thom paused, fan to chin, then smiled winsomely till the hubbub died down.

"To all the beautiful ladies, beautiful gents and beautiful

LGBTQs out there, this song is for YOU. Hit it jumpers!" The spotlight encircled Thom as Frogee cued the record. With arms extended, Madame Pompadour wriggled seductively across the stage. Her destination of choice, the flipper snapping emcee.

He stopped, twirled mid-stage, then burst out in a deep baritone. "When Madame Pompadour was on the ballroom floor, it was very plain to see she had a rather ah, well developed personality." Thom embellished the lyrics considerably while caressing his voluptuous body. Whistles and shouts of "YOU GO GIRL!" broke out. Kay, Alex and Rain exploded with laughter. "She's a tremendous hit," Alex managed to choke out.

Kay gasped and nodded. "Tremendous is the operative word here, and look, look." She pointed to the stage. "Alex, Alex, you know who the backup zombies are?"

Alex squinted and lowered his voice. "Don't have the froggiest."

"Ugh, that's really terrible," Kay said, laughing. "It's Teri and Brooke. They came, after all."

"I'll be damned. They sure kept it a secret. Oh man, I wonder who's at the house tackling the trick-or-treaters?"

"Oh Emerson, don't be a bore. I'm sure they arranged something," she said, and clapped to the beat.

After the Zombies, Frogee and Thom took their bows, the applause and roars of "more, more, more" died down. Thom salaamed from the stage. He stopped to accept an outsize glass of champagne, adjusted his wig, and triumphally raised the bubbly to the cheering crowd. Laughing and bowing, he wove his way through handshakes, hysterical accolades and slaps on the back. The audience shouted: "Encore, Encore," but soon Frogee spun a hot Cuban number, the yells faded, and everyone danced.

Thom, glass sloshing, wobbled up to Rain and company, who were almost hysterical. They hugged him. He stood back. "Now Dahlings, where can this hoofer rest her dawgs? They are a barkin'."

With a wide grin, Rain pointed to the stairs. "It's quieter in the office loft. Wick's up there having an Alka-Seltzer, and Ujima's joined him." He shook his head. "Man, up there, they had an unobstructed view of your famous act."

"Dears, I always knew I was destined for the theater." Thom

finished his champagne, then with a haughty air, tossed Rain his empty champagne glass.

Kay grabbed Thom's elbow. "Here, I'll guide you up the stairs. It appears one of your heels is loose."

Thom looked down. "I thought it was the champagne. I think someone put a Mickey in it." He sniffed. "I hope he was cute."

Supporting the waving and exclaiming Thom, they started up the haunted staircase. After the first four steps, it bleated, groaned, and vibrated.

Thom patted Kay's arm and smiled grandly. "I'll never, never forget my marvelous debut this evening…" then he stopped and gritted his teeth, "and particularly these goddamn flatulent stairs. Whatever possessed them?"

Laughing ensued. "Wick's the guilty party," Alex and Kay rhymed.

Alex wiped his eyes. "He and his friends thought it was a great idea. They adjusted this morning, and they were fine. But later, part of the mechanism broke. It's difficult to get at. I mean, who thought it would sound like a farting cow?" Alex paused. "Woof. Well, you guys go on up, gotta see a man about a dog." He turned and waved his hand. "I'll see you all later."

At the top of the stairs, Thom pulled out his lorgnettes and focused on the yelling crowd below. Madly batting his eyes, he threw kisses at his shouting fans.

CHAPTER 45

The Envelope Please

Ujima opened the door for Thom. "Saw everything from up here… utterly unforgettable." She smiled and pointed to a well-used easy chair. Groaning dramatically, Thom flung himself on the cushioned seat, tore off his wig, and kicked loose his high heels.

"Merde! Those shoes cost a mint. Of course, you know Sabra, these were just the thing." He inspected his feet. "I don't think I'll ever be able to walk again." He paused until he had everyone's attention, touched his bosom delicately, then smiled. "However, I enjoyed myself immensely. Was Moi convincing enough?" He asked and batted his huge lashes.

Wick shook his head. "Thom, it took away my migraine. The stage is definitely calling… again. Here. Drink your coffee." Wick bowed. "Even with my throbbing head, I've decided. You must emcee Toady's next spring Musicale. 'Thoroughly Modern Millie', it's your venue. You've really got to… Thom, you're a star!"

"Well, I…," he simpered with modesty. "I…I".

Suddenly the door burst open, then slammed shut, violently. They all froze in a tableau.

Magnificently costumed, the Phantom of the Opera grinned malevolently. Rock steady, he aimed a large gun, silencer attached, at Wick.

"This is not a prop, and none of the mob out there will hear if I use it. Everyone over beside the floozy in the chair and try nothing!" There was a loud "pop." A bullet slammed into the wall behind Thom. "This includes you, Sherriff Washington! All hands up, where I can see them."

"Okay, we hear you," Ujima said calmly, and raised her hands high. "What do you want?" He's as mad as a Hatter, she thought, but crap, he handled the German luger like a pro.

"We don't keep any cash here," Wick blurted out. "All our proceeds for the night go into a chute that's next to the ticket-taker. The money is stowed in a safe."

The mouth half of the phantom's smile was crazed. "I don't want your evening's pathetic proceeds. You know what I've come for." He steadily pointed the gun at Wick. "Where is it?"

Ujima only moved her eyes. "Does anyone know what he's talking about?" A bullet whizzed past her head and blasted the woodwork. "Sheriff, carefully put your piece on the floor and slide it to me." Helplessly, Ujima obeyed.

His gun swung back at Wick. "Thanks sweetie, now cut the crap. Where are the directions? She said they're in a white envelope. How appropriate." He sneered at Wick. His voice was icy. "This is the last time I ask. When these lovely 9mms. fly, poof! You're all dead. Then I'll take this place apart."

"Sir," Wick said, wide-eyed. "I don't know who you are, but I think I know what you mean." Everyone stared at Wick.

"Speak," the phantom commanded, his voice a controlled menace.

"Two days ago, I found a large sealed white envelope on my desk, there." His raised arms moved slightly as he nodded in the direction. "It was weird. Addressed to be opened by AVATAR INC. only! Anyone else would be cursed. I'm a puppeteer, so I thought it was a…"

"She wrote cursed?" He cackled hysterically. "Well, in a way, you may all be. That envelope's mine. Where is it?"

"At the risk of being shot, I'll have to find it. I put it in the file cabinet under 'A'. Naturally, I figured…"

"Shut up and move. Otherwise, you're one dead puppeteer."

"I have to lower my hands, and you might think I have a weapon of some sort in the file."

"If you do, it won't do any good. I'll take care of you first, then the others. Of course, I can get it myself." He sneered. "If you haven't noticed, I'm an excellent shot. Move!"

Wick sidled over to the cabinet, opened it, and removed a large white envelope. Kay noticed the letters on the back. They were all different and cut from glossy magazine paper.

The masked man curled his lips. "Put it on the desk, then move back with the others. You'll form a nice shot group."

Ujima's mind raced. By the time she launched herself at the Psychopath, he'd shoot her and, most likely, someone else. But just maybe...

Kay was angry. She recognized the phantom's voice, but the person was too tall, costume too tight and the figure far more athletic than she recalled. If she could provide only a small distraction, like in the movies. But someone would get shot...Christ!

Thom was seething. Maybe he could toss-kick his wig, cause a distraction, then one guy could tackle the loathsome ape. However, that white mask was quite dashing... and where did he find that marvelous cape?

Wick didn't believe in auras, but this man radiated evil. He tensed. He could launch himself forward. If he got shot, maybe he would survive, and the others would live. The distance wasn't that far, then he could...

"Everyone, bite the dust, hands in front, palms down." The shot that followed chunked behind them. Immediately, they were on the floor. The phantom yanked the door open. Below, the crowd noise had ramped up. It was a western stomp, romp, and shout.

Okay, the idiot would not kill them, Ujima thought and looked sideways at Kay. But how would he...

The roar increased, then the door slammed shut. The rug muffled Ujima's yell. "Stay down! Don't anyone move. He'll do less damage if he's not threatened by us."

Thom wiped a watering eye. "Gott em Himmel, how long could they abide this miserable position? His boobs had deflated with a loud pop and now the lorgnettes were stabbing into his pecs, not to mention the eyelashes poking his eyeball... and Mein Gott! Did Wick ever vacuum this rug? Was für ein Scheißkopf!" When extremely angry, Thom swore in German.

CHAPTER 46

Flight

Gun in holster, and envelope stashed in his belt, the Phantom paused on the balcony. He waved to the enthusiastic dancers, then gripped the rope attached to the railing.

A shout arose from the dance floor. "Look, look. Wow, it's the Phantom of the Opera!" Clapping broke out. The crowd yelled and stomped even louder. What a great topper for the evening's entertainment.

"What's he gonna do?" Chorused over the rousing music… then someone yelled, "He's got a knife!"

Froggie's mouth fell agape. The green emcee grabbed the mic. Hopping excitedly, he shouted through flapping lips. "Look out, look out below. He is cutting the rope to the chandelier!"

The phantom sawed steadily at the thick hawser. Wrapped in black and orange crepe-paper, the decoration and hemp fibers yielded easily to his knife. The ornate overhead fixture began to sway and rattle ominously.

The dazed group in the office struggled up to peer out the window.

"He's nuts," Kay said. "He's wrapped the excess rope around his wrist. That rope won't hold. He'll fall."

"That's not a pity… unless he hits someone," Thom said dryly and kicked his shoes under Wick's desk. "Useless things. Hah, now I'm fit and ready to rumble."

Wick stared at the phantom. "It might work. We made a chandelier of paper mâché and doodads. It only weighs about 155 to 170 lbs. And there's a fifteen-foot length before it loops over the pulley. Even though it's attached to that heavy beam, he's taking a devil of a chance."

"Thanks for the briefing on weights and measure," Ujima snarled through her teeth as she tugged at the door. "Damn, he's wedged it shut."

Kay was excited. "The idiot's hands are occupied. Somehow, we've got to stop him."

"Stand back," Wick yelled, then jump-kicked. After several whomps, the frame splintered, and the door shot open; it back-slammed against the adjacent window; glass shattered.

Poised on top of the railing, rope clutched with both hands, the Phantom leaped into space. Cape fluttering, he swooped dramatically toward the crowd. The gigantic chandelier, with the attached disco-ball, was ponderously moving to the ceiling.

"Everybody, everybody, to the sides of the room!" Froggie yelled. He jumped up and down as he pushed his limbs in a swimming motion.

Ujima snarled. "Christ, these god damn farting stairs; if I ever get my hands on the bastard who did this…throttling is too kind."

"Urp," Thom gulped. "It's terrible. They're undulating again. I'm …I'm going to be sick."

Kay clenched her teeth. "Thom, I thought, you were ready. Just hold the barf till we hit the floor. There are people beneath us."

The phantom continued his swing across the room; released the rope, then gracefully made a running landing.

The untethered chandelier plummeted to the floor.

Ujima's eyes had never left the fluttering figure. Reaching the bottom of the stairs, she shouted, "Come on, Kay!" The crowd parted as the two rushed toward the tall double-dock doors. They were open, and the phantom vanished through them.

People pointed to the parking lot. Ujima stooped to help a tall, but portly man struggled to his feet. "You, okay?"

"Yeah, yeah lady. That creep couldn't hurt a fly." His breath wafted in a fog of alcohol.

"Hey, thash a great police outfit." Smiling lopsidedly, he extended a hand. "Shay, I'm Doc, one of the sheven dwarfs." His lopsided leer quickly turned to surprise as his enormous frame stumbled backward, crashing into his friend.

Tool belt, rattling loudly, Kay helped Ujima push Doc and his swearing companion upright.

"Lotta action tonight," muttered Doc's friend. "Shay Ma'am, who are you shupposed to be? Shome kind of kinky dentisht?" He grinned and poked Kay. "Names Bashful, honey." He wobbled and pointed at the retreating caped figure, "Whatt a crazy shtunt, could've killed himshelf." Bashful looked at Ujima. The emanation of fumes was overwhelming. "Shay, you're cute."

"Shut your yap, Bashful", Doc said in a censoring baritone. "Don't you recognize … Holy crap!" The sound of shots echoed across the parking lot; a motorcycle revved up. "Thash guys got a real gun."

"Shit," Ujima exclaimed. "More shots! Damn, he has extra clips for that luger." She had been counting.

CHAPTER 47

The Chase

Smiling, Alex stepped out of the men's room and bumped into Rain. "Man, it's uber noisy out here. Why's the music stopped?" Rain seemed agitated. "Hey, what's up?"

"Didn't you hear those shots? They came from outside." The green-man mask muffled Rain's words.

"Ha, ha bro, you've got a serious case of mush-mouth. But yeah, I heard. Who brought the firecrackers?" Alex said jokingly.

Rain shook his head and uttered something in disgust.

"What? Sounds like a motorbike revving up." Alex shook his head. "Man, you can't hear yourself think in here. Let's get outside. Hey, what's the crazy chandelier doing in the middle of the floor? Man, why's that mob crowding the entryway?"

His questions fell on deaf ears. Rain's lithe, green-clad body was already out the side door to the parking lot.

Alex muttered to himself. Crap, something urgent must have come down. Cursing and shoving, he bulldozed through the crowd after Rain.

Rain ripped off his mask and tossed it toward a loudly swearing lawn dwarf. Desperately, he searched the lot.

"Toady's dirt bike is gone. It was parked next to my sidecar… look, there goes that madman!" Rain pointed at the perimeter road.

"Cripes, you're right. It's that creep. The Phantom of the Opera guy. He wouldn't speak to anyone tonight. See his cape flapping? And he's looking back in that weird mask. What's his problem?"

"Damn, he's not gonna get far." Rain shouted, running to his sidecar. He leaped on and kicked the engine into life.

"Here," Alex said and tossed his pith helmet at another dazed dwarf. "Wait for me," he yelled. Then ran and vaulted into the sidecar's seat.

"When did you get this rig?" Alex shouted at Rain.

"Last week. Use it for hauling plants and making deliveries." He strapped on his helmet. "Hold on!" He shouted over the roar of the engine and the sound of flying gravel. "There's a helmet on the floor. Shit, your weight's gonna slow me down."

Alex, bouncing back and forth, finally put his helmet on and tightened his seat buckle. Then he bellowed. "What an offensive comment. That guy has a gun and you're going to need all the weighty back-up you can muster." There was a haughty pause. "Besides, I've lost ten pounds this month." The bike jolted again, then shot out of the parking lot.

Across the tarmac, another engine fired up. A siren screamed. Flashing blue and red lights lit up the night.

"Sergeant Reynolds has clocked the guy too!" Alex shouted as the patrol car tore out of sight. "Yahoo, we just got ourselves some real firepower!"

CHAPTER 48

Bring On the Posse

Ujima's cell phone chirped as varoom sounds and screeching tires resounded from the parking lot. "Yaahsss. What now Sergeant Reynolds!?" she drawled, helping Kay shove another pawing dwarf aside.

"Some guy in a white mask has appropriated Raymond Toda's motorcycle. Alex and Rain are in pursuit. Rain's bike has a sidecar," he said excitedly. "The caped yoyo is armed and dangerous. Shot a few car tires out as he left the lot. Umm, wasn't that your blue Toyota truck parked by the entry?"

"Yes, Merde! That jerk pinned us down in Wick's office, and ape-swung from the chandelier to escape. We just got down here. I'm at the entrance now. I'll commandeer another vehicle."

"I'm right behind you," shouted Kay, "we'll take my car. It's near the ticket booth."

"Thanks, I just heard from Sergeant Reynolds. I told Isaac earlier to swing by the parking lot on his rounds," she panted. "He'll nail the turd. Where's your vehicle?"

"Right here," she gestured as they rounded the corner. Ujima froze, "Not the Packard!"

Kay yanked open the driver's door. "It's okay. Starts with a switch under the dash."

The engine's growl changed to a hum as Kay settled into the bucket seat. "Bobo Bentley, what a sweet guy, says it can do 100 on the straight-away. He's souped it up."

Ujima scrambled into the passenger jump-seat and slammed the door. "Hey, there is no seat buckle?" Ujima, head down, mumbled something unintelligible. "You're sure you know how to drive this crate?"

Kay neatly double-clutched into gear. "Ujima, what a question. Alex made me learn to drive this thing from day one."

"To answer your second question. Nope, it's a classic." She shook her head. "It's got four gears forward. Hold on to your back teeth, we'll be up to speed in a second... er... maybe a little more. And, this 'crate', as you call it, has a 'grandma gear'; why we can climb mountains."

"I truly hope it doesn't come to that," Ujima muttered. "No seat belts, eh? Good God, we're going fast." She punched her phone pad.

Kay switched on the head and fog lights; The road lit up. "Notice, a new power generator and battery, but still stock," she said excitedly.

"What are you doing? Trying to sell me this heap?" Ujima's phone beeped. "Ten-four, Sergeant Reynolds. We are in pursuit. Keep us informed."

"Copy," his voice jerked back. "The perp just took a left off Cedar Point Road. He's on that logging shoot-off. The one that goes by the old Kraken mine, then up the mountain. Hope you appropriated an off-road vehicle."

"Whew, er, yes," Ujima exclaimed, "er, we're in the Black Mariah!"

There was a prolonged silence with plenty of static. "Great vehicle, built like a truck." His voice was firm and reassuring. "You sit high off the road. And you guys got a Grandma Gear too...uh, who's driving?"

"Kay," Ujima said too forcefully as they lurched onto Cedar Road.

"All right!" He sounded hyped. "She's an ace. Oops, lost sight of Rain and Alex."

"Sounds like we won't get a decent signal here." Kay said, then made a long pause. "Er, Ujima, did I hear a reference to Alex and Rain?"

"Damn dead spots," Ujima exclaimed. "It might get better when we gain elevation. Oddly enough, this road leads to Sayther's bog and there's no outlet. We got him."

"Um, true, but, again, what's this about Rain and Alex?"

Ujima sighed, collecting her thoughts. "I meant to tell you

about the guys. No, really." She made her voice sound casual. "It seems they spotted our perp first and went after him."

"Oh great. Super-duper great. Do they know he has a gun?"

"Yes." Ujima's teeth chattered. "But it's rather difficult for our caped flyboy to shoot back when he's romping up this washboard."

"Sayther's bog? The locals call it the Bog of the Medusa. It's surrounded by real hilly territory. I remember, it was our first summer on the island, Willie Cloudmaker took us there."

Kay gripped the wheel. "Real gloomy place, and it's weird, has lots of quicksand." Kay's voice became lower. "Willie said it was the haunt of the Hooting Woman. Cripes, I wasn't paying attention; just wanted to get the hell out of the there. Never thought of it until now."

Ujima rolled her eyes. "Well, hoot-de-do. We're chasing the Phantom of the Opera into the waiting arms of a Medusa, or the Hooting Woman? Take your pick."

Ujima groaned, head in hands. "Oh, why didn't I grab a desk job in Seattle when I had the chance?"

"Stop whining, girl; we're hot on his trail." Kay paused with a grin. "Hey Chief, gonna deputize me?"

CHAPTER 49

In Sight

"I can see his taillights," Rain whooped and gave his bike more throttle.

"Good show," Alex exclaimed, then clenched his teeth and held on with a death-grip. The erratic jolting had increased.

The motorcycle's steering light flashed briefly over a bullet-ridden sign. "Isn't that the Kraken Sand and Gravel fiasco? Weren't they going to dig a mine here?" Alex yelled.

"Yeah," Rain shouted back. "But the islanders and environmentalists shut em down. It's a crazy place...ends in a bog."

"A bog? Willie once showed us a weird place and..."

Shots zipped over their heads. Rain applied the brakes. The bike spun on the gravel, hopped, then launched into the brush with a roar.

Silence.

"Holy shit, I think I wrecked my bike!"

"You don't say." Came the droll reply. "How about me? I'm picking rocks and shrubbery out of my teeth," Alex groaned. "Ow, cripes, my old back injury. I'll need a year's worth of traction, along with dental surgery."

"Man, I'm...I'm really sorry. Are you okay?" Rain frantically began pulling branches and brush aside.

"Lips cut, body bruised, but I can wiggle my toes and fingers...I'm okay." Alex spat twice as he carefully extracted himself, then paused. "But remember Sunny, okay, is a relative concept."

Rain fumbled for his emergency flashlight and set it low.

"You have cuts on your face and arms. Look! There're bullet holes in my windshield."

"Shut the damn light out. He could spot us down here." There was a click. Alex chuckled then whispered, "Rain you won't win any beauty contest either. You've got blood all over your face."

"Yeah, but our helmet, goggles and this dense brush saved us from worse."

Alex grinned and lowered his voice. "One could look at it that way. But Rain, that was really one hell of a ride." He surveyed the shallow ditch they were standing in and made a quick gesture. "Follow me, keep low, watch your footing. We've got protection, but if I say drop, you flatten. We're going to see what this flying Erik-dude is up to."

"What the hell is that eerie light?" Rain hissed.

"It's the Moon. Gibbous phase tonight. Keep in the shadows. Egad… still dizzy." Alex turned and steadied himself on Rain's shoulder.

"Woof, there he is. Up ahead," Rain whispered and elbowed Alex, who inhaled sharply, smothering a yell of pain.

Both men lowered themselves into crouching positions and watched the Phantom dismount from his bike. He picked up something white from the road, cursed, crumpled the object, and tossed it to the ground. Pointing his gun, he disappeared into the rocky entry to the bog.

"What the hell was that?" Alex whispered. "We're going to have to move closer, yikes!" Alex exclaimed. There was a click. Both froze, straightening.

"Raise your hands, buckoes. Hold it right there," said a deep, surly voice behind them. "Slowly turn, no funny business." A large, silhouetted form stood in the road.

"Christ, Reynolds, it's us," Alex hissed. "Almost had a cardiac arrest. And where's your damn squad car?"

Reynolds patted the ground, they all quickly squatted. He whispered, "My car is blocking the road, blew a tire. And I'm sorry, I wasn't sure who you guys were… after I heard the shots. Thought maybe masked man had partners."

"You knew we were ahead of you," Alex replied.

"Yeah, but you blended into the ground and shadows. It doesn't help that you're covered with leaves, blood, and crap. Man, what in the hell happened?"

Alex nudged Rain, "Ask Green Man here. He has the penchant for shrubberies!"

"Oh," was all Sergeant Reynolds said. Then a faint, hollow mooing sound echoed far down the road.

Alex ran his hands over his face and groaned. "Oh, please don't tell me that's what I think it is." There was a long pause. "Why didn't Bobo Bentley ever fix that horn?" Alex looked to the heavens. "Who's driving that accursed vehicle, anyway?"

"Er, Kay, but not to worry. Ujima's armed, and I've got contact." Sergeant Reynolds smartly pressed his phone, a quiet crackling issued forth. "Hmph, reception isn't worth a shit here either."

"Why did they use that damn horn?"

"Probably signaling my vehicle is blocking the road." He shrugged. "Go figure."

Rain heaved himself up. "How far back is your police car?"

"About 350 feet. The road gets nasty from there on."

"Nasty? There on? Do tell," Alex said, eyeing Rain. There was a pointed silence.

Reynolds gestured. "We'll use the cover of those rocks on the left and maybe get a view. I hope I arrest the jerk before the ladies show up." He gestured with his gun. "Better get a move on, see what's going down."

Rain stuck out his arm. "Hey guys, I'll immobilize his bike. That's easy. Then I can crawl behind that rock face on the right side. I'll be able to see everything from there."

"Not if you get your ass shot off, you won't," Reynolds replied.

"Sergeant, it sounds like a good idea. Rain can use your gun, maybe wing the bastard."

"Not possible. No loaners. And a gunfight at the not-so okay bog isn't my idea of capture."

"You want to capture that evil creep?"

"I just said so."

"Look guys, I've been here before," Rain hissed. "Climbed all over the place, even know why the locals call it the Bog of The Medusa."

"Why?" Alex muttered robotically, as they eased forward. "Cause," Rain hissed again, "see those formations? Kinda looks like stone giants; mucho eerie, but there's a cool trail behind them."

Stealthily, they approached the rock-lined entrance. Sergeant Reynolds gestured with his gun at the opposite ledge.

"Look Rain, you've got an okay idea, but not with my gun, against police procedure. Sneak up there, see what's happening, then get back, double-quick. If you're right about the trail, part of that higher rocky overhang should cover you."

"That's what I said," Rain snorted.

"Don't get huffy, young man, and don't pull any hero crap. You've got a five-minute window, then get your ass back here. I'll cover. Got it?"

"Yeah," Alex cut in, "We'll debrief; then Sgt. Reynolds can tell us what's up next."

Rain crawled over to the bike, took the keys out, shook it at them, then scampered silently to the foot of the rocky cliff.

CHAPTER 50

Reconnaissance

"Man, the dude is crazy," Rain whispered to himself. The Phantom, gun in one hand and a branch in the other, was testing the ground in front of the bog.

The place always gives me the creeps, Rain thought. If one tried to cross from the grassy edge, it was curtains. Although clumps of grass appeared to mark a path across the mire, it was unstable. He'd tested it by heaving larger and larger rocks. The small missiles would splat, the heavier ones sucked in with a slurping sound. Also, the place stank of rotting vegetation. Rain shook his head. The bog was a horrid place.

What was the cape-man staring at? Ah… ahead. Something moved in the thickening fog.

There it was! Suspended over the bog's surface, a large, nebulous shape slowly drifted from side to side. Rain squeezed his eyes and blinked to focus on it. Long hair surrounded the hideous face. It wasn't a Medusa, but the Hooting Woman. She clutched an enormous basket in her pale hands. Rain had seen the exact creature in Wick's play, only puppet size.

* * *

"Psst, what the hell are you guys doing?"

Alex gasped, wide-eyed. "Cripes, Kay, you guys can't creep up on someone like that. Man, instant brown shorts!"

Ujima held her pistol, pointed at the ground. "Sorry boys. Can't help you with any laundry problems." She smiled to herself. "Now, what's the situation?"

Reynolds pointed at the opposite rock formations. "Rain

went behind there to scout things out. He'll be down to report…
in a minute, I think."

"Here he comes," Kay whispered and gestured toward a
pale figure.

Rain swallowed hard and spread his hands as he approached
them. "Jeez, the guy is just standing there and pointing his gun
at some sort of apparition. Man, it looks just like the Hooting
Woman. But, enormous."

"What?" they all exclaimed together.

"Yeah, it's obviously a fake. It's exactly like the puppet in
Wick's play, and it's holding some sort of woven basket. Couldn't
make out too much, as the fog is patchy." He shook his head. "I
think that crazy man is gonna try to cross the bog."

Ujima turned to Kay. "I'm definitely going to reapply for that
desk job."

"Where's the Packard?" Alex asked out of the side of his
mouth.

"A good walk back. We would have gotten much closer if
Sergeant Reynolds hadn't blocked the road." Ujima sneered and
rolled her eyes.

"I had a flat," Sergeant Reynolds hissed back defiantly, then
two shots reverberated over the bog. They dropped.

"Christ, he's shooting again," Ujima exclaimed. "If I'm right,
and he hasn't a third clip, he's about out of ammo. I'll sneak up.
Reynolds, cover me. I've been wrong before." A scream echoed
over the bog.

"Come on, guys, we'll tackle him," Alex shouted and charged
forward.

"Wait, wait. Take it easy!" Ujima panted, as she struggled to
hold Alex back. "This isn't army scrimmage time. It sounds like
he fell into the bog."

Alex, Rain and Reynolds, wide-eyed, agreed.

Ujima nodded an affirmative, then showed a quiet approach.
In the lead, and gesturing, she followed the rocky edge. Then
peered cautiously around the last corner.

Faint moonlight still illuminated the swamp. But a thickening fog was creeping in.

Roughly, about twenty feet into the morass, Ujima could
make out the hooded head of the Phantom. There was no struggling and with the cape spread out behind, he was slowly sink-

ing into the mud.

Rain shouted, "Quick, find a sturdy branch, about 10 feet long. I…I think I can reach him from that rock ledge to the left. I've been out there before".

"No, don't, don't," Kay said, shaking Rain's arm, "It's useless, useless. He's gone."

"Ye gods," Ujima exclaimed and pointed, "That's the thing."

At the far end, in and out of the fog, glided a white shape. Strands of gray-black hair framed a greenish face, owl-like eyes stared above a tulip shape of blood-red lips.

A wicker basket, partially submerged, floated beside the monster's shape. The spilled contents of what looked like paper files seemed to float, but they, too, were slowly sinking into the mire.

"Look. Look up there," Rain said with a shout and pointed. Strung across the bog, from branch to opposite branch, hung the remains of a large fishnet.

"It has to be what's left of whatever moved that Tsonoqua thing," Rain said excitedly. "See, it was suspended from those trees. I bet, if we searched, we'd find ropes and pulleys." He took a breath. "Now if that hair was snakes…"

"Thanks, Rain. We don't need any further analysis," Ujima said dryly. Then, pondering the situation, she shook her head.

"Okay, everyone. Listen up. Whatever happened here, tonight, we're finished." There were a few mumbled protests. "No, the fog is getting thick, fast. And I'm not losing anybody else. There's nothing useful that can be done now."

She poked the stunned Sergeant Reynolds. "You and I will be here tomorrow morning, bright and early. The hook and ladder boys will be here, too. They can drag the area; recover the body and whatever else."

Ujima took a deep breath. "No one, and I mean no one, is going to risk their necks in this mud-trap tonight."

Reynolds gulped. "Shouldn't someone at least say a prayer?"

"Whatever floats your boat," Alex said and turned his back to the entrance. "Ujima's right, though. We can't do, or see, a damn thing."

Kay spread her hands in agreement. "With this fog, we're going to have a real fun time just following the blasted road back." She paused, then turned to Rain. "You're right, whatever happened tonight was a set-up, a bait… and the phantom, the victim. But we can't forget that he almost shot everyone over that stupid message!"

"We hear you, Kay," Ujima said, then flashed her hand-light off and on. "This high-intensity torch isn't worth a crap in this fog. Sergeant Reynolds, is yours any better?"

"Nope, turns everything into a white glare."

Ujima pointed hers at the ground. "Well, at the very least, these will help us see the road."

Kay grimaced impatiently. "You'll have to admit, that woo-woo thing back there was well crafted. But who fired and who screamed?"

"The phantom most likely," Ujima answered, "or the manip-ulators. I have a hunch about who they are. And I'm sure there long gone." She hesitated. "Did everyone see those papers strewn across the bog?"

Rain held out a crumpled white wad. "Ma'am, I just picked up this one crumpled near the motorcycle. And it is strange."

Ujima flattened the thick paper and flashed her light. "It's a photo of a child. This is interesting… beside it and below are statistics, and then detailed descriptions."

"The picture looks like baby Renée," Kay exclaimed, as she looked over Ujima's shoulder. "It is! Read what it says."

Ujima scanned the sheet. "You're right! It's quite a detailed compilation of information on Renée. The letterhead reads, Angelic Avatars Animations."

"Here, ma'am, I pulled another out of the mud."

"Thanks Rain. This one's a bit more difficult to read."

"The paper looks really old," Kay said. "But it's another photo of a child, with stats and everything. Wow, the date! Is that 1975?"

"I can't believe it," Kay said, aghast. "This document is dated around the time Brooke was stolen. That rotten man must have many more in the files out there…"

A muffled roar echoed over the bog. Everyone looked up.

"It's another motorcycle!"

"Yeah, a Harley," Rain said excitedly.

"Confirm that," Sergeant Reynolds chimed in.

"But where's the revving sound coming from?" Alex was puzzled.

Rain pointed. "Behind that ridge I just climbed."

"Yeah, so?" Alex growled.

"There's another old logging road."

Alex threw up his hands. "Crap. Obviously, someone is getting away."

"No doubts about that buster." Ujima exclaimed, hands on hips. "And…" three shots echoed over the bog, followed by another roar… with a highly discernable rattle.

"Good God! Now what the hell is that?" Alex exclaimed.

"I'd say a truck that needs a tune-up, and possibly an overhaul," Rain said.

"What do we have…a circus back there?" Sergeant Reynolds sputtered, looking at Ujima.

She scratched her chin. "Hmm, I think I'm seeing what's going on." She flashed her light at everyone.

"Okay, let's move. We've got a tire to change, and pull a bike out of the brush, and then Kay will turn the Packard around and you'll all play follow the leader. Her rigs got fog lights and the ability to crawl like a caterpillar." She paused. "Don't we Kay?"

"Yes, ma'am!"

Sergeant Reynolds turned to Alex. "After I put on the spare, we can horse the bike out. I've always wanted to use that extendable tow bar, the one Bobo Bentley made for me. It's in the trunk."

"What about me?" Rain asked.

"Why, man, you're our main muscle," Alex chirped. "After all, us older folks are forbidden from any heavy lifting."

CHAPTER 51

Plans

Jinx Buckwass released his seatbelt, closed his eyes, and listened to the drone of the plane's jets. He smiled. The newspaper in his lap brought back memories of headlines from over a month ago.

'Unidentified body found on Alki Beach', the front page of the Seattle Star shouted. Naturally, the body would be hard to identify. The currents had carried it a long way. Jinx laughed aloud. Talk about getting the lead out. Seated next to him, the lady who snubbed him since she came on board looked askance. He covered his mouth. True, it was not a charitable thought, but lead was the only way to sink the body.

Fish and saltwater, not to mention crabs and other creatures, would have satisfied their appetites. He shook his head. But there had been no other solution. The Magpie had to disappear. He would have destroyed everything. All the planning, all his years of work. Jinx chuckled as his bony hands rattled the paper he'd picked up at the terminal's kiosk. Ach, and in trying to blackmail me. The Magpie made a fatal error. It was the irony, the irony of simple justice.

Jinx made a derisive sound. Then there was the inept duo, monster Maureen and the sham of a shaman, Mary. Those two witches thought they could capture him alive and turn him into the police, destroy his work of genius, his reputation. Jinx smirked. He knew long ago that Maureen had stolen some of his paper files. She must have planned to use them at an opportune time. But what she didn't know was early on, he'd trashed all the electronic evidence. At the very beginning, he'd been careful with children's dossiers. The electronic files contained nothing traceable. He'd deleted contacts and evidence weeks before the delightful escapade to the bog.

He was far cleverer than they, his powers were much greater. Even if someone had made traceable copies of plans to expose his operation, they would never find him. Nor does his thumb drive. Long ago, he'd developed strategies for such an eventuality.

The Bog of the Medusa on Hallowe'en night was a superb place for his grand exit! The witches set up a silly trap. But it was the thrill of the unknown. The challenge of facing and solving the glitches that would inevitably arise.

It was so easy to weigh the pockets of his cape, then carefully ease it into the bog. Delighted, he hid in one of the many clefts in the rocks to watch it being sucked down.

It had been comical to see the woman's frantic attempts to manipulate the overhead nettings, and then fail to snare his supposed body, before it sank.

He guffawed again when Sherriff Washington and her amateur posse departed. It was easy to restart his emergency motorcycle. But the cursed fog was a hindrance. He had to drive down the mountain road.

Then the two witches made their last attempt to capture him. He thought he'd have time to trash Mary's distributor, but she was a cagey creature. Then when he got to the flats, he easily outdistanced them. And he'd made sure he had plenty of time to catch the alternate ferry from Burn to Tacoma.

His plan had worked perfectly. He'd stashed his other bike earlier, on the other road. Nothing like extra insurance.

He folded his newspaper and looked out the plane window. It would be delightful to see Roma and distribute his gifts and greetings. Afterward, before his final last exit, there would be much work to be done. Picking up his fake passports, thus making complete his identity shift. Then shutting down any minor European contacts, payoffs… ach; then to my special remodeled Villa on the island of Sardinia, to settle permanently.

Sardinia. Its pre-history was like the island of Bradestone. There still existed evidence of ancient trading sites. It was, and now too, a major place of social and material exchange among multiple peoples and civilizations. Jinx nodded, from before the last ice age, if he remembered correctly.

And today startups were new happenings. Jinx rubbed his hands in expectations of future exciting opportunities. The island was in a strategic part of the Mediterranean. And was still a place for illicit trading. Indeed, it was where multi-lingual bartering of goods and services, and funding of wars happened. He looked forward to this crux of many cultures and world travelers.

Jinx squirmed in his seat. Wasn't that ironic…yes, from Bradestone to Sardinia? Two islands that had ancient tribal negotiations, and today's methods of trade, were in common. Although Bradestone was small potatoes. Ach, over the entire planet, interactions and the deviousness of mankind's nature never varied much.

Jinx frowned. His attempts to implicate Maureen in the sales of children. Then, pulling his last brilliant coup, the kidnapping of baby Renée all failed. He shrugged. But it was exhilarating to see the media guessing who the phantom at the party was, the supposed sequence of events, and the "no comments" of the badgered Sheriff Washington.

Jinx chuckled to himself. But Sheriff Washington was a wily one and, in the end, she and Kay winkled him out. He nodded; they could be as devious as he.

Turning and putting on his best people's smile; Jinx offered his newspaper to the lady beside him. She held up her hand, shook her elaborately coifed head, and thought, 'how could anyone accept anything from such a horrid little man?'

The woman, Claire Armstrong, glanced back at her friend Elsa, in an aisle seat. Elsa motioned for her to sit in the now-vacant seat beside her.

"Pardon … excuse me," Claire said in a grim authoritative voice, and as graceful as she could, stepped into the aisle. She waved at Elsa.

My word, she thought. That cadaverous little man, besides his newspaper, had offered her a measly bag of chips. How uncouth. Well, I deserved it, traveling on a lower-class airline. She couldn't wait to tell Elsa about her horrible and unmannered fellow passenger.

Jinx leaned back and sighed. Ah, a little more room, he

thought. Then a burly gentleman asked if the seat beside him was taken. Jinx reluctantly mumbled no. He'd known his brief feeling of space wouldn't last.

The man held out a large hand. A smile lit up his handsome, weather-beaten face. His clothes were neat and clean. The sleeves of his blue-checked shirt casually rolled up to the elbows. His limbs were deeply tanned, with a large anchor tattoo on his left forearm. Jinx nodded; this friendly fellow, no doubt, was a man who spent most of his life at sea. Definitely a clueless tar.

"My good friend, my name is Sven R. Fossland. At your service," he said in a deep, smiling voice.

Jinx wanted to scream; his hand was being crushed. Concealing the pain, he smiled widely. "Very pleased to meet you. I'm J. L. Buckwass retired business consultant." He blithely lied and quickly yanked his hand back from the numbing grip.

"I'm a seafarer myself," Sven said. "Worked ships and docks all over the world. That's why I'm on my way to Sardinia. I'll be interviewing for an Arabian outfit." He winked. "Oil, right now is king, and this outfit means big bucks for me."

"Sardinia, curious… that's where I'm intending to go… eventually. I must take care of a few things in Italy, then I'm on my way." Jinx had looked down the aisle to see where Mrs. holier than thou had gone. Then he spun back and found Sven staring intently at him.

The man quickly studied his large hands. "You know, friend, your voice, even your face, seems familiar. Are you from the states?"

"You could say that. I'm actually from Canada, but I worked, err… used to spend a considerable amount of time in Europe. No end to problems. Finally, heading into retirement. I need a well-earned rest," Jinx paused. "Not to brag, but even though I was busy, I was much in demand. I worked only on the East Coast. Specifically, in New York and its surroundings."

Sven shook his massive head. "I never forget a face. My mother said it was my cross to bear." He paused for a considerable length of time. "Do you know Byron Roberts? He lives on an island in the Pacific Northwest, called Bradestone and is a student at a university between Tacoma, Washington, and the Sea-Tac airport." He looked intently at Jinx. "Interesting name, Tacoma. It comes from Tahoma, which is the English interpretation of the local Salish name of their sacred mountain. Now the city, Seattle, is named after a Duwamish tribal chief who…"

Rarely had panic mixed with hatred combined in his mind. Jinx's thoughts became incoherent. They kept bumping into each other. Who is this man? What does he know? Never seen him in my life! How does he know about Bradestone? Is he a police officer? Did that country bumpkin of a Sherriff send him here?

Jinx shook his head. "No. But my geography is not very good. Bradestone, you say? Sounds English to me, and I don't know any Byron what's-his-name." His smile became ingratiating. "Sorry, you've confused me with someone else." He made an indulgent chuckle. "Now, if you'll excuse me, I'm going to take a nap. I can't be concerned about what I don't know, and I want to be reasonably refreshed when we get to Rome."

"Oh, Mr. Jinx Buckwass. I think you know a lot more than you're saying. Does murder come to mind?"

Jinx gasped and clutched the arms of his seat. "What are you talking about? You know nothing," he hissed.

Sven's expression of bonhomie instantly became threatening. "Oh Mr. Buckwass, but I do. I agree, this may become troublesome for you. But, months ago, I saw a newspaper write-up in the Seattle Star. Something about a body being discovered on Alki beach." Jinx sputtered.

"Shut up, you little monster," Sven growled back. "You see, I saw you push that man into the bay and watch him sink. I was that drunken sailor you waved to on the dock. I knew something was up and pretended to stagger away, but I hid in the shadows of the hotel. You were dressed like a tall woman, but I could see the way you walked. You were faking it."

Jinx became white with fear. "This, this is preposterous. You're harassing me. I'll call the steward."

"No, you won't, because I have this." He brought out a snapshot. It was Jinx and Maureen when married; much younger, but their faces were clearly discernable.

"Let me see that," Jinx demanded and snatched the photo; it disappeared. His smile was smug again. "Now you see it, now you don't. Ho hum, whatever it was, it's disappeared forever." His sneer was akin to a crocodile's smile.

"Mr. Buckwass. I know all about your stagey tricks. That was only a copy. And there are many more original pics in the safe deposit box of a certain bank; along with a complete folder related to the murder. Included are documents covering the other incriminating things you got up to on Bradestone Island." Sven shook his head. "Oh, don't start plotting my funeral. You see, I have a contract with the bank. If they don't hear from me monthly, I contact them, but in a special way. If there's a glitch, all the material in the box goes post-haste to Sherriff Washington. She'll know what to do," Sven said, with his own crocodile smile.

"Why this, this is impossible," Jinx whined. There was a long pause, and he lowered his voice. "What, what is it you want from me, blackmail?"

Sven's smile became cordial. "Well, it's simpler than that. You've just hired a trusted companion, me. A person to ease your path along the highway of life. One who assists in your golden years, such as they are."

"But this is preposterous. I'll take legal action," Jinx sputtered.

Sven held his finger to his lips. "Shush now, you wouldn't want anyone to witness the first signs of your descent into dementia. Do you?"

Sven leaned back and smiled with satisfaction. "Yes, I thought so. Of course, I've had great help in keeping tabs on you. Remember Byron Roberts, the reporter who interviewed you for the newspaper? Ah yes, I see you do. Isn't he a very resourceful and savvy scout?" Sven nodded at Jinx's sour face and smiled. "Me too, and my guess is, he'll go a long way in life."

Sven turned an innocent smile on Jinx. "I had a chat with him recently. Found he was also doing favors for Chief Washington." Jinx mouth was dry, and he was trembling.

"I want you to know that my salary will be extremely generous, but welcome." He exhaled. "Naturally, there will be other, err… unexpected monetary expenses." He became contemplative, then philosophical. "Hmm, it seems life can deal a man with a loser's hand; especially when one spikes his cards … with murder."

CHAPTER 52

A letter to Kay

"Thank you for handing me the first page. Me oh my… this appears to be a lengthy tome," Alex said, then cocked an eye as he sat down next to Kay. The old veranda loveseat wheezed. Its only redeeming feature was its view of Scoon Bay.

Kay nodded and brandished the other pages. "I thought so too. After a quick peek, I immediately bolted for the kitchen and put up a large pot of tea. Our favorite, Murchie's # 10. It should have steeped by now. Needs a well-muscled arm to lift…oh, and there's scrambled eggs with sausages in the warming oven, and don't forget the jam and brioche. I feel we're in for a lengthy breakfast. So, while you play the speedy fellow, I'll sort through this other post."

"Alas, I'm relegated to the role of butler." Alex moaned and slapped his forehead. He smiled and bounced up into a military stance with salute. "What would madame desire, sugar, a pitcher of cream, warm plates, appropriate utensils to go with it?"

Kay sighed. "Get a move on, or I'll demote you to Master Michael Finsbury's butler, Mr. Peacock, one of your favorite characters. Oh, and don't forget the napkins."

Alex slumped his shoulders then muttered in a high, shaky voice, "Very…very… well, m-m-m madame. I'll just…just t-t-take a moment to collect myself, sigh, then shuffle off to get a t-t-tray and…was there any anything else?"

Kay stared over the top of her glasses. "Move it, or I'll demote you to Igor."

Alex threw another hasty salute. "Aye, aye!" Smiling, he disappeared in a flash. Kay got up and moved a large coffee table nearer to the loveseat.

* * *

Nestled in with mugs of tea, and nibbling on breakfast, Alex adjusted his new glasses. "Shall I go first, since I have the top page?"

"That, my dear, is a Prince of a suggestion."

"Oh, now I'm a Prince, am I? Got promoted, eh?"

"Get on with it. This can't take all morning. Warm November days end in chilly evenings. I'm sure you've noticed."

"Very well then, ahem." Alex cleared his throat.

Dear Kay and Alex,

Thank you for your hospitality and for bearing up with me during my visit. As you know, I was on the verge of a nervous breakdown. Part of it I'm sure, because of changing my life. Downsizing, then moving back to what's left of my village, and reuniting with my friends, who are still there.

I admit I was full of trepidation, but knew in the long run, I would be happier. Then the worse, the impossible, happened. I discovered my husband, Jinx, was alive and had returned to Bradestone. Possibly again, to ply his criminal and hideous trade. It is only right that I tell you about his villainous background. It started everything.

"He was evil personified!" Kay blurted out.

Alex snorted. "Do you want to read this?"

"No, no. Sorry, you're doing fine."

When my mother was young, she inherited, then operated, a gold mine. It was traditionally passed down through her Tlingit mother's family. The location of the mine was a secret, its initial discovery a tribal legend. Because it was a revered, almost hallowed place, only women worked the mine.

My father was from Norway, and being an adventuresome person, learned to speak many languages. He had left his homeland at fourteen to explore the world. Even though he was white, he became an important player in our tribal area of western coastal Canada. My mother, who was part Tlingit and Russian, possessed a powerful personality and, because of her inherited wealth and privilege, was also an important force.

It was during a confrontation on the coast where my mother met my father. His amazing strength, size, and intelligence attracted her. Too, my father's philosophy of life was much like hers.

An amusing legend is that she knocked him out, threw him over her shoulder, then took him back to her people, and married him. When anyone related that tale, my father would only smile and nod his head in agreement.

Alex peered over the top of his glasses. "So, we have not only indigenous persons in our family, but a Viking as well?"

"Quelle surprise. Nobody's perfect. Carry on, my dear."

Their marriage was a ceremony of legend. Naturally, there were many objections to their union. Horrendous intimidations from the braves, our powerful shaman, and the elders. Before their marriage, my father had quietly approached, then eventually enchanted our shaman. Too, I believe, my mother's offer of gold swayed the powerful man. Naturally, there remained much dissent among the elders. But my father's success in most contests with the strongest men, and also bonding with certain influential tribal members, gained him great esteem.

After the backing of our shaman and a contentious four-day conference with our chief and the elders, my father was chosen to be our spokesperson to the white man's world. My parents became a powerful force to be reckoned with. The tribe flourished after their union.

Even though prosperous, we lived simply. Luckily, our tribe's winter village and its environs were small and remote. My father, mother, and elders, through a variety of schemes, formed a cadre of individuals to help keep outsiders away. To maintain this protective group strategy, meetings were held in an abandoned salmon cannery, miles from our village. The privileges granted and the dispensations of responsibilities were like what our great chieftains accomplished in earlier times.

Naturally, our tribal life aroused suspicions and unwanted attention. Therefore, we relied on an already ancient legend of a prehistoric tribe, ghost people, who lived in a perilous place by the sea. The members of this tribe appeared to be normal travelers, but if encountered would bring disease, misfortune and death to you and your tribe.

We had the wealth and skills to perpetuate this myth. The name of our tribe inherited from ancient times was kakikt-pipel-ev-awaesala.

"Egad. I can't pronounce this," exclaimed Alex.

"Hand it over. It can't be that difficult." There was a rattling of paper. "Oh… I see. It's obviously, er…k um pipe exceptional salad. See, it's easy," Kay muttered.

Alex's jaw dropped. "You don't say? That was amazing. Do carry on. I can't possibly match your acumen. And your versatile skills at articulation are beyond me."

"Now you're being sarcastic."

"You don't think? Okay, tomorrow we show it to Willie. Bet he'll know how to say it, and what it means."

Kay paused as she arranged the rest of the pages. "Humph, sorry, that was lousy, but…"

"That had crossed my mind," Alex said, closed his eyes and sat back.

"Now, if you would kindly not be so snide and let me finish. I actually know what it means."

"Sure, sure, and the moon is a wheel of Parmesan cheese."

"Well, my dear. If you had just read further."

Alex opened one eye. "Yes?"

"It says here that meaning, roughly translated, is the reapers of the foam of the sea."

"Really? Well, that's pleasant. Read on… McDuffie."

I was fifteen, and naturally very excited about life. Many considered my height, facial features, and demeanor in my tribe and surrounding peoples as attractive… with signs of latent powers.

One spring, a far distant tribal group, more inland and to the north, gave what one would call a fantasia. All the friendly people who lived near and in the woods were invited. Actually, it is also called Potlatch. But could not be called such, since the celebration was illegal.

Again, this was because of the sad notions of the white man and his religions. And if the celebration was discovered, there would be horrific consequences. Unsurprisingly, as a teenager, I wanted to go. Fortunately, since my father was white and had traveled most of the world, he was well aware of the consequences and dangers. Thus, he advised me, the tribe and the elders as well.

"Damn, those Vikings not only got around, but they were also persuasive to boot. Possibly the first to see the continent from the Atlantic side."

"Alex, your observations astound me. I saw where archaeologists found a site, north of… or in northern Canada, I believe, and...."

Alex waved a hand. "Yes, yes, the finds are still indeterminate. But please continue, this story is fascinating."

My parents finally yielded to my pleas, and as long I was chaperoned by my aunties, I could go.

We all used disguises and misdirection to avoid the white man sniffing around. There were territorial police, vigilantes, and troublesome outsiders to deal with. Missionaries were dangerous and malicious.

Alex sighed. "Nothing ever changes, does it?"

"No, my dear. Stupidity and extremism never come to any good."

The dance was dazzling. Many tribes attended. Performers and audiences wore their native costumes. There was feasting, gift-giving ghost stories and plays with masks and puppets. Many of the presentations were in the traditional ways we do things.

We communicated through dependable individuals who traded with all tribes. Remember, any native rituals, teachings of languages, and cultural preservation were illegal by the white man and again fraught with horrendous punishments. They took away children, used terrible beatings, incarceration, even killing some of those who had given or taken part in a Potlatch. Many of the missionaries used the worst punishments.

"Curses. Why do humans not treat others as human? Don't they see we all suffer from pain and can bleed when injured?" Alex shook his head in disgust.

"At the risk of sounding pessimistic, humanity seems not to care. But there are pockets of good," Kay said and nodded.

"You're like me, Kay, always an optimist...but with experience."

We were not naïve. There were always spies and sellouts in these gatherings, but the younger warriors took care of them... in various ways. Toward the middle of the evening, some of the younger braves introduced white-man jazz-dancing. I remember vividly, there were strong objections from the elders. But our chief and his close advisors quelled them. The young people had brought a wind-up phonograph with 78 rpm records from America and Europe. I was ecstatic, and that was the beginning of my misfortune.

Attending was a pale young man. A friend of an important guest who vouched for him. He was handsome, shorter than I, and with sharp features. He had the demeanor and enchantment of the hawk-raven, and jet-black eyes that seemed to explore one's very soul. His manners were exceptional, and he danced like the American Fred Astaire. He sought me out and taught me every move, every nuance of the dance. It only took a few moments, and I could follow him instinctively. It was as if we were one being. I was instantly in love. My father and mother liked him, but our wise shaman was wary.

When I became pregnant, my father convinced Jinx to become a member of our clan and marry me. In the first few months, I was ecstatic. Too, Jinx had a dynamic way with my father and was welcomed by the chief and his group of elders and advisors. However, our shaman still held his distance.

"A smart shaman," Alex remarked.

"There are very few that aren't," Kay shot back.

It was during this time that I rescued a girl and her younger brother from a rock ledge near the sea. My husband took a great interest in them and their strange abandonment. With his contacts and charming manners, he found, from various witnesses, that the parents had gone to get supplies and gasoline but changed course and anchored near a small island. They had seen smoke, and a person hailing from the beach. There, they encountered, some said, an island hermit. The rumors are that he suggested they go to a nearby village to get gas and rations.

Before departing, they rowed the children to the beach, where I found them. The parents promised to return for a picnic after refueling, but never did. And there is no village anywhere near where the two children were dropped off.

Surprisingly, we found, the young people's native language was Norwegian. And they spoke excellent French and English as well. This impressed my father, and he helped them with translations of our tribal language and speaking and understanding our ways.

My father, and our chief too, used trustworthy contacts to make discreet enquiries at the few villages along the coast. Their efforts came to nothing. Shortly afterwards, it was decided we would adopt the two and make them members of our tribe.

At first, they were homesick and crying. My mother's family and I cared for them and learned a little more about their background. Then my husband also took an interest in their plight and told my father he had connections and confidants on Canada's east coast and could glean more information, maybe find clues as to the poor children's relatives.

My husband was as wily and as clever as my father. And with my mother's help, petitioned the tribe for permission and money to pursue my husband's admirable proposal of locating where the children were from and who they were.

In less than a month, he returned from Montreal with photos of a farm and a family that lived in Norway. They had a similar surname. Then, with more research, the farm turned out to be owned by the uncle of the lost children. Through tears and much questioning, the children affirmed that the family in the picture was indeed their father's brother and wife, who owned the adjoining farm.

After endless legal wrangling with officials, all papers and ancillary problems were taken care of in Vancouver and Ottawa. Money is indeed a great persuasive factor.

My husband nobly offered to escort the children to the east coast, where they would be put on a ship to Norway. It seemed an admirable and heroic gesture. However, I didn't realize until much later that my husband had amassed a considerable amount of money for this venture. That is when, for the first time, I noticed the beautiful look in his coal-black eyes turn to something furtive and sinister.

"Tsk, tsk, the needy are greedy. They can never stop wanting more," Alex said.

Before our marriage, my husband made use of a man who traveled between tribes, even tribes that carried on long, ongoing disputes. The man was simply known as The Magpie. My husband, Jinx, assured me he was a friend. However, he was regarded as an anathema but still valued for the secrets and stories he traded; including any new information he brought from the outside world. It was later I discovered my husband employed The Magpie for providing information on Canadian and Alaskan children.

Some tribal idealists felt that with the proper information that people like The Magpie provided, they could lawfully rectify the terrible things and injustices they had endured since the coming of the white invaders; and at the very least, some devastations could be legally addressed. But as we know, history shows how futile and inequitable that was.

"Whew, just read the native people's accounts."

"I have, I have," Kay said. "It tears one's heart to shreds."

We lived in a small house, a gift from the chief, on the edge of our village. I was raising our son, Ned, and was thrilled. My husband worked for several tribes and developed business contacts on his own. It was then he was away for long periods. Occasionally, he would bring a child of a relative or friend home and ask me to babysit. I was more than delighted, as it gave Ned children to play with.

The parents of these children always had difficulties, and my husband developed a certain cachet of being able to reconcile families and help them amicably resolve their problems. He said that he was first inspired by the rejoining of the two children with their uncle in Norway and it was emotionally rewarding for him. Later, he resolved to make it his pursuit. A charitable way of restoring abandoned or homeless children… possibly even to their rightful families. Failing that, Jinx would locate magnificent homes that would adopt them.

It took me a long time to realize that his so-called 'altruism' had warped into actually stealing children to meet the demands of wealthy couples who could not adopt or have children themselves. Thinking back, I could see why the children were mainly of Caucasian extraction or could easily pass for white.

There was a little girl, in my care, a very sweet and delicate thing. She lost her arm in a terrible accident, and it was my fault.

We were picking berries and she and Ned were playing near a defunct ore-processor. I heard a noise, then a scream and a cry for help. When I found them, Ned was in shock. Part of a ramp had collapsed, and the girl's arm was crushed. I've never forgiven myself. In trying to help the girl, she died. Jinx told me she was an abandoned orphan, and I had been careless and neglectful, and I had to bury her myself.

"That beast. Remember the incident at The Madrona Inn with the doll's arm that Ujima had to resolve? That was when my aunts, first breakdown happened."

"I do indeed. Jinx was even more despicable than I thought."

Since then, my husband has held this horrifying accident over me. He threatened to tell the chief and my father whenever he found it useful to do so. He prevented me from revealing the misery of our marriage and even his dreadful occupation by saying he would take away our son, Ned.

That other night at the bog, Mary and I tried to capture him and expose his crimes to the police. Sadly, because of his trickster nature, he easily escaped. Your chief of police, Ms. Ujima Washington, knows the entire story. Cousin Mary e-mailed her a copy of this letter and the information she requested.

Life can be marvelous, serene, and horrible, as all Earth's people can attest. I love the natural world but have a little hope for this creature called man. I've traveled to seek my destiny; in a place where I first found happiness. I hope the Fates are kind to me and my few friends.

One of my favorite translations regarding human life is from the pen of the great Persian poet, Omar Khayyam.

"Tis all a Chequer-board of nights and days Where Destiny with men for Pieces plays: Hither and thither moves, and mates, and slays, And one by one back in the closet lays."

Your loving Aunt, Maureen D'Moresby

"Jeez, that explains a helluva lot," Alex exclaimed. He became thoughtful. "Kay, I feel it would be very beneficial to share this letter with Teri, and particularly her friend Brooke. If you think it would be appropriate, that is."

"Alex, I was thinking the same thing. It brings the multitude of incredible events together. And with Brooke, it would relieve a lot of her own self-doubt and guilt concerning her parents... and herself."

Alex grimaced, then nodded. "Amen, it would indeed do all that, and maybe more. As someone once said, let the healing begin."

CHAPTER 53

New Year's Day

Kay wrapped her robe tightly and stepped out of the kitchen door onto the veranda. It was a snowy morning, and icy cold.

Edgar and his mate were eyeing her from their apple-box roost under the eaves. It snowed harder; Edgar quietly landed on the blanketed porch rail. He ruffled his feathers and, with a bobbing head, made a soft throaty sound, "Mah, mah." Kay replied, "Mah… mah" back. It was their special conversation. He wanted food.

Snow filled the flowerpot attached to the railing. Kay scooped it out, took a plastic bag from her robe pocket, and filled the pot with seeds, bread bits, and dried meat. Cawing excitedly, both crows glided down. Edgar's mate was shy and held back, but Edgar's powerful beak pecked away. He would bring food to her, but not today.

"There you go, and Edgar don't be such a pig," Kay whispered. "Now, coffee is calling me, or I'll be a zombie for the rest of the day." Stuffing their beaks, they nodded, as if they understood.

Kay stretched into a yawn and firmly shut the kitchen door; then poured a generous cup. She sipped, inhaling the rich aroma of hazelnut, then hesitated. Stealthy footsteps sounded in the hall. A specter, clad in a hooded robe, crept. It groaned, then peered at Kay with an ashen, haunted look. The threat dissolved as it also raised a steaming cup to its lips. Alex had gotten to the coffee first.

The specter spoke. "I looked for you in the living room.

Oh Mama Mia, my head feels like it's the size of a respectable watermelon… and liable to fall off." With a free hand, the wraith steadied itself at the kitchen table, then gingerly sat down.

"I've heard of one being melancholy. You know, body like a melon, head like a collie; but I'm not so certain about the opposite," Kay said innocently.

"Don't, don't even make me chuckle. It's one of those long heavy buggers. If I reach up, I can touch both ends." He swallowed. "I must keep it carefully balanced."

"That bad, eh? Could I offer you two aspirin, or an Alka-Seltzer?"

"Both. I'm dying anyway."

Kay hastened to the pantry. "I really hate to be the prophet of gloom and doom. But it's not dazzling to keep up with Rain and your son. They're twenty-plus years younger."

"I know, I know, we were chatting. It was interesting, and I lost count."

Kay shook her hand. "It's best to keep track as we enter our autumnal years." She handed him the foaming seltzer and two Bufferin. One gulp, and it was gone.

"Thank you, oh sage one. I might live a little longer."

Kay sipped her coffee and pointed to the hall table. "Hopefully, long enough to help me muddle through that." She gestured with her cup. "You just stumbled by a mountain of correspondence we have to go through."

Alex groaned and cast a bleary eye at Kay. "It'll be mostly ads." He took careful swallows from his cup. "I don't think I can face anything. I'll need three more javas and probably some food before I can attack anything." He had a woebegone look. "Is it still attached? My head, that is."

Kay chortled. "Hasn't hit the floor yet. But it really was a fun party." She stood, listening carefully. "Ah ha. Nobody else is up. Let's you and I enjoy some Danish." She hugged him, then put a finger to her lips. "I've kept a box hidden just for us. Luckily, the girls didn't find it." She went over and gathered the post. "I'll get the circular file. We can quickly go through this mess at the table."

Fortified, with more steaming cups of hazelnut java and a plate of lemon-cream pastries, they sorted. Gaudy grocery announcements, tacky hardware flyers, magazine promos, all were offering the same schlock. Then there were envelopes, with paper inserts begging for whatever, and 'reply to this immediately' scams. "What a waste of trees." Alex grimaced, and the junk-mail hit the waste-recycle.

"Hmm, you must be feeling better." Kay paused, then picked up a blue-edged missive. "Alex, have you seen this?"

"To answer your question, marginally." He read the back of the letter. "It has an interesting return address. This is all the way from jolly olde England. Weird, why don't people use our modern email address?"

Kay shrugged, then slit open the envelope. "Don't grumble, hey it's our first real snail-mail reservation, no less. The gentleman wishes to book a room, ensuite, with a view, and a walk-in closet. My, my, and through all of next summer."

"He's describing our primary bedroom. It's the only one with a walk-in closet. Geez. But not a chance. Besides, all our bedrooms are ensuite."

Kay rubbed her chin. "I don't know. We can get top rates for our room, and it seems he's not concerned about the cost." She paused in thought. "We could convert that large storeroom-come-pantry next to the kitchen. It would make a decent bedroom for us. It even has a sink." Alex frowned as Kay continued. "I know. The window stares directly at the bank in the back, but it is on the northwest side; so, it's pleasantly cool." Alex's frown deepened.

Kay shrugged. "Look, my friend, it's roomy, opens to the kitchen and is on this floor. I've thought about it several times. Particularly when we were laying out the plans for the upstairs. And another thing, the spices and dried herbs give the room a delicious aroma."

Alex rolled his eyes. "But the closest toilet is the first-floor powder room, and it's just that, a fancy powder room. I will concede it's roomy, but no shower... I vote, tough agates. We'll send a tactful reply that only regular rooms are available. Man, they're spacious enough."

"Look Alex, it's for this coming summer, only. He requests four months, starting May 1st." She shook the letter. "Says here he's a writer and working on his tenth book... set in the San Juan Islands; hmm...and wants to immerse himself in the Northwest milieux and mingle with the muggles'." Kay smiled impishly. "I added that but look at this fancy letterhead."

Alex scanned the sheet. "Elliott W. Lafond? Never heard of him. But you're right about this logo, it's cool." He laughed. "A raven wearing a top hat, while rapping on a tavern door, looks at his fancy cane. It's clever. Hmm, appropriate address too: 'Raven's Knock Pub, Nettlewood, England'."

He smiled and took Kay's hand. "We'll have to come up with a design similar to this, only with a jaunty Edgar, and maybe an umbrella? We can hang it near our gate by the main road."

"I really like that. And we'll ask Wick to do the design. I know he'll love it." She paused. "So tonight, let's google the gentleman and this address." Kay's eyes lit up. "We'll have a 'writer in residence,' how de rigueur."

"Yeah. But I still wonder why he didn't contact us on our website. It's so much quicker."

Kay shrugged. "He or his travel agent may have. There've been plenty of site hits and queries. In fact, along with snooping after Mr. Lafond, you and I are going to screen and answer the legits this evening. It doesn't look like we'll have any trouble filling rooms."

Alex groaned. "Ah, my capitalist friend; hate to nag, but there's still the shower situation, or lack thereof."

"Bah, don't be such a baby. We'll use the basement shower. I'll admit it's open. But maybe you and Chuck McKindley could build some sort of enclosure... next month?" She grimaced. "And don't look like a squashed rooster. It's only for this coming summer."

Alex resigned himself and closed his eyes. "Yep, I suppose we can accommodate. After all, running a B&B will engender many unreasonable sacrifices... along the way, eh?"

"Now that's the man I know."

He snorted and showed the tabletop. "Any other way for us to avoid getting tons of this thrilling junk-mail?"

Kay smiled. "It's not all junk. But Byron said he'll set us up to pay bills online and that should be expedient." She peered over her cup of coffee. "It would be also helpful if you visited the post office more often." She removed a letter from her pocket. "I've saved this one for last. It's from Willie's Cousin Mary in Oregon. I just had to read it." She waved the lilac-colored paper at Alex.

"Humph, from Willie's cousin, eh? What's the old girl saying? She apologizes for that fiasco at the bog?"

Kay smiled devilishly. "Ujima really raked her over the coals concerning that mud trap. And since no actual harm was done, Ujima had Mary fill out her statement of events, then advised her to return to Oregon, post-haste."

Alex chuckled. "How did the marvelous wizard of psychic wisdom take Ujima's suggestion?"

"With great grumblings, Willie said. However, it appears she'd like us to visit her in Oregon sometime this summer."

"Is she crazy? Can't be much of a seer or even a logician… she'd know we'll be very busy. And for many a summer to come."

"Willie said the same thing. He suggested the winter slow season. It's the best time to visit, for us, and Willie's going too."

"Sounds like a plan." Alex hesitated, then listened carefully. "Is that someone knock, knock, knocking at the kitchen door?"

"It's the Raven of Nevermore," Kay whispered in a tomb-like voice.

Alex listened intently. "Yup, it's gotta be Rain, never uses the doorbell. I'll get it."

"You sure you can make it in your delicate condition?"

"Ha, ha, funny. Just steer me in the right direction."

CHAPTER 54

Harbinger

Rain stood in the swirling snow; a large manila package in one hand.

"Come in… egad, you look like the abominable snowman. Rain, don't you ever wear a cap or a hoodie? It's gotta be 40 below out there."

Rain grinned. "Hey, Mama Alex. This leather jacket may be old, but it's lined." Snow and ice fell to the mat as he shook like a dog in the doorway. "Besides, my Great-Grandfather swore our family descended from Vikings."

"Okay, swearing, Norseman, shed your gear." Alex slammed the door on the winter blast.

Kay laughed at the disheveled Rain. "I'm surprised, oh rugged man of the northern climes, that you just don't wear an animal skin, or maybe a kilt."

"Ha, ha, not a bad idea," Rain said as he thrust the manila package into Alex's hands, then abruptly sat down on the hall rug and began unlacing his boots. "Poor Edgar greeted me at the door. He cawed, probably for attention, or is he hungry?"

Kay sighed. "What a bottomless pit. I just fed him. And not 40 minutes ago. I'll get more dried liver-pellets from the pantry." Her eyes fell on the package. "What's that?"

"That," Rain nodded, "was delivered to Toady a couple of months ago. We ran across it last Wednesday, stuffed in our storage boxes. You know, after the fire at the restaurant? It's addressed to you guys and," he grimaced, "Toady thinks, from the postmark, it may have arrived in October."

Alex peered at the colorful cancelations. "It's hard to make out…but hey, it's from Cairo. Gotta be from good ole buddy Role." Excitedly, he tore at the large envelope's flap and skillfully caught a legal-sized sheet of paper as it fluttered out. Silence. "It is!" He shouted. "Wow guys, listen up."

Dear Alex and Kay,

This was meant to be a short one. We are catching the next plane out of here. Did I say we? Holy merde. In the last year, I've become an adoptive father of a 14-year- old. The result of a pledge I made to Mohamed, and oh mercy, with all the demands and obligations that come with it. You cannot imagine the nightmare of bureaucratic idiocy I've had to endure.

Her father, Mohamed, is my best bro, and the finest 'fellah' in our North African digs. Since the get-go, we've worked side by side. He's a brilliant man and in charge of just about everything.

We were devastated when his wife became an innocent victim of a crowd shooting in Cairo. She was shopping for goods when a skirmish broke out.

After her mother's death, Chione (that's her name) lived with Mohamed's family. Then we were struck by another devastation. My beloved friend, Mohamed, was partially paralyzed in a bus accident in Ethiopia.

Chione's extended family is large and very poor. I was and am currently funding the girl's education. What can I say? She is a genius, and since she was a little child, she's had a keen interest in Egyptology.

Mohamed used to bring Chione to our work sites. She was full of questions and had a sharp eye for artifacts. Amazingly, at only four, she understood things quickly. As brilliant, if not more so, than me and Mohamed put together.

He was worried about Chione's future. Didn't want her to become the usual subservient woman. So, he asked me if I would consider being her guardian. He is an au-currant Muslim. He speaks several languages fluently, and of course his daughter does too. Working alongside our team, she became quite an archaeologist in her own right. Obviously, we regarded his daughter as more than exceptional, which she is.

The young lady has an intellect as sharp as her mother and father. And now wishes to continue her education in America. It could have been England, but I'm definitely not living there.

Chione hasn't decided which school to go to yet. But with her intelligence and background, I wager she will be accepted anywhere she applies.

Anyway, I finally could finish and get the visas and necessary paperwork and am a nervous wreck.

Being not one to dally and to avoid any further bureaucratic obstructions, we are leaving for the states tomorrow.

However, I have a few important things to finish at the museums in New York and Chicago; you know who they are, the angels who provide lucrative grants for our fieldwork. After that, we'll head your way. Hope your inn is up and flourishing.

Love and knishes,

ton frere dans la vie, Roland

P.S. Chione is using my laptop at the moment. Thus, the handwritten missive. She thinks I'm extremely old school, anyway.

Kay clapped her hands. "Oh Alex, he's well, and I'm flabbergasted… has the guardianship of this young lady? Look at these photos. She's beautiful."

Rain peered over her shoulder and nodded. "Indeed, she is." He paused. "Does Roland mention a window… when they'll get here?"

Alex shrugged. "Roland? Ha. With him, it's impossible to say. If he gets tied up with his reports to the museums… we'll never know till we see the whites of his eyes. Strange, he's never mentioned the woman he was searching for. I guess it came to a dead end."

Kay sputtered in frustration. "Alex, that's really an unfortunate comment. But seriously, what are we going to do? They'll have to stay at our inn." She tapped the letter. "Did Role ever tell you he was the educative patron of Mohmad's daughter?"

"Role can be tight-lipped. But we'll find out more when they get here. And my dear Kay, when they get here, we'll do like we did in the Army, punt. Yes, that's exactly what we're going to do. Punt."

Rain rolled his eyes. "You always say that when things get difficult."

Kay returned to studying the photos. "Chione, what a lovely name. It's so appropriate. She, she looks so…so ethereal. And what a splendid picture of Role. I've never seen him look happier."

"Let's have a gander." Alex squinted and adjusted his glasses. "Humph, Role looks the same, but what's that thing in the background?"

"It looks familiar," Rain said, intently studying the blur. "I saw something like that in a history book. Hmm, now I remember. I think it's called Cleopatra's Needle?"

Kay nodded slowly and looked up. "You're right."

"Ahem," her voice assumed a decidedly professorial tone, with an overzealous British accent. "But the name is erroneous. It is an obelisk. The very one that was constructed in the reign of the great Pharaoh Thutmose. Ramses II, of course, appropriated the thing for himself. Indeed, there are three with that incorrect label. One in London, one in New York City, and one in Paris. And Cleopatra had nothing to do with any of them. And they should return them to Egypt. I have spoken."

"No kidding," Alex said, as he studied the photo. "Egad, I know where this one is. It's in Central Park. Role and company must be already in America." Alex cast an inquisitive glance at Kay. "How do you know about all this Egyptian rigmarole?"

"A moment, my dear." She raised a finger and went to the bookcase under the stairs. Selecting a large tome, she shoved it at Alex. "Besides the internet, this is my go-to reference on Egyptology."

"Woof, if this dropped on a person's foot, they'd be down for the count."

"Could I see that?" Rain asked.

"Most certainly," Alex grunted and handed it to Rain.

"Hmm, 'Pharaohs, Pyramids, Tombs and the Lives of the Everyday Ancient Egyptians'. Man, what a formidable collection." He thumbed through the pages. "Wow, these temple sketches are outstanding."

Kay closed her eyes, a sly smile on her lips. She assumed her professorial tone. "Note, my dear Emerson, it's not rigmarole. Before going as Amelia Peabody for the Hallowe'en party, I felt it incumbent on me to know at least something of Egyptology."

"Humph," Alex replied, as he looked down at her. "I don't

even want to go there."

"Oh, don't be a curmudgeon. We had a lot of fun at the party. Okay, maybe not so much after…that wasn't so jolly, the fog and all, and crawling home in the morning, but we were safe."

Kay stepped on the toes of his slippers. "You know, you make a masterful Radcliffe."

"You don't say? Er, we have to change, before the girls come down. And Rain, are you staying for breakfast?"

"Thanks, but no, gotta go." He turned the pages quickly. "There's an interesting bit of info here." Rain brushed back his drying hair and pointed at the item.

"This says that 'Chione', in Egyptian, means a 'daughter of the Nile'. Well, whatever; that's interesting though. But thanks for the brekky invite but got to get back. It's my turn to fix breakfast." He replaced the book and headed for the hall.

Kay gently poked Alex, then looked at him meaningfully.

"Oh, er yeah…we've been meaning to ask, Rain. Do you think you could give us a little help this spring? Gosh, planning our grand opening is mind-boggling. And even before we open, there'll be lots of little niggly things to do."

"Naturally, we'll pay you for your work," Kay added.

Rain sat on the floor, pulling on his boots. "I'd like that. Even though Toady's music festival is this spring; and I'll be revving up my organic farming project." He hesitated, a thoughtful smile on his face. "You know, Toady's getting his restaurant up and flying. Of course, I'll help him. And the Toad; will be super hyper."

"Well, if it's too much…"

"No, it's okay. That's if you don't mind me proselytizing about our local organic movement, I'll be happy to help. It'll be good to have a complete change." He stood up. "And more publicity helps too. We'll be testing and cultivating the seeds of our ideas right here on Bradestone. Hopefully, as Toady says, the program should not only grow here, but on the mainland, as well." Rain guffawed at his pun.

"Sounds like you're sowing acres of corn," Alex replied.

Kay rolled her eyes. "Rain, you really are the Green- Man. I'm sure with your expertise and eagerness it will…" she stared at Alex, "Indeed, take root."

Alex and Rain groaned. "Not you, too."

"I couldn't let you both have all the fun, but seriously, it is going to be one busy summer. Role and Chione show up, then meet our first guests; including that curious writer from England. Says he's staying all summer, but..." Kay slapped her forehead. "Crikey, how could I forget... Rose and Isaac are getting married, too?" Her expression changed from astonishment to determination. "I'm going to insist Rose have her wedding here."

"Whoops!" Alex said. "It even slipped my mind."

Rain shrugged on his jacket. "Not surprising. There's a lot on you guys's plate. Thankfully, Toady's done the musicale before, and we only have to get The Bloated Toad up and, er...well, hopping," he said with a silly grin.

They groaned again.

"Also, whatever you two do, there'll be the inevitable and atypical complications that arise." Rain gave them a knowing look.

Kay raised an eyebrow. "Rain, there is a great solution to the unforeseen, er... things that happen to us. We will consult Willie's, Cousin Mary."

Alex's eyes widened. "No, no. I mean, Mary's okay, but no, no."

"What's your problem?"

"Hey, I agree Mary and Aunt Maureen's ingenious contraption over the bog was amazing. Quite the dynamic duo, those two; even though Jinx gave them the slip." Alex spread his hands. "However, to see what might happen in the future? No, no. If one could, where would all the fun and challenge of the unexpected be? That's what life's all about, isn't it? The challenge of meeting change?" Then he wiggled his eyebrows. "It's just daily dealings with entropy, says the existentialist in me."

"Okay, no woo-woo stuff this time. We can meet any challenges without the aid of mystic prognostications." Kay crossed her fingers behind her back.

"I should hope so," Alex said, and kissed her. "So far, life around here has been always interesting, never dull."

"Amen to that," Rain mumbled, "Or should I say Amen-rah to that?" He paused; a puzzled look came over his face.

Outside the frost-covered kitchen window, a shadow moved along the sill. Tap, tap, tap. Edgar cocked his head and peered through the frosted pane.

Rain, hand on the doorknob, arched his brows. "There came a tapping. As of someone rapping, rapping at my chamber door."

Kay shivered. "Good God, old Edgar Allan Poe...Edgar's namesake."

Alex puffed up. "Elementary, my dear Kay. Lifted from The Raven, if I'm not mistaken."

"Edgar is a cousin to the raven," Rain said. "So, I would suggest he's implying Evermore, not Nevermore." Rain turned. "Ah, methinks a fit omen for the unforeseen… since it's always coming our way."

"Uffda," Alex muttered and looked wide-eyed at Kay. "If I were into auguring, I'd say, whatever lands in our laps, and this is based on past years, we can handle."

"And if we don't?" Rain snorted.

"Ah, you're such a pessimist. Remember what I've always said?"

"No!" Kay and Rain chorused.

"Tsk-tsk. You guys really have a serious case of someheimer's." Alex shrugged, then spread his hands. "We'll punt, okay?"

Rain opened the porch door. Snow swirled in. "I'm out of here. Feet do your stuff." He shut the door firmly behind him.

"Quite the character," Alex said and double-checked the door.

"Yes, he's a great friend." She turned, then hesitated.

"Look, there's something under the table." Kay pushed a chair aside and stooped to pick it up. "It's a sealed envelope. Must have fallen out when you frantically tore open Role's package."

"Frantic. Me?"

She turned it over. "Hmm, something on the back. The writing's cramped."

Alex reached for it. "Here, let me read it. I still have my glasses on. Hmm, it's titled Update."

Kay shivered. "I don't like this."

I can see why. Below Update, it says, a little something you should know. "Hmph, difficult to read. Role's handwriting is never the best."

"Just get on with it."

"Now who's being frantic?" Alex opened the envelop

un-creased the note and held it under the light. "Hum must have been in a hurry. Ahem,"

"Alex, I've noticed we're being followed. I'm sure it's Mr. H, and he is up to something. And that's curious as my search for Juba and Selene's library came to zilch. So, if you notice or sense something untoward, contact me on my cell immediately. Knowing H, I think he feels I've absconded with something."

Alex snorted. "Typical. What does Role think he can do, miles away?"

"I take it Mr. H is actually that Mr. Hugo, the jerk that almost got you and Role killed?"

"Yeah, the same. Though Ujima found it was not his intention. Evidently, one of his, er, associates, hired a pair of malicious thugs. They were supposed to give us a warning shot, not kill us. Regardless, Alex shrugged, "it's an old Army term; H is a devious bastard. We've been involved with him before when we were stupid and reckless, on-site shovelbums. You know, thought we could make some extra money."

"You and Role actually worked for this creep?"

"Well, yeah...sort of. Hey, we were poor, and starving students."

"Oh, give me a break." Kay took out a hanky and dabbed her eyes.

"I weep. Such a sad story. Blah, you were nothing but a pair of felons, miscreants, blah and blah again."

Looking as superior as a judge, Alex rose to his full height. "Mock you may. But any way we slice it, we'll have to be extremely alert. I'll fill Ujima in and you can warn the girls. They're sharp at noticing the unusual, or when something is not copacetic."

"Ah, more thrilling days and another spanner thrown into the works. Honestly Alex, you and Role can be so non-caring about what you do and then cavalier about the results."

"Now don't get testy."

Tap, tap, tap, came again.

Kay pulled her robe tightly. "Alex, I've got a strange feeling about Role coming here. I mean, I want to see him and Chione, but..."

Alex wrapped his arms around her. "Come on Kay, you're not Cousin Mary. And there's me, Role, Officer Ujima and all our friends. We work as a team, and we've always muddled through…somehow."

Kay held him close and looked up. "That's true dear. But I think you've forgotten; it's usually the muddling that can be very difficult and extremely dangerous."

Tap, tap, tap…

Finito

Acknowledgements

Oh Lord Peter Wimsey, where to begin?

Obviously, the writer's group, Rain Daze, composed of Gwen Knechtel, Llynda Peters, Kate Thompson and Charlie Thompson: and the amazing two Newfs publishing house.

So far, all of the above, have not given me the boot. Of that I'm thankful. All encourage me to be alert to my spelling problems (frantic phonetic) and to try and overcome my abysmal ignorance of proper punctuation (most likely, never). Otherwise, I pass their collective scrutiny. They are a great and thinking bunch of people.

However, I must mention the High School teacher, la Belle McKenzie, who initiated my efforts in evaluating everything with a critical eye, and my striving to become the mature person, not the immature person (still struggling).

Also, I was assisted by tripping over the works of the elusive Homer, the philosopher Camu and the Presian polymath Khayyam, all at a tender age. The trio helped a lot (drove me to drink and think, or is it think and drink?). But seriously (not), so far, life possesses all the amusing incongruities of things it's cracked up to be.

As Omar, via Fitzgerald, asked: Who is the potter, pray, and who the pot?

L. C. Mcgee

L. C. Mcgee lives with his wife and a rascally cat in a coastal village near the Salish Sea. He is the author of The Amber Crow, the first in the series, where the reader meets Alex, Kay, and Edgar, along with the other various characters who reside on Bradestone Island. L. C. is a member of Rainy Daze Writers and a contributor to their short story collection, New Halem Tales. For further adventures involving Edgar and crew, read the first books in the series, The Amber Crow and The Black Mariah.

www.ingramcontent.com/pod-product-compliance
Lightning Source LLC
Chambersburg PA
CBHW061057100726
47911CB00012B/265